SEAN KENNEDY

Heretic Squad

Evolution Trials Book 2

First edition

This book was professionally typeset on Reedsy.
Find out more at reedsy.com

To Quinn
who broke my heart by growing up and going to college. You're
one of the great dreamers.
I envy the future you'll create.

Contents

Acknowledgement

Thanks to my amazing family and friends who have supported me through this whacky decision to be a full time writer. Thank especially to my awesome street team— Whitney, Quinn, Marc and Joe: heretics all.

Map of Grendar

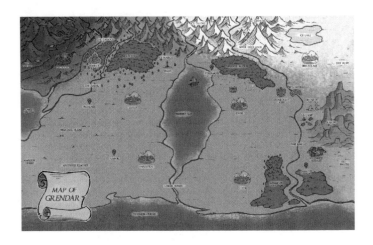

1

Kavi

Kavi lifted a foot and the metal end of the staff whistled under it.

"See, that's what I mean," said Clara. "Sparring against you is pointless. I'm not getting any better because there's no positive feedback."

Kavi tempered his speed and swung his staff at her left side. Clara barely brought her staff back in time to block.

"That's not fair. I offer encouragement all the time," said Kavi.

"Not that kind of positive feedback, you ass." She struck twice at his face.

He blocked both strikes then pushed into the second to force her to reset her feet. Her footwork was still sloppy.

"No matter what I attempt, I never get to score with you." Kavi smirked.

She scowled. "Yes, I heard it when I said it. You know what I mean. If I know that whatever I try will be countered, how will I ever know what the right attack is?"

"Did you know the best Krommian sprinters train with

weighted belts?"

"What?" She caught her breath, planted the staff and leaned against it. "Oh, is this you being the mystical master of the staff? Fine, mighty stick master, why do they train with weighted belts?"

"Why do you think?" he asked.

"Because Krommians like to punish themselves? A fashion statement?"

She struck three times in rapid succession, and this time her feet moved in harmony with the weight transfer required for each strike.

He nodded. "Better." He struck twice, faster than his previous attacks.

Her eyes widened, but she managed to put her staff in the way of both attacks. He struck three more times, even faster.

Still, she blocked. Fierce lines of concentration rippled on her forehead, making her angular features more pronounced. Sweat dotted high cheek bones to run down her narrow face to pool in the small cleft of her chin before dropping to the sand below.

He increased his speed again, and she blocked on instinct. He smiled as he continued to press and she continued to react. Then she lunged in an attack of her own and Kavi had to sidestep to miss the strike. When she struck again, she overreached and this time Kavi's staff took her in the left shoulder harder than he meant it to.

"Ow, shit," she said, rubbing her shoulder.

He stepped back. "Sorry, my mistake. But seriously, why do you think they train with weights?"

"So that when they take the weights off, they move faster."

Kavi nodded. "And what happens when you spar against

2

others after fighting me?"

She shrugged. "Everybody seems to move a little slower. I'm able to process a little faster."

"I've never seen you move that fast. What did you do differently this time?"

"I stopped fighting against you. I tried moving with you, mirroring and reacting."

"It's why my mother calls it the deadly dance," said Kavi. "She always pushed me and my brother to fight people better than us, mimic their moves until we found weaknesses. You don't improve by fighting people below your level."

She stared at him.

"What? Do I have something on my face?"

"No, I've never heard you talk about your family before. You have a brother?"

Pain settled over his shoulders like a familiar blanket. He let it rest there for a moment. It had been months since he had the horrible recurring dream of the time he lost his brother Brink. There had been so much other death and pain since. Brink's death had lost some of its sting.

"*Had* a brother," he said.

"I'm sorry. I didn't know." She dropped her staff and stepped forward to give him a hug.

Kavi stiffened.

She pulled out of the hug and looked at him, puzzled. "What? Did I do something wrong?"

Ever since he was captured, forced into slavery, and brought to this hell that was Company Sugoroku, he had stopped caring what other people thought about how he expressed himself. When they lost Trixie, he cried in front of the entire Ghost Squadron and didn't feel the least bit of shame. Then, when most of his friends died in the last Quest, he embraced the pain so fully he was able to tap into something primal and divine. A power that allowed him to briefly reverse time.

A secret he shared with no one. Only he and Rose, the fifth Sage, knew about this new power. Rose called him an agent of change. She meant it in the broad, world shaping sense, but Kavi felt it on a personal level too. Everything that happened to him over the last six months required him to adapt and change, often on a daily basis. He embraced it, knowing change was key to his survival.

Embracing his mortality in the Pool liberated him and the other Ghosts to live entirely in the present in their daily fight for survival. This primal focus gave the survivors access to skills and powers once considered things of myth and legend. Even with these powers, they took losses. Ghosts were given the name because so few survived a single season on the fodder team for Company Sugoroku, where they competed with other teams of the League to finish Quests divined by the mentally unsound, deific Sages the League had captured and exploited. The Ghosts were considered already dead until they survived an entire season.

Their last Quest ended over two months ago. The League had taken so many losses due to the rise of the Marked— twisted creatures and monsters considered dark fairy tales by most of Grendar only months ago. The Marked had evolved into something incredibly powerful thanks to a newly discovered substance Rose called trunite.

The Marked weren't their only source of losses. Members also died in skirmishes with other teams. Many League warriors also defected to the Liberators, a group run and operated by Rose. Liberation was an option Kavi and one of his closest teammates, Pip, were given. They turned it down. Many of their fellow Ghosts, and the entire professional team, took the offer. Pip and Kavi refused to leave the rest of Ghost Squadron in the hands of the League.

With so many losses in the first two Quests of the season, not a single Company in the League had a full roster. As a result, they put the season on hold, while the League came out of the shadows and began to actively recruit volunteers.

So, what was wrong? Kavi wasn't sure where to begin.

"No, nothing wrong," Kavi said. "It just surprised me. I've never talked about it before, and I'm not sure I'm ready."

She smiled. "Maybe you're human after all. Find me when you do want to talk."

"Thanks." Kavi picked up his staff and walked to place it back on the rack. He looked over at the Coaches who hovered over the other sparring circles, shouting pointers and issuing threats.

"What time's your meeting today?" asked Clara.

"Third bell. They're pulling me out of work duty."

Clara looked over at Pip, still sparring with Boost. "Pip going with you?"

"I doubt it. They questioned us so many times separately. Then they interviewed us together. They tried every technique to uncover our 'grand plan.' They're convinced we're working with the Liberators, but we just keep telling the truth about what happened. They can't believe we came back for our team."

Clara shrugged. "I get it. When your entire life is spent on selfish pursuits, the idea of someone being selfless sounds like a lie."

Kavi kept his eyes on the match between Pip and Boost and answered. "I guess so. I'm sure it didn't help that Rake made new things up each time he was interrogated." He smiled. "It's got to be killing Rake that he can't remember a thing."

"Fucking cockroach," she said. "I don't know why evil bastards like Rake survive the longest."

Kavi grinned at her passion. He made his peace with the hand the fates dealt Rake, but it didn't mean he had forgiven the man responsible for the death of Trixie and others on Ghost squad.

"I guess they finally realized the guy whose story kept changing might be the one who wasn't telling the truth," said Kavi. He faced Clara. "You're on work detail with Stix today right?"

Clara laughed. "Will you relax? Everyone will be there tonight. Rumor has it Healer Brand even convinced Doctor Cleary to show."

"Not really a secret meeting anymore, huh?"

"It affects everyone in the Nest. Not sure it should be a secret."

"Yeah, but what if the Coaches break it up?" asked Kavi.

"Stop worrying," said Clara. She put her own staff on the rack. "I wouldn't be surprised if the Coaches try to join us. Everyone's wondering how their job is going to change with volunteers coming in. I still remember Olsen's face when he told me about the first idiot who showed up at intake."

She dropped and softened her voice in a passable imitation of Healer Brand. "This kid walks right up to me and says - So ah, is this where I sign up to fight monsters and solve Quests?"

"Why do you think she picked me though?" asked Kavi, switching topics to the other thing worrying him.

Clara playfully bumped her hip into his. "Because you're the golden boy. Of course our illustrious owner wants to meet with you. I wouldn't be surprised if Pip got called in too. He's the pretty face after all."

Coach K blew his whistle. "Enough warm up," lisped the big man through his giant underbite. "Forts, you're back in the boneyard with Coach M. Dancers to the Gauntlet with me. Strikers and Guards, you're running plays with Coach L."

Clara hugged him and this time he relaxed into it. "See you tonight," she said, then winked.

Kavi grabbed his kit while keeping an eye on her retreating form. The fabric of her sparring uniform hugged her body in the most distracting ways.

Pip and Boost joined him in packing up their gear. "I don't know why you don't take your shot with her," said Boost.

"She made it pretty clear she's not interested," said Kavi.

Tess snorted as she joined them.

"What?"

"You're an idiot," said Tess. "She made it clear she wasn't interested months ago when we all didn't know if we were going to live to see tomorrow."

"Right and I just found out a week ago that half of Ghost Squadron was hooking up with the other half whenever they got the chance," said Kavi. He shrugged. "If you're gonna die tomorrow, might as well live today. If she didn't want anything to do with me then, why would she want to now?"

"You *are* an idiot," said Pip. "Clara's got higher standards. She didn't mess around with anyone back then."

"I still don't understand why nobody told me the squad had became a warren of teenage rabbits," said Kavi.

"Because you're intimidating," said Boost. "Nobody wanted to disappoint you. Even me, and I hated you."

"Wait a second, you were hooking up too?"

"What? I have game," said Boost.

"Yeah, but you were such an asshole."

"Not to Leesta or Piety," said Boost with a leer.

Tess snorted. "Leesta, really? I thought she had taste."

Pip laughed and Kavi and Boost joined him. "You definitely have a type my friend," said Pip putting a hand on Boost's shoulder.

"Something about those tall ladies," said Boost. He trailed off, lost in a memory. He turned to Kavi. "You think they're doing okay?"

Kavi nodded. "For the first time in a long while, I think they're doing better than ok."

* * *

The dining hall in the Ghost quarters was filled to capacity. It hadn't had this many people in it since...since ever. Kavi thought back to when his class of Ghosts showed up for the first time, and the battles for food and beds. Even before people started dying, they never filled the dining hall up like this.

Kavi looked at Stix who nodded. "That's all the double As that could make it. The rest are on shift. Believe it or not, I think everybody enjoyed walking these stairs again. Like a walk back in time."

"Speak for yourself, Stix," said Doctor Cleary. "I swore I would never walk these stairs again."

"Yes ma'am," said Stix automatically. "Sorry for asking you to break that oath."

Doctor Cleary smiled. It was impossible to stay annoyed with the affable double A.

Healer Olsen Brand sat next to Doctor Cleary, both in chairs. They had saved more lives than anyone in this room could count. They earned their respect.

Kavi looked at Olsen. "Gibbons couldn't make it?"

Olsen shook his head. "He took call so Doctor Cleary could come."

Kavi nodded to her. "Thanks for being here, ma'am."

Doctor Cleary tilted her head.

"And what about a triple A representative. Did they send anybody?" asked Kavi.

"I don't know," said Stix. "They told me they would."

"I'm here," said a voice from behind Stix.

"Well, I know you're here, dumbass," said Stix as he looked at his long time friend, Stonez. "But that wasn't the question was it?"

"Yes, it was," said Stonez in a deadpan voice.

Stix paled. "No, you didn't, Stonez! Tell me you didn't join the triple As, you dumb son of a bitch."

"It's not like they gave me a lot of choice," said Stonez. "You know how low they are on Guards. Besides, the kid inspired me."

Stix was about to continue when Kavi held up a hand. "Mind finishing this later?"

Stix nodded, but the look he gave Stonez promised a

prolonged argument.

Kavi stood and moved to the front of the room. "Clara, Pip, mind giving us some privacy?"

Clara stood and activated two silence runes above the door and the fireplace. Pip's eyes went dark and sparkly as he summoned a void dome around the room and tied it off. The non-Ghosts looked impressed.

"They're going to find out about this conversation anyway," said Doctor Cleary.

"I know," said Kavi. "I'm sure the League knows we're here and I can almost guarantee someone is going to spill what we talk about, but maybe not until after I meet with our owner."

"Until then," said Pip, "enjoy spitting in their eye. It's gotta make the League angry. They know we're meeting but can't see or hear what we're saying."

That brought smiles all around.

"I meet with Sugoroku tomorrow for lunch," Kavi said. "The little leverage we have with her and the rest of the League is that most of the professional teams have been decimated, if not completely destroyed. We know the League decided to come out of the shadows by accepting volunteers. They started a program to create future heroes of Grendar. Which leaves us with one big question."

"What happens to all of us?" asked Doctor Cleary.

"Exactly," said Kavi. "Worst case scenario, they clean house. They eliminate every one of us and start fresh with volunteers."

Kavi looked around the room and saw grim faces. They all knew the League was capable of such an atrocity.

"This type of brutality would solve a lot of problems for

the League. Especially now that they're trying to portray themselves as saviors. Nothing like accusations of slavery to pop that bubble."

"Do we start stockpiling weapons?" asked Stix.

"That's always a good idea," said Kavi. "But I'm not convinced they're going to purge the teams."

"Why not?" asked Stonez.

Kavi held up two fingers. "Two reasons. First, if news got out that they massacred hundreds of their own players? That's it. The League is done. One can recover from a history of slavery if those that perpetrated it were forcibly retired then portrayed as relics from a bygone era. A massacre though? Different story."

"If it got out," said Olsen. "That's a pretty big if."

"Yes, it is. That's where we have another powerful ally in our corner. The fifth Sage. Rose and her Liberators would make sure it got out, and the League knows that. They're smart enough to fear her."

"Rose? Are you on a first name basis with the Sage now, Ghost?" asked Stonez.

Kavi raised an eyebrow. "Ghost?"

"Sorry, force of habit."

"As a matter of fact, I am," said Kavi. "And Sugoroku knows that. They also know I declined her offer and came back."

"I tagged you as smarter than that," said Stix. "It's a shame someone with so much talent was cursed with so little common sense."

"Hey, comedy relief, shut it until we hear what he has to say," said Doctor Cleary.

Stix and Stonez hung their heads and muttered, "Yes,

ma'am."

"Go ahead, boy," said the doctor. "I'm looking forward to hearing that second reason."

"Thank you, doctor. The second reason is greed. The League sunk a ton of resources into everyone in this facility. There are hundreds of collective years of experience in fighting monsters and solving Quests in the current Companies. You can't just replace that, even with volunteers. The owners of the League don't seem the type to burn the loot on the way out."

"And if they don't burn us all down..., well..., we're going to have to give them a reason to trust we're not going to do the same to them," said Doctor Cleary.

Kavi pointed at her and nodded. He wasn't surprised it was the doctor who got to the heart of the matter. "Which means we need a reason not to destroy them the minute we taste freedom," said Kavi. "So, what do we want from Sugoroku?"

Ideas were thrown around for hours. Slowly, a plan began to form. Kavi had ideas ahead of time but he was glad he brought all the groups in on a decision this big. Not only did it build buy-in, a lot of these people were smarter than him. Thank Krom for Doctor Cleary. The woman had a knack of putting pins in ideas that wouldn't float without destroying enthusiasm. She wrangled the best ideas to the fore. It didn't hurt that everyone in the room respected the hell out of her.

When the ideas slowed to a trickle Kavi was confident they had what they needed. He stopped to wrap up the meeting when Pip stood.

"I agree, the likelihood of them going scorched earth is low, but everyone needs to know there's a plan in place if that does happen," said Pip.

Kavi nodded. "Pip's right. We built a communication system using our skills. We're not going to share the details of how. However, if you ever hear someone from this Squad say—Pass the Firecracker Chicken—it means it's time to drop everything and defend yourselves. And your teams. Ghost Squad will meet with the heads of each team at dawn tomorrow to share the plan. It's up to you to distribute it to your groups before lunch. Understood?"

"Understood." Most in the room were yawning. It had been a long night.

Doctor Cleary ended it by standing up. "I must say I'm impressed with Ghost Squad, but I need my beauty sleep. You got what you need?"

"I do," said Kavi. "This is what I'm going to propose tomorrow..."

"I don't need to hear it. Probably better if I don't. I trust you and I think the group does too. Good luck tomorrow."

2

A new role

Kavi's attention drifted to the meeting ahead, to Grim and the Ghosts that escaped with Rose, to his family in Stonecrest. His muscle memory took over but without attention, his form was riddled with holes.

"Ow," said Kavi when Sliver's strike took him in the arm.

"Yes!" yelled Sliver. She did a little a dance, spiky hair bouncing up and down as she ran in a small circle. "I scored a point on Eleven!" She flexed, showing a good amount of ropy muscle.

Kavi smiled at the small Bricker. "Nice move, Sliv," he said.

"Gotta take my chance, you being distracted and all."

Kavi looked around the sparring rings. So few of the original Ghosts left, they could only fill seven circles. He knew that was about to change. If Sugoroku didn't outright eliminate them, there would be consolidation with other teams. The sparring in each circle was not the normal graceful dance of Ghost Squad. It was tense and worried.

Everyone was nervous about Kavi's meeting.

Coach L had enough. He blew his whistle and yelled, "You're wasting my time. If you're not going to fight, you're going to run. Three laps around the Rim."

Kavi breathed a sigh of relief. It was much easier to think while running. He set a slow pace. The giant practice facility was eerily quiet. Some triple As—the pool of alternates who volunteered and were qualified for the pro team—worked the Boneyard, a tilled area where Forts practiced building defensive structure. That was it.

As they finished their second lap, Coach K walked over to them. He looked at Kavi. "It's time."

Kavi made eye contact with each of his Strikers in turn. They nodded back.

Pip grinned. "You got this."

He turned to Clara. She smiled encouragingly. "Give her hell, Kavi."

"Let's go, Eleven," said Coach K. "We do not keep the owner waiting."

Kavi followed Coach past the main floor dining hall and coaches' rooms. They avoided the pro team coaches huddled in hushed conversation. Coach K led them to a narrow stairway leading down. These stairs had a handrail. The walls were wood paneled.

"Fancy," said Kavi as they descended, running his finger along the paneling.

Coach K grunted. "Don't be cute. Not with her. Or you might get us all killed."

"Your life is meaningless to me," said Kavi sharply. He thrilled at throwing the words Coach K had said so many times back at him, even if they were untrue. All life held meaning to Kavi, even one as tainted as Coach K's.

Coach K ignored him.

After several minutes descending, they came to a landing with a door. They walked through it and followed a hallway lined with small alcoves decorated with sculptures tastefully lit from magelights ensconced above. The walls without sculptures hung priceless pieces of art.

Clara would love this place.

At the end of the hall lay a trio of glass doors which led into large conference rooms. Coach K acknowledged the six guards, clad in Sugoroku colors of black and green, with a grunt.

The largest of the guards nodded to Coach K. "We'll take him in," he said in a nasal voice. The guard had a flat, crooked nose common to boxers and he eyed Kavi like a prize fighter sizing up an opponent. The scars on his face told of a military history, but they were the old scars of a Krommian warrior who hadn't gone through an evolution. Until he accepted his own mortality so completely that his body and mind manifested a new level of existence, where summoning powers was not only possible but commonplace, he simply wasn't a threat.

Kavi stood patiently as they frisked him for weapons. Scenarios flitted through his head of how he would disable each of the guards. He wouldn't even need to slow time. He'd start with the big guard, a spear hand strike to the throat would lay him low before he knew what happened. The other guards would respond, but not before Kavi spun and took out the second with a hook kick to the left ear, followed by a fake kick to the nuts to the third to bring his hands and head down, making a knee to the nose an easy follow up. The other three would shrivel and flee while he focused on

Coach K. That would be a fun fight. It would be easy, but it wouldn't solve any of his current problems. To do that, he would need to play nice.

Coach K handed the leader of the group a suppression collar and the man carefully placed it around Kavi's neck and clicked it into place. Kavi felt the access to his evo skills fly out of reach like they were placed on a high shelf. Kavi bared his teeth at the sound and smirked when the boxer flinched.

"Would she like me to wait here?" asked Coach K.

"We'll bring him back up."

Coach K walked off without a word.

The lead guard opened the door to the conference room and ushered Kavi in.

* * *

A small Harpstran woman sat at the head of a large, polished stone table. She wore a black silk, strapless gown with the Sugoroku crest embroidered over the left breast, like she had just come from a League gala. To her right sat a man in a carefully tailored black and green suit. He held his pen like a weapon over a leather bound book.

"Would you like us to remain in the room, ma'am?" asked the guard.

She shook her head. The man handed her the baton that controlled Kavi's collar and left the room.

She stared at him for a long moment. "So, you are Kavi Stonecrest," she said, her voice mellifluous and smooth—a carefully tuned instrument. "Please, sit."

Kavi sat to her left, across from the man in the suit. On the table were a variety of platters with mouth-watering aromas. Kavi forced his face to remain placid when he recognized one of the dishes.

She raised thin eyebrows and squashed a smile. "Not intimidated at all, are you?"

"You're hardly as intimidating as an Ach'Su, ma'am."

"Defiant *and* polite, what an intriguing combination. Can I offer you tea or lemonade before we dig into lunch?"

"Lemonade sounds swell," said Kavi, reciting lines in this first act.

"Tom? Would you mind?"

Her assistant stood and grabbed three glasses. As he poured, Sugoroku fingered the baton in her hand and clicked the lowest button on the device. Kavi's collar clicked open. At the sound, the pouring stopped for a moment then resumed.

Kavi nodded his thanks and tightened his gaze. Sugoroku may as well had shouted she was not intimidated either. He removed the collar and set it on the table. He accepted the glass from Tom and took a long sip. Delicious.

"Please, try the Firecracker Chicken, it's one of my favorites."

Kavi nodded. "Thank you, it's one of mine too."

Someone had talked. They had carefully chosen that code name last night. Or the owner could see and hear into their rooms even with the protections they put in place. The question was: why did she want him to know that?

He thought through this as he ate, feeling like an animal in a zoo. His every move watched, cataloged away to be used against him later.

The chicken was divine. The mozzarella countered the dark red spice perfectly and the grease from the dark meat made each bite a silken paradise. He chewed slowly, savoring the taste. He helped himself to another serving knowing it would annoy his host.

"I met your mother once," said Sugoroku. "She's an intimidating woman. In another life, we could have been friends." The woman tapped her fingers against the table. "In this one, I'm sure she would happily slide a sword through my ribs."

Kavi nodded. "I doubt she'd enjoy it, but she would definitely see you as someone who needs killing."

"And you? Do you see me as someone who needs killing, Eleven?"

Ever since he was pressed into the League, he had no reason to play the games of high society. He went with truth. "You enslaved me and had a number of my friends murdered. So, yes, it's hard to see otherwise. Wouldn't you if our roles were reversed?"

"Perhaps, which brings us to the heart of the matter," said Lady Sugoroku. "The League has chosen to become a softer, gentler organization. A hero factory, as it were. While we launch our new identity, we are faced with how to manage past transgressions. As you correctly reasoned last night, most of us are unwilling to...How did you say?"

"Burn the loot on the way out," supplied Tom.

Kavi held her eyes. She was belaboring the point. It made her less intimidating.

"Burn the loot on the way out," she said. She broke their gaze to share a smile with Tom. "I like that, and you're correct. Most of us won't simply drop such an investment in time and resources. Not to mention the experience the squads built along the way."

She reached across the table to lay a hand on Kavi's wrist. "Can you imagine if that level of unethical behavior were to be unearthed?" she asked as if he were a confidant. "We haven't completely parted ways with our ethics, you know."

"Forgive me if I don't put any faith in your ethics," said Kavi. Why was she recapping their arguments from last night? It didn't make sense to keep playing the same card. She was fishing for something. Kavi wished Pip or Tess were here with him, they picked up on these things quicker than he did.

She laughed. "That's a relief, because I don't either. Ethics limit one's options."

Kavi finished chewing and finally pushed his plate aside. "What do you want from me? From us?"

She leaned towards him and squeezed his wrist tighter, green irises flashing with aggression. "A reason not to destroy you and everyone in the Nest. A reason to trust you to keep your silence until the League can get in front of our slavery problem," said Sugoroku.

"*Your* slavery problem?" Kavi said with a laugh. "With any luck, one day you'll wear the chains. Then, you can experience a true slavery problem."

Kavi took a moment to think this through. He realized she wanted him angry. But why? Then it struck him. Destroying all of them wasn't ever on the table. Kavi had seen this act in warriors who didn't want to fight. All bluster and no battle. She wouldn't be pushing this hard to make the point if it wasn't a bluff. Another force had already removed that option from the table.

Krom, he better be right about this, or he really was going to get them all killed.

He donned a cheeky smile and extricated his wrist from her grasp. "We want it all. Starting with reparations. We know you have plenty of gold. We want each unwilling member, or slaves, of Company Sugoroku to get a year's pay of a Colonel in the Krommian army for each month served as a Ghost. They will receive a year's pay of a Major for every month served after that. This will be delivered to our families with a letter we write telling them we are committed for another full year. After that, your volunteers will be up to speed and those who want to leave will be given their freedom."

Sugoroku looked outraged. Kavi couldn't tell if it was feigned. She whispered something to Tom who wrote something in the notebook. Probably asking how much each of these officers made. Kavi imagined him doing the math right now.

"You commit for *two* years and you receive the pay of a Major and a Captain at the end of that service. We get to read the letter before it goes out," said Sugoroku.

"You can read the letter," said Kavi. "The pay is of a Colonel and a Major for time already served. It will be paid on signing an eighteen month contract. We fully understand you have the power to eliminate our families. Unless, of course, we treat with the Sage and her Liberators."

She raised her eyebrows. "I thought you didn't have a way to contact her."

"I don't, but if you think she hasn't foretold this meeting, you're more a fool than you look. She'll contact me," said Kavi.

"Is that it?" she asked sarcastically.

Kavi smiled. "Please don't play the victim. It only makes it easier to up the stakes."

"Very well."

"We get a say in how we are deployed for the next eighteen months. We'll go on the missions you ask of us, but we decide who goes and in what role."

She nodded. "Fine. I could care less as long as the objectives are completed. I'm unwilling to fire any of the coaches but I'm okay with them working exclusively with our new volunteers. What else?"

Might as well throw the dice and go for the big ask. "You will set up a meeting between me, two people of my choice, and the Collective."

She grinned. "You are a cheeky one, aren't you? I can make the request, but I can't assure it will be honored."

"I'm sure if you explain the terms...," said Kavi.

She lay both hands flat on the table. "Here are my terms. There is no requirement to complete Quests, but whoever you and your cohort decide will be the new professional team will be deployed once a week to put down Marked incursions."

Kavi's eyes widened. He had no idea there were that many Marked. If the governments were calling the League, people must have died. A lot of people. "What do you get out of us putting down incursions?"

"Image," she said with a raised eyebrow. "We will truly help people with these missions, something I imagine appeals to you and your friends."

Kavi nodded thoughtfully. "While providing a counter narrative to the Liberators."

"Exactly, but so what? Helping people is helping people. I

believe your friend Rose will be pleased. Also—you, and the rest of your professionals will submit to interviews when and where they are requested."

"Interviews? Like what you put me and Pip through over the last two months?"

She laughed. "No, these will be of a public nature. We're going to make you heroes."

"So we can endorse your behavior?" asked Kavi.

"Only our new behavior, which will be on the level."

Kavi considered. "One a week. Maximum. Tie the interview clause to the meeting with the Collective."

"Done. Tom will draw up the paperwork for you to sign by the end of the week." She stood and pulled a black shawl around her shoulders. "With any luck, we'll never meet again."

And with that, she walked out of the room.

3

Strong bond

"So who decides who makes it on the professional team?" asked Stix.

"We do," said Kavi.

"I understand that, but the team still needs a tactician," said Stix. He rubbed a hand over his face. "Without the coaches calling the shots, someone is going to have to make these decisions."

Kavi looked around the main dining hall, packed full of people. Unlike the mess in the Ghost dormitory there was room for everyone to sit. There was a lot of righteous anger seething below the surface in the eyes that looked up at him. It wasn't directed at him but it *was* intimidating. The deal Kavi negotiated gave each unwilling Sugoroku member an exit plan, but eighteen months, with the dismal survival rates of this place, felt like an eternity.

"And why would anyone volunteer to be on the profes-sional team?" asked Rance.

Anytime the former leader of the no-neuros spoke, Kavi wanted to choke him. But the question was a good one and it deserved an answer.

"Hazard pay and the chance for the world to see you as a hero. Plus, we'll actually be helping people. All that bullshit the coaches said about us protecting people from things that go bump in the night? It's true now," said Kavi. "And we'll need to run two pro teams, not one. Going out and fighting Marked every week is too much for any one team."

"I know this will be an unpopular idea," said Stix "but what if Rake runs one of the teams?"

The man perked up when he heard his name. Rake had laid low since realizing his entire professional team had deserted him when they joined the Liberators.

Kavi couldn't help the rage that bubbled up anytime he looked at the man with the blue scaled tattoos. When Rake stood, Kavi almost cut him off. It took everything he had not to. But the man had more experience than anyone in the room when it came to life and death situations.

Rake spoke and the murmuring in the room silenced. "No. I'm not going to lead a team. I've decided to join a new program the League is offering called Project Midnight."

Just what the prick deserved. Kavi knew the sentiment was unworthy. The man at least deserved a warning. "They're going to turn you into even more of a monster. It's not worth it," said Kavi.

Rake shook his head. "There's nothing left for me here. I have no family, so there's nowhere for money to be sent. They all died in the race riots of eighty-one. My only friends were on Team Sugoroku and they left me for dead. The League is offering to make me a god. How could I turn that down?"

Kavi couldn't square his feelings for this humbler version

of the man who killed his friends. He almost felt sorry for him until an image of Trixie and Pete flashed in his mind. *That* squelched any sympathy.

"You always were a selfish idiot," said Kavi.

Rake turned to him. "Maybe. But take a last piece of advice from this idiot. Don't throw it all out. Use the professional and triple A coaches. They have a lot to teach and they don't get hung up on the ghost thing."

This brought jeers from the room and Rake smiled. "I don't care if you listen to me or not. I'm on my way out. I'm just channeling what Tack would have said." Rake sat back down.

Stonez stood up and the jeers quieted. "I hate to say it, but he's got a point. What if we asked the Coaches from the pro and triple A teams to run try outs?"

Kavi let the grumbling continue this time. He wasn't crazy about working with the coaches either. Not just because it was Rake's idea.

Stix held up a hand and Kavi nodded to him. "How many spots do we have to fill? Didn't you say that some of your Ghosts have to fight?"

Kavi nodded. "Sugoroku singled a group of us out as the faces of this new campaign. Me, Jansen, Tess, Pip, Boost, Clara and Sliver *have* to deploy."

Several of the Ghosts in the room let out heavy breaths. Kavi had already spoken with those that had to go but hadn't shared the news with those that hadn't.

Stix did some math in his head. "So, seven of you means there are twenty three spots left if we're going to field two teams. Do we have that many volunteers?"

Kavi smiled. "I don't know, but tons of people volunteer

for the army for a lot less pay. In the army, there's almost no chance of being a hero and Sugoroku is hellbent on turning us into them. Remember, this time we get to help people."

Stix shook his head. "Never been much for fame. Maybe we need a head count. How about everyone stand up who wants to volunteer for this lunacy. Mind you, you'll be fighting Marked."

Kavi grinned when half the room stood. The entire triple A team was on its feet and Stonez was doing his best to pull Stix to his feet but the man wasn't having it.

Pip stood up and Tess joined him. "Since we're the ones being forced to fight," said Tess. "We'll build our own roster from those the coaches deem worthy."

Jansen stood. "Let's work out schedules for using the training facilities. I need to get my time in the Pool."

Clara looked at Kavi. "When do we deploy?"

Kavi stood and held up his hands for quiet. "We get deployed in two and a half weeks for our first peacekeeping operation. The team I lead will be deployed for the first mission. Let's get to work."

* * *

"No, you're going to have to explain it to him," said Boost.

"I lose him too quickly when it gets technical," said Sliver.

"But I don't fully understand it yet," said Boost. He threw a spanner into the wooden crate next to his pallet. They were packing up to move to their new quarters. "Half the theory you and Hiram toss around is a click over my head."

"Come on Boost, it's fifth year math," said Sliver.

"It's not the math I don't get. It's the physics and the neuro-twiddlies." Boost wiggled his fingers.

Sliver grabbed the pillow she won on a bet with one of the double As several months ago and threw it into her crate. The Ghost quarters felt empty when they returned from the second Quest months ago, but now with all of their personal effects removed it looked like the grim skeleton they encountered at the start.

"Is it weird to say I'm going to miss this place?" asked Sliver.

Clara shook her head. "No. Not all the memories here were bad." She stared at Trixie's old bed. "Now we have to say goodbye to those too."

Clara stood on her bunk and traced her fingers along the Harpstran death rune she made after their first time in the Pool. The rest of the Ghosts stood, lost in their own thoughts.

"Quit stalling, Sliver. Just explain it already," said Boost into the silence.

"Explain what?" asked Kavi and Tess at the same time.

"I'm getting a little tired of you two Brickheads yammering back and forth," said Tess.

"Fine," said Sliver. "I think Boost, Hiram and I figured out how to fuse powers in the Pool."

"Who's Hiram?" asked Tess.

"Triple A neuro-mage," said Pip. "Nice guy."

Kavi marveled at how Pip seemed to know everyone in the Nest, where Tess knew almost no one. They fought so well together yet were so different. "What do you mean by fuse powers?"

Sliver grabbed the chalkboard the Dancers used to track

their trap disarming scores and wiped it clean with the sleeve of her uniform. She mounted it back on the wall and drew three circles on the board.

"Do you remember when we got in the Pool that first time?"

Everyone stopped packing and gathered around Sliver and her chalkboard.

"Kinda hard to forget," said Jansen.

"When we first got thrown in the Pool we were each put into our own simulations. I couldn't see Jansen getting his ass kicked by the banglors and he couldn't see me getting gutted."

Jansen's face darkened. "Too soon, Thirteen."

"The next time in the Pool," continued Sliver, "they linked us together so we were all in the same simulation."

Sliver drew two lines between each of the three circles. "When they put us in as a group, they linked our minds. They created what Hiram calls a 'weak bond'. That bond shared our position with everyone nearby."

"Why two lines?" asked Pip.

"Because each of us has to share our information with everybody else. See if this helps." She added a directional arrow to each line. "The number of connections required is n, the number of people, times n minus one."

"You lost me," said Jansen.

"Do you understand the pretty picture?" asked Sliver with a condescending smile.

Jansen nodded.

"I'll leave the math out of it."

"Why a weak bond?" asked Kavi.

"Damnit, Eleven, I'm getting to that. Don't jump ahead,"

said Sliver. "It's weak because that's the only information shared, stuff that—if it were not a simulation—anyone could see if they were watching from a distance."

"What about the communication between us?" asked Jansen.

"Are you trying to grow a brain on me, Twenty-two?" Sliver bounced as she pointed at Jansen. "The audio takes place on a different channel." She drew two dotted lines between each of the three circles this time. "Everybody with me so far?"

Jansen glowed as everybody nodded.

Boost fidgeted until he couldn't hold it anymore. "But it doesn't actually work like that," he said.

"Do you want the chalk, Nineteen?" She held the chalk out. "You asked me to explain it so I'm explaining it."

Boost shook his head. Sliver turned the chalkboard over and this time she drew five circles.

"Look at what happens when there are five of us in the simulation. All of a sudden we have twenty lines between us and that's before I add the audio channels. Imagine fifteen of us in there. Boost, how many lines would I have to draw?"

He looked up for a second. "Two hundred and ten."

She held out her fist and he bumped it. "That's right: two hundred and ten. What we call the tinkerer's ass crack."

Blank stares met her statement.

"A hot sweaty mess. Keep up people."

Sliver flipped the board back over and erased the three circles. This time she drew five circles on the bottom and one big circle at the top. She then drew two lines from the big circle to each of the little circles.

"So, the Vonderian neuro-mages who invented the Pool

built a big brain to keep track of everything. Instead of sending that information to each other every time we do something, we send it to the big brain. The big brain sends the information about each of us back down. So, instead of having to maintain n times n minus one connections, now we only have to maintain—"

"Two n," said Kavi.

"Not bad, Eleven," said Sliver. "Two n. So, with fifteen people, instead of maintaining two hundred and ten channels, the Pool only has to maintain thirty. "

"What I asked Hiram," said Sliver. "Is what happens if we created a strong bond between only two of the circles in the Pool?" She drew a thick line between two of the circles that had an arrow on either end. Then she paused.

"I'll bite," said Tess. "What's a strong bond?"

"A strong bond is when we open a neural channel between minds," said Sliver.

"No, no, no, *no*," said Pip. "You're talking about mind share. My parents do that with each other. It's disgusting. Zero privacy. You have to expose everything in your head to the other person. All your dirty little secrets. They all come out. Once you go down that path, there's no hiding. Not from yourself, not from the other person." He had a big frown on his face as he shook his head. "No way! I'm out."

"Relax, Twelve. I didn't say it would be easy. I just said it was possible. Imagine what we could unlock if we got in each other's brains. We might be able to fuse skills together," said Sliver.

"It's an abomination," said Pip.

"Worse than dying?" asked Kavi.

"Maybe," said Pip. "Think about what happens if one of

you dies. Which, by the way, will happen in the Pool over and over again. You're going to experience your own death *and* that of your strong bond."

"It might be nice to have some company," said Clara.

Kavi held up a hand to stall Pip. "I get it, it's dangerous. But if it gives us an edge that keeps us alive in the real world, it's worth trying." He looked to Sliver. "How would it translate to the real world?"

Sliver nodded to Boost.

"We don't know yet," said Boost. "It may require a neuro-mage to make it happen or it may be like the skills we unlock. Once we figure it out in the Pool, we can talk about taking it into the field."

"Will the Company let us tamper with the Pool?" asked Tess.

"As long as the golden boy asks, I'm sure it won't be a problem," said Sliver.

Kavi nodded. "Do we have volunteers?"

Boost and Sliver looked at each other.

"We were going to try it anyway," said Sliver.

Boost grinned. "Reckless experimentation is kind of our thing."

4

Grim

Grim sputtered as the cold water hit him. A second splash followed the first.

He held out a hand. "Stop, I'm up. I'm up!" he yelled. "What the hell are you doing?"

Nettie dropped the wooden bucket and stared at him. "What the hell are *you* doing? It's been two weeks. Two weeks of you getting drunk off your ass then waking up, outside, in a puddle of your own...filth. Enough!"

Grim sighed and pressed his hands to his ears in an attempt to stop the pounding in his head. "I know, I'm a useless piece of shit. That's well established."

"Will you quit feeling sorry for yourself? You saw horrible stuff. Whoop de doo. We all did. You killed other people. Most of us did that too. It's atrocious crap we have to live with. Do you want to know what helps? What actually helps, instead of getting black out drunk?"

Plugging his ears did nothing to block out her yelling. "Leave me alone, Nettie."

"Doing something about it. Bringing justice to the monsters that did it to us."

"I can't fight anymore, Net. I can't kill more people."

"No one's asking you to kill." She got close to him and stuck a finger in his face. "But you will fight. You will fight by helping this group that took you in. You will make weapons and armor. You will train those going out in the field. Every single one of those kids could benefit from someone trained by the Suli Elites."

She stood up and wrinkled her nose at his stench then threw a wet cloth at him. "Wipe your face. No...you're going to need more than that. Head to the bathhouse. No more of your wallowing in self pity bullshit. We start in an hour. Meet me at the forge, and don't make me send Carlin after you."

The baths were built around a natural hot spring. When Grim walked in, several Liberators stepped back to give him room. His reputation as a berserker preceded him. He ignored the stares and stripped off his stained clothing. He sniffed at his shirt and winced. Nettie was right. He was disgusting.

He sunk into the cleansing bath and grabbed a slab of soap and a pumice stone. Nettie had built clever filters around the cleansing area so used water was exchanged almost as quickly as bathers could dirty it. Grim had no idea how they worked, he was just happy they did.

As he sluiced off dirt and vomit the hot water began to dissipate the brain cloud that hung over his head for weeks now. Clarity brought shame. He was tired of being a disappointment. He didn't deserve yet another second chance. This would be chance number five, six? Why did people keep giving someone so worthless the benefit of the doubt? Pity. It was the only logical explanation. He didn't want their pity. He wanted to be left alone.

He grabbed his discarded clothing and scrubbed it in the bath. He ignored the dirty looks as the muck that came off the clothes turned the water a greenish brown. The filters burbled in an attempt to keep up. He gave himself one last scrub and hopped out of the cleansing bath, taking a perverse sort of pride in bending over at the waist to set his mostly clean clothing on the drying racks, treating the other bathers to a full moon. Huffs and grumbles accompanied the slip-slap of wet feet fleeing for the exit.

When he moved into the separate rinsing and relaxing area of the hot spring, he was blessedly alone. He rested his head against the edge of the bath and closed his eyes.

Images assaulted him. His axes cutting through monsters. Cutting through friends. Blanton lying in a pool of his own blood as Grim stood over him laughing in hysterical rage. Albin, Shon'Ji, Caitlyn, and even young Amanda who stood barely taller than a child. All dead now.

All his fault.

He banged his head against the edge of the bath, harder and harder with each image. He couldn't remember which ones died in the Pool at his hand or out in the field. It didn't matter. They were all dead now.

"By Krom's hairy...stop it. Grim! Stop!" yelled Carlin, his voice growing louder with each word. "You're bleeding all over the place."

Grim opened his eyes and looked into Carlin's worried ones. "I'll clean it up," he said. Anger flared, another one of his *friends* come to heap on more pity. He dunked his head under the water and felt his rage knit the cut on the back of his head. Another useless skill which benefited only him. He'd never had the ability to heal others. He was a taker, never a giver. His head broke through the water and he stood. If Nettie sent Carlin, he must have been in the bath longer than he thought.

"I'm fine," said Grim.

"Boy, you are as far from fine as I am from the moon. Nettie thinks a day's honest work will be good for you. I agree." Carlin threw clean clothes at him. He looked over at the torn and stained clothes drying on the rock. "You need to burn those."

"No," said Grim. "Those are my favorite pants."

Carlin walked over and delicately picked up the pants with thumb and index finger, holding them at arm's length. "There's a huge rip in the crotch. Favorite pants...yuck."

"What? I like the ventilation."

"They're borderline pornographic." Carlin dropped the pants back on to the rack. "I'm burning them. You best get down to the forge in the next couple minutes or Nettie's coming herself. You're not going to like how that ends."

Grim stood and walked out of the bath. He toweled himself off and noticed for the first time that his chiseled muscle had started to turn flabby, especially around the midsection. He shrugged. That's a liquid diet for you.

Carlin held a hand over his eyes. "Will you please stop waving that meat pipe around and put on the new pants."

"You like what you see, old man?"

Carlin grabbed a towel and snapped it towards him, missing the meat pipe by centimeters.

"Not funny, Carlin," said Grim. "That was too close."

"Get moving. If you keep messing around she's going to

yell at me too."

"You still scared of that little Bricker?" Grim asked with a smile.

Carlin raised his eyebrows. "Damn right, and if you had any sense in your head, you'd be scared of her too."

"It wasn't too long ago that I wiped vomit off *her* face," said Grim. He thought back to when he helped Nettie through her dangerous suli withdrawal. "Simpler times. You ever wish we told her to take that journal and go screw herself?"

"Pretty much every day," said Carlin.

* * *

The forge, like all the buildings in their little community, was surprisingly nomadic. The Liberators spent a good amount of their existence planning how to flee at a moment's notice from the Collective's impressive roster of assassins and crack troops. This required them to use a combination of technology and skills to allow them to pack up and disappear in minutes.

One of the previously unknown skills Nettie unlocked as a Fort for Company Wari was battlefield architecture. Pretty useless as a Ghost, but an incredible boon when it came to managing a war camp. It was an ability she used again and again in their flight from one camp to the next. She tapped her foot impatiently as she waited for Grim and Carlin to make their way down to the forge. She was about to demonstrate her architecture skill to a group of Liberators.

37

"There they are," said Cliff as Grim and Carlin walked down the path. Even Cliff was nervous around Nettie when she had a full head of steam. Her insults were terrifyingly personal. Often, they didn't bother you until a couple hours later when you caught your reflection in a mirror or someone else made a comment of a similar nature. The only person not bothered by her sharp tongue was Grim. Then again, the huge Krommian berserker didn't seem bothered by much.

Nettie glared at both men right up until they joined the circle standing around the forge.

Her glare focused on Grim. "It's amazing someone with that large of a head has so little concept of time."

"Easy. We're here now," said Carlin.

"And only fifteen minutes late, will the miracles ever cease?"

Grins lit the circle, but they were relieved rather than amused. Relieved that Nettie's scorn was not being heaped on them.

"Today we're going to discuss nomadic architecture," said Nettie. "You've been here long enough to know we might need to flee at a moment's notice. Those who spent time in the League understand the overwhelming...capacity of the Companies in the League. Company Wari has an underground fortress where you can walk for an entire day without being able to go from one end to the other."

The Liberators who hadn't spent time in the League looked at her in disbelief. One of the small Brickers near Nettie snorted.

Nettie narrowed her eyes at the Bricker. "What? You don't believe me, Ears?"

The small Bricker self-consciously pulled wild hair over

his ears. "The name's Flask. I believe you, I just envy your underground fortress. At the Nest we had to climb one thousand, two hundred and twelve stairs to get to bed every night."

Nettie gave Flask a rueful grin. "Our stairs went down and as you dropped it got so damned hot."

Flask smiled. "We had the opposite problem-"

"Is this going to turn into a one up session?" asked Grim. "Maybe you could have had *that* contest in the fifteen minutes you waited for me to get here?"

"That huge melon of yours getting bored?" asked Nettie.

"Yeah, it is," said Grim with as much contempt as he could muster.

"Moving on then," said Nettie. "What you probably didn't know until you got here was the group backing the League, the Collective, is even bigger. Has even more reach. Our favorite Sage is the Collective's enemy number one. When she gets a premonition that we're about to be attacked, we need to move. Not in hours, in minutes."

"The engineers who preceded me created these amazing buildings that can be put up and taken down in minutes. Those engineers used two primary tools - replaceable and collapsible parts. Something those of us trained at the University call...?"

Nettie looked around but everyone stayed silent. She shook her head derisively. "Come on Flask, fourth year engineering was all about this."

"Modularity," said Flask.

"Exactly," said Nettie. "Modularity. Why didn't you speak up?"

"Because I find you terrifying," said Flask.

She looked at him in disbelief then looked to the others standing around the circle. They nodded and shrugged in solidarity with Flask. "Okay, I'll take the insults down a notch."

Grim snorted in disbelief.

"Except with you," said Nettie. She put her hand on one of the crossbeams which supported the small roof over the anvil. Only one wall kept the anvil mostly open to the elements but protected it when it rained. "What do you notice about this crossbeam that you wouldn't see in a regular building."

"It's made of three different pieces with those little bracket things between 'em," said Carlin.

Nettie nodded at Carlin with encouragement. "Good, what else?"

"The three pieces are identical in size. Actually they're identical in every way," said Flask. "That way we can use them for this structure or any other. They're like blocks."

Nettie nodded. "Thank you, Flask. Exactly right but please let the non-University trained answer the rest of the questions."

Flask nodded but held his hand up.

"Go ahead," said Nettie.

"Doesn't modularity make the structures weaker?"

"Absolutely," said Nettie. "If any of these buildings were permanent structures, building them this way would be a terrible idea. Build permanent structures out of solid wood or stone. The Liberator engineers who came before me realized that when you are shuffling between five, six, even ten camps, you need another option. If everything is made from the same four or five buildings blocks, all you need to do is move the blocks. Or...teach people how to make the same four or five blocks quickly so every camp is stocked with them."

"We've all evacuated, at least once, through those portal thingies. So, you know the buildings in each camp," Nettie spun around to look at the camp, "are made from these blocks. If something breaks we replace it. If we need to move quickly, we pull the stabilizing pins and the entire building collapses in seconds. We fold the pieces, toss them into the portal and away we go. Impressive engineering."

There were nods in the audience but not a lot of enthusiasm. Most of them understood the basics.

"We getting to the good stuff soon?" asked Grim.

"Keep your pants on," said Nettie.

"The new ones," added Carlin. "We're all sick of the old ones."

This brought real smiles, even from Nettie. "So, why the long preamble?" Nettie asked. "You get the basics. I understood the theory, too. I just didn't care. I was an overeager wannabe Quest adventurer before I got snapped up by the League. I'm guessing I wasn't the only one."

There were a couple of nods, but mostly shrugs. This group was long past Quest idealism. "I learned the hard way, like most of us," said Nettie, "that Quests are big business and big business doesn't give a shit about who it grinds up on the way to results. Even when I got captured and made a slave, I held out hope I would be promoted to one of their Cracker positions. After all, I figured out Korbah's Conundrum. Then I found myself in the Pool. Everyone died anytime we set foot in that thick, glowing water. Then, one day, as we were being overrun by a horde of disgusting lizard creatures, I accepted I was going to die. Why not make the best of a horrible situation? One of our Forts said, 'I wish we could build towers instead of hiding behind these tiny little stakes. Then we'd have real protection, if only for a minute to catch our breath'."

Nettie's voice dropped as the memory struck. Everyone leaned in to hear. "So, I looked at the materials us Forts had summoned. I thought about the most effective tower to protect against these flying frog thingies that spit acid at us. Suddenly, plans for a perfect tower popped into my head. It had to have a sloped roof, so the stakes we already had would do fine. Then I began to play like children do. This piece would go here, this one would go there. The other Ghosts on my team said I began to spin, whirling around like a mini tornado. Before I knew it, I was standing atop a perfect little tower, completely protected from the lizards."

Nettie snapped from her reverie and resumed at a normal volume. "The problem, of course was, not only did I take all of the resources, I also pulled the palisades protecting our front line. The stakes the Forts sunk earlier and pretty much everything but the traps our Dancers laid. A lot of people were pissed when we woke up. Of course, it was the first time I woke up last because I was pretty safe in the tower I built. Safe enough that the lizards killed me last."

"I remember a scenario like that," said Flask. "Was there a big tree in the jungle? That's where the first of our Ghosts unlocked a skill."

Nettie nodded. "The tower faced the tree but from what I heard, Sugoroku spent a lot more time in the Pool than we did."

"Yeah, we had this crazy guy who kept pushing us back in

the Pool," said Flask. "His name was —"

"Kavi?" asked half the people standing around the circle.

"We were with you on that Quest, remember?" said Cliff. "Only guy I've ever seen fight that monster," he pointed at Grim, "to a standstill. Was the damnedest thing." Cliff bit the inside of his cheek in a bid to scatter those memories. "Anybody else from your group of Ghosts unlock skills?"

"One or two others, but we only got in the Pool for a week or two before the first Quest," Nettie said. "I lost most of my team that day. If it hadn't been for Rose, we all would have died."

Her grim look was mirrored in the faces around her. Everybody in the Liberator camp had their fill of violence and the League.

"So, how'd you do it?" asked Cliff.

"Not completely sure," said Nettie. "It started with me accepting I was going to die, but I was thinking about protecting the Forts around me."

"That does seem to be the recipe—embrace mortality, protect your team," said Flask. "That's what Kavi believed. After that, it seemed to require passion about something. For me it was alchemy."

"That sounds right," said Nettie. "For architecture, I need to focus on two things: a blueprint or plan has to be crystal clear in my mind. Then—absolute belief I could build the structure with the resources I had. That's why these modular blocks are so valuable. I can build so much with so few pieces. Watch!"

Nettie focused and the Liberators jumped back as the forge began to deconstruct in front of their eyes. Nettie spun like a top, pieces of the forge bouncing in her wake. Within seconds, those pieces reassembled into a different forge ten meters from the original. The entire process took maybe ten seconds. She stopped spinning and looked to the group with a smug smile.

"Cooool," said Flask. "Can you teach it?"

Nettie shook her head. "I don't think so."

"Then why are we here?" asked Grim. "You need muscle to bring the anvil over to the new spot?"

"Not as much muscle there as there once was, huh?" asked Nettie, looking at the paunch Grim now sported.

Grim smiled, held his belly and burped. "I get it, you're showing off. A lot of us have cool skills, you know. Should we have a show and tell?"

"No, you doofus. I brought you here because you've all unlocked talents in the Pool. The only way the Liberators will unlock new talents is by constantly pushing ourselves. Constantly facing our mortality. So how we going to do that without a lot of people dying?"

"You want to build a new Pool," whispered Flask.

Every face in the group blanched.

Nettie nodded. "Not just a Pool. A nomadic Pool. One that can travel with us. How else are we going to compete with the Collective?"

5

Liberator Camp

"What am I doing here?" asked Grim for the second time. He hadn't had a drink in four days and while the hangover had mostly disappeared, his stomach was off. Everything was irritating.

"You're guess is as good as mine," said Carlin. "But when Rose requests your presence, attendance is mandatory. Even if she's too nice to say it herself."

"Does she know I've been drunk in the gutter since I got here?" asked Grim, surprised to find he cared what the fifth Sage thought about him.

"She knows," said Nettie. "She wants you here anyway." Nettie reached up and fixed Grim's collar. "You're going to do fine. Don't speak unless someone asks you a direct question, and keep the snark to yourself."

"He's only snarky around you, girl," said Carlin. "Grim knows how to behave in front of a superior officer." Carlin looked sideways at the big Krommian as if trying to convince himself of his own words.

Grim gave him a nod. "I won't embarrass you."

They stood outside the one permanent building in the Liberator camp. Every nomadic camp had a large, enduring structure that acted as the command center. This one was an abandoned fort that Nettie and her team of engineers rebuilt. They intentionally left the exterior in as much of a state of disrepair they could. They wanted the site to look abandoned when they packed up camp, so the outer walls of the fort still had broken segments of wall and crumbling towers.

The abandoned look was an obvious façade the moment one walked through the 'crumbling' gate. Every wall was reinforced. The broken walls were artfully crafted so that boxed ramparts and bulwarks could be slotted on top from the modular building blocks that lay beneath the walls.

Nettie caught Grim's eyes drift to the building materials and smiled at him. "Between me and three Forts, we can put a five-meter defensible wall in place in under ten minutes."

"Around the entire fort? That's got to be over a hundred meters of wall," said Grim.

She shrugged. "I do three quarters of it and the others focus on jointing the corners."

"And if you're not around?"

"It takes twenty engineers ten minutes. We drill on the defenses twice a week. They're getting faster. Imagine if we had two more architects. We could turn any battlefield into one-sided siege warfare."

Grim nodded, impressed in spite of himself. Nettie's skills would change how battles were fought across Grendar. He hoped her defensive approach would protect the poor citizens who inevitably ended up as collateral damage and he said as much.

"That's what Rose hopes too," said Nettie. "She really does care a lot more about the people than any of the Garden City governments."

Grim snorted. "I haven't learned much, but one thing that stuck with me is that things which sound too good to be true, normally are."

"Give her a chance, lad," said Carlin. "She's got as strong a moral compass as the Lioness."

Grim shook his head. "Case in point Carlin, I don't think anyone but me understands what the Lioness put Kavi through."

Carlin opened his mouth to protest.

Grim didn't let him. "Please don't tell me you're naïve enough to believe Lady Stonecrest has a lily-white conscience or clean hands."

"She did right by you, boy," said Carlin.

Grim nodded. "She did, but there were plenty of strings attached. To me, and to control Kavi. Don't think for a second otherwise."

"Leadership meeting starts in five," said Nettie interrupting Carlin's response. "We better get in there. The Sage is never late."

They walked through the wooden back door with rotted wood on the outside, reinforced by steel on the inside. The small keep was well lit. There were blue magelights in sconces placed every meter around the main hall. A large fire roared in a repaired hearth on the northern end. The keep had one main hall with two rooms segmented by walls accessed by arched doorways. The larger room was where the Sage slept when she was in camp. Rose's quarters were highly defensible and had a permanent portal structure that

Rose or any Vonderian guard could activate for a quick exit.

Half the leadership team already sat at the large wooden table at the center of the big hall. Younger Liberators carried food and drink from the kitchens below the fort walls.

"What's the berserker doing here?" asked a small Bricker woman with shaved hair and a fierce gaze.

"Easy Tack, Rose asked him to join us," said a huge man sitting to her right.

"You gotta quit calling me Tack, it's confusing. There are four tacticians here now. Seriously White, it's Promo now."

"How about General?" asked a man with long hair tied up in a topknot.

Promo smiled at the man, but shook her head. "I told you, Gavin. I'm not accepting the position until I see every squad fight."

"That could take months," said Gavin. "I don't know if we have that time."

"Then you wear the general hat," said Promo.

Grim didn't remember much from his first encounter with Team Sugoroku's professional tactician, but the fact she didn't want command was a mark in her favor. He liked her bluntness and her confidence. If she was as talented as Cliff made her sound, she'd make a strong military leader for the Liberators.

Gavin shook his head. "Never again. I'm an excellent bodyguard, but a terrible leader. My job is to keep Rose safe."

Carlin and Nettie took their seats around the table leaving a spot between them for Grim. As Grim was pulling his chair back in, everyone else stood up. He paused, not yet sitting.

"Remain seated please. No need for ceremony on the leadership team," said Rose, strolling in. Her black silk shawl was upgraded to a fabric that looked less like lace and more like metal filigree. As Rose moved to her chair at the head of the table, the shawl made a tinkling sound that caught the Sage's attention. She pulled it from her shoulders and set it over the back of her chair.

Rose looked at Promo. "I love how it looks and it still feels like silk, but it's too loud when I move. Anything you can do for that?"

Promo held out a hand for the shawl. "Does it chafe your neck?"

Rose shook her head. "Other than the sound, it's perfection—an amazing work of utility and style."

"As long as it fits, I can add upgrades to silence it," said Promo.

"Thank you." Rose turned her attention to the table. "Thank you all for arriving on time. We have loads to cover, so let's keep the status part short. Carlin, what are your eyes and ears picking up?"

Grim looked at Carlin with surprise and a new level of respect. He hadn't realized the huntsman had taken over so much responsibility. Could he really be managing the entire information network for the Liberators?

"All the Garden Cities, save Loam, have bought in to the League's message. With the governments behind it, the League will have more volunteers for the grinder than it knows what to do with," said Carlin.

Rose looked disappointed. "We all know what they'll do to those poor fools. Have we identified the corrupt politicians?"

"Most of 'em," said Carlin. "It's pretty obvious. They've made massive new purchases, home renovations, acquired new mistresses. They're not trying to hide it. Those already in power are benefiting the most. In Krom, the civilian council and the military received huge sums of money. In Astra, it's the theocracy. In Vonderia they bought the masters at the Academy. The League knows which levers to pull."

"Is anyone in power pushing back?" asked Rose.

"Pushing back against the League is very unpopular right now," said Carlin. "But there are a few. Lady Stonecrest, who you might know as the Lioness of Valun, a couple of other minor nobles and merchants, the VNC, and the entire guild of Harpstran stage performers. The actors seem to pick up on a scam faster than others."

"The VNC?" asked Promo.

Carlin nodded. "The Vonderian Neural Conglomerate. They believe the League is stealing their technology." Carlin shrugged. "Which, of course, they are."

"And what of the gods? Have there been any sightings yet?" asked Rose.

"No ma'am. I'm not sure how your divinations work, but my people haven't seen signs of them yet."

"Gods?" asked Grim, unable to hold his tongue.

"Yes, Master Grim," said Rose in a tired voice that made it clear she'd gotten the response more than once. "The gods will make an appearance, sooner than any of us would like."

Grim apologized and shut his mouth.

"Nettie, thank you for subbing for Bernard," said Rose. "He should be returning from his meetings with the VNC early next week. Tell me, how are the plans for the rapid defense deployment systems coming?"

Nettie's eyes lit up as they did when she had the opportunity to talk about anything that excited her. "The plans are done Sage. Madam Sage. Sage Rose?"

"Rose is fine, Nettie."

"The plans for the defense deployment system have been done for a week. The problem is power storage. We can't assume someone will be around to power the turrets when Bernard, Callum, or Quon'Ji are not around. It's terrible engineering to rely on any one person for power."

"The suli capacitors didn't work?" asked Rose.

Nettie shook her head. "It was a wonderful idea, but while sulimite is great for power enhancement and acceleration, it's terrible for storage."

"Have you tried experimenting with the trunite Promo brought in?" said Rose.

Nettie held her hand to her mouth. "Oh no, Rose, I couldn't. Bernard would never forgive me if I used even a milligram. We have so little."

Rose smiled. "I'm sure Bernard appreciates you being protective of our trunite reserve. Don't worry, we'll acquire more soon. It's critical we automate these defenses. The Collective will be ramping up their attacks and I'm nervous about the progress they're making with Project Midnight."

"I still haven't picked up anything about Project Midnight ma'am," said Carlin.

"That doesn't surprise me, it's one of the Collective's most closely guarded secrets. If there's one thing the Collective does really well, it's keeping secrets."

Rose turned back to Nettie. "What about your other idea? The mobile Pool technology?"

Involuntary shudders rippled through the room. Nobody doubted the results of the Pool, but they all hated it.

"Early stages still, ma'am," said Nettie. "One of the Sugoroku Forts, a Bricker named Flask, thinks we should open communication with Kavi and his team. They have a void mage who can communicate over long distances, but we have to figure out how to initiate it. They know the Pool better than anyone but its creators. If Bernard fails in his talks with the VNC, it may be our only option." Nettie fidgeted for a second.

"Ask the question, Nettie, I won't get upset."

"Well, we were thinking Sage Rose, that maybe...um...you could initiate the communication with Kavi? Like send him a vision or something? If you can do that sort of thing. Maybe?"

"Kavi has his hands full, but he and the rest of Team Sugoroku are well." She smiled as the news lit Nettie's face with a smile. She turned her gaze to Grim and Carlin then Promo and White. "However, he and his companions will face a new peril sooner than I expected."

"How can we help?" asked Grim and Carlin at the same time.

"I'm afraid you can't," said Rose. "If Kavi and his team don't face this danger alone, their future is even darker. Anything we can do to help is already in motion, like exposing the League and the politicians who enable them." She held up a hand to stall more questions about Kavi. "Kavi Stonecrest is incredibly capable, more than he realizes. Have faith, he and his companions will prevail."

Nettie nodded. "Let's hope Bernard succeeds with the VNC then."

"Let's hope," said Rose. "Now, Tack...sorry Promo, what is your initial analysis of our armed forces. Don't pull any punches."

"Pulling punches isn't my thing," said Promo.

White raised a hand and pointed down at Promo. "Nominee for understatement of the year."

Promo ignored her second. "They're a complete mess, but I understand why. The Liberators have been operating a guerrilla campaign for the last ten years. Communication has been relegated on a need-to-know basis with small groups of five or six. This is an effective way to protect information and the lives of individual cells. It's a fucking disaster when it comes to running a military force larger than a knitting circle."

Rose held her gaze. "Understood. How would you proceed if you ran the Liberator armed forces?"

Promo shook her head but smiled. "Don't think you can trick me into accepting the role, Sage." She pointed to her temple. "I know the mind games you play."

"Hypothetically then. Please."

Promo gave her a sideways glance then nodded. "Squad based structure, similar to how the League deploys. We'll never be an army, nor should we be. This group values autonomy too much. Eliminate the autonomy and you eliminate passion and inspired thinking. However, these cells *have* to learn how to work together. The League is now out in the open and so are we. If we want to be effective as a large fighting force we have to let go of protecting identity within our own ranks. We have to bring the cells together so they can learn to fight together."

"That's a bitter pill to swallow for most Liberators. They joined under the promise of anonymity," said Gavin. He looked to Rose. "We knew this was coming someday though, didn't we?"

Rose patted Gavin's hand affectionately. "We did. And I said that when we found the right commander, we would make the transition."

"You think Promo is the one?" asked Gavin.

"I'm sitting right here," said Promo.

Rose smiled. "She's the right one." She turned to look at Promo. "You speak truth to power, but know when to hold your tongue when it matters. You have the most brilliant mind for strategy I've ever met and I've been in the minds of most of Grendar's military commanders. You're tough enough to make difficult decisions, but you haven't lost that big heart of yours that makes you special to family and those closest to you." The evaluation was delivered in a matter-of-fact way that didn't leave room for doubt.

Promo squirmed at the compliments. "Is this a vision thing? Like, do you already know I'm going to say yes?"

"Very little is preordained, my dear. That would make life incredibly boring, don't you think?" She raised an eyebrow at Promo.

"So it's my choice?"

"Of course. It's always your choice."

"The deck is stacked against us. Why would I say yes to such a bad bet?"

Rose smiled. "Because there's a hole inside of you. You have an amazing set of skills that are begging to be used. This role will allow you to stretch those skills to the limit. Challenge you in a way you've become used to being challenged. What you're missing is purpose. That's what I can give you. That's what I give all the Liberators. A way to change Grendar for the better. If it's not the League or the

Collective, it's somebody else taking advantage of the have-nots. We can do something about that."

Promo nodded."When do you need an answer?"

Rose smiled. "Today. There are too many irons in the fire for us to hesitate. If you're not going to accept the offer I have to move on my second choice. We're out of time."

Promo nodded. "Okay, I accept."

White looked at Promo with wide eyes. "Are you sure? What about seeing how the rest of the squads fight?"

"Her actions back up her words," said Promo. "I've got a good feeling about her and I don't get a lot of good feelings. Haven't had one for years."

White nodded. "Good, I'm starting to like the nomad life."

"The last piece of business regards you, Master Grim," said Rose and all eyes turned to the largest man at the table.

Grim sat up and nodded to her.

"We need an audience with your father."

Grim's eyes widened and he snorted derisively. "I'm the last person that can get you that. My father disowned me. How do you not know that? In his eyes, I'm a pathetic weakling that should never have been born."

It was Promo's turn to snort. "A pathetic weakling. You? By the tinkerer's polished knob...has he ever seen you on the battlefield?"

Rose said gently, "I know you wouldn't believe it if I told you, but your father does feel regret. I'm not sure I believe it myself, but this is a demon you need to face, and we badly need to share some information with him. Two birds, one stone."

Grim clasped his hands together in an effort to still their trembling. "You've got the wrong person, ma'am. Carlin would be a way better advocate. He could use the Lioness' connection with my dad."

"I already tried, lad," said Carlin. "So did the Lioness. We need shock factor. We need you."

"The Krommian Council is entirely in the Collective's pocket. The only one who did not take their blood money is your father. General Broadblade has done many things I find atrocious," said Rose with a sympathetic glance at Grim. "But the man has his own set of principles. I believe we can share selective information about the Collective that could turn him into a sympathizer. We need people on that Council who aren't owned by the Collective. The Krommian army is too powerful."

Grim nodded. "I understand, but I'm the wrong guy. Look at me, I'm a mess. How can you give something this important to somebody who's such a disaster?"

Rose nodded with each self-deprecating statement. "Now's the time to clean up that mess. I know exactly who you are. It's time you figure it out too."

6

Stress & purpose

"When's the last time you took a break?" asked Clara from the doorway.

She leaned against the door frame of his new room. Kavi had taken Tack's old room as the tactician of this new pro team. The room wasn't huge, but it was large enough to fit a real bed, a desk, a small table and two chalkboards hanging on the walls around the table. Diagrams of formations were scrawled across the boards in Kavi's messy script.

Kavi looked up from his desk and scowled at her. "A break? A week and a half, Clara! A week and a half until we are back to fighting for our lives. What do you expect me to do, go for a midnight stroll around the Rim? I don't take breaks and neither should you."

"Don't snap at me, you ass," said Clara. "I'm trying to help. And now that you mention it, yes, that's exactly what I expect you to do. All these problems are going to be waiting for you when you get back. If you take a break, maybe even talk about what's bugging you for a second, you'll be able to look at everything in a new light."

He leaned back in his chair and looked at her. The green mage light flickering from the hallway accentuated her narrow features. The verdant glow cast her as some otherworldly, sylvan creature. Gorgeous. When they lived together in the one big room, the idea of pursuing any of his fellow Ghosts felt perverted. Sneaking off late night to the stairs or their disgusting privy...yuck. Kavi was too private for that.

Since they moved into their new quarters, Kavi had begun to isolate himself. The thought of losing more friends drove him to do everything he could to keep his squad safe, but he spent time in the army. He knew safety was impossible. When thrown in harm's way over and over again, people were going to die. But this wasn't the army. This was his squad, his rules, his responsibility. If he lost people now, after they made it through being Ghosts....well, he didn't think he could live with that. And he knew, no matter what preparations he made, it wouldn't be enough.

Maybe she was right, he needed a new way to look at the problem, or the stress would kill him long before the Marked. He let out a long sigh and stood up.

Clara held out a hand. "Well, Kavi Stonecrest, will you escort me on a midnight stroll around the Rim?"

His identity as the young lion, long hidden, was no longer a secret. "Well, I don't know Clara, have you lined up a chaperon? I would hate to have my reputation sullied."

"Are you afraid I'll do something untoward?"

"A guy can dream," he said with a grin.

He took her hand and felt a frisson of energy pass between them. Gooseflesh pimpled his arms and his eyes found hers. She felt it too. He wanted to blame it on a scuffed rug but the

Nest had none.

Having the freedom to walk the main floor at night was still a novelty. The past five months were a nightmare of restrictions. To be able to walk free after lights out, with a beautiful woman at his side made him feel unstoppable. Alive. How had he not done this until now? He could feel the weight lifting off his shoulders.

"What was it like, growing up as the son of two legends?" she asked. "The pressure must have been incredible."

They walked past the vacant dining hall and the entrance to the Gauntlet. Kavi hardly glanced at them as he thought about that pressure for the first time in months.

"With my father it was easy. He was the glue that kept us together. He was curious about everything. When he talked to you, you always had his full attention. Like there was nothing more important than you. He made me feel like I mattered."

Clara smiled. "I had an art teacher like that. She made me feel like I could do anything."

They walked in silence for a moment. When they reached the expansive training cavern they blinked at the perpetual daylight emitted by the three large spheres hovering below the ceiling. The bright yellow glow burned in contrast to the relaxing green of the hallways, too searing, less prone to revelation. They instinctively moved to the far edge of the Rim to find softer light.

"What's your mother like? She seems...intense," said Clara.

Kavi snorted. "Intense is an understatement. She floats on an ocean of rage. You never knew when she was going to snap."

"Did she beat you?"

"Only in the sparring circle and, even then, it was instructive." He thought back to all the time spent in the ring. He had grown up on those sands. He missed sparring against her. He felt a tug at his hand.

"Kavi?" Clara stopped. She stared at him.

"What?"

"I said that doesn't sound too bad."

He smiled at her. "Sorry." They started walking again.

"She prided herself on sparing us the switch," said Kavi. "She would talk about how disgusting it was when somebody would hit a small child and the child had no way to defend themselves..."

"I agree with her."

"Oh me too, but that was her moral high ground," said Kavi. "She preferred verbal violence. When she started yelling it was like...being in a tornado. You had trees and cows of pure wrath circling around you, but never quite striking you. The implied violence was so high, it was almost like it would have been better if she just hit me. That moral high ground was so...hypocritical. She acted like words couldn't be violent when in reality her words tore away all your self-worth. To be the target of such rage...you felt an inch tall."

They walked together in silence for a moment.

"You know what I finally figured out?" said Kavi. "It took me being a slave and losing all my freedom to understand it."

"What?"

"She's an asshole," said Kavi. "People who completely lose their minds to rage are assholes. Once you get that angry, you turn into something that stops seeing people, only objects to scream at. There's no chance to listen or understand another point of view." He shrugged. "An asshole."

"So the Lioness of Valun is an asshole. Huh, I wouldn't have guessed. She's always portrayed as icy calm."

"Maybe to the outside world," said Kavi. "Maybe that's why she has so much anger. Anytime she would lose it on my brother or my father, you know what I felt?"

"Relieved?"

"Yeah, that too, because it wasn't pointed at me," Kavi said. "But more recently my feelings shifted. A couple of weeks before I got captured, I saw her lose her mind at her favorite horse. She's throwing straw around, stomping her feet, and screaming at the top of her lungs at this animal. I felt something different."

"What?"

"Embarrassed. For her, for my family that has to deal with such an asshole," said Kavi. "I never would have said it then because it was so terrifying to me as a child. That leaves scars. But looking back, she looked like a clown. Her lack of control was pathetic."

Clara looked at him. "That explains a lot."

"How do you mean?"

"Well, you have zero tolerance for anybody that loses their temper whether we're in the Pool or in the field. I get it now. Is that why you came down on Sliver yesterday?"

Kavi shook his head. "No. Sliver struggles with social cues. She had been going on and on about how disgusting Boost was after ten seconds in his mind. She didn't pick up on how bad Boost was feeling. You don't get it, Clara, guys constantly think about sex. I can't imagine the thoughts in Boost's head are anomalies. I think it was a bad idea mixing sexes for our first experiment with the strong bond. There are too many differences in how we think and the stakes are too high."

"You were harsh on Pip, too," said Clara.

"The 'I told you sos' weren't helping. We have to be able to take risks. Risks are what got us this far in the first place."

"Who do you think could handle a strong bond? It's so... intimate."

"Me and Pip, if he were up for it. You and Sliver maybe? I'd go in there with Boost but I think Sliver really hurt him by airing the things in his head. I don't think Jansen could do it, there's too much trauma there. Maybe Stix and Stonez if we can ever convince Stix to join the squad."

"I heard what you said about the different sexes, but I don't agree with it. What about you and me?" asked Clara.

"I don't think you'd like what you'd see." Kavi tapped his temple twice. "There's really dark stuff running on repeat up here."

"We all have dark stuff running around upstairs," said Clara. "Maybe that's the secret to the fuse. We have to accept the darkness. Without judgment. It's as much of a part of us as the things we like about ourselves."

"That could take a lifetime," said Kavi.

Clara shook her head. "I don't think so. I was one of the ones who thought you were crazy to go back in the Pool again, but it forced the issue. It made us accept our mortality. Sink or swim. What if this is the same thing? We accepted we're going to die. How much harder can it be to come to terms with our own darkness? Especially with this group. We shared so much trauma as Ghosts. That's the beauty about facing mortality. You drop the pretense of polite society. Maybe it's time to make the next jump."

"You might be on to something," said Kavi, nodding. "But it still feels like we're missing a key ingredient."

"Like what?"

"Motivation? Survival threw us back in the Pool again and again, but we're not Ghosts anymore. We have resources now. Support teams."

Clara nodded. "Survival is the best motivator. You think we need something more. Purpose?"

Kavi nodded. "We're locked to our contracts, but we need something to push us. Helping people is great, but we have to find something more to drive us."

"Maybe the strong bond will help," said Clara. "Help us uncover what that is."

They were coming to the end of the lap around the Rim. Kavi stopped, looked at their entwined hands then turned to look Clara in the eyes. "I don't know what this is," he said. "But I don't want to screw it up. I'm afraid if you look in the dark corners, you're going to hate me for it. I don't think I can handle you thinking as badly about me as Sliver thinks about Boost."

"I'm better with social cues than Sliver." She held up her free hand. "But I understand. All I ask is you think about it."

"I will. Would you be willing to go in with Sliver first? Maybe I can talk Boost into going in with me."

She looked deep into his eyes, searching for something. He felt another frisson of energy run through him as he fell into those green pools. So beautiful. She edged closer to him. He was about to lean in for a kiss when inspiration struck.

He smiled and the moment was broken.

"You were right," he said.

Clara looked disappointed but offered a half-hearted smile. "Three of my favorite words. About what?"

"About taking my mind off it. I know how to get Stix on board."

7

Building the team

The Aerie was a hive of movement and information. The first time Kavi walked up the wide stairway past the coaches' quarters he was struck by how many people moved in and out of the command center on an hourly basis. If the giant training cavern was the heart of the Nest, the Aerie was its brain.

Long linen sheets covered the entrance to the research lab. With the progress the Ghosts made last season, the Company was expanding the lab. The sheets kept most of the rock dust out of the briefing rooms, but not all of it. The AA construction team had almost finished hanging the new door to the lab. It would match the door that led to the Web and the Rookery on the far side of the briefing rooms. The Coaches demanded the door after the cacophony from the falcons and messenger pigeons grew loud enough to interrupt Quest briefings. The final passage out of the briefing room led to the Crypto Quarter where the Crackers spent time making sense of the gibberish they received from the Sages.

Kavi wasn't the only one impatient for them to finish the

damn door. They were all tired of inhaling dust and the constant hammering of pickaxes frayed everyone's patience.

Kavi sat on one side of a broad table with Pip, Stonez and the head coach of Team Sugoroku. Coach Sug, as he was called, was an older gentleman with pale skin and hair that had gone white over the years. Kavi knew no one in the Company that predated Coach. Even Lady Sugoroku had less tenure. His face was a tableau of wrinkles and scars that hinted at legions of stories filled with war and pain. Kavi had yet to hear the man raise his voice or issue a threat. He didn't need to. Those around him were sucked into the vortex of his presence.

The four of them stared at the craftsmen hanging the door until Stonez couldn't take it any longer.

"Damnit Lolly, you've been on construction for three years and you still don't know how to line up a hinge. Pathetic!" yelled Stonez as he walked over to the three AAs holding the large door.

Stonez grabbed the edge of the door and slowly guided it towards the wall. "Don't you dare drop that pin before I get the knuckle lined up," he barked. "Ok, now! Quickly, this thing is heavy. Now...the top. No...same process. I swear to Krom, if you drop that thing one more time I'm going to drop you."

Stonez stepped back and nodded once as the double As swung the new door back and forth to check the seal. "That'll do, now close the fucking door and give us some quiet!"

"Don't know what they would do without you, Stonez," said Pip. "You sure you want to give up the construction gig?"

"I can finally hear my own thoughts," said Stonez. He spat

on the floor then looked up at Coach with a slightly horrified look. "Sorry Coach, this dust is brutal."

Coach smiled. "The moment you start caring about manners is when I start to worry, young man. Ready to get back to work?"

"Before our next candidate review," Kavi said. "I'd love to get your thoughts on deploying a fifteen-person squad instead of an eleven. Since these are peacekeeping missions, we don't need to follow League rules."

"Thanks for bringing that up," said Coach. "Our strategies are built for eleven person squads but the whole damn playbook is going to have to be rewritten if you pull off this neural bond. We have the playbook so we can communicate quickly, the bond would make communication instinctive. Use it."

Kavi tried to find Pip's eyes, but the Striker refused to look in his direction, still unwilling to even discuss a fuse with someone else. "We're going to attempt it again tomorrow, Coach. The hard part is finding willing volunteers."

Coach grimaced. "Some things need to be ordered."

Kavi shook his head and shrugged. "We're free men now."

Coach shrugged. "Ostensibly."

"Freedom's a fragile thing," said Kavi. "The minute the team feels like they lose their voice, they're going to break."

"They're tougher than you think," said Coach. "But it's your show." Coach cleared some paper notes on the table until he exposed two small silver domes in front of him. He raised his eyebrows at Kavi. "Ready to look at some sims?"

Kavi nodded and joined Coach, Stonez, and Pip in placing his hands on the two silver spheres built into the table in front of each chair.

The world shifted and they were in a pre-recorded Pool scenario. Over the last couple of weeks Kavi had gotten used to observing. It was far better than a two-dimensional broadcast. They couldn't change the outcome in a pre-recorded sim, but they could stop the action whenever they wanted and observe from any angle or position within the recording. They also had their own communication channels so they could continue to speak with each other regardless of how furious or loud the action was in the sim.

This was a battlefield scenario where a small team of warriors faced off against a much larger unit. It was an open field where hay bales and rock walls provided minimal coverage on either side. Kavi recognized some of the AAs in the smaller group on the near side of the field. He didn't recognize anyone in the larger group. Both sides were currently frozen in the sim.

"Two folks I'd like you to pay special attention to," said Coach. "Tristan, the Loamian Guard on the far right. And Jory, the Harpstran Striker just left of the Guards. Jory's skills are...interesting."

"Don't forget about our honey pot," said Stonez. "Crystal is five steps back. She's a hybrid like you, but Astran-Harper."

Kavi made mental notes of each. He also noticed Stix on the line as a Guard, anchoring the line in front of Crystal. "Let's go."

Coach Sug flicked the small controller in his right hand and the action started at triple speed. The force with superior numbers charged at a comically fast pace. Kavi briefly wondered if he looked that silly when he slowed time. The two Guards set their feet. Neither Tristan or Stix carried shields. Strange for Guards.

Crystal rapidly built a structure behind their line. Odd, why not build a defense in front? At triple speed the structure was quickly revealed as a raised ballista. Impressive. It had a clever screw and pully mechanism that loaded one gigantic bolt while queuing up a second. As soon as it was complete, she shouted something unintelligible at triple speed and fired over Stix's head.

The gigantic bolt skewered the charging Krommian at the head of the larger force. The bolt passed right through the man and had enough power to remove the arm of the Krommian behind him to lodge into a tall, spindly Bricker behind him. Crystal cranked a hand winch and the second bolt slid into place. She fired and another two charging warriors were ripped apart.

When the charging forces closed, Jory pulled something off his back that looked like a...lute? Maybe it was a mandolin. Kavi frowned. A musician on the field? Then Jory's fingers raced over the frets as he played a dark and angry tune. Moments later half the remaining force charging them stopped and ran the other way, screaming in fear.

This gave Crystal the chance to fire two more bolts with devastating effect. Two of the ranged Strikers on each end, a Bricker and a Loamian, fired at their retreating backs. They were good, but not nearly as good as Tess or Boost. Still, another five of the attackers fell.

"A troubadour? Really?" asked Pip echoing Kavi's own thoughts.

"Shh," said Stonez. "Watch him fight when they close."

When the effect of Jory's music wore off, the other side—now with nowhere near the overwhelming numerical advantage—charged again. This time more cautiously.

"Why did the sim create such weak warriors on the other side" asked Kavi. "I'd like to see these candidates perform under pressure."

Coach Sug laughed. "They're not from a sim. Those are our new volunteers. Super green, but they're eager."

The unit on the far side still outnumbered the defenders three to one, but it was starting to look like a lopsided battle. In favor of the defenders. Then, two Vonderians on the far side summoned flame and lit up the two Strikers on either edge of the defenders' line. The Bricker died in screams. The Loamian kept firing even as he burned.

"The Vonderian in the back of the challengers' line is talented," said Coach Sug. He fiddled with the controller again and the speed of the battle slowed to normal. "His name is Varseid. We would have already given him a volunteer squad if he wasn't such an arrogant ass. That's the reason for this exercise, to teach these overzealous idiots some humility."

The charging Strikers and Guards finally met what was left of the defenders' line. As the first Krommian to reach the line raised his sword to attack Tristan, the lanky Loamian transformed into a giant cat. With a swipe of his paw, he removed the attacker's head in one blow. He then pounced on the woman behind the headless victim. She died just as quickly.

On the other side of the line, Jory defended himself with short sword and dagger. Kavi was impressed. The man took the bigger strikes on his sword, deflecting, then swiped the knife up to find exposed necks and sides. He was fast. Three attackers already lay dead at his feet.

Crystal drove a spear in the openings between Jory and

Stix. She found exposed flesh at least twice while Stix kept everyone at bay with his two wicked sabers. Stix defended with speed and timing. He was always in the right place at the right time—to defend a strike meant for Crystal—or to launch a strike of his own as an attacker overextended. It looked fluid and easy, like the man was not even breaking a sweat. Stix smiled as he fought and Kavi was almost certain he saw him whistling once as he struck.

Eventually an attacker did get through with a spear thrust that caught Crystal in the leg. Stix's demeanor shifted instantly. "You little bastard," he growled. Then he began to spin. He became a literal whirlwind of steel which ripped through the remaining attackers. When he stopped, only the Vonderians and ranged fighters in the back of the attacker's line remained. Stix pointed a sword in their direction and yelled, "You're next!"

Tristan bounded towards the survivors with Jory and Stix right behind them. Crystal laid her hands on the wound in her leg and it slowly stitched up. She grabbed her spear and began to jog after the three men.

Tristan reached the two Vonderians first and his claws made quick work of both of them. Stix and Jory took out the archers with little effort.

Stix looked to the sky and screamed in triumph.

Coach Sug hit a button on the controller and they were once again in the Aerie conference room.

"Not bad," said Kavi. "I want to spar Tristan, Jory and Crystal in the circle." He looked at Stonez, impressed. "Great finds. If they can show me they're willing to learn, I want all three of them."

"That leaves just the one spot left," said Pip.

"He'll come around," said Kavi.

* * *

"Fuck you too," said Stix. "You dragged Crystal into this because you thought it would get me to sign on?"

Kavi had never seen the AA angry. His face was blotchy and his normally calm demeanor had been replaced with something demonic.

"No, Stix," said Stonez. "You know she can fight. When she heard about how much it pays, she came to me, not the other way around."

Stix pointed at Kavi. "And you, skulking around behind my back doing everything you can to get me to sign up."

It was the wrong thing to say to Kavi. His hackles raised as he stood and faced the man across the table. "I don't skulk. First, I told you straight to your face that I would do everything I could to get you on my squad." He pointed when Stix tried to respond. "No...It's time for you to shut your mouth. Second, I'm going to do everything I can to keep my people alive out there. That means recruiting the best. I've watched her in the Pool. Not only can she fight, she can heal. I'd be an idiot not to take her. Third, go fuck yourself. I don't want you on my squad if you're going to break down the minute something doesn't go your way. You've been a double A too long, you've forgotten the stakes."

Stix threw down the roll he was eating and stormed out of the dining hall.

"That went well," said Sliver.

"At least he sounds like a Tack again," said Tess with a smile.

Stonez held his arms out and looked at Kavi in disbelief. "What the hell, Eleven? You didn't even tell him he would be able to drop in on his family in this first deployment."

"You saw how angry he was. Nothing we said would have changed his mind. If he joins this squad, he's got to understand what's acceptable."

Stonez stared at Kavi. Kavi stared back. Stonez slowly nodded his head. "Okay, Tack. I'll work on him when he cools off."

"See if you can get him in the Pool tomorrow," said Kavi.

"That may be asking too much," said Stonez. He held Kavi's gaze. "I know, we're running out of time. I'll work on him."

"Have you seen the new volunteers shuffling in?" said Boost. "They're strutting around like they own the place. Apparently, the draft this year was a martial tournament in each of the Garden Cities. Sugoroku landed the Harpstran champion and the Vonderian runner up."

"Yeah, one of those idiots bumped into me in the dining hall this morning then said he was going to kick my ass," said Jansen. "I couldn't take him seriously. It *really* pissed him off when I started laughing. Then, the rest of the dining hall started laughing too. One of his buddies had the sense to usher him out before it got out of hand."

"I've seen them strutting around," said Tess. "I can't believe I'm saying this, but this particular group of idiots will benefit from Coach K knocking the snot out of them."

"Categorization is day after tomorrow," said Pip. "You

going to sit in, Tack?"

Kavi shook his head. "No, I'm in meetings most of the day when we're not in the Pool. The Snoops have new information on the incursion. So far I haven't been impressed by these volunteers but we have to do our diligence. Can you take Tess and scout for talent?"

"I need to be there if there's new info," said Pip. "Tess, mind taking Boost?"

Kavi did everything he could to appoint Pip as the tactician for the team. Pip had a better head for strategy and was a natural back line fighter. Sugoroku wasn't having it. Kavi Stonecrest would be the face of the incursion squad which meant he was tactician. Kavi and Pip trained the team in the Pool to accept orders from either of them, especially when Kavi had to plug holes.

Tess nodded. "We'll come back with a report. None of the volunteers have unlocked a skill and Coach Sug made it clear they're only to be used for Quests, but I get it. We need to know how the development squad looks."

"What about the neural bond tomorrow?" asked Kavi

"We're calling it a neural hug now," said Sliver.

"I didn't agree to that," said Boost.

Sliver rolled her eyes. "You will. Clara yelled at me for talking shit about Boost."

It was Clara's turn to roll her eyes. "I didn't yell at you. I just explained how bad it might feel if I exposed some of your secrets."

"So, Clara yelled at me," said Sliver. "And I realized she was right. I apologized to Boost and we're going to try another neural hug in the Pool tomorrow."

"Can we try two neural hugs tomorrow?" asked Kavi. "I

don't think I need to repeat this but..."

"We're running out of time," said the whole team in unison.

Kavi laughed. "Can we?"

Sliver shook her head. "I haven't heard anyone else volunteer, but Hiram thinks it's a bad idea. The neural hug is resource intensive and he's not sure what even one of them might do to the simulation."

"Let's have a back-up ready if yours fails," said Kavi. "Any volunteers?"

Clara raised her hand and looked at him. "The offer is still open, Tack."

"I've been thinking about it," said Kavi. "I'll try it with you when we get a successful bond. But I need to be focused on team dynamics in tomorrow's runs. Don't think I can test new tech at the same time."

Tess raised a hand. "I'll join you Clara, if the Brickers can't make it work."

8

Neural Hug

Kavi looked forlornly over his empty room. Over the past six months he got used to being surrounded by people *all* the time. He'd been so busy the last several weeks, he worked until he collapsed. Then, he got up and did it all over again. He avoided free time that allowed him the chance to brood about keeping his team alive.

It wasn't working.

He had the recurring dream last night. He watched the kobold slip the dirty sword in Trixie's back while Rake's javelin slid through Pete's. The pain and fear lessened in the morning light, but never went away. He looked over at the twisted, sweat-soaked sheets and took a couple deep breaths.

Sugoroku promised to deliver the letters to their families the day they deployed on their first peacekeeping mission. He looked over at his desk with the crumpled papers of many failed starts. What to say? How does one explain all of *this.* Carlin would have communicated he was still alive, so it needed to be more than a status update. The censors would never allow intelligence or disparaging sentiment of the League or Collective through.

The angry child in him wanted his mother to choke on the lack of information, but that wouldn't accomplish anything. He could encode a message with references only his family would understand, but that might put them in danger. How did one explain the loss of freedom? How did one share the revelations from accepting mortality and his ever shifting role in this world of Sages, Quests and fantastic powers? No letter could do all that. Maybe just a warning he would be in the news in a couple of weeks.

A knock on the door interrupted his thoughts. "Come in," he said.

Pip walked in with Tess. "Stonez got Stix to show this morning," said Pip. "We have a full roster for the first time... provided the newbies can actually fight."

Kavi clapped his hands together. "Let's get to work."

* * *

They lined up in front of the Pool. Coach Sug stood with two assistants in the booth. They promised a town defense scenario that would parallel their next peacekeeping mission. Coach refused to tell them what they would face. He wanted to see how the team improvised.

As they walked to their seats, Stix met his eyes. "Sorry," said the Harpstran Guard who'd been a philosophical mentor to Kavi over these past months.

"Water under the bridge," said Kavi. His shoulders relaxed

with the apology.

"No, I screwed up," said Stix. "You're right to do everything you can to protect your squad. *Our* squad. I don't go looking for fights, but if Stonez and Crystal are in the field I can't be sitting on my ass in the Nest."

Kavi nodded, relieved Stix found his own reasons to join.

"Promise me you'll do what you can to keep them safe," said Stix.

Kavi found the arm rests in the Pool and sat. He looked at Stix taking his own seat. "I always do, but I can't promise I'll be successful."

Stix held his eyes for a moment then gave a tight nod. "That will have to be enough."

Boost and Sliver sat next to each other in the Pool. When they strapped in to their seats, they scooted close so they shared an armrest. Kavi raised an eyebrow at Sliver.

"Hiram thinks it will enhance the neural hug," said Sliver.

Hiram grinned from the booth and gave them a thumbs up.

"He's going to activate the hug as soon as we get in. If it doesn't work we'll still be able to salvage the run," said Boost.

"Good luck," said Clara.

Kavi raised a finger above his head and spun it around letting the coaches know they were ready. He put his arm back on the rest and felt the strap lock him in place. The glowing ball of light descended from the ceiling.

"Here we go," whispered Jansen with a fierce smile. Ghost Squad had been training in the Pool since Kavi and Pip returned to the Nest, but this was the first time with a full team.

The landscape shifted and Kavi found himself on a hill overlooking a small village. Far to the east he could make out the Harpstran skyline. He looked at Boost and Sliver as their bodies went taut.

They're expressions shifted from pained to ashamed. Then, they took a breath in perfect unison.

"Why do men have to be so frigging disgusting," they both said at the same time.

Kavi looked at both of them in surprise.

"Ooh, that was creepy," they said at the exact same time. "So was that."

"Can you communicate separately?" asked Kavi.

"Hang on," they both said. "Boost has an audio channel with Hiram. Not easy to process looking out of two sets of eyes."

"Not easy hearing your voice coming out of two mouths either," said Tess.

Sliver and Boost laughed in Sliver's super-fast chortle.

"That's worse," said Clara. "No more laughing."

"Take what time you need," said Kavi. "Pip, ready the team in a spread formation as we move into town."

Pip started issuing orders.

"Oh, thank the tinkerer's crispy bunghole," said Boost, through his own mouth. "We still share senses but Hiram talked me through separating audio channels. Damn, this is freaky. I have two sets of eyes, noses and...whoa, never thought I would have a pair of those," said Boost as he and Sliver looked down at their chests.

"That's exactly what I mean," said Sliver. "Eyes on the road, Nineteen."

They tried to follow the team but their bodies moved in

79

jerks and starts. "We'll catch up," said Boost. "We have to figure out how to move. If you need us playing our roles immediately, say the word and Hiram will cut the bond."

Kavi shook his head. "No, we have to see if the gamble pays off. Figure out how to walk and meet us at the inn."

Kavi followed his squad, observing how they moved. He smiled as Pip yelled at their new troubadour to get in formation. Pip had the man sharing point with their other Dancer, Amity, a Ghost from their class who volunteered to join the squad. She was a quiet woman that got along famously with Clara.

Then again, who didn't.

Their troubadour, Jory, was a ghost four seasons ago who had become interested in going back out in the field when he heard they would be playing the role of peacekeepers.

Jory had an open face with dimples the ladies found irresistible. He had tattoos of twin lyres on either side of his face. When he smiled, it looked like his dimples played the inked instruments. He let his dark brown hair grow to his shoulders so was forced to wear a leather cap to keep it out of his eyes when in the field. He carried his short sword as he led the group down the hill into town. His lute was strapped to his back without a case.

Amity stopped twice to point out potential traps. The rest of the squad waited patiently, most of them wondering if and when Jory would pull the lute off his back and do something musical. They'd seen the recordings, but the idea of using music in combat was more peculiar than a dog reading poetry. Then again, they'd seen stranger since joining Ghost Squad.

"What are we going to call this new squad?" asked Pip as

Kavi caught up with the group.

"Why not stick with Ghost Squad?" said Tess. "The Ghost era ended with us."

"True, but not everybody on the squad shares that history," said Clara. "I vote for something new."

"Focus on the mission please," said Kavi.

Clara rolled her eyes. "Even with a defense scenario, Tack? The chance of hitting traps are slim to none. Now's as good a time as any to establish identity."

Kavi stared at the village below, but acknowledged Clara's point. They passed several villagers working the fields and Kavi could hear the ring of a hammer on an anvil from the farrier below. If there were active traps down there, the villagers would have triggered them long ago. He relaxed a little. "I'm fond of Ghost Squad for nostalgic reasons, if nothing else," said Kavi.

"I was thinking more like Pip's Predators or Pip's Pillagers," said Pip with a toothy grin.

"How about Pip's Pacifists or Pip's Squeaks," muttered Stonez.

"I wouldn't mind Peacekeepers," said Tess. She looked at Pip. "You could tell your mom it's Pip's Peacekeepers."

"If we change the name, it can't be ordinary," said Stix. "It's got to have bite. We have to see how the team fights together."

"Agreed," said Jansen. "A squad name is like a nickname, it can't be forced. Ghost Squad fell on us. If we plan it, it's gonna suck. That said, I like something with Marked in it. Marked for Greatness, Marked Martyrs."

"It's not a band name Twenty-two," said Tess. "Marked Martyrs is terrible. You realize martyrs only get that way after they die?"

Jansen snorted. "Says a Striker from Ghost Squad."

Tess looked at Jansen with something bordering on respect. "Huh, hadn't thought about it like that."

Amity and Jory jogged back to the group. "Don't think the area is trapped, Tack," said Jory. "If it was, there'd be a lot more dead villagers." He flashed a cocky grin.

Kavi grinned inwardly when he caught Tess staring at those flashing dimples. "Pip, mind asking the farrier if there've been any raids on the village recently?"

Pip jogged over to the building with the sign of a horseshoe swaying in the breeze. He ran back a moment later. "East side of town. The villagers built a wall and manned it with a lookout."

Kavi shaded his eyes and looked in that direction. "Let's move."

The wall was more impressive than they expected from a village this size. It had four ladders that led up to a broad walkway which ran the length of a wall. On either end were elevated covered towers that housed lookouts armed with wide drums. A group of villagers with crossbows could easily hold the wall against a large group of bandits.

"But they're not bandits," said the lookout. "It's them damned razorspines you gots to watch out for. They come out the grasses low and silent like. That's why we cut the grass back so far. Damn things creep me out."

"What's a razorspine?" asked Kavi.

"Kinda like wolves with a lower profile, weaselly almost," said the lookout. "When they're on the prowl, their hackles are sharp barbs they can throw at you. They normally hunt in pairs, but since we built the wall around this side of town most attacks stopped."

"Why'd they send for us then?" asked Kavi.

"Ty swears he saw one of them things standing on two legs issuing orders like they was planning a major offensive. But they're animals. They don't plan. Ty's been known to hit the bottle pretty hard, but his pa's the mayor so he called for help."

"You see any other types of creatures out here?" asked Pip.

"Outside of squirrels and rabbits?"

Pip nodded.

"Every once in a while, a lookout claims to see small, bat looking creatures flying by, but they have tails and don't move like bats. Never seen one myself so I'm guessing it's a trick of the light. But it *was* Cricket saw one last time. He's not one for making up stories."

Pip turned to Kavi. "What are you thinking?"

"Sounds like we have a group of razorspines driven by a Marked. Maybe some imps?" said Kavi.

"It's not like we're getting out of the Pool without a fight," said Pip.

"Clara, take Crystal and Felicity and shore up the defenses," said Kavi.

Clara summoned a cart of supplies. "I'll have them plant stakes while I draw runes."

"Can you plant traps in front of the gate behind another round of spikes? We want to leave room for the Guards to maneuver while we draw them in," said Kavi. "Forts, especially Crystal and Felicity, stay on this wall. Be ready to heal. Amity stays low to heal serious injuries."

"Is the big guy anchoring our line?" asked Stonez.

"Remains to be seen," said Kavi. "Don't know if we can count on Sliver and Boost."

As if on cue, Boost and Sliver walked in to view. Their bodies moved independently of each other, but it looked like they had to put a lot of concentration into each step. As they closed on the wall, their motions slowly became more natural.

"Holeee shit," said the lookout, never shifting his gaze from the fields to the east. He ran to the tower and beat the drum.

Kavi looked out on the long grasses but couldn't see anything at first. Then he noticed unnatural ripples through the grasses, like predatory fish slicing through water. Every few seconds a tail would stand above the grasses like a furry periscope.

"Forts, behind the walls!" yelled Kavi. "Guards, hold that gate. Ranged, on the wall with me!"

Sliver and Boost ran up the ladders and slid into position.

"Would be really nice having Herman anchoring that line," said Kavi.

"Working on it," said Sliver.

Boost unslung his hand cannons. He moved to the north side of the wall opposite from Tess who knocked an arrow to her bow. Jory anchored the center of the wall and pulled a crossbow from a duffel he summoned from the Pool.

Stonez and Jansen pulled shields off their backs and moved in front of the gate. Stix and Tristan—their new Loamian Guard—stood on either side of the shield holders. They would use speed to prevent anything from getting around the line.

The razorspines cleared the deep grasses and broke into

the open. There were hundreds of them, each one the size of a small wolf. Tess's arrows found eyes and throats. Where they struck, razorspines fell. More dropped as the booms of Boost's cannons echoed against the buildings.

As the beasts neared the wall, Jory dropped his crossbow and pulled the lute from his back. He played a haunting dirge. When the notes struck the front line of razorspines, the center of that line yelped in fear and turned tail.

Clara sprinted to activate the fire runes on the far side of each wall. Flames spewed outward and lit four of the weasely creatures ablaze. After the first were set alight, they ran around like guttering torches in warning to the others to avoid the edges of the wall. The spines slanted towards the gate protected by the Guards, right in the path of Jory's song. More creatures fled.

"How long can you keep this up?" asked Kavi of the troubadour.

"Hours," said Jory between verses. "That's not the problem. The fear song loses it's effectiveness once the creatures understand it's not inflicting harm. It's an illusion."

"When does that happen?" asked Kavi.

"Depends on how smart they are," said Jory. "It looks like they're figuring it out already. Time to change the tune to something more destructive!" he yelled.

The lute music shifted from melancholy to loud and discordant. When the new music struck, slashes appeared on snouts and shoulders with every jarring chord. Tens of animals fell.

Jory changed it up again, switching from chords to notes. After the first three notes, three of the closest razorspines looked up at the troubadour. With each pluck of the strings the three razorspines moved in synchrony with the notes. Jory's hands moved faster, finding notes with blinding speed as the three razorspines turned and attacked their brethren. They died quickly as hundreds more of the razorspines continued to charge, as if driven by something more fearsome in the grass behind them. When the charmed weasel beasts fell, Jory took a breath then shifted the music back to loud and discordant.

The stakes placed by the Forts did their job, slowing and injuring the first wave of beasts. There were too many to fully stop the charge. Kavi heard a scream and looked for the Ghost who lost their cool, but it was the lookout.

The man yelled, "By the gods I've never seen so many. I'm not ready to die today!" The man banged the drum as if his life depended on it.

The first wave of razorspines hit the Guards protecting the lone gate. Stonez and Jansen planted shields. Jansen activated his Guard skill, Shield wall. The sound of a hundred fur padded skulls striking the golden barrier resonated in a giant clang. Many of the beasts who hit the wall at a sprint didn't rise again, skulls crushed on impact.

The razorspines who followed approached more carefully. Slowing down meant more time flayed by Jory's chords of pain. With no better option, they charged forward and met the impenetrable wall of the four Guards holding the gate. When the beasts couldn't advance past the coordinated defense of Jansen and Stonez, they slunk around, hugging the wall, trying to avoid the influence of Jory's song.

When the southern flank became too much for Jansen to manage, Tristan shifted into a giant orange and black cat with curved fangs. Any razorspine who leapt too close was batted out of the air by powerful claws.

On the northern side, Stix had foregone his sabers in favor of two peculiar, matching daggers. The handle of each was in the middle of two curved blades which arced outwards, like miniature sharpened windmill blades. Stix stabbed and sliced razorspines in punching motions, thick leather bracers protected his arms and wrists from the second blade. His hooks and uppercuts left a mounting pile of dead razorspines at his feet. When the press of beasts became too much, he invoked another dervish skill. The blades began to twirl until they spun so quickly all Kavi could see was a circle of steel in place of Stix's fists. When he punched with the whirling daggers, ground chunks of razorspines flew in all directions.

Pip looked at Kavi and offered a fist bump. Neither of the squad leaders had engaged yet, still observing.

"I don't think that's a cloud," Kavi said, pointing to the horizon.

"Let's find out," said Pip. "I'll open a small gate in the middle with an exit directly in front of us. Ready to fight what comes through?"

Kavi drew steel and nodded.

Pip summoned the gate and two purplish winged creatures flew through. Kavi struck and both creatures fell to the ground, dead.

Pip closed the gate and examined one of the creatures. "Imps. I knew it. That cloud is huge, there's got to be thousands of them."

"Sliver!" yelled Kavi.

"I know!" yelled the young Bricker. "I don't know why it's taking so long to summon Herman. Quit fighting my skills, Boost!"

"Not trying to, but I'm a little busy," yelled Boost as he fired bursts of hot lead into the horde of razorspines.

"Two seconds. I need you to focus!" yelled Sliver.

The barrage of fire from Boost's side ceased and the razorspines pressed Stix and Stonez. A claw slipped through Stix's whirling daggers and the man fell back with blood covering his left side. Amity jumped forward and healed Stix while Stonez summoned his own shield wall.

"They're running out of time!" yelled Pip. "Kavi, you want to move down? I'll keep an eye on the field."

"Three more seconds and I'll go," said Kavi.

"Finally!" yelled Sliver as a golem materialized in front of her. It didn't look like Herman. This golem was twice Herman's size and made entirely of midnight black steel. It stood taller than the wall and had four arms instead of two. Giants cannons were mounted on either shoulder and it's lower two arms ended not in hands but in barrels that pulsed with energy. The one on the left crackled with electricity and a small pilot flame winked from the one on the right.

"What in the hell is that?" asked Kavi.

"I don't know," said Sliver. "I think it's an upgraded Herman."

"I thought Boost could only upgrade armor and weapons."

"Embrace the fuse!" yelled Boost and Sliver with one voice.

"Why did you summon it on our side of the wall?" asked Pip, looking down at the huge golem trapped behind the wall.

"Because the old Herman could have walked through the gate," said Sliver and Boost through two mouths.

"You gotta stop doing that. It's freaky. Get him out there! Let's see what he can do," said Kavi.

Sliver nodded. "Guards, make a hole. Jory, I'm going to need you to pick a side, the only way Herman is getting out is through."

When Herman moved, Jory and the Guards jumped out of his way. The behemoth walked through the wall and began laying waste to razorspines in front of him. Giant rounds shot from his shoulders. Where they struck, they left craters as dirt, rock and razorspine body parts flew into the air. The beasts that closed on the golem were met with bolts of electricity from the left and waves of flame from the right.

The Guards retreated behind what was left of the wall and joined the rest of the squad, watching Herman single-handedly destroy an entire wave of razorspines.

"Unbelievable," whispered Kavi. He turned to Sliver. "How much juice does the new Herman have?"

"The Hermonster? No...how about the Hermemoth?"

"How much juice, Sliver?"

"Fine, work in progress," said Sliver. "Look at his back. The Hermiathan has got dual suli cores. A while."

"More than a while," yelled Boost from his spot on the wall. "What Sliver can't see is that those large suli cores house a matrix of independent cores. He could last all day."

"Good, we need him to," said Kavi.

As the cloud of imps neared they blotted out the afternoon sun. The temperature dropped and the shadows cast from the fire runes became dark and menacing. Herman eliminated the last of the razorspines and turned his weapons to the sky.

The imps attacked in a chaotic swirl of miniature fireballs

and poisoned darts. They were so tightly packed together that every ranged missile shot into the cloud found a target. Imps fell like purple hail.

Jory's music had little effect on the imps so he strapped the lute to his back and drew his dagger and short sword.

Herman mowed them down by the hundreds, but there were so many of the creatures that hundreds more got past the golem to close on the defenders.

Boost was first to fall. After Herman, he did the most damage with his hand cannons and became the focus of hundreds of the little creatures. There was no dodging the barrage of fireballs and darts which peppered his position. His scorched corpse leaned over the back of the wall, a pincushioned mess. It happened so fast, Kavi doubted he felt much.

When Boost fell, Sliver screamed in pain and fell to the ground, catatonic. Moments later Herman stopped functioning. When the golem fell, their defenses were quickly overrun.

When he woke in the Pool, Kavi looked over to the booth. "Coach, any idea of how to defend against that many flying opponents?"

"Nobody's ever made it that far," said Coach, his voice tinny through the speakers. "But I've got notes."

Kavi looked over at Boost and Sliver who were slightly more green than usual after a run in the Pool. "You two ok?"

"Not really," said Boost and Sliver at the same time. This brought a fit of coughs that turned to chuckles.

"That bond is intense," said Boost.

"It's like I died twice," said Sliver. "Next time in the Pool, I call dibs on dying first."

"We'll be fine, give us five minutes before we go back in," said Boost.

Kavi nodded. "I'll give you ten. We need ideas."

Stix shuddered. "I'll never get over how quickly you guys jump back in the Pool after dying."

"You're gonna have to," said Kavi. "Once Coach shares his ideas, I want us brainstorming how to fight an army of flying creatures. Coach, lay it on us. We go back in in ten."

9

To Krom

"Is it possible she's trying to get rid of me?" Grim asked.

Carlin smiled. "Definitely. She's been trying to get rid of you the moment you walked into this place. I mean, look at you. What use does anyone have for a giant who fights like a god and knows how to make weapons and armor?"

"He may be past sarcasm, Carlin," said Nettie. Nettie handed Grim the new clothes she had commissioned for him several weeks ago.

Grim took them and placed them into the travel pack on top of his other things. "I don't know. It feels off, like I'm being set up for something."

"Like what?" asked Carlin.

Grim shrugged. "No idea, but I don't think Rose is sharing everything she knows with us."

Nettie laughed. "Of course she isn't, you giant headed monstrosity. She sees the future. She knows more about Grendar than any person alive. She's supposed to share all of that with you to get you to trust her?"

"That's not what I mean," said Grim. "I don't think

she's sharing everything she knows about my father and the dynamics in the Krommian Council. It doesn't make sense she would send me unless she knows something about our relationship that I don't."

Nettie reached to put a comforting hand on Grim's shoulder. "I haven't been a Liberator for long, but in the time I've been here, I've only seen Rose do things that help other people. Even when, at first glance, her requests look like they may be harmful to that person. She always has multiple agendas running at once. That's how she operates. She is a force of good in this world."

"I'd like to believe that," said Grim. "But it seems too... convenient, I guess."

"Did I tell you the story of how she helped me recover after my brother?"

Grim looked up and shook his head. When he met Nettie, she had been devastated by the loss of her brother in a fight that Grim, Carlin and Kavi had been moments too late to prevent.

"She sent me on a humanitarian mission to a small village eviscerated by one of the Marked," said Nettie. "Everyone in the village lost somebody. When I arrived I was surrounded by shock and pain. Most were openly sobbing, but the worst were those who sat silently. Vacant stares into nothing. A twelve-year-old girl sat holding the hands of her dead father and mother with no expression on her face. When I came to check on her, she snarled at me like a feral dog. The pain of losing Pick crashed like a wave. Pain I kept tamping down when I was a Ghost so I could survive. I sat there and held this child, and I started crying. She felt me crying and it opened the floodgates in her. We sat there and cried for hours. I didn't do a damn thing to help with the clean up. All I did was hold this devastated child and sob. When I finally stood up, a huge burden had lifted from my shoulders. And you know what?"

"What?" whispered Grim.

"The child finally let go of her parents' hands and came with us. She's in school now, training to be an engineer." Nettie wiped the tear that came unbidden. "And I couldn't be prouder. Sometimes Rose sets us on a path to help the Liberators and sometimes she sets us on a path to help ourselves. Most of the time, it's both. So, no, I don't think she's trying to set you up. I think she's trying to help you and it's been so long since someone has tried to help you that it feels like a set up."

Grim looked to Carlin.

The huntsman shrugged. "I agree with Nettie, she changes all of us. In most cases for the better."

"Okay," said Grim. "But no killing."

"It's a diplomatic mission," said Carlin. "Why would there be killing?"

* * *

They gathered at dawn.

Rose planned multiple delegations from the ranks of Ghosts turned Liberators to the different Garden Cities. Each had their own mission, but part of that mission was to share experiences about the League.

Those headed to the western Cities would go by portal.

Grim would travel over land with Flask, Carlin and Grundle.

When Flask was at the University he apprenticed to Chief Architect Stilton, a master tinkerer and a contemporary of Kavi's father, Tribar. There was no love lost between the two men, but there *was* mutual respect. Flask would meet first with Tribar, then Stilton to understand more about why the University had thrown in with the League.

Grundle was the son of one of the Keepers of the ancient Groves in Loam. His mission was to understand how the Collective and the League approached the Keepers.

The four men mounted quietly and left the camp at a walk as the sun's first rays struck the top of the small fort. They planned to travel north for three days until they reached Stonecrest. There, Flask and Carlin were going to break off to meet with Tribar and the Lioness while Grundle and Grim continued on to Krom and Loam. Grundle chafed at having to travel so far north before traveling to Loam, but the Mill Bridge was the only place to cross the Rhune for hundreds of kilometers in either direction.

Grim shrugged. It was nice to have the company.

They were asked to stay silent and keep a low profile until the fort on the hill had been out of sight for at least an hour.

They traveled in an easy silence until mid-morning, each of them comfortable residing in their own thoughts, except for Flask. Carlin had to shush the Bricker three times as his curiosity bubbled out any time a random thought popped into his mind.

"But look how high up the hill the fort is," whined Flask the last time Carlin shushed him. "It's going to be in sight for hours."

"And you're willing to be responsible for letting our

enemies know that Rose and our Liberator friends are camped at the fort because you can't shut the hell up for three hours?" asked Grundle.

Grim and Carlin shared a smile as Flask pouted. Grim liked the big Loamian. He sized the large man up and wondered how they would match up in a fight. Hopefully, they would never have to find out.

They traveled along a game trail which never diverted too far from the river. They would remain off any major road until they were close to the Mill Bridge. Grim gave his large bay gelding its head and let himself enjoy the trip. The light breeze of early spring rippled through his hair and Grim took a deep breath through his nose. The wet air smelled of new life and new beginnings.

He hadn't seen his father in almost four years. He didn't miss the old bastard. Not for a second. His early years growing up weren't what anyone would call enjoyable. His father ran their household like a military camp and when Grim's mother left, it hurt. The man expected to be instantly obeyed in all things. When he wasn't, he used the belt. On Grim and on his mother. The regular beatings taught Grim to distance himself from pain, to step outside of his body and travel to a place without violence.

The beatings broke his mother.

Her last words to him, before she fled, were seared into his mind. She gently stroked eight-year-old Grim's face as she put him to bed for the last time. "Someday I hope you'll forgive me. I didn't sign up to be a soldier."

"Forgive you for what, momma?" asked eight-year-old Grim.

"For what I have to do. He might forgive a slave disappearing, but would never forgive his only son disappearing with her."

"What slave? We don't own any slaves," said young Grim.

His mother smiled and kissed him on the forehead. "Sleep tight my sweet boy. Don't let him turn you into a monster. I love you more than anything in the whole world. Now sleep."

That was the last time he saw her. In the fifteen years since, he transformed all the hurt of being abandoned into a white-hot anger at his father. His father earned that rage every day Grim lived with him. The beatings increased when his mother left. There was no one there to divert his father's anger. The only moments of solace were when his father was deployed or when he was able to spend time with Kavi and his parents. It was such a relief when he turned old enough to enter the Bastion.

"Okay, it's been a full bell and then some since the fort passed out of sight," Flask said, interrupting Grim's memories.

"Waited a couple extra breaths, did you?" said Grundle.

"It wasn't easy," said Flask. "Have any of you ever been on a diplomatic mission before? This is my first."

"Do we look like diplomats?" asked Grim.

"No, but that's why we're perfect for the job. Nobody wants to talk to diplomats. I met a diplomat once. He wore nice clothes and talked about himself for hours. Boring. We look more like spies."

"Why do you say that?" asked Grundle.

"Because we all know how to fight, we each have a secret mission and we all just stayed absolutely silent for almost four hours."

"None of those things have anything to do with how we

look," said Grundle.

"Huh, you're right. Maybe we look more like an elite squad of warriors who wander the land, fighting for justice and protecting the helpless. Like Max Leaguejumper and his band of rakish ruffians."

"I loved that book," said Carlin.

"It's what got me chasing Quests as a sprout," said Grundle with a smile. "Grim, you a fan of *The Travels of Max Leaguejumper*?"

"Who wasn't," said Grim. "Me and Kavi used to act out half the scenes. We waited in the Draydale for six hours one night hunting the elusive snipe."

Flask laughed. "Me too! I was pretty upset when I learned there was no such thing."

"What do you mean? There were pictures right in the book," said Grundle.

Everybody laughed. "Nope," said Flask. "The author made them up, parents have been tricking kids into snipe hunting ever since. Did you really think a small, dumb bird that couldn't fly wouldn't have gone extinct years ago?"

"So the invisibility thing was bullshit too?" asked Grundle. "I'm pretty sure my whole family thinks they're real."

Grim laughed as hard as the other three. It felt good to be out on the road again. To have a purpose. Even if it meant he had to talk to General Asswipe.

* * *

They made good time. After two days of traveling, they saw

nobody but an old shepherd looking for lost sheep. They traded stories and the shepherd shared they were only half a day's travel from the Mill Bridge. He cautioned them that since the Lioness got serious about patrolling the bridge, the bandits had relocated several kilometers away in either direction.

"Stay by the river or head up to the road?" asked Grim.

"If we're in for a fight, I wouldn't mind having some room to move," said Grundle.

Flask and Carlin nodded and the foursome turned their horses east to the road. They moved north even faster on the trade road. Grim knew the area well enough to know they were only a kilometer or two from where the road split to Brickolage to the North and Stonecrest to the West when they encountered a tree which had fallen across the road.

"Careful," said Carlin in a low voice. "That tree didn't fall naturally. Damnit, we should have stayed by the river. I see two of them in the trees. One's holding a crossbow."

Just then a man stepped out from behind one of the trees lining the side of the road.

"Well, well, well, if it isn't the coward and the old man," said Roanik.

10

Stonecrest

"They haven't arrested you yet, Roanik?" asked Grim.

Roanik shook his head and put on a large, artificial grin. "To arrest me, they have to catch me."

Roanik signaled into the woods, and fifteen men came out from beneath the shade to stand behind the mercenary.

Grim tamped the anger that threatened to rise. He was certain that if he went into a berserker rage the rag-tag group in front of him wouldn't pose much of a challenge. He was also certain he would hurt one of his friends and break his vow.

No more killing.

"You know this clown?" asked Grundle.

Grim nodded. "We served together once upon a time. That was before he sold me, Nettie, and Kavi into slavery."

Grim turned back to Roanik and looked him up and down. The man's clothing was stained and torn, and the sword at his waist had spots of rust. Rust on a weapon was a hangable offense in the Suli Elites. The bandit role looked less an act and more a way of life.

"Rough winter, Roanik?" asked Grim. "Now that the League isn't paying for slaves anymore, you go full high-wayman?"

Roanik laughed. Grim had to hand it to the man. Confidence was never an issue for the ex-Elite. "As I said before, coward, people pay a premium for those that need killing. And there are always those that need killing."

"Care to share who put the bounty on us?" asked Grim.

Roanik shrugged. "No bounty for you fools. I guess you're not important enough. That's why we're just going to take your gold and weapons and let you go on your way."

Carlin chuckled. "Fool me once, Roanik." The huntsman stood up in his stirrups and addressed the bandits standing behind the bandit leader. "The three riding with me are League trained warriors. Believe me when I say you have no chance if this turns bloody. If you throw down your weapons and come with us, I'll put in a good word with the Lioness to grant you leniency. Hell, she might even offer you a position in her service. Stonecrest is growing fast. They always need strong workers."

Roanik laughed and some of the men behind him joined in, but their laughter was forced and nervous.

"Oh huntsman, the stories you tell. I was glad to hear you got away from my men. I never had a quarrel with you. You were just a tool to bring that one under control." Roanik pointed at Grim.

"How about you and I settle this in one-on-one combat, Roanik?" Grim said. "For old time's sake. Suli Elite rules. We'll draw a circle and fight to first blood. You might even walk out of this situation alive. At the very least, your men will survive."

"You never could stomach blood, could you? That's why me and the boys in the Elites called him coward," spat Roanik. "But why would I risk it when I have the numerical advantage." Roanik brought a hand down and three crossbow bolts plugged into the earth at the hooves of their horses.

The horses nickered and stepped back in fear.

"Now that was stupid," said Grim. "We both know it takes at least thirty seconds to reload one of those things. Flask, can you take care of the group behind our mercenary friend?"

Flask reached into the belt around his waist and grabbed a small vial. He threw the vial into the group of bandits behind Roanik. The bandits jumped back as a green smoke began to waft up from the broken vial.

After several seconds of nothing happening, Roanik began to laugh. The other bandits joined in and this time their laughter was genuine.

Roanik turned back to them, still laughing. "That's it? That's the extent of your League training?"

Grim looked at Flask, raised his eyebrows and held his hands out in the universal gesture of 'What the hell man?'

Flask gave him a wide smile and pointed his chin towards the bandits.

The bandit closest to the broken vial collapsed. Then the rest of them slowly began to fall. When Roanik turned to see his men collapsing to the ground, his laughter stilled and the grin left his face.

"Bit of a time delay there, huh?" asked Grim.

"I could have killed them instantly, but I figured we try to do this without bloodshed," said Flask calmly.

"You don't look it, but you're pretty scary, you know that?"

asked Grim.

"I never wanted to be." The Bricker looked disappointed. A thought came to him and he brightened. "But I guess since we're spies now..."

Carlin unstrapped his bow and shot several arrows into the branches where the crossbowmen perched. Cries of pain echoed through the trees.

"Don't worry," said Carlin. "None of the shots were fatal. Grundle, you mind tying up our friend here? I've got rope hanging off the back of my saddle."

Grundle and Grim dismounted. Carlin held a knocked arrow pointed at Roanik.

Roanik looked ready to flee. They could tell he was judging his chances when Carlin shook his head.

"You're never going to outrun the arrow. So, either let the big guy tie you up now, or let him tie you up when you have an arrow sticking out of your leg. Your choice."

"Fine, I accept your offer of a duel Grim, but I want to fight this other big guy," said Roanik.

"Sorry, offer expired," said Grim with a smile. "But you wouldn't stand a chance against Grundle."

Grundle tapped into the edge of his talent and released a very bear-like growl.

Roanik's eyes widened in fear.

"Put your hands behind your back and we can avoid most of the pain," said Grundle.

"Please, don't be gentle," said Grim.

They found more rope on the bandits and decided to bind those sleeping to the injured men who had sniped from the trees. They sat them on the side of the road.

"What if predators show up?" asked one of the injured

men.

"Don't worry, we'll send a wagon once we make it to Stonecrest. The guards will be here to pick you up soon."

"That could take hours," complained the injured man.

Carlin grinned. "Probably should have thought about that before making such a terrible life choice."

* * *

"It's good to see you again Grim," said Brodie. "Stonecrest has been a lot...sadder since you and Kavi left."

Brodie oversaw the contingent of guards protecting the Mill Bridge. They took Roanik into custody and Brodie issued orders to send a caged wagon to pick up the rest of the bandits. Brodie escorted them back to Stonecrest, knowing Carlin would want to make a report.

"Guard Captain now Brodie? Impressive," said Grim. "You deserve it." Grim looked down at the man's hip to see the sword he made for him all those months ago. "How's the sword holding up?

"Like it was blessed by Krom." The newly minted guard captain smiled at Grim. "Would you believe I'm the veteran around here now?"

Grim shook his head. "How'd Jax take the news?"

"He bitched until I made him my lieutenant."

Grim and Carlin laughed at that.

"So am I taking all four of you in to see the Lioness?" asked Brodie.

"I don't think so, me and Grundle have to keep moving. I

need to be in Krom day after tomorrow," said Grim.

"I was hoping for an audience with Tribar," said Flask. "Can you make that happen?"

"I can put in a request, sure. Grim, if you don't stop in and see the Lioness, or at least Tribar, they're going to be hurt," said Brodie.

"Look at you. They put a gold badge on your chest and all of a sudden you're the wise old captain. I approve," said Carlin. The huntsman turned to Grim. "Brodie's right. If I go in there and make a report alone and she finds out you were in Stonecrest and didn't stop in to see her? She's going to be angry with *me*."

Grim shook his head. "I don't think I should, Carlin. I'm on a shorter fuse these days. I'm going to struggle to be civil."

"You bit your tongue for two years. You can do it for another hour."

"Besides, the kitchen is serving chicken cacciatore tonight," said Brodie. "This new chef Tribar hired is an artist. All of you should stay for dinner and get a good night's sleep. Maybe we feed you before sending you in to meet with the Lioness. One of the perks of being Guard Captain is I can pop into the kitchen for an early meal."

Grundle and Flask eagerly accepted. The idea of a meal that wasn't hardtack sounded glorious. They thanked Brodie for the offer to put them up in the guard barracks for the night. A bed and a meal would make the following day's travels more pleasant.

"Don't mention it. Friends of Kavi's are friends of mine. How was he doing last time you saw him?"

"I don't know how else to say it," said Flask. "Kavi thrived as a Ghost. He was the best of us. He propped people up and made us care again."

"He's also a total badass," said Grundle. "Nobody on the squad, except for Pip on his best day, could hold a candle to Kavi in the circle."

"Really? I mean Kavi was good—hell he was Bastion trained—but he was never as good as Grim. Not even close," said Brodie.

Grim snorted. "Not anymore. Last time we met on the field he whooped my ass."

Brodie laughed. "Now that's a story I want to hear in detail over dinner." He handed the reins of his horse over to the stable hand and they all dismounted. "I've got to make my rounds then report to the Lioness. Head to the kitchens and grab a bite, I'll meet you there in an hour."

"If we have a full hour, I have to stop in on Master Brixon," said Grim.

"So, you'll see the blacksmith but not your surrogate mother?" asked Carlin. "That's messed up."

"The blacksmith actually cared about me," said Grim.

The others looked uncomfortable with the tone of the conversation. Brodie broke the silence. "I have to make my rounds. Carlin, you remember the way to the kitchen?"

"I lived here longer than you, boy," said Carlin.

"Yeah, but you're getting to that age where you start to forget things." Brodie left with a grin before Carlin could respond.

* * *

Grim took a deep breath as they stood outside of Stonecrest's briefing room. Carlin looked over at him, puzzled.

"No different than a hundred times before, lad," said Carlin. "She's not going to bite your head off."

"That's not what I'm worried about," said Grim.

At that moment, Tribar came running down the hallway. He locked eyes with Grim and gave him a huge smile.

Before he knew it, Kavi's dad engulfed him in a hug. "I missed you Grim. How's my boy doing?"

"Kavi was fine the last time I saw him sir," said Grim.

"That is wonderful news but I wasn't talking about Kavi."

Grim broke free from the hug and looked at Tribar. "Who do you mean then?"

"I'm talking about you, you big idiot. You've always been a son to me. How are you?"

Grim almost broke down right there. All the anger he was holding for the Lioness fled, if for a minute, at the kindness and acceptance in Tribar's eyes. "I'm actually pretty shitty, sir. But thanks to your son and close friends like Carlin, I'm turning a corner."

Tribar nodded and pulled him back into a hug. Grim sobbed once, cheek atop Tribar's head. It felt good to feel a real emotion, even for a second.

Tribar patted his back. "I know. It's been a rough stretch. For all of us. But the night is always darkest before the dawn."

"I hope you're right sir," said Grim.

"I'm right. Now let's get in there. I'm looking forward to hearing your account of the last six months." Tribar knocked on the door to the briefing room.

A curt, "Come in," answered the knock.

Grim took a deep breath to compose himself and entered with Carlin and Tribar.

Lady Marie Stonecrest, the Lioness, had aged ten years in the six months Grim had been gone. The small grey highlights in her shoulder length hair, which once made her look dignified, had taken over her entire mane. They now framed her features in sooty thunderclouds. The severe lines of her face that had always stretched thin over high cheekbones now looked skeletal. Her scars stood out from her face in unnatural protuberances. She looked like she ate once a week, but her manner hadn't changed one bit. If anything she was more intimidating. She mastered the art of staring down at people even while sitting.

Grim felt all the extra pounds he put on in the last couple of months while living out of a bottle. The extra weight felt decadent and depraved in her presence. He shook the feeling and worked to reign in the anger that built when he saw her.

"Husband," said Marie nodding to Tribar.

Tribar nodded and sat to her right at the briefing table.

"Carlin, nice to see you again," she said, a whisper of a smile turning up the corners of her mouth. She looked to Grim and her face hardened, if that was possible. "Young Broadblade, you look as you did when you crawled into Stonecrest years ago. I figured the League would have hardened you. Have you come seeking my leniency again?"

Her acerbity didn't bite nearly as hard as it once had. Lady Stonecrest had nothing on slavers or League coaches when it came to disdain. He *almost* found her words funny. So, he treated them that way and pasted on a Roanik-worthy, fake smile.

"No milady, that was a one-time performance. I wanted

to pay my respects before heading on to Krom as soon as my horse is fed and watered," said Grim. He was impressed with himself at how well he handled her glare. Grim could tell his easy manner bothered her and his grin widened.

She took it for the disrespect for which it was meant. "So these Liberators have taken you in. Why?"

"I suppose the fifth Sage sees something in me you must have missed, ma'am."

Her right eyelid ticked twice, and Grim was surprised to realize her anger took over before his. It felt like a victory of sorts.

"What happened to you, Grim?"

"Would you like a full report of the last six months or is that a hypothetical meant to express your disappointment at my wasted potential?" Grim didn't know where the words were coming from. The icy calm that had taken over lent him an eloquence he didn't normally possess.

"We'll get to the report later," said the Lioness. "Let's first talk about your wasted potential."

"Well ma'am, my father happened to me," said Grim, the grin plastered on his face. "You're friends, so I'm sure you know of his love for beating his son and wife. He was so accomplished at hurting people. When he almost killed my mother for the fourth time, she finally left. Then I discovered I was very good at hurting people too. As a matter of fact, I was a wonderful killer. Each time I killed or really hurt somebody it broke a little piece of me. So, I crawled into a bottle. After that I suppose, *you* happened to me. You came across as caring, giving me a chance, but I learned later that you were really trying to control my best friend. That number you did on him by putting the blame on his shoulders for his brother's death.... That would have made my father proud."

Her face was white with rage. "Do you find this amusing, disrespecting your elders?"

Grim nodded. "A little."

"Careful," whispered Carlin at his side. "Don't burn this bridge."

Grim turned to him. "It was never a bridge. It was a trap disguised as a lifeboat." He turned back to the Lioness, winter snow replacing his veins. "But back to your question. *My* elders are not worthy of respect. Sure, you and my father are wonderful killers and decorated soldiers but you are truly awful people."

"And due to your years of experience, you've got it all figured out," said the Lioness, holding back the rage.

Grim's smile widened. "Not even close, but at least I can admit that. Your generation loves to talk about how experienced you are. But look around—the League, slavery, the corruption in the Council—all this happened under your watch. You know what also comes with experience? An unwillingness to change. A yearning for the glory days. The inability to dream of a better future because, frankly, you don't have much of it left. So, you don't even think about listening to those of us that have to live in the mess you created, because we don't have *experience*. Instead of handing over power to those who could do something positive with it, you hold on to it with shaky fingers."

"And what would a drunk like you do with that power?" asked the Lioness.

"Oh, not me. I'm talking about leaders like your son. I'm well versed in my own character flaws, thank you very much.

But your son, he is five times the leader you are. He went back into the lion's den of the League because he refused to leave his people behind. His team respects him and he would never put his best friend to death without trying to understand his reasons first. He saved my life when he should have taken it."

This put the Lioness over the top. "Shut your fucking mouth," she screamed, spittle flying out with each word, her entire body shaking in rage. "Did Kavi tell you that?"

"Shut my fucking mouth or share where I learned about your pathetic decision?"

She moved in front of him and raised her hand to strike his face.

"Strike me Lioness, and know that it will be the last thing you ever do," said Grim, his eyes never leaving hers. "I am a far better killer than you or my father."

"Tribar, do something!" yelled Carlin.

Tribar shook his head. "No, Carlin, these words need to be said. On both sides. That's the only chance we have of healing this rift, before it's too late."

Marie lowered her hand, seeing something in Grim's eyes she had never seen there before. "Tell me who told you about me executing my best friend," she whispered.

"It was my father. He bragged about it. 'Duty is more important than friendship.' That was the lesson. I almost believed it. Thankfully, I learned what a load of horseshit it was before it was too late."

Lady Stonecrest barely made it back to her chair before she collapsed. She folded in on herself and Grim could see, for the first time, how unnaturally thin she was. "I'm sorry," she whispered over and over again, sobs wracking her body.

111

Tribar was there in an instant. He pulled a handkerchief from his breast pocket and wiped the corners of her mouth. When he pulled it back, it was splotched with blood.

"What's wrong with her?" asked Grim, pale now.

"She's dying," said Tribar.

The ground dropped from beneath him. All the hateful shit he said pressed down on him with the force of a mountain collapsing. "I...I didn't know. I wouldn't have...I'm sorry. I didn't know."

Tribar smiled and nodded. "I wouldn't have told you. What you said needed to be said. She needs help understanding what's important before she goes. Please. If you can. Forgive her."

Coughs had taken over for the sobs. She looked so small. Grim couldn't square in his mind the overpowering figure of the Lioness with the broken thing that sat curled before him. It was too much. Tears ran down his face.

"How much time does she have?"

"Six months, a year? No more than two."

"Why can't she be healed?" said Grim.

"It's the wasting sickness son, it's in her bones. Once it reaches the bones, there's nothing any healer can do."

"I'm sorry," said Grim, wet eyes finding Tribar's. "You don't deserve this. Not after all the pain."

"It's life, boy. It's not about deserving. It just happens."

Grim knelt down and engulfed the sick woman in his giant arms. "I do forgive you. And I do love you."

She looked up at him with wide eyes. "Thank you, Grim. I'm sorry for how you were treated by your father. By me."

They cried together for a time. Then, Lady Stonecrest patted his arm and looked up to him. "Your father knows you're coming. They've set a trap for you and any Liberators who travel with you."

11

Caster

Caster looked at the two men writhing in their restraints. She couldn't understand it. They were top candidates. They both unlocked multiple talents in the Pool. One of them even served on a professional team for over a year. So why? Why would the trunite cause men with so much potential to turn feral?

Caster wished she had access to her peers, but the work she was doing was confidential, even from other members of the Collective. There was no chance she could discuss her research with any traditional academics. Sure, the Collective recruited researchers from the University and the Academ D'Arcana every week, but the established Masters had no reason to move. Tenure was a powerful thing. It caused brilliant minds to stagnate.

She would love to bounce ideas off her old mentor, Tribar. She knew how deeply he would disapprove of her work, but she had yet to meet another mind as brilliant as his. If the man would sacrifice even a fraction of his rigid moral code, he and Caster could solve the problem in weeks. If she could find even one tinkerer with half the brain of Tribar, the stuff they could accomplish with the resources of the Collective would change the world.

She undid her ponytail and ran fingers through wild hair. She excised some tangles and watched as dark brown strands fell to the floor. The motion brought clarity. It was time to face the reality.

She was stuck.

It had been over a month since she and her team had made a stride forward. Project Midnight was floundering.

She could ask the Thin Man for help, but the mere thought sent shudders through her. The man was terrifying. It had been years since anyone made her feel so helpless. Not since the time when she stayed with her favorite uncle during the summer of her sixteenth year...

* * *

Uncle Cam had a cabin on the northeastern side of the Whisper Sea. Caster was so looking forward to that summer and it started so well.

The locals in Tobermoss had the standoffish friendliness of any seasonal town. They relied on the income summer tourists brought, so they knew to be friendly without crossing any lines. City folk tended to take a dim view of any sailor trying to ingratiate themselves into their circles. Most Brickers, and even the militaristic Krommians, saw the dockhands as under-educated servants and treated them that way.

Uncle Cam was different. He treated everyone as if they had something important to teach. Caster would find him in deep conversations with the dockhands about knots, fishing techniques, even the makeup of fibers for the ropes the sailors used. He never talked down to anyone, and because of it, the locals in Tobermoss treated Cam like one of their own.

Caster had grown so tired of the arrogance of the Bricker kids in her classes. Most of the boys, and some of the girls, endlessly bragged about their intellectual exploits. The long, bland stories detailing elaborate pranks played on a teacher or parent made her want to pull her hair out. In a society where intellect was the meter stick for status, snark and sarcasm were so commonplace they became boring.

As she watched the young men from Tobermoss tying boats to the docks or repairing nets, she noticed they didn't try to make each other feel stupid. They worked, made jokes and laughed while wearing nothing but shorts. Their bronze skin accentuated ropy muscles that ran across backs and down sculpted arms.

Their physical prowess and easy attitudes were refreshing. Most of them were easy on the eyes, especially Matteo, the youngest of three brothers. He couldn't have been more than a year older than Caster. He had shoulder length dirty blonde hair that turned almost white over the course of the summer. His smile was brilliant enough to compete with the sun. Whenever he turned those liquid brown eyes in her direction she felt slightly dizzy.

Caster's marks were exemplary and she knew she'd place into the University two years early. So, if she was to have any fun in her life it would have to happen this summer.

When she looked at the tanned shoulders of the young man waiting to wrap a lanyard around the cleat of the dock, a new definition of fun entered her mind. She loved puzzles and decided then and there that she would work to understand the pieces that made this young man tick. If one of those pieces involved having those strong, calloused hands bringing her face in for a kiss, all the better.

"He's cute. Would you like me to make an introduction?" asked Uncle Cam, tracking her eyes. "His dad is working on a project with me."

Caster blushed. "Oh no, I would never..." No. That was Brickolage Caster. Tobermoss Caster had to take risks. Otherwise, she would miss out, and another summer would pass in a mental barrage of what might have beens. "Maybe... yes, would you mind?"

Uncle Cam smiled and walked over to the men standing near the large fishing vessel. She busied herself in a book the moment he walked away. When he waved her over she looked up from the book, as if surprised, before setting it down. She walked over nervously, not sure how she felt about the attention as all eyes turned to her.

She didn't *not* like it.

Uncle Cam laughed when she joined their circle. "I know, that's why I'm going to keep an extra close eye on you," he said as she walked up. He put an arm around her shoulder and drew her into the group. "And this is my lovely niece, Caster Ada Vigner, prodigy and soon to be one of the great Masters of the University. Caster, this is Master Clarence and his sons, Nestor, Rafe and Matteo."

Caster spent the next six weeks helping around the docks. Everything was fresh and new. She learned how to crew a two masted ship, helped with the basics of ship repair, she even helped when the three brothers were hired to take Brickers out on tours. She dreaded the arrogance of their Bricker clients, but soon came to appreciate how the locals managed their demeaning treatment. They made up nautical terms that pilloried the snottiest of their clients without them ever knowing it. Her personal favorite was 'trim the brown sail two spans from the mizzen' which meant: watch as I hit the wave just right to spray the arrogant asshole near the mizzenmast.

The best part? Every activity in those six weeks was another chance for an 'accidental' brush of fingers or shoulders as Caster and Matteo passed on the boat. Each touch sent a ripple of heat arcing through her. Matteo was too much the gentleman or, more likely, too intimidated by her city dweller status to take it further than light touches and furtive, steamy glances.

If things were to move to a new stage, it would be up to her. She had three weeks left before being sent back to the city so if she was going to make the move it had to be now. It didn't take her long to come up with a plan.

Uncle Cam traveled to Krom every two weeks for a standing meeting with investors. He was working on funding a project to observe the natural sulimite absorption of marine creatures within the Whisper Sea. He was convinced there were large deposits of suli off the coast. His theory was based off data he pulled from the catch the fisherman hauled in. Cam had narrowed down maximal absorption to a species of grouper and a specific red snapper. He had enlisted Master Clarence to help him identify their spawning points.

If Cam was right, he would be wealthy beyond his dreams.

If he was wrong, a lot of extremely angry, militant investors would be looking for blood. He hadn't received positive data in several weeks. He was not looking forward to the upcoming trip.

Caster stopped paying attention to Cam's data weeks ago. She didn't want to be a part of research projects this summer, so she was only peripherally aware of his higher levels of stress. Cam was such an easy-going guy that stress came off as mild annoyance. Besides, her attention was not on her uncle. Caster only cared that he was going to be out of town for two nights and the cabin would be hers.

The morning after he left, she put on a flowery, yellow sun dress and looked at herself in the mirror. Her brown hair had lightened and her skin had turned a golden brown over the last six weeks.

She looked good and she knew it.

She briefly ran a finger over her lips and thought of how Matteo had lightly brushed them with his own last night. She had maneuvered him to the edge of the dock after his brothers had already gone inside. With how close she stood, she left him with two choices, kiss her or jump in the water. He finally found the courage to lightly caress her face and brush her lips with his own before ducking under her arm and following his brothers. But not before she caught the hunger in his eyes.

She wasn't the only one looking for something more.

Matteo's older brothers got called out on a trawler to help with a big catch late in the afternoon leaving Matteo to manage the shop and dock on his own. It wasn't much of a challenge—there were no scheduled tours or boats coming in that evening. Matteo had instructions to shut down the small bait and rental shop at six bells.

"Uncle Cam's in Krom until tomorrow," said Caster. "Why don't you come up to the cabin and I'll fry up a striper and some potatoes. Maybe you can read me some of that poetry I caught you looking at behind the shop."

"Caster, I can't imagine anything I would rather do," he grabbed her hand with his and gazed deep into her eyes.

"I sense a but."

"But, my brothers will castrate me," said Matteo. "You and Cam are different than the tourists who come into town, but what you don't know is that these kind of...," he waved his hands about trying to find the word. "...summer romances, can be dangerous for us. My brother Nestor got mixed up with a Krommian girl when I was six. Her father beat him within an inch of his life and when Da confronted him, he beat the crap out of him too. Then, the man went and told all of his Krommian friends not to do business with us. I can't risk..."

"Matteo, I'm here for three more weeks," said Caster, "and I'm not leaving Tobermoss without kissing someone. I want that someone to be you, but I will move on to my second choice if I have to."

Matteo looked confused for a second then his eyes widened in surprise. "You mean Paulson? Even with the mole on his chin with those little red hairs poking out of it?" He put his knuckles against his chin and wiggled his fingers.

She nodded and bit down on her smile. "Yes, even with the mole on his chin. Only you can save me from mole whiskers."

He grinned and broke their gaze. He looked to the sea as if it held answers.

"Besides," she said. "Who's going to find out? Your dad

and brothers are on the water until early morning and my uncle doesn't come back until tomorrow. My cabin, seventh bell."

He nodded reluctantly and she kissed him. This kiss was much less chaste than the brush on the boat last night. It left them gasping for air.

"Seventh bell," he whispered.

She spun to leave and the sun dress flared, exposing toned and tanned upper legs. She didn't look back as she made her way to the cabin knowing it would fuel Matteo's desire.

The night went exactly how she hoped. Matteo was right on time and he even brought a bouquet of flowers that he picked from the gardens of the Bricker Club off Haulson Road. She filled a glass with water and placed the flowers in the middle of the small dining table.

He also brought a cheap bottle of reddish wine he must have pilfered from his father's store. He poured the wine as she served the food. The fish wasn't half bad and the potatoes were amazing. After they each had a glass, Caster's belly began to warm and any remaining cares she had slipped away.

As Matteo read poetry she let herself be swept up by the flowery promises of love and faithfulness. By the third poem the words began to get a little repetitive so she took the book from him. Their knees touched and a frisson of energy coursed through her, making the small sun-bleached hairs on her arms rise. His hand brushed her face in a caress, calloused fingers tracing the contours of her face. Their lips met and she felt her pulse pounding in her ears. It was the perfect moment.

The front door slammed open. Uncle Cam stood in the

doorway, eyes red with drink. "You!" he yelled pointing a finger at Matteo.

Matteo jumped up from the couch and held the book of poetry in front of him. "I haven't done anything Master Vigner, you have to believe me," he said in a voice wobbly with fear.

"Get out of my fucking house! I'm so tired of you curs sniffing around as if she was a bitch in heat!" Cam yelled.

Matteo didn't need to be told twice. He sprinted for the back door and fled into the night.

"Why Prita, why?" said Cam as he walked towards her. "Every time I leave, I come back to find you with another man."

Prita? Caster looked at her uncle confused. That was her mother's name. Did they have a relationship before her mother married her father? As her uncle closed on her she could smell the stale odor of alcohol and mistweed. She stood from the couch and gauged the distance to the back door. *Should she make a break for it too?*

"At least this time, it's not my own brother," said Uncle Cam. He stared at her, eyes filled with hurt and rage.

"Uncle Cam, I'm not Prita. I'm Caster," she said, nervous as he grew closer.

He grabbed her arm and began to squeeze. She looked to the door and regretted not following Matteo into the night.

"No. No more pet names and no more of your lies, Prita. Tonight, we have one last hurrah then you and I will have no more to do with each other."

He reached under her sundress and rough fingers pushed aside her small clothes. A finger entered her and she gasped in surprise and pain.

She slapped him in the face. "No Uncle Cam. I am not Prita, I'm your niece. Stop!"

That brought him up short for a moment, and she thought he returned to his right mind. Then his other hand wrapped around her neck. Her body went stiff and cold. She couldn't breathe. She was completely powerless. This man, who she loved and trusted, could and would do whatever he wanted with her.

"No, no, no," she sobbed, a lamb being toyed with by the wolf.

Uncle Cam reached down and began to fumble with his belt.

I can't believe this is happening. Why is this happening? Time seemed to slow, drawing each breath out. She briefly stepped outside of herself to watch this paroxysm of horror take place in slow motion. His pants dropped to the ground and she whimpered.

Then he passed out. He fell to the ground, pants around his ankles and began to snore.

Caster stood there, shaking and violated, too frightened to scream and wake the beast who turned her into this quivering, disgusting void of power.

She looked down at her uncle and stilled the urge to kick him in the face. How could he? How could he take a night with such promise of real romance and turn it into such an ugly thing?

Never again. Never again would she feel this way. Powerless. Helpless. She would dedicate her life to tinkering devices that put *her* in control. The physical strength of a man, of any being, would never put her in a position of weakness again.

She packed her things and walked into the night.

* * *

Caster rubbed her knuckles against the lab bench until they began to bleed. *Stop it. STOP IT!* This was not productive. *What was the matter with her?* Rumination wouldn't solve the trunite binding problem.

She had to contact the Thin Man.

The Thin Man always had answers but could rarely explain the mechanisms for those answers. Any time he helped, she ended up in the lab reverse engineering one of his brilliant insights for weeks or months. He always seemed to know what was possible, but could never explain how.

She bit her lip and stood. It was the only way to get past this blocker. She needed to face the demon one more time.

12

Project Midnight

The Thin Man sat in his office. It was on a small island two hundred kilometers south of Harpstra, deep in the Tranquil Ocean. The chain of islands was known as the Krechiti Archipelago, named after the islander tribe who first settled it. They died off long ago. Besides the Collective, the only residents of the archipelago were birds and turtles.

The Collective moved their headquarters to the islands four hundred years ago after most of the continent of Grendar had been explored. He knew it was cliché to have a base on an island, but clichés became so because of the advantages they offered.

The Thin Man's office was a hundred meters below the island in a large room without doors, windows, stairs, lifts or any access save for air vents the Thin Man had put in many years ago. Only he could travel to the office through the vents when he assumed his darkness form.

He looked at the maps which lined the southern wall, a compliment to the rows and rows of screens that lined the western wall. These screens displayed images from magic eyes strategically placed in rooms of enemies or potential enemies. The eyes were invisible and positioned all across Grendar. When he needed to, he could take control of an eye and move it about the room or use it as a teleportation conduit. The Eastern wall had another bank of screens. These images were from eyes turned on allies and those in the Collective itself.

Privacy was not high on the list of the Collective's principals.

If the Collective had a driving principal it was tightly controlled knowledge. As the knowledge of the indigenous residents of Grendar grew, the Collective tightened its noose around knowledge it may have freely shared two hundred years ago. Information traveled too quickly now.

The Thin Man recognized eons ago that the only true power is knowledge. Another cliché. Another truth. If pressed, the Thin Man would say that knowledge consisted of three things: information, the skills to use it, and the timing to use it effectively. Real-time information was the most valuable thing an organization like the Collective possessed.

The Thin Man stared at a screen centered on one of his people. Caster Ada Vigner. His most brilliant researcher and tinkerer. She was softly banging her head against her lab bench as two men in restraints writhed behind her. He admired her sharp mind and ruthlessness of character. He ran a finger down the screen, tracing her features. Such power and intelligence. If she could overcome her *condition*(her word), the woman would be unstoppable.

He winced when he saw the blood well up on her knuckles. She had fallen into a cycle of rumination and self-recrimination. It only happened when she was stuck. She would be calling for his help soon, but not until she had exercised every potential solution she could dream up. She always beat herself up before a major breakthrough whether she called for his help or not.

He was just as frustrated about Project Midnight's lack of progress. The first prototypes happened with lightning speed. The creation of the Ach'Su was equal parts hard work and serendipity. They were just so damned...unmanageable. Since then, no strides had been made in working with trunite. The moment the substance touched the candidates, they immediately went into a frenzy, nothing like the Mid-Knights of his old world. Those were beings of chaos, but *they* could be controlled.

The Thin Man looked to the fourth and final wall and saw the countdown in large block numbers. His brethren would be here soon. If he didn't unlock the secrets of trunite, he might not hold the advantage he held the other times they appeared in Grendar.

He looked back to Caster. He knew if he visited her unbidden, she would clam up. His presence was too strong. Her condition would worsen and they would lose days of research. Days they could not afford.

He looked back to the wall which held the images of his rivals. Three new eyes had been placed in the Liberator camps in the last two days—all of them still operational. No sign of the Fifth Sage. Wait, there she was now. She smiled as she walked towards the eye. His eyes met hers through the screen.

Her hand reached out and grabbed the invisible device. She rotated the eye until her face took up the entire screen.

"I'm coming for you," she whispered. Her hand squeezed and the eye popped. The screen went blank.

The Thin Man smiled. He loved her tenacity. Female Sages might as well be goddesses. Their spirit, their knowledge, unparalleled in all but the divine.

He couldn't wait to break her.

He looked back to Caster. She better call him soon or he *would* arrive unbidden. Just then she turned to the wall and bowed her head.

"Ogronoth the Enlightened, please lend your assistance to this unworthy servant," she whispered.

About damn time.

The Thin Man made sure to materialize on the far side of the lab from Caster. Even when he reined it in, his authority was strongest in his vaporous form. He quickly shaped himself into his least intimidating human form and turned to face his favorite tinkerer.

He glanced at the bound figures lying prone on the table and breathed in the power they offered. Only he could see the small lines of energy coursing from them to his inner core. The trickle was frustratingly tiny, but the power it held was real.

"Thank you, milord Ogronoth," said Caster as he moved towards her.

He nodded his head. It wasn't his true name but no one on this world would ever know that.

* * *

She did her best to slow her rapidly beating heart by breathing deep through her nose. His suffocating presence brought her back to that night. She moved her bloody knuckles to press into the underside of her lab bench and forced herself to focus.

"Still struggling to find adaptation with the trunite?" The Thin Man asked.

She flinched and steeled her will. "Struggling is an understatement. There is no adaptation gradient. The body resists for as long as it can but is ultimately dominated by the tru. There is no middle ground. Without middle ground, there's no controlling mechanism we can put in place."

"Dilution of the trunite has no effect?"

She shook her head. "We've diluted it to trace amounts using every solvent I could think of. We even used different compositions of sulimite as diluents. It doesn't matter. Even trace amounts of pure trunite seize control of cognitive and motor functions within the first three hours of introduction."

The Thin Man turned to look at the cages holding various transformed animals Caster and her researchers have been working with. Most of the animals were either soundlessly biting at the bars of their cages or throwing themselves against them, looking for weaknesses in the containment. The researchers finally contracted a rune scriber to place sound dampening runes to let them think while in the lab.

"Any luck with biological dilution through breeding?"

Caster shook her head again. "Maybe if we could get them to breed. Once the trunite touches them, all they want to do is kill. They're not killing to sate hunger. They're killing because they enjoy it. That doesn't leave much room for romance."

This didn't produce the smile she hoped to see. Had she ever seen the Thin Man smile?

"Yet, we have seen Marked in the wild that are not mindless killing machines," said the Thin Man. "We have seen them communicate and even control troops. They are dramatically transformed, but not mindless. There is an evolutionary dilution or transformation to the substance we haven't found yet."

Caster nodded. "Agreed. For those that have successfully transformed without turning into killing machines...do we know anything about their environment? The conditions under which they evolve?"

It was the Thin Man's turn to shake his head. "I see much, but not all."

"We're going to have to send another team to the Wastes, aren't we?"

The Thin Man nodded.

"I know just the person to lead the expedition," said Caster. "In the meantime, I will focus my research on trunite that has been altered by biology. Our most promising trials have been from injecting the blood of a creature transformed by trunite into a creature that has yet to be exposed."

"Define promising."

She shrugged. "The loss of logical thought and cognitive function took four hours instead of three."

"Feeding a trunite exposed animal to an untainted one doesn't produce results?"

Caster shook her head. "We had high hopes, but it does nothing. We believe the acids in the stomach are too strong."

"And the protections the contracted neuromancers put in

place were a dead end?"

"That was the most disappointing result of all. We had a neuro-mage put defensive barriers around the mind of our most promising candidates. It took less than two hours for the man to go fully feral."

The Thin Man raised his eyebrows. "It accelerated the problem? Interesting. And the counter experiment?"

"No joy. We had the neuro mage hold the man's mind open to influence, as if he were being charmed. Same results as the control. Acceptance to the adaptation is not the key."

"Or not the only key," said the Thin Man.

She shuddered as the Thin Man put a hand on her bench and leaned towards her. She consciously gulped down the fear. "Exactly. Like any general research, we are dealing with a nearly infinite number of variables. Are there any other examples you can think of where transformative power was controlled?"

"I've heard ceremony like oaths of loyalty can be effective," he said quietly. He pulsed the strength of his authority. With something so speculative, Caster would surely have questions he didn't want to answer.

Her eyes widened with her fear. "Yes, milord Ogronoth, we'll look into that too. If there are specific ceremonial elements we should start with, please let me know." Her last three words came out in a squeak.

"I'll send you my notes," said the Thin Man. He vanished in a black fog.

When the fog dissipated Caster took a full three minutes to breathe. Maybe this was a good thing. A reminder that no matter how powerful she got, there was more work to do. Not until the gods themselves licked at her boots would she be satisfied that her condition was under control.

She left the lab on a hunt for Drew. She had him moved to a different department so there would be no conflict of interest. The thought of having gods licking her boots made her yearn for release. Drew loved being submissive, in the bedroom and outside of it.

She looked forward to putting on the tall leather boots and considered which underthings would look best with the footwear. Then there was the riding crop to consider. She might even pull out the spurs tonight. As the thought of each accessory popped into her head, the fear and helplessness dissipated bit by bit. She grinned at the thought of the sharp black spurs. The last of her fear popped like a soap bubble on the edge of a spur.

13

Kavi

Kavi made his way to breakfast. He nodded absently at those he recognized. He was focused on the peacekeeping mission tomorrow. So many things could go wrong. Thanks to the fuses, Team Sugoroku had to increase the power to the Pool on three different occasions in the last week. They could now support three neural fuses in one run, but they still had no idea how to take the fused powers out of the Pool and move it into the real world. It didn't matter. Their team cohesion and creativity in a fight while mixing skills was worth every bit of experimentation.

Their neuro-mage, Elana, worked overtime with Hiram, Sliver and Boost to understand what it might take to build a strong bond outside the Pool. They were making progress, but only if Elana was part of the fused duo. Kavi hoped they'd make a breakthrough soon. He grinned when he saw Clara.

She smiled at him and his darker thoughts fled like insects skittering for cover when the rock they called home was upended. She fell into stride next to him and they walked in a comfortable silence for a moment.

"Big day today," she finally said.

"Really, what happens today?" he asked.

"You're an idiot," she said.

He chuckled and held the door to the mess hall open for her. "You sure you can handle what you find up here?" He pointed to his head.

"If Sliver can handle what's in your head, so can I. You sure *you* can handle me being up there?"

Good question—one Kavi had been thinking about non-stop for the past week. "I wouldn't have agreed to it otherwise. The team is so much closer now since we started the fuses."

"I never thought I would get close to someone again after we lost Trixie. Then I accepted the neural hug with Sliver. It was like I was never going to be lonely again. Two people sharing one mind, closer than sisters. When she died in the Pool and the bond was broken, it was like losing half myself."

Kavi scooped eggs on to his plate then moved to the potatoes. "Yeah, it's deeper than family, isn't it? My brother and I were close when we were kids, sometimes we could even finish each other's sentences, but we were never as close as the Cranston twins, schoolmates of mine before I shipped off to the Bastion. Those kids seemed to share a mind. At least when they were little. The fuse though...it's like sharing a womb. I don't know if there's a comparison that can do it justice."

"Blood brothers," said Jansen. He put a huge scoop of potatoes on his plate. He was listening in as they walked through the line. "Only comparison I got. Back when I was with the Fourteenth, we were always bleeding from something. We were shoulder to shoulder holding those damn shields, swapping blood. Like the blood brother thing you do when you're kids."

Jansen made a pile of bacon on top of the potatoes that was so high he had to hold a hand over it. "Welp, when you thought you were gonna die, they *were* blood brothers. They were a part of you, another limb. You'd unload your secrets on them because you didn't want to die with those secrets weighing you down."

Kavi shook his head. "Never got that close with anybody as an Eagle," he said.

"Of course not. You hoity-toity types were too good for us grunts. You weren't allowed to get that close. You want that piece of bacon?"

Kavi shook his head and Jansen took the last piece.

"Didn't know what I was missing until the fuse," said Kavi.

"Damn straight," said Jansen. "Now it feels like I've been fighting with Stix and Stonez for years. When you and me gonna fuse Kav?"

"Not until after I get a shot at him," said Clara.

"Oh ho, that's right," said Jansen, grinning and bouncing his eyebrows up and down, "you two love bugs gonna go through with the neural hug today?"

She threw a potato at him. Jansen laughed and popped the potato in his mouth.

"Just saying, don't think I'd have the guts to share everything in my head with somebody I had the hots for." Jansen laughed.

"Kill me now," said Kavi.

"Ignore him," said Clara. "Sometimes that works."

"Sit your ass down, Twenty-two," said Pip moving into the line.

Kavi gave him a grateful look.

"These two idiots have enough to worry about with you piling on," Pip continued and Jansen extended his knuckles for a bump. "I don't agree with the grunt often, but he's got a point. Opening yourself up like that to somebody you have feelings for seems like a dumb idea."

"I think it's romantic," said Tess.

Everybody stopped talking and stared at her. It was the last thing they expected from the stoic ranger.

"What?" Tess asked.

Pip started to laugh.

Tess hit him. "You're an idiot," she said. She stomped away and sat next to Jory.

Pip looked at her, puzzled. "Never would have thought she had a romantic side."

Clara shook her head. "You *are* an idiot."

Kavi waited until everyone sat down before addressing the team. "Today is our last day in the Nest before we ship out. The Snoops assure us we're dealing with only a small incursion led by a single Marked."

"If you believe that," said Stix. "I have a snow drift I'd like to sell you."

"My thoughts exactly," said Kavi. "We need to prep for the worst. This morning is our last shot at the Pool for at least a week. We can support three strong bonds now. Today those bonds are me and Clara, Tess and Jory and Stonez and Boost."

Sliver raised her hand and Kavi nodded to her.

"I got a theory I'd like us to try. When we're embracing mortality today, I'd like you think about the mortality of your teammates. What would it be like if we got back from our mission and they weren't here anymore?"

The team looked sick over the idea.

"What's the theory you want to test, Sliv?" asked Kavi.

"We unlocked a bunch of crazy powers when we accepted we were going to die. Then, we started fusing with each other. Now, I can't imagine losing you, Clara or Boost. We got so close when we did the neural hug. Maybe too close? It's too painful to think about you not being here, like losing a part of myself. It almost feels like when I first struggled to embrace my own death."

Kavi nodded and he wasn't alone. Everyone had fused at least once by now, even Pip.

"The thought has been nagging at me like a loose tooth," Sliver continued. "Since we embraced death, not a whole lot scares me anymore. Except losing you all. So—"

"What would happen if we embrace that too?" said Stix, finishing the thought. He looked at her with respect. "It's a good idea."

Kavi nodded. "Agreed. Accept it but don't let it paralyze you."

"It's got to paralyze before you accept it," said Sliver. "Or I don't think it's going to work. Focus on one person to start. Really think about not seeing them ever again. What would you miss? What would you say to them now if you never had the chance again? I'm not saying it's going to be easy but I know it scares the shit out of me. That tells me it's worth doing."

Jansen raised his hand and the group turned to him. "I don't think it's that simple. Let me start by saying I'm all for trying this, but this is pretty much the opposite of what we learned in the military. Back in my grandfather's day, they wouldn't let men and women serve together because they were afraid attachment would cause soldiers to disobey orders or abuse rank. I'm not saying it's right, but there were solid reasons behind it. If we get too close, couldn't that cause the whole squad to implode? Make it too difficult to make life and death decisions?"

Sliver looked at Jansen, not with the typical condescension she reserved for the Krommian, but really looked at him. "You're not as dumb as you look, you know that? If we lost you, I would miss your strength and willingness to speak your mind without thinking it though. You live closer to the present than anyone here. I admire that."

Jansen looked stunned, like he had no idea what do with the rare compliment from Sliver. "Thanks?" he finally said.

Sliver continued. "Jansen asked the hardest question. Kavi and Pip, if you get close enough to anybody on the team, can you order them to do something that will put them in danger? Clara, if you and Kavi finally hook up, like we've all been waiting for—for freaking months now by the way—is that going to be a problem?"

"In what way?" Clara asked.

"Can you still take orders from him in a battlefield situation without wanting to know why?" asked Sliver.

"I thought you knew me better than that," said Clara. She looked hurt.

"I know you better than that, now," Sliver continued. "But that's Jansen's point. All that changes if any of us ends up in a deeper relationship. We've all had friends who hop the ship to crazy island the minute they start dating someone."

"I've never served in the military and I won't answer for Kavi," said Pip. "But I don't think it will be a problem for one huge reason. We're not the military. Jansen makes a good point, but the military of any Garden City, is a massive operation. They have to make rules that the dumbest, least talented members can understand. Like Jansen here."

"Fuck you very much," said Jansen.

Pip grinned. "We're more like a small mercenary company. They make their own rules." He looked to the ceiling for a second. "No, we're more than that. There's not a mercenary company on Grendar that could hold a candle to us. We've all been Ghosts. We've all lost friends. Hell, we've seen each other die hundreds of times. We've been through more shit in six months than any mercenary company has in their entire history. What's the one thing we've always done, better than any outfit in the world?"

Kavi smiled at Pip and nodded.

"Kavi knows, but he's letting me keep the floor because he's a hell of a leader," said Pip. "The one thing we do better than anybody is push back against conventional wisdom. We don't follow the rules. We break them. Then we remake them. When we remake them it makes us stronger. Every. Time. Not just because we like to rebel but because there are no rules for the situations we're forced to deal with. If we followed conventional rules we'd all be dead by now. We're the rule breakers, the heretics, the apostates of the normal."

"Nice speech," said Kavi.

"There might be a new squad name in there," said Jory. "Heretic Host, Apostate Army. Let me work on it."

"I agree with Pip," said Kavi. "We've all come out the other side by defying the conventional. Jansen, your point's a good one and we need to keep an eye on those concerns. Let's give Sliver's idea a try and lean in to her philosophy.

If something scares you—and it's not suicidal—it's worth trying. We get in the Pool in half an hour, so let's make today's session count. We're back in the field tomorrow."

14

Kavi and Clara fuse

"Fuse commencing in three, two, one..."

Kavi found it best to close his eyes during the countdown. It could be dangerous if the Pool scenario threw someone in immediate peril, and the disorientation of the fuse did that anyway. He braced himself for the onslaught of images.

Kavi was a young girl in a small apartment above a bustling city street. The ruckus from below promised excitement, action, and motion. All she wanted to do was run down and be a part of it. She looked over to see her mother still asleep on the small bed in the corner. Wine blotched the front of her light brown tunic and stained her teeth a red that could just as easily be blood. She knew when mom woke, she would be in a bad mood. She was always in a bad mood these days. Kavi didn't know what she was doing wrong that made her mom so mad all the time. At least she came home alone last night. They wouldn't have to deal with a stranger waking up with her. She looked over at mom and wished it could be like it was before Da died.

She looked around for her last nub of charcoal and began

to draw.

A flash of light.

Kavi was in a classroom with five other Harpers around her same age. The big slate blackboards offered endless drawing possibilities. If she didn't like what she drew, she could erase it and start over. She wished she had one of the slates at home. Three of the other children played and talked together in one of the corners of the classroom. Kavi didn't like the two boys. They called her names like guttersnipe and whore-spawn. Never within earshot of the teacher of course.

She felt a touch on her shoulder.

"You're it," said a small voice. The black haired girl who tapped her started to run.

Kavi laughed and chased after her. Tricia was her best friend in the whole world. Kavi never had a sister, but if she did, she bet she would be just like Tricia.

A flash of light.

"Shhh, sweet girl. He's gone now," her mother whispered as she held Kavi in her arms. She smelled of stale wine and cheap perfume.

Kavi cried and pressed the cool rag against her eye where the man hit her. She knew she shouldn't have done anything but when the man hit her mom again, she couldn't help it. She had to do something.

A flash of light.

The room around Kavi was far more opulent than the small apartment. Her mom wore a flowing gown that showed too much of her boobies. They had been living in the bordello for two months and life had gotten better, just like Mom said. Until this morning.

She showed her mom the cloth speckled with blood. Mom's face paled, but she put on a fake smile.

"You're a woman now, hon. Congratulations."

Kavi felt another pain deep in her stomach. "Is it always this bad?" she asked.

"They're just cramps." Her mother's face softened at the pain on her face. "They shouldn't last too long, but keep this to yourself, okay? The other women will want to celebrate your first bleed, but it's best you stay a girl as long as possible. Especially here."

"Can I tell Trish?" Kavi asked.

Her mom nodded. "As long as you're not around any of the girls from the Petal when you do."

A flash of light.

She and Trish were so excited. It was going to be their first Harvest Ball as women. Trish had gotten her a job in the kitchens that paid enough they could share a small room over Hunter's square. Their place smelled of piss and rotting flesh from the two tanneries that shared the square, but it was theirs. Kavi would choose that smell every day over the cheap perfume and depression that lined the walls of the Pink Petal.

"You look great," said Trish as Kavi primped in front of the mirror. She hated the small cleft in her chin, it made her look mannish. She refused to put on any makeup. Makeup was for whores like her mother. She knew her narrow features wouldn't win many suitors, but maybe a young merchant with non-discerning tastes could get her out of the slums.

"Let's goooooo," said Trish, holding her head up and dragging the word out like a wolf howl. "Come on, I would kill for cheek bones like yours. One of these days you're going to have to stop hating yourself and accept you're a beautiful woman."

"I know you're just being nice, but thank you anyway" said Clara.

"I'm not just....Fine. Let's goooooo," Trish howled again.

The ball was as magical as she hoped. Clara couldn't believe men actually wanted to dance with her. She had more partners that night than Trish did. It didn't make sense. She had just started her third dance with a young merchant by the name of Pieter when they heard the yelling.

"Fire! Fire! Oh my god, it's the Astrans! Run!"

Chaos descended and Kavi grabbed Tricia's hand and bolted for the doors. The streets weren't any better. In the flickering of street lamps it was hard to tell friend from foe. The Astrans weren't wearing their traditional garb of long hooded robes. After the initial panic it became more obvious as the Astran garb was plain and utilitarian compared to the Harvest ball finery the fleeing Harpers wore. The Astrans also carried clubs or long wooden staffs.

She and Trish darted from shadow to shadow until they made it back to Hunter's square. One of the tanneries was on fire. Kavi knew they had a decision to make. "We need to head out of town for a couple of days until we know more. Grab whatever food we have left. Quickly!"

A flash of light.

Kavi blinked his eyes twice and could almost make out the rest of the team.

"You back with us yet, Kavi?" asked Pip.

Kavi gritted his teeth but could not bring the present into focus.

A flash of light.

Kavi squatted in the small cave as Trish slept. She looked through their supplies. She knew counting what little food they had left wasn't going to increase the stash, but it was better than doing nothing. She stared into the gloom outside the cave and knew they would have to move come first light. The soft patter of rain drops whispered a dirge that promised wet and slippery travel.

She grabbed a small piece of charcoal from the expired fire and drew on the wall of the cave. She noticed something she hadn't when they first explored the cave. She pushed on a small rock wedged into the cave wall and gasped as the wall creaked backwards to reveal a small passageway leading into the darkness.

"Trish," Kavi whispered. "Come look at this."

They stood and stared at more gold than either of them had ever seen. They would never have to work again. They would never have to beg for a man's help.

"How are we going to get it back?" asked Trish.

Neither of them noticed when the slavers stepped behind them. The blackjacks struck their heads in a rapid staccato of pain.

A flash of light.

Kavi looked at the dormitory room and choked back a sob. Maybe she and Trish could find some beds close enough to the fire that they wouldn't freeze. She sat down on the small pallet and fought against sinking into despair. It wasn't as bad as the slaver caravan at least.

The small Bricker wearing number nineteen came over, mechanical arms flailing wildly. Tricia had to jump out of the way as a metal arm grabbed her bed. Why was he so angry?

Kavi dodged as the splinters of bedding shattered against the wall and hurtled back at her. She jumped back and dodged two of the projectiles the small Bricker shot towards her. She grunted as the third struck her stomach.

Another man came over wearing number eleven. He was cute. He traded angry words with the Bricker. Kavi winced in pain when looking at this man. The image in front of her started to split and she couldn't focus on the man's face. She shook her head. She marveled at how quickly the man moved as he deconstructed the device on the Bricker's back.

She felt gratitude for this man for saving her, but wondered what he would want in return. This place. This Nest. This was not a place for selfless acts. His face, his name became clearer. Kavi. She looked at him and was pulled towards him, in a violent undertow of subjugation. She screamed and her vision began to pulse.

A flash of light.

"Kavi. You back with us yet?" Pip repeated.

Kavi opened his mouth wide, stretching his jaw. "I think so," he said and heard his voice come out of both his and Clara's mouth. "Hiram, how are we doing with separating the audio channels?"

"One more second," came a voice from the sky. "There we go, how's that?"

"Better," said Kavi. His voice came out of only his mouth.

He looked over at Clara and she beamed him a smile. He frowned and wondered how the smile could be real. The fuse was a two way bond so he knew what she saw of his past. How could she smile after that horror show?

Because I understand everything a little better now, came Clara's thoughts in his head. *But we are going to have to talk*

146

about the whole time reversal thing.

Kavi nodded and saw her head bob up and down in concert. This part always took some getting used to. *Please keep it to yourself for now*, he thought. *I made the others I fused with promise, but I trust you. I have no control over the power and the Sage warned me to keep it private.*

I will, but only if you consider discussing it with the team. We might be able to help you figure out how to control it.

"Kavi, I'm going to set a perimeter and send Sliver and Crystal to scout the immediate area," said Pip.

"Do it," whispered Kavi. "We've almost got control of the fuse. Two more minutes."

Pip started yelling orders. They had a rule that only Pip *or* Kavi could fuse in any one scenario so the command structure would have one strong tactician in place. There was a hierarchy in place where Boost then Tess could take over if Pip and Kavi fell, but the most important role of tactician was in the beginning of a Pool scenario. They had to evaluate the threat, quickly put together a strategy and execute it without time for a discussion. That couldn't happen if both tacticians were working through the disorientation of a fuse.

Kavi forced himself to focus as Pip directed the squad. He enjoyed watching the man work. He was so confident, so sure of his decisions. It didn't hurt that he was also gorgeous.

Where did that thought come from? Kavi wondered with a smirk at Clara.

It's true, but don't worry, he's too pretty for my tastes.

Ready to get to work?

In response, Clara summoned her paints and walked towards the fortifications.

They were in a deserted city. Freshly painted row houses

lined neatly cobbled roadways. Street signs labeled each intersection. The blue sign with white letters above Kavi's head declared they were on the corner of Dahlia and Twelfth. Flowers were planted in tight, geometric patterns between the cobbles and the row houses. The flowers were perfectly round and perfectly spaced from one plant to the next.

Not only were there no people in the immediate area, there were no animals, no insects buzzing from one flower to the next. This city was completely silent but for the movement and communication between members of Ghost Squad.

Kavi looked at the barriers the Forts put up with satisfaction. The area was easily defensible. Pip had Boost, Jory, and Tess on the rooftops of the row houses. He wondered how Jory recovered so quickly from his fuse disorientation. Kavi kept getting glimpses of what Clara was seeing as she helped put up the fortifications. It made concentration difficult.

Time to see if I can make use of your speed while we're fused.

I've been wondering the same thing, mused Kavi. *Now's the time to experiment. If only I had some artistic talent.*

Clara began to paint. Kavi felt time slow but it was Clara pulling on the temporal stream, not him. He watched through her eyes as runes formed on every open surface. Clara flitted from one rune to the next like a hummingbird. A larger mural of runes began to appear on their fortifications all at once.

It was an artistic rendering of an idyllic cityscape. A tableau of form and function. The art added life to the dead city. The patterns took on a vitality of their own. The runes interacted with each other, flowing together then bouncing back in a dance of color and texture. The runes accounted for their surroundings. Flowers, cobbles and row houses were incorporated into the greater artwork so it was hard to tell the difference between the art and the reality surrounding it.

It was almost like she created an alternate reality, thought Kavi, bringing the dead town back to life. It was so much more than her runes of the past, the art was fluid, moving and flowing. There! A bee buzzed on the painting, landing on a painted flower. Then, the bee flew off the painting and on to one of the real flowers.

Sliver came running back with her automaton spiders surrounding her. "I have two contacts about a half click south of here and...what in the hell is that!?" she asked, stopping short as she encountered the fortifications. "Those patterns are making my eyes go all wobbly, like the walls are alive. Are you still in there?" She stopped moving entirely— a feat for Silver—and stared.

"That, is what happens when our rune scriber fuses with speedy," said Pip stepping out from behind one of the walls.

His words pulled her out of her mesmerized stare. "Wow, that is trippy," said the Bricker woman, wiggling the augment in her ear with a finger. She pulled at one of the small yellow spikes of hair as if pulling could counteract the hypnotic nature of the mural in front of her. "I can't look straight at it without feeling all sorts of funky."

Pip cocked his head at her.

"Seriously, come out where I am and look at this thing," said Sliver. "You can't take your eyes off it."

"How quickly are the contacts moving and are they heading our way?" asked Pip.

Sliver stared at the mural.

"Sliver!"

She looked back at Pip. "Sorry, they should be here in five minutes. They look like ordinary people, but confused. When they saw one of my spiders, they went into a rage and started kicking and pounding on it with their fists."

"Did they see you?" asked Kavi.

"No, but they didn't see much of anything. They were walking around in a daze, nobody talking to each other, nobody touching. They just walked in silence. But they're coming our way and it's safe to assume they mean us harm."

"We *are* in the Pool," said Pip.

We have five minutes, it's your turn. Embrace it. Embrace your mortality and try to create. Clara's thoughts came across as a command.

Kavi took a deep breath and concentrated. *I don't know how to create. I only know how to destroy.*

Nonsense. Kavi could feel Clara's frustration through the bond. *You've created this, Ghost Squadron. Your art is bringing people together, making them better than they are alone. Now CREATE!*

Kavi sought the mantra he rarely needed anymore. Speed came naturally to him, but creation? That was new. *Move like wind.* They were all going to die shortly anyway, what was the harm of trying to create something? He thought about how many times he had seen Clara create things of such beauty that they moved him from feeling awful in one moment to feeling alive and invigorated in the next. He couldn't imagine life without her. The Ghost Squadron, the Nest, all of it would be a darker place without Clara.

He drew both swords and began to move. He slowed his movements to a performance. It wasn't dance, but it was close. He played off Clara's art to build an expression of life.

He thought of home when he started the most basic sword kata: *thread the needle*, followed by simple dual wield katas: *weave the loom* and *till the field*. Only then did he start to improvise.

Strike like fire. He thought of all the Strikers he encountered. He thought of Strikers on his team and how different life would be without them. How terrible. His movement shifted to a memorial of each. He sensed it when the threat arrived but continued his performance. His katas turned catlike as he moved like Tess, then mechanical as he fought like Boost, and finally fluid and unpredictable as he fought like Pip. An image of the three appeared in his mind's eye as they fought a group of ordinary people. Citizens, city dwellers that did not look like warriors but fought like demons when riled.

Pip shouted orders and Tess and Boost fired projectile after projectile as these urban demons shifted barely enough to dodge every strike. Tess and Boost shared a look colored with dread but kept firing. Pip stayed calm throughout, an island in a turbulent sea. His calm kept the team functioning as he summoned void gates that confused and angered the demons coming their way. They were close now.

Defend like earth. Kavi's thoughts turned to the Guards. Jansen, who lived and fought with his heart. Anger and fear as obvious as joy and pride on the big man's broad face. His ability to live in the present would outlast them all. Tristan moved beside him. The Loamian morphed back and forth between cat and human as he plugged gaps with sword and shield then struck with claw and teeth. To those that didn't know him, Tristan was as aloof as the giant cat he turned into. One-on-one? He was thoughtful and caring and worried about each of the squad members nearly as much as Kavi.

Kavi's thoughts moved to Stix, their warrior philosopher. His speed was second only to Kavi's but his knowledge of battle and people put him in the precise spot in a fight where he had the most impact. Then there was Stonez, the anchor on the line. He was a tough man to like but an easy one to love. His grouchiness was outweighed by a fierce loyalty to friends and family. He shrugged off any insult to him, but if you dared insult one of his tribe? You better run because he was coming for you.

Kavi saw the four men form an impenetrable wall as the city folk advanced. His katas became defensive in nature as his improvisation matched his thoughts. Herman wedged himself into the middle of the line and the five held as the urbanites attacked. They went back and forth for what felt like hours with neither side gaining an advantage. The demons watched then mimicked what they saw. Their styles mirrored and anticipated what would happen next. Kavi continued to move until he felt a pain as one of the urban demons pierced through Jansen's guard and a blade sliced the large man's hamstring. Jansen fell to one knee and as he did, the city dweller that struck him paused for a moment as he saw the runes behind the big man. Paused and stood mesmerized until a strike from Stix pulled him back in the fight. Clara's art could slow, but it wasn't enough.

Parry like water. This was not a battle that would be won traditionally. This would require the creativity of the Forts and Dancers or something else entirely. Kavi continued to move, erratic now, switching to a kata he never used in battle—*cart on a bumpy road.* He reveled in the bluntness of Sliver. The tenacity the small Bricker took to every problem she encountered. No problem existed that didn't have a solution. Failure was just an idea that didn't work yet to the piercing laden Dancer.

The answer would be in the supporting cast, those that couldn't be readily emulated. He thought of the quiet Elana, their neuro mage who shifted to ebullient the moment you linked with her mind-to-mind. She was a beauty, with caramel skin and raven hair, but she struggled with confidence. She hated her own voice, a shame because she always had something interesting to add, yet rarely participated. She turned her powers to one of the smaller urban attackers who stopped and stared at Clara's runes. One of Tess's arrows took the woman through the throat and she died silently. Kavi continued his erratic dance.

The art was the key, but it needed more.

His movements smoothed as he improvised around his Astran teammates. Amity, Crystal and Felicity moved from wound to sprain to break. They saw more blood in a battle than any Striker. They turned gore and violence into smooth skin and cool relief. They saved Kavi and the Ghost Squadron so many times. He wouldn't have a life without them.

Kavi's movement became jerky and discombobulated as he thought of Jory. The troubadour was easy to talk to and comfortable to be around. The turbulence came from his own thoughts about the man. The women, including Clara, found him irresistible. His charm, amazing voice and skill with the lute made him an almost mythical creature to the opposite sex. Plenty of men felt the same and Kavi could see why. When he sang, he painted stories in the air and brought them to life with his alluring voice. It was intimidating, but he wouldn't trade the bard for anyone else. His songs brought joy. As he thought about the stories Jory told, he noticed the city demons were not immune to the music. With a flash of insight he knew how to beat these creatures.

He was about to stop his dance of steel and explain his thinking to Pip and the team when the world fractured in two. He could still sense and see everything in the sim but a new vision flickered in front of him.

Kavi was in two places at once. Here in the sim and somewhere else entirely.

In this alternate vision, Kavi stood with his squad in the farmlands west of Harpstra. Across the fields stood a horde of goat-like creatures. At the head of the enemy host stood a giant, scarlet beast. Unlike its brethren, it stood upright. It had goat hooves for feet and the arms of a man. Those arms had muscles that rivaled Grim's. Its red face was built around its goatee, its features long and pointed like its beard. The demon's face was capped with black hair and swirling ram horns. Every bit of exposed skin was bright red, a caricature of the devils Kavi read about when he was a child.

The creature was surrounded by thousands of farm animals converted into something twisted and horrible. They were mostly goats, but Kavi saw pigs, dogs, cows and even a couple of grotesque chickens. Ghost Squad wouldn't have a chance against those numbers. The alternate Sliver handed Kavi a looking glass and Kavi stared at the devil for a long while. He soaked in every feature. The devil lifted its head to yell an attack when Kavi noticed a small black rose tattooed to it's throat. Kavi issued orders that had the squad looking at him curiously, but they did what he asked.

The alternate Tess pulled an arrow from her quiver and

handed it to to the alternate Clara. That Clara carved a rune into the shaft and painted another one on either side of the arrow head blisteringly fast before handing the arrow back to Tess. Alternate Sliver stood in front of the Squad and sent her spiders running towards the goat devil.

Alternate Tess knocked the arrow to her bow, pointed it to the sky, and loosed. As the arrow flew, alternate Jory played power chords on his lute to push the arrow even higher. Boost sent projectiles over the heads of the spiders. Then the image froze in time, like a tapestry hanging on a castle wall.

Something in Kavi snapped, like a string from Jory's lute breaking. The fracturing of worlds ceased. All his focus returned to the sim. He looked down, expecting to see his squad fighting for their lives, but there was no battle. The enemy had not attacked yet. Then what did he see? Did he dance into the future? And what the hell was that vision of the devil creature?

What was that? Where did you go? came Clara over the fuse.

I have no idea, Kavi thought back. *But we have more immediate concerns.*

Kavi stopped moving. "Pip! New plan. Something I saw in the fuse."

"You better hurry," said Pip. "We have maybe three minutes before these creepy looking city people attack."

Kavi smiled and noticed the squad for the first time since he stopped moving. They shot him sidelong glances while pretending not to look at their erratic leader practicing forms. They prepared for the imminent attack, but moved out of his way when it was obvious Kavi was in a trance.

Crystal arrived a moment later from the opposite direction from Sliver. "I made it a full click out and didn't see a single living thing," said Crystal. "It's creepy. Nothing but endless city streets recently renovated, immaculate landscaping, everything freshly painted. It felt like walking through the set of a play."

Stix smiled at Crystal, glad to see her back safe. "We're in the Pool. If it's a play, we know it's a tragedy," said Stix.

Kavi faced the group. "We need to pull everyone behind the fortifications. Clara, can you and Felicity put a small tower up in the next minute so we can elevate Jory while keeping him protected?"

Clara nodded and started grabbing materials from the cart the Forts summoned the moment they entered the scenario.

Stix and Crystal moved to help.

"Here they come," said Pip. "If we're going to execute the plan, we better do it now."

"Tell me when to summon Herman," said Sliver.

"No need," said Kavi. "We're going to beat this one with art and music."

Puzzled looks met the statement.

"Trust me," said Kavi. "Jory, get up in the tower and play something calming, something that will get these city dwellers to keep their focus on the mural Clara created and not us. Can you do that?"

Jory nodded and the rest of Ghost Squad peered through gaps in the fortifications to watch as the urbanites shuffled towards their position. When they caught sight of the wall, they paused. Kavi could tell the art gripped them but the idea of something blocking their way infuriated them.

"Hold!" shouted Kavi when he noticed Tess drawing her

bow and Boost aiming his hand cannons, the clockwork in his legs whirring as he planned to leap to the balcony of an adjacent house. They lowered their weapons and looked at Kavi doubtfully. Kavi ignored them, focusing on the urbanites below. His shouted command had raised their anger again. Where the hell was that troubadour. "Jory..."

Jory began to play. The soothing notes wrapped around the urban demons. Kavi could see their shoulders lower and their eyes shift back to Clara's art. The life she created resonated with them and slowly the rage began to dissipate.

Some sat and stared at the mural. When Jory started the second verse of the soothing lullaby, those staring at the mural shook their heads as if waking from a long sleep. They began to notice the people around them for the first time.

Old friends hugged and pointed at the art. Spouses kissed and laughed while children shook their heads to clear the daze before rushing to play with friends. All the while, Jory's calm song engulfed the area in a musical hug.

The building next to Kavi started to flicker. The flowers in the closest flowerbed disappeared.

"Kavi, are you doing this?" asked Pip.

"No. I don't know what this is."

Moments later the building disappeared. It left a blank white void in its place, like a carbon copy of one of Pip's void gates. The urbanites began to disappear next.

"I don't like this," said Jansen. "I'd rather fight something then get sucked up by this void."

With a flash, everything went white.

The Ghost Squadron woke up in the Pool. "What the hell was that?" asked Kavi.

Hiram's voice came across the speakers. "I think you

broke it."

"Broke what," said Kavi, "the scenario?"

"No, the Pool."

15

Harpstra

Ghost Squad left the Nest before dawn. There wasn't a single complaint as they humped up the stairway to the dock without gear. The stairs flew by without the extra weight. Rank had its privileges. They boarded the airship and launched minutes after. The League had no need for the obfuscator, the Bricker tech that hid the giant zeppelins, anymore. So, the launch took a fraction of the time.

Kavi stood on the main deck and enjoyed the feel of the wind through his hair. Thoughts of the bureaucracy and busywork he endured at the Nest blew away in the icy winds of the Talons. The others had gone inside for warmth but Kavi needed a moment alone. A moment to recalibrate.

He thought of the chaos in the Aerie he left behind. Kavi was the only one smiling around the conference table in his last meeting. The researchers were up in arms about the Pool. The Snoops were upset with the incomplete intelligence they received about the next Peacekeeping mission, and the coaches complained about the slow progress of Quest candidates who weren't given access to the Pool after Kavi and his team broke it.

"What are you grinning about?" Coach Sug had asked.

"None of this is my problem for the next two weeks," Kavi said, leaning back in his chair as he watched the chaos.

Who'd have thought a peacekeeping mission would feel like a vacation. Kavi gripped the rail. It wasn't a vacation though. He would be putting the lives of his squad in danger. Again. He didn't know much about this new threat other than the Snoops telling him they were dealing with a Marked that might be demonic. He wondered about the strange vision in the Pool yesterday. Did it have something to do with the peacekeeping mission? The black rose at the creature's throat made him think it was a message from the fifth Sage, but he wouldn't know more until they got to the site.

He was sure their mission would be deadly, but at least it wasn't a Quest.

Kavi couldn't believe how foolish and naïve he, Nettie and Grim had been those six months ago when they went looking for a Quest on their bid to be heroes. Idiots. They learned their lesson the hard way. At least Grim and Nettie were safe with the Liberators. As safe as one could be when hiding out with a rebel group. He wondered when he would see them next.

Thoughts of Grim led to thoughts of home. His letter should have made it to Stonecrest a week ago. He wondered how it was received. Dad would have been happy, maybe his mother too. When the next mission took him near Krom or Brickolage, he would stop in. It wasn't as if there was a pressing need. It had only been six months. Stonecrest was fine without him. He'd love to see his dad, but he knew both he and the Lioness could use the time apart to reevaluate their relationship.

Kavi looked up as snow began to fall. His breath misted in the lightening sky and he forced himself back to the present. He had the deck to himself as the pilots for Team Sugoroku demanded an indoor helm with all the mountain flying they had to do.

Five more minutes and he'd head inside back to his team. Back to his responsibilities.

* * *

They landed in a large field outside of Harpstra. The government knew when and where they would arrive and sent a contingent of politicians and press to meet them.

An officious looking minister was the first to greet them as they walked down the gangway. The man wore a military uniform littered with trinkets, ropes and ribbons. His round, amicable face hadn't seen hardship in years. He looked like an actor playing a soldier.

"Welcome Sugoroku and thank you for your assistance in our time of need," said the man. He pulled out a piece of paper and Kavi rolled his eyes. A speech, really?

Then Kavi noticed the recording crystals floating behind and above him. Not only was he here on an official capacity, he had every intention of gaining political capital for this welcome.

Kavi had been groomed by the public relations people of Team Sugoroku. They taught him what questions to steer clear of, what questions to give canned answers to and how to give an answer that didn't actually answer anything. They assured him it wasn't lying, but flirting with the truth. When he called them sneaky little scumbags, they pulled out his contract. He finally relented to some of their guidelines, but he couldn't help but feel dirty doing it.

As he looked down on this politician from the elevated gangway, he realized he underestimated the scale of his public relations role. He expected the PR to happen in his scheduled meeting with the Harpstran Post. He did not expect to be met by politicians with an agenda and media platform.

"You're going to need to turn those crystals off around the airship. We're unloading sensitive and confidential materials," said Kavi.

"Don't worry, we signed a non-disclosure with Sugoroku's owners," said the official.

"That may be, but that non-disclosure does not cover recording our equipment in a crystal. Shut them down," said Kavi.

One of the man's aides whispered something in his ear. The man smiled and turned back to Kavi. "You must be Team Sugoroku's tactician. Kavi Stonecrest is it? I didn't expect you to be quite so...salty."

Kavi smiled back, showing a lot of teeth. "I can be friendly," he said. He took a deep breath and time slowed. Kavi reached up and grabbed both crystals before they had the chance to adapt to his movement and avoid him. "But please don't test my patience with tricks. We have come to help you and your people so I will ask you to respect the terms of our agreement without trying to unlawfully gain information."

The man looked at the crystals in Kavi's hand and his grin widened. "You're as fast as they say you are."

"If there are more recording crystals pointed in our direction, I will ask you to turn them off now. If I find out about more you haven't disclosed, I'll be forced to confiscate them."

A young aide standing behind the official whispered to him. The official shook his head and whispered back.

Kavi nodded to Pip who did a quick scan into the void to look for signals. He held up two fingers.

The minister looked straight into Kavi's eyes and lied. "No, those were the only two. Would you mind passing them back?"

Kavi sighed, disappointed but not surprised. "I assume you are a politician, Minister...?"

The man pushed out his chest and held out a hand. "Yes, I am Defense Minister Kwan, nice to meet you."

Kavi took the man's hand and squeezed, just hard enough to make an impression. The man squeezed back, slightly harder and Kavi nodded. He broke the handshake then squeezed with his other hand until both of the hollow recording crystals shattered. "I don't like being lied to, Minister Kwan. Please hand the other two crystals over before we decide to retract our support and move to a Garden City that will work with Team Sugoroku in a more... professional manner."

The defense minister scowled when one of his aide grabbed the concealed crystals and handed them to Pip. Kwan pushed out his chest and said, "You'll be sorry for that, young man. Each of those recording crystals costs over two hundred gold. I expect to be reimbursed."

"No, I won't be sorry," said Kavi. "And you won't be reimbursed. You obviously haven't been working with the League for long. If they found out you lied to us and recorded our technology, what do you think they would do to you?"

The man didn't answer.

"Consider the four hundred gold an investment," said Kavi.

"In what?"

"In living to see your next birthday," said Kavi. "Now, please show us to our quarters. We've been traveling for three days and all I want is a warm bath, a hot meal and a cold beer. Can you make that happen?"

Defense Minister Kwan scowled again and gave an order to the aides behind him. He turned his back on Ghost Squad and walked to his carriage. He shouted at the driver and they wheeled towards Harpstra.

"Making friends already," said Stix with a grin. "My family is going to love you. You already have one thing in common."

Kavi grimaced and wondered for the hundredth time why Sugoroku picked him to be the face of the Peacekeeping campaign. He sucked at this diplomacy stuff. Pip would have been a better choice. "What's that?" he asked.

"You can't stand Defense Minister Kwan. That guy's a snake. Always has been."

The tallest of the three aides walked over to Ghost Squad and gave a dramatic bow. "My apologies, Milord Stonecrest. Minister Kwan had a difficult morning trying to broker a peace with the Astrans. He's normally far more respectful."

Stix snorted and the aide glared at him.

"We all have bad days," said Kavi magnanimously.

"What's next?"

"We can help unload your gear into the covered wagons behind us if you'd like," said the aide. "If you would prefer to unload it yourself, both of those larger wagons are yours for the duration of your stay. We've provided each of you with mounts or seats in the elegant carriages to take you to Harpstra. We've reserved the top floor of The Vondam for your team which is only a stone's throw from the palace."

Stix whistled. "They reserve those rooms for visiting royalty. I take back all those terrible things I said about you, Kavi. I'm going to like being a part of this team."

"Until we face the Marked," said Pip.

"Don't bother me with details," said Stix throwing an arm around the Vonderian's shoulder. "Tonight, we live like kings."

* * *

The Vondam was once part of the Harpstran Palace compound. Harpstra still had a king, but his power was tempered by a parliament. The old nobility still had a say with the House of Royals but the House of Citizens had equal power to the nobles in what the government decided. The government had been in place for a generation so the Harpstran people had grown accustomed to it. King Harlan IV still held an inordinate amount of power, especially when it came to the military, but his father, Harlan the third, started the process of giving power to the people. Once the people got a taste of that power, taking it from them would cause wide-scale rebellion.

During the transfer of power, some of the palatial struc-tures were transformed into government buildings and some were put up for auction to the wealthiest citizenry. The Vondam was one of the latter. It was purchased by a group of merchants and actors who now rented rooms to visiting dignitaries. The king had the right to commandeer rooms for political guests, but the primary difference was the crown had to pay for those rooms.

Palatial. It was the only way to describe the rooms on the top floor of the Vondam. Each of the twenty suites had its own bathroom and these bathrooms had been recently upgraded with a combination of the latest Brickolage and Vonderian plumbing. With a flick of a wrist a hot bath could be summoned in minutes. The chamber pot had been replaced with a comfortable chair with a hole in the base that would take away human waste.

The door to his suite burst open and Clara rushed in while Kavi was still in the bathroom. He was glad he hadn't sat down to use it.

"This place is incredible," she said, voice breathless. "Me and Trix always imagined what it might be like to stay here. When we were little girls, we would play dress-up and the Vondam was where every pretend ball took place. Even the working girls dreamed of a magical night in the Vondam."

Her face fell. "I wish she lived to see this place. She would have loved it." Her eyes moistened, but she didn't let the tears fall.

Kavi engulfed her in a hug. "I'm not going to judge you for crying. I don't know that hanging on to it does any good."

She leaned into the hug, then pushed him back. "No. If I

don't hang on to some of it, she's going to be gone for good. I'm not ready for that. I can accept she's gone without being ready to let her go."

Kavi's own eyes moistened. "I get it. She had a huge impact on me and I only knew her for a couple of months." He sniffed twice. "I'm no expert. When I lost Brink I did everything in my power to be a good Krommian warrior. Stoic. No emotion, toughness a wall around the pain. That way I never had to touch it. I know you're not avoiding it like I was. Still, when I finally let the storm hit and run its course, it was like someone gave me permission to start looking at his death in a new way. Instead of it running through my head exactly the same over and over. It didn't mean I had to let him go, it was more like taking a break from the old story and starting something new. It was a wise woman who told me to take a break and look at things from a different perspective."

She smiled at the reminder of their walk around the Rim. "You're right."

"Two of my favorite words." Kavi cocked an eyebrow. "About what?"

"She sounds like a *very* wise woman." She reached up and brushed away a stray lock of hair that had fallen over his eye. "You've come quite a long way from that arrogant Krommian git that tried to save me and Trix that first night in the dormitory."

"Arrogant? That wasn't arrogance."

"Fine, over-principled git."

"What's wrong with principles?"

"We never asked for your help and you came charging in like a fairy tale knight. Would you have helped if we weren't two seemingly helpless women?"

Kavi scowled. "You were in my head, you know me better than that. Yeah, I would have helped. It was less about you and more about not letting Boost be a giant asshole to everybody in the Nest."

Clara smiled. "I know, but you're cute when you're annoyed." She moved her hand to the back of his neck and drew him down towards her.

Kavi tensed. All the feelings he had for Clara, especially after spending time in her head, were built around grief and pain. This felt so foreign, he was blindsided by it. Foreign but good. He leaned into the kiss.

"Excuse me," said a woman standing by the open door. "Are you Kavi Stonecrest?"

Clara whipped around. "And who the hell are you, mystery woman with horrible timing?"

Kavi looked at the newcomer standing outside his door. She was tall and impeccably dressed. The heels on her shoes added to her height and the formal Harpstran gown accentuated curves only slightly diminished by the silk shawl draped over her shoulders.

The woman looked Clara up and down disapprovingly then dismissively. "Are you Kavi Stonecrest?" she repeated.

Clara gaped at her then growled. "Oh, I'm going to enjoy kicking the—"

"A moment, Clara," said Kavi, interrupting her. "Who's asking?"

The woman looked at both of them, waiting for an answer.

Kavi shrugged. "You're standing outside of my room, interrupting a private moment. Declare yourself or Clara will show you how Ghost Squad deals with an enemy."

"Ah, the rune scriber," said the woman looking down at Clara with a bit more respect. "So you *must* be Kavi. I am Patrice Elden Baroque, head of public relations for the League. We need to discuss your stay in Harpstra and the image you need to project. No more of this—," she waved a hand to encompass both of them, "public display of affection in front of open doors. You are greater assets as single heroes then you ever would be as a couple."

Clara snorted. "Why would we care—"

"I could care less what you do behind closed doors, my dear, but you are about to become a very public figure and your time in the public is mine for the next eighteen months."

"Oh, I hate her so much," said Clara in a stage whisper to Kavi.

Kavi laughed then turned back to Patrice. "We're not supposed to meet until tomorrow morning."

"I'm incredibly good at what I do, Lord Stonecrest. If I waited until tomorrow, this—," she made the hand waving motion again, "would have already become a disaster. Honestly, I don't care if the two of you are sleeping together, but have the decency to do it behind closed doors. Imagine if a servant saw you. I would be cleaning up the mess for weeks."

Kavi's face flushed. "No, we weren't about to—"

"You don't know that," said Clara, interrupting him.

Kavi's face got even redder.

"Ooh, I *like* that angle. The 'will they or won't they' thing always plays well for the peasants."

"Who are you?" said Pip.

They all jumped. None of them heard the void mage

169

walking down the hall.

"None of your business," said Patrice, turning to Pip. She stopped and stared, readjusted her shawl and tried to regain her composure.

Pip's lips twitched up at her discomfort.

"I'm Patrice, head of relations...public relations that is... for the uh...for the League," she said.

"I love it when pretty girls see Pip for the first time," said Clara in the same stage whisper. "They look and act as stupid as men do around them."

Pip had replaced his battle gear with a dark blue, loose-fitting tunic with an open collar that managed to show blond tufts of chest hair peeking between sculpted pectorals. His hair was swept back in a look so effortless Kavi was sure he spent twenty minutes in front of a mirror.

"Nice to meet you, Patrice," said Pip, "but we've got a mission to attend to."

Patrice raised her eyebrows. "The mission isn't for another two days," she said.

"Tonight's mission is different, we're gathering intelligence," said Pip. He looked at Kavi and Clara and spread his hands. "What the hell are you two doing? We leave in fifteen minutes. Let's go! Stix is going to kick the crap out of you if you're late."

"Why wasn't I notified of this mission?" asked Patrice.

Pip turned and gave her the same once over she gave Clara earlier. Patrice reddened at the treatment and Clara smiled. Pip pointed at Clara then to the door.

"Fine, I'm going," said Clara. She gave Kavi's hand a squeeze and walked out.

Pip turned back to Patrice, eyes meeting hers. "You must

not have security clearance. Now please, we'll meet you at the scheduled time tomorrow morning."

Pip stepped inside and shut the door in Patrice's face.

"I don't know how you do it, Twelve," said Kavi. "She would have followed you to your room if you'd asked."

Pip grinned. "It's not *that* easy," he said. "With a beautiful woman like her, she is so unused to men being rude to her that she's going to spend the next two hours wondering why I didn't find her attractive. I have become a mystery she needs to solve."

"Sounds evil," said Kavi.

Pip slapped him on the back a little harder than necessary. "We're no different than monkeys, my friend. This is just another mating ritual. Now put your stuff on and let's go meet Stix's family."

16

Thickbloods

They left the Vondam as a group. This was the first time anyone from Team Sugoroku had been given leave to visit family. Everyone in Ghost Squad treated the trip as if it were a visit to their own family. The mood bordered on jubilant. Kavi couldn't help worrying. It seemed the perfect setup for an ambush.

Two men dressed in dark clothing slipped behind the group as they exited the outer walls of the hotel. Kavi looked at Pip.

"I don't think anyone would be dumb enough to try anything," said Pip in a low voice.

"Those two are an escort from the League," said Tess breezily. "It's the two in front of us that may actually be looking to start some trouble."

"Three," said Boost. "The first one, with the goofy tough guy hat, disappeared before you walked out, Tess."

Kavi gave a relieved chuckle. "And I was worried you let your guard down."

"Seriously?" asked Sliver. "We're going to visit Stix's

family, which is amazing, but there ain't a Ghost alive capable of letting their guard down. Ever. Again. I got six spiders crawling the rooftops ahead and behind us. If there's any real trouble, we'll know about it long before it gets dangerous. Relax, Tack. Nothing in the city can pose a threat to us."

Kavi started shaking his head. *Damn it Sliver, don't invite trouble.* Then he smiled. She was right. Street thugs had no chance against Ghost Squad. His team naturally assumed a scouting formation as they walked down the street. The fancy new clothing the Vondam provided couldn't hide the menace his team emanated. Not a single weapon could be seen through the ruffles and lace, but every Ghost was armed.

The Harpstran theater district was always crowded. They walked through it right before the evening showing. The streets teemed with people. Moving through theater-goers was like managing the current of a strong river.

Stix and Clara took point. As native Harpstrans, they navigated through these currents like master ferrymen. Ghost Squad exuded an aura of danger so most everyone rushed to move out of their way.

Stix pointed at several larger boys who scanned the crowd for easy marks. He gave each a subtle shake of his head. *This group is not worth your time or your lives.* The boys offered innocent pantomimes before nodding back.

For all their skill navigating a crowd, it was slow going. When they finally broke free of the theater district and into the residential neighborhoods on the hill, an hour had passed.

"Ma's going to be pissed," said Stix. "I tell her I'm

bringing fifteen people to dinner then I show up late."

"Double time," yelled Pip. "Point the way Stix, we'll make it."

"We still have a tail?" asked Kavi.

Sliver nodded. "Spiders have a line on all five of them. If the three in front are going to make a move, they'll do it next time the streets narrow so they can take us a couple at a time."

"Boost, Tess, find high ground," said Kavi.

The two Strikers broke from the group and scaled the buildings on either side of the street with uncanny speed. Boost wasn't wearing his full rig and the augments in his legs whirred as he frog-leapt his way to the top. Tess didn't have her bow, but Kavi knew both wore throwing knives.

Let's hope it doesn't come to that.

The larger townhouses on the hill transitioned to a series of row-houses on narrow streets that weren't nearly as well lit. When the man with the bowler hat materialized in front of Stix and Clara, no one was surprised. Clara let out an unintended giggle at the man's disbelief that his entrance hadn't created a response.

The man hid his disappointment quickly as he scanned the Squad. "You lot look like you know how to handle yourselves, which is why we warned the cutters and shrikes off. But I can't let a group of trained whatever-you-are walk through Thickblood territory without meeting the boss."

"How are you planning to stop us?" asked Kavi. His eyes flitted upwards where Tess and Boost had cornered the other two thugs.

The man smiled, but there was a falseness to it. "You found the men you were supposed to find," he said, his words an easy drawl.

While the man in the bowler hat spoke Stix looked at him strangely, as if trying to solve a puzzle. "Red, is that you?" Stix finally asked.

This caused the man to start. He squinted back at Stix. "Ho-lee shit, Bernie?"

"Bernie?" asked Stonez in a voice on the edge of cracking. "Nobody else is finding that hilarious?"

Stix grabbed Red in an embrace. "What's it been, ten years?"

Red held him at arm's length. "At least! Damn, Bern, you put on some muscle."

"You running with the Thickbloods?" asked Stix. "Didn't expect that from you."

"It's more complicated than that," said Red. "I only got involved when your Ma did, once Kwan started coming down hard on Easties."

"Easties live in the poorer neighborhoods on the east side of town," whispered Clara to Kavi.

"He sent the Guard to evict everyone he could after Minister Wharton doubled taxes." Red's face reddened in anger. "That was after the two of them struck a deal with the landowners to triple rents. They're clearing out common folk to do something big. We don't know what it is but there's a lot more people living on the streets. It's bad, Bern."

"Wait a second," said Stix. "My ma's part of the Thickbloods?"

Red snorted. "She's not a *part* of the Thickbloods, she's running the gang."

That rocked Stix back on his heels. He whistled. "This is

going to be one hell of a dinner."

"She had us tailing you since you landed last night. When you met with Kwan, I thought you might be enemies, until that one," he pointed at Kavi, "sent the Minister off in a huff. What your Ma didn't mention is that you were a part of the group."

"She didn't mention a lot of things," said Stix. "But I can't blame her for being cautious. Mind giving us an escort?"

Red whistled and five men came out from hiding spots along the narrow street. Kavi nodded in appreciation. He hadn't seen two of them. The Thickbloods weren't half bad.

"I would appreciate it if you held up the other two following us while we eat with my family," said Stix. "Don't hurt them. They're with the League and they don't mean us harm, but it's going to be hard to have an honest conversation if they're listening in."

Red whispered to the Thickblood closest to him and the man ran off. "They won't bother you for the rest of the evening," said Red.

Stix gave him a hard look.

Red held up a hand. "We're not going to hurt em, hand's blood."

After hearing the oath, Stix nodded. "Lead the way."

* * *

Stix looked dismayed as he looked at his old home. The row-house was never extravagant, but now the dilapidated façade was openly decaying. Red led them through the front door.

176

Stix shook his head at the mold and exposed plaster in the main room. The stairs leading up were an invitation to a broken leg.

"By Harp's sagging gams, Red!" said Stix. "Nobody around to do a little maintenance?"

"Hold on to your panties, cuz. You're seeing exactly what you're supposed to." Red moved into the next room and put first his hand, then his entire arm through a hole in the wall. When he pulled it back out, the wall slid on runners cleverly crafted so they could only be seen from the other side of the wall.

When the wall stopped, Ghost Squad looked into an entirely different home. It was well furnished, not with anything expensive, but every piece of furniture had been well made and lovingly used. It felt like a home. The most notable thing in the room was a tall woman with flaxen hair shifting white. She had a broad smile on her face. Her facial tattoos were a constellation of hearts and stars. She wore an apron over sensible clothing and her hands were dusted with flour. She wiped them on a dish cloth as she surveyed the group.

"Mama?" said Stix.

"You better get over here and give me a hug, boy," said the woman, eyes filling with tears.

The rest of Stix's family came from the kitchen near the back of the big room. There were four sisters and one older brother. Tears, laughter, and hugs came together in a mess of joy and limbs that surrounded Stix.

When he finally came up for air, Stix asked, "Where's Dad?"

A dark cloud moved over his mother's face. "All in good

time, Bernie."

Stix's face drained of blood. "He's dead, isn't he?"

Mom shook her head. "No, but it's not good. We'll talk while we eat. First, you better make introductions. Especially to this woman and best friend of yours you mentioned in your letter."

Stonez held out his hand in greeting which she pushed aside to fold him in a hug. "If you must know, my name is Esther," she said, "But you will call me Mom, or Mamma Esther. My boy told me how you saved his life more times than he could count."

Stonez rested his chin on her shoulder and leaned into the hug. "The life saving was mutual, Mom. He's more a brother to me than my own blood."

"Which makes you part of *my* family," she said. "Now come in here and meet the rest of your siblings."

Esther fussed over Crystal next. "You are a beauty, my dear." She tucked a strand of hair behind her ear and looked deep into her eyes. "And there's kindness in you. I get what he sees in you. We'll have to put a little meat on those bones though. You make sure to take at least two servings tonight, you hear?"

Stix came from a family of storytellers and they gave a montage of every embarrassing moment Stix suffered while under this roof.

Stix gave as good as he got. The room roared with laughter when Stix told the story about his older brother's attempt to adopt one of the dirty mutts running around the streets. When they finally cleaned the dirt off the poor thing, they realized it was the same fox who killed four of their chickens. The fox escaped the family in an explosion of feathers as it ate one more succulent hen on its way out.

Mamma Esther served a delicious yellow rice dish with bits of chicken and shrimp that enhanced the onions and garlic. She cooked the meal in a large sloped pot in the outside courtyard next the kitchen. The flour dusting her hands was from the most delicious rolls Kavi had ever tasted.

As Stix's siblings began to clear the food, Esther turned to Kavi. "Tell me, young Lion, is the League really here to help?"

Kavi shook his head. "Please call me Kavi, Mamma. The League can't *ever* be trusted. They will help as long as it's in their best interest. Right now, their best interest is to show the world they are a benevolent organization. Not one that, as recently as last year, imprisoned and enslaved whoever they wanted in order to make them fodder for their Quest division. While we're here, we represent the League. But the organization, and the one backing it, are rotten to the core."

Mamma Esther sighed. "The League took my boy from me over five years ago. I expected as much. I just hoped...well no matter."

"What is it Ma?" asked Stix. "What happened to Dad? Just because the League might not be able to help, doesn't mean I can't lend a hand."

"That goes for all of Ghost Squad, Mamma Esther," said Kavi. "We have to complete the peacekeeping contract for the League, but our contracts don't prevent us from helping others along the way."

"I appreciate that young Lion, sorry...Kavi." The matriarch of the large family stood and looked to her family. "I need you to clear and clean, okay? We'll head down to the tunnels. Kavi, there's only room for two besides my sons."

Her look included Stix and Stonez. "I'll tell you the whole story then."

They walked down a set of narrow cellar stairs between the courtyard and the main house. The bunker below was spartan, but well lit. It went on for almost a full hundred meters. It must have included all the cellars under the row houses on either side of the narrow street. Thickbloods trained with weapons as they taught younger members of the gang to fight.

There had to be a hundred people in the training area and all of them put full effort into their strikes. There were rows of weapons hanging on the walls. Kavi raised his eyebrows when he caught Pip's eye. This gang prepared for war.

They walked to a small, cordoned off room near the southeast corner of the large underground bunker. They squeezed and settled around a wooden table.

"Quite an operation you ha—" said Kavi.

"Tell me what happened to Dad," interrupted Stix.

Pip held up a hand for silence and he stood from the table.

"What is it?" asked Esther.

Pip held a finger to his lips. He stood on his toes, reached up and ran his fingers along a small crack where the wall met the ceiling. He pulled out a listening crystal that was no larger than a thumbnail. He concentrated and wrapped a small void gate around the listening device, placing it into a dimensional pocket. "I sensed a nearby signal. Chances are, all conversations over the last couple of weeks have had an outside audience. I can destroy the crystal if you like, or you can use it to feed bad information to whoever is listening. Either way—"

"We have a traitor in our midst," said Esther. "Damn it."

Pip nodded and sat back down. "The device won't be able to pick up anything we say while I keep it in my dimensional pocket but if we leave it there for too long, it will be a dead giveaway we found it."

"Red, the Vonderian's right. We can use it to feed bad info. Would you mind taking it to the other end of the hall so it sounds like no one's in the meeting room?"

Pip handed Red the crystal and the man jogged it to the other side of the training hall and placed it on a small shelf that held ammunition for the Thickbloods' ranged weapons.

Esther waited for Red to return before she started speaking again. "Your father was taken by Kwan's goons two weeks ago. It was a trumped up charge for years of *supposedly* not paying back taxes. When he called out the guards, they roughed him up in front of a crowd of Easties. The Easties responded by throwing rocks, and one of the guards lost an eye. After that, they changed his charges to inciting a riot and sedition."

Stix took a shaky breath. "When?"

"They're supposed to hang him three days from now, at noon in Independence Square."

"What can we do to help?" asked Stonez as Stix processed the news.

"Thank you, Stonez," said Mamma Esther. "We need to know why the Ministers are driving Easties out. It will work best if we can confront them with that truth on the day of the hanging. If it's as bad as I think, it will be enough to start a true rebellion, which will take down these grifters we call Ministers. In the chaos, we should be able to save your father. The biggest problem of course—"

"You don't have access to the circles the Ministers run in,

which is the only way you can get the information you need," said Pip.

"Exactly."

"But we do," said Kavi. "Say we do this for you, Esther? We expose the ministers, the Easties rebel, we save your husband, then what?"

"This is a chance to do something good, for real," said Stonez with a growl. "Like you're always talking about."

"Yeah, but a lot of people die in rebellions," said Pip. He held up a hand to stall Stonez' outburst. "Kavi's not saying no. He's thinking like a tactician. Let us do our job."

Mamma Esther looked at the two tacticians then back to Stix and Stonez. "The Lioness was a thinker too. That's what made her effective. You two are lucky to be led by thinkers." She turned back to Kavi. "We've made political connections with prominent players in the House of Citizens and the House of Royals. There's a plan to oust Kwan and his toady Wharton, our squirrely Minister of Finance, but none of it will happen without the momentum of an uprising. That's as much as I'm willing to share until I know we can trust you."

"And to earn that trust, we provide you with the information you need?" asked Kavi.

Esther nodded. "The League is an unknown factor. I have no idea how much control they exert over you. It's not a stretch to think they're threatening your families to ensure your good behavior."

"They've absolutely threatened our families," said Kavi. "And if there's corruption in your government I wouldn't be surprised if the League is exploiting it, if not driving it. You have every right to be cautious. What we do have is an insurance policy. We have some leverage over the League that we can call on if things get really bad. Have you heard of the Liberators?"

Esther snorted. "You don't actually buy into their nonsense of a female Sage do you?"

Kavi smiled. "I've met her. She's not only real, she's an ally. If you're trying to do your best for the people of Harpstra, you can't discount the Liberators."

Kavi turned to Stix's cousin. "Red, do you know how to get in touch with the Liberators in Harpstra?"

Red nodded. "I know who to contact to set up a meeting."

Esther held up a hand. "Whoa kid, this plan is too complicated already. Bringing another party in this late is a recipe for disaster."

"They may not be able to help with a rebellion scheduled for three days, but they'll share information I'm sure will be valuable. And the best part?" Kavi held Esther's gaze for a long moment. "We know with a hundred percent certainty that they are at odds with the League's agenda."

"Bernie? Thoughts?"

"Kavi and Pip are two of the most talented strategists I've ever worked with," said Stix. "I trust them. If Kavi trusts the Sage, I do too. One more thing..."

Esther looked at him expectantly.

"If we're going to war, you need to call me Stix."

Esther smiled. "I like it. Can you set up a meet with Red tomorrow night to share any new information?"

Stix looked to Kavi who nodded.

"Tomorrow's going to be a media circus as the League tries to make me the face of this peacekeeping campaign," said Kavi. "But, there are fourteen other members on my team. We'll get that information and we'll deliver it before we ride out to meet the Marked the next day."

When they returned upstairs, the rest of Ghost Squad was having a wonderful time. Wine flowed freely. Kavi looked to his squad, then to Pip, and raised his eyebrows.

Stix intercepted the exchange. "Let them have a little fun. Harp knows they've earned it."

Pip nodded. "We don't fight until day after tomorrow. I don't mind keeping my wits about me. I'm not a big drinker."

Stonez laid a heavy hand on Kavi's shoulder. "It would do everybody good to see you loosen up a bit." He grabbed a glass, filled it to the brim with wine, and passed it to Kavi.

Kavi took a big enough sip to prevent it from spilling and immediately felt a calming warmth in his belly. Kavi was never a big drinker, but he hadn't had a drop of alcohol since he was taken captive by the League. He looked about the table and noticed Clara sat next to an empty seat. He weaved through Thickbloods and squad mates and sat next to her. He took another sip and turned to face her.

She gave him a large smile and patted his knee. Her teeth were slightly red from the wine. Her hand lingered for a long moment before she removed it. "Was wondering if you were ever going to make it back," she said, words slightly slurred.

Even with the red teeth, she was more beautiful than Patrice on her best day. Several strands of honey-brown hair had escaped her ponytail to frame that gorgeous face. His eyes flicked to the cleft on her chin, then up to her lips. At that moment, all he wanted was to pick up where they left off when Patrice interrupted them. He wasn't great with non-verbal queues, but he was pretty sure the hand on his knee signaled Clara felt the same.

Kavi took another sip and let himself relax in what felt like the first time in months. He looked at his squad and felt immense pride. Not in himself, but in his team. The men and women at this table had become prodigious fighters. When they fought together as a squad, they were truly magnificent.

He gave a self-satisfied grin. He'd made this. Ghost Squad. He never felt this way about his men as a Silver Eagle. The members of Ghost Squad were elite. No, elite wasn't strong enough. They were the best. They came from so many different backgrounds, but they shared a will to improve, to survive, and to watch each other's backs.

He felt truly blessed.

Kavi smiled at Boost when he leaned over and filled Kavi's glass again. "Do you remember how much we hated each other?"

Boost laughed. "You were so damned smug."

Kavi laughed with him. "You were such an asshole. And you sucked with those hand cannons. Who'd have thought you and Tess would become the best ranged fighters in all of Grendar."

Boost beamed and Tess sat up straighter in her seat.

Kavi felt Clara's hand find his thigh. He took another sip and grinned. "And what about Clara. She came from such a humble background, to become the League's premier rune scriber."

Clara squeezed his thigh.

Kavi was on a roll. "I mean, her mother was a whore, for Harp's sake, and look how amazing she turned out."

Boost slapped a hand over his eyes and shook his head.

"You're a fucking idiot. No wonder you never got with anyone back in the Nest."

Kavi furrowed his brow in confusion. Clara removed her hand from his leg.

"Dipshit move, Tack," said Sliver. "You fused with Clara, you know how sensitive she is about her mother."

It finally caught up to him. He just called Clara's mom a whore in front of all of Ghost Squad. He was a fucking idiot. "No, no, no," he said so rapidly he thought he might have slowed time. He entertained reversing time to take back what he just said, but knew he couldn't pull it off. "Clara, I'm so sorry. I meant it as a compliment. Boost is right, I'm an idiot who can't hold his wine."

He scowled at Stix and Stonez laughing behind their hands. Screw those guys.

Clara patted his hand and gave him a lopsided smile. "I agree. You are an idiot, but I know your heart was in the right place."

She got up to hit the bathroom. When she returned she sat in a different seat.

What a moron.

17

Harper politics

The reunion continued into the wee hours. Everyone had too much wine. Kavi knew he blew his chance with Clara, at least for tonight. Any hopes Kavi had of salvaging romance faded when she threw up in the bushes on the walk home. Sliver had to summon Herman to carry both Clara and Amity back to the Vondam. Neither had any real experience with alcohol so, 'one more glass of wine' ended up taking them well past Drunkstown and straight to Vomitville.

Morning hit Kavi's room with a flurry of activity. He was sound asleep when the blackout curtains swept violently open. He reached for the dagger under his pillow and jumped out of bed.

He had stripped naked the night before to get out of his wet clothing before dropping into the sheets, utterly spent. It took Kavi a second to recall. It wasn't raining last night. He groaned as he remembered. Boost bet him he couldn't use his speed to run across the surface of the fountain in the courtyard of the Vondam. He groaned and felt an embarrassed flush. *So stupid! He couldn't afford getting that drunk. Ah well, the Ghosts got a laugh out of it.* Jory even promised to write a song memorializing how their fearless leader was actually human.

The incident led him to his current situation—naked, armed only with a dagger—staring at Patrice Elden Baroque. She looked him up and down, unimpressed. Kavi folded a toe under his foot to make sure he wasn't dreaming. Only then did he move to cover himself. After a second, he decided against it. If she could handle it, so could he.

"It's not like I'm seeing anything new," she said in a calm voice, eyes not leaving his body.

He fumbled at the dresser and took out dark pants and a white tunic.

"Why are you here, Patrice?" asked Kavi, hoping the question would allow him to regain a measure of composure.

She pointed at the clock. "Nine bells, young Lion. I'm never late."

"At least let me get some coffee before we start."

"Way ahead of you," Patrice said. "Coffee and breakfast will be here in one minute. I wanted to make sure I got here before a servant had to wake up to the tactician of the Peacekeeping force of Team Sugoroku. No reason a servant needs to see you buck naked and brandishing a weapon the size of my middle finger."

Kavi looked over to the nightstand where he set the dagger. "It's bigger than that."

"I wasn't talking about the dagger."

"Harsh," said Kavi.

She glared at him. "I'm not your lover. I'm not your friend. I'm your publicist. My job is to be harsh so you keep your cool when the media tries to trap you into answering something we don't want you to. The questions I ask this morning will prepare you to handle the tough questions that mob is going to throw at you today."

"You realize I was a slave and a Ghost," said Kavi. "I'm not afraid of a difficult question."

"Fear has nothing to do with whether or not you come across like an idiot. Lose your temper up there and the Harpstran media will eat you alive quicker than the Ach'Su you supposedly slew."

"Supposedly," he grinned. "I see what you're doing."

"You can learn," she said. "Whoop-de-doo."

A soft knock interrupted them. Patrice moved to answer the door and took a tray from the servant who stood outside. She put it on the small conference table and poured Kavi a cup of coffee.

Kavi pulled on the clothes and sat. He took a long sniff of the brown liquid in the cup before taking a sip. Glorious. The Vondam had mastered the art of brewing coffee. He grabbed several slices of bacon and two pieces of toast. He slathered the toast in butter and tucked in. The grease calmed the boiling in his stomach. After several minutes he felt almost normal.

"I'll want Pip here for the prep," said Kavi. "He does as good a job as you of making sure I don't get too big a head. Plus, I need him to set a couple of things in motion while I'm stuck with you. You think you'll be able to keep your cool if he's in the room?" Kavi asked with a satisfied smile.

Patrice held his gaze. "Please, Lord Stonecrest, I'm a professional."

"Well, you *are* the head of relations," he said, not losing the smile. "Give me a minute, I'll go wake him. Not sure what might happen if you go in there and he's in a similar state of undress."

Pip was already up, drinking coffee and reading the Harpstran Post. He looked to Kavi as he opened the door. "I heard you walking down the hall." He set the paper down. "These interviews should be a breeze. The writers at the Post are practically salivating over how wonderful the League is to send them a Peacekeeping force. I wouldn't expect any difficult questions."

Kavi nodded. "Tell that to Patrice, she's in my room spewing doom and gloom. You should have seen how she woke me up."

"You were too tired to put anything on after that stupid bet you made with Boost, weren't you?" said Pip. "Did she see your wee-wee?"

Kavi blushed and Pip laughed. "She did, didn't she? Clara's going to be super pissed that Patrice beat her to it."

"Don't you dare," said Kavi, pointing at him. He shook his head and looked to the door as if it led to the gallows. "Let's get this over with."

Pip was still laughing as they walked out of the room.

They ran into Tess in the hall.

"Where you off to?" asked Kavi. "Looking for a way in with the Ministers?"

"Not yet. My bond is pouting. I'm going to head outside for clear communication with Feather so he knows not to come into the city," she said quickly, as if the words were rehearsed. "He knows, but it's been too long since I've seen him so he needs soothing. He can wait one more day until we're out in the plains."

Kavi looked at her with concern, but knew they were all a

little off their games this morning. No more drinking until *after* the mission.

"You should take Boost," said Pip.

"I know my way around a city. I'll be alright."

"You better be," said Kavi. "We need you back here by noon."

Tess nodded and continued to the stairs as Kavi and Pip made their way back to Kavi's room. When they walked back through the door, Patrice looked up. Her lips were glossed in scarlet. Not a hair was out of place.

Pip nodded to her but she ignored him. "Finally ready to get started?" she asked.

The grilling lasted two hours and was more excruciating than time in the Pool. Patrice teased out every one of Kavi's insecurities and tried her best to make him lose his composure. It only happened once. Kavi was used to being known as the rich kid so nothing there rattled him. The loss of Brink was an old wound, so when Patrice picked at it, it hurt, but he didn't lose his cool.

When Patrice asked, "Rumor has it you're dating the daughter of a whore. What would the Lioness think of you dating someone so below your station?"

Pip had to restrain him when he grabbed her by the throat. Kavi didn't even remember getting up from his seat—regret from his own foolish words of last night and anger that she would target Clara had taken over.

"There it is," she said. "When these jackals figure out they can't break your façade they're going to go after your friends. If I found out about Clara's history, they will too. Pip, how should he have responded?"

"By deflecting or making a joke."

"Such as?" she asked.

"The Lioness wouldn't mind, I mean it's not like I'm dating a journalist," Pip said.

Patrice smiled.

"I don't like it," said Kavi. "Why should I let these jackals, as you call them, take shots at my friends when I would never allow it if they said the same thing in private? I'm not a politician, I'm a soldier. Soldiers aren't known for their charm."

"He's got a point," said Pip. "What makes Kavi a good leader is his moral compass and his sincerity. Not his charm. He should be prepared for these type of questions, but if a journalist crosses the line, Kavi should give them hell. The League can be benevolent without looking weak."

Patrice tapped her pen against the table. Then she nodded. "You're right, charm is not his best quality. The young Lion can roar but can't lose control. Let me ask the question again and you answer it without trying to kill me."

Kavi took a deep breath and prepared his answer as she re-asked the question. "I won't let anyone take cheap shots at any of my team when they're not here to defend themselves. Actions have consequences and that includes asking questions meant to provoke or disrespect someone who isn't present. I'll set up a meeting for later today where you can ask her that same question. Then, I will sit and cheer her on as she beats you to a bloody pulp. Next question."

"That's better than my answer," said Pip with a smile.

Patrice nodded. "Definitely better for him. Let's go through the questions about your family one more time..."

* * *

When the two hours of prep were finally up, Pip and Kavi ran out of the room. They moved immediately to the larger meeting room on the same floor. They were heckled by the team as they walked in a minute late for the briefing for tomorrow's mission.

"I know, I know," said Kavi holding up a hand to still the jeers. "Public relations is brutal."

Kavi sat down next to Stix. "Any luck discovering what Kwan and Wharton are after?"

"Not yet," said Stix, "but Kwan offered to take you out to lunch to smooth over the 'misunderstanding' from our first meeting with him."

Kavi groaned. "I was really looking forward to a meal with the squad before these press interviews." He took in Stix's crestfallen look. "I'll be there."

"Good," said Stix. "I already accepted on your behalf."

Pip pulled out the map they made before leaving the Nest. When unfurled, it took up half the conference table. He outlined the plan again, paying particular attention to how they would set up their defenses when they hit the plains.

He turned to Tess. "Did Feather find signs of the Marked?"

Tess shook her head. "He found a lot of what he calls rotten goats. No sign of the Marked."

"Rotten goats?" asked Pip.

"Something tainted," said Tess. "Maybe evil, maybe just sick. He didn't like how the goats looked. He growled at me and made it clear he would never hunt something so dirty."

Clara pointed at Kavi. "You've got to tell them," she said.

"About what we saw in the fuse. It can't be a coincidence."

"Tell us what?" asked Pip.

Kavi let out a breath. "It felt like one of those evolution dreams. Almost like a vision. I didn't know what to make of it. Honestly, I forgot about it until now."

"Damnit Kavi, you said we were going to share evo dreams when they came up," said Tess.

"Wait, this type of dream happened to you before?" asked Clara.

Kavi nodded and frowned at her. "Not exactly like this, but I thought we all got them after evolutions."

She scowled at him. "My mother was a whore, I guess that made me exempt."

Kavi winced. "I'm sorry about last night, Clara. I didn't mean to—"

"You really had visions after your evolution?" asked Sliver.

Kavi nodded. "So did Tess and Pip. I thought we all did. Maybe you just didn't remember?" He looked around and noticed some of the others were nodding. Looked like some of them did, maybe the others just forgot. "Anyway, I apologize for not bringing it up. I've been so busy and haven't even tried to process half of what happened while in the Fuse. That's no excuse. I'm sorry."

Stix put a hand on his shoulder. "We're good, mate. Now get on with the damn vision."

Kavi shared the story of the goat-horned Marked and the legions of tainted farm animals. Then he shared how the team had worked together to charge an arrow for Tess to fire.

"Oh and that's it?" asked Jory. "I'm supposed to play

some chords to guide the arrow towards this beast's throat? No pressure, Jory, but don't screw up or it's all our asses. A little warning would have been nice."

"Hold on a second. This should not change our plan of attack or defense at all," said Kavi. "We have no idea if it's real. I've never had a vision of the future. If we rely on this as the primary plan, we're bigger idiots than the Coaches ever made us out to be."

Clara stood and moved behind Jory to put a hand on his shoulder. "Don't worry. The over-indulged mama's boy didn't tell me either. I guess we're not important enough to trigger his need to please."

What the hell, Clara? She pulled that directly from the fuse. He could only apologize so many times. He felt his blood rise. "You were in the fuse with me!" snapped Kavi. "If I remember correctly, you saw what I saw, so don't lay this all on me, Thirty-three."

Clara opened her mouth to retort when Pip stood. "Enough," he said quietly, holding Clara's eyes. "Kavi, you should have discussed this with me, but I accept the apology. It's been a busy couple of weeks. You're right. The plan hasn't changed. Clara, Kavi is having lunch with Minister Kwan and then he's going to be interviewed by the Post. Do you think you can remember enough to sketch out the vision?"

"I think so."

"Good," said Pip. "Those of you not gathering intel for Stix's mother will work with Clara to interpret this vision of Ghost Squadron at its finest. If we can use it, we will. If not, the plan stays as we drew it up earlier."

* * *

The central dining room in the Vondam was opulent without being ostentatious. Tasteful paintings of bucolic scenes shared the new daises with poses of the goddess Harp in all of her lascivious glory. The white marble chastened the nude poses, but no one would mistake Harp for any deity but the goddess of fertility.

Pip and Kavi walked to the officious looking maitre'd protecting the entrance to the dining tables.

"And how can I help our esteemed League guests?" purred the man.

"We'll be having lunch with Minister Kwan," said Pip. "Has he been seated yet?"

"No sir, we received a note he's running five minutes late. I've set aside one of our finest tables overlooking the veranda for the four of you. It should leave you with privacy without putting you on display."

"Four of us?" asked Kavi.

The maitre'd looked puzzled. "Of course, Lord Stonecrest. Minister Kwan invited Minister Wharton. I thought you knew. Will that be a problem?"

"Of course not," said Pip. "We were simply unaware that not one, but two of the esteemed gentlemen from your majesty's government would join us. I assume they would have arrived five minutes late regardless of the time of *our* arrival?"

The maitre'd smiled. "I wouldn't deign to understand the schedules of powerful men."

Kavi slipped him a thick silver coin. "Of course you would.

You appear to be a master of the doings of powerful men. If it comes to it, please let the Ministers know we are on a tight schedule. I have an interview with the Post in an hour and it wouldn't do to be late."

After the maitre'd sat them, he left to grab some 'aperitifs for the discerning gentlemen.' Kavi turned to Pip. "Where did you learn to speak pretentious nobleman?"

"My parents were regularly called to treat mental health issues of the Mage Council and their family members. The Grandmasters consider themselves far more intelligent than politicians, but talking down to others is a pastime of the rich and powerful. Work with them long enough and you pick up the cadence. Big, flowery words seem to be the standard language of condescension, regardless of locale. It's almost as if they believe vocabulary is a replacement for wit."

Kavi snorted. "Not in Krom. Use big words and you're gonna get a fist to the teeth. Krommians pride themselves on straightforwardness when, in fact, they run towards violence instead of big words whenever the tone of conversation is not to their liking."

Pip raised an eyebrow. "You're able to hold your own around the posh."

Kavi shrugged. "Officer training. 'An Eagle must comport himself as a gentleman when visiting foreign lands.' How am I doing?"

Pip took the water their server offered, took a sip and turned back to Kavi. "Terribly. I'm afraid you'll never be a gentleman. Play the role though. Do it well enough and we've got all the leverage we need on these two."

Kavi didn't answer, eyes fixed on the maitre'd leading the two Ministers over. "Lords, Ministers and Gentlemen, I leave you to your luncheon. Please call me if the servers are not meeting your needs."

Kavi and Pip stood and handshakes were exchanged. When they took their seats, Minister Kwan began. "I apologize for my behavior two nights ago, Lord Stonecrest. I had just concluded another frustrating day of unproductive negotiations with the Astrans. I needed a win and resorted to backhanded techniques to get one. Thank you for saving me from what I'm sure would have been difficult repercussions from the League."

Kavi looked at the man for a long minute. He seemed sincere. He could never be sure with a man like Kwan, where lying seemed to come as easy as breathing. "Water under the bridge, Minister Kwan."

Kwan breathed a sigh of relief. "If there's anything I can do to make up for my indiscretion, be sure let me know."

"Perhaps there is," said Kavi. "The League is looking for investment opportunities."

Wharton gave Kavi a sidelong glance. "The League's finances are a closely guarded secret, but it's common knowledge they have more gold than they know what to do with," said the finance minister.

"Rich men always want more wealth," said Kavi.

"Truer words have never been spoken," said Wharton with a smile.

"The League *is* looking for monetary returns, but more important is influence. Power."

Kwan smiled furtively and looked around the room. "It sounds like you are about to offer a bribe, Lord Stonecrest, in the middle of the Vondam dining room."

Kavi laughed, fully embracing the role of power broker.

"Oh, nothing so pedestrian as a bribe, Minister. I wouldn't dare. I'm merely offering an opportunity for you, both of you, to tie some of your reputation and prestige to the League's rising star. For example, I'd be happy to do my interviews today with the two of you present in the room as advocates and supporters."

"In return?" asked Kwan.

Kavi matched the man's oily smile. "I'd like to invest in whatever the opportunity is that you're undertaking in the East side of the city."

Both men narrowed their eyes. The silence held for a full minute. The two Ministers looked at each other and finally Wharton nodded. Interesting. Kavi expected Kwan to hold the power. It made sense. Kwan was too much of a hothead.

"And you're representing the League when you say you'd like to invest?" asked Kwan.

"Not yet," said Kavi. "I would be investing as a Stonecrest. When I understand more about the opportunity, I may bring it to the League."

"Your intelligence is good but incomplete," said Kwan, twirling his butter knife in his hands.

"That's what makes the opportunity intriguing," said Kavi. "You've done an admirable job of keeping the information from the government and the public. It's only a matter of time until word of what you're doing leaks. Now is the perfect time to invest. Once the project becomes public the overall value of the project will rise by, what? Sixty percent, seventy?"

"I have it at fifty seven percent," said Wharton. "Do you mind if I ask where your information is coming from?"

"Of course I mind," said Kavi. "Information is the most

valuable currency of all."

Wharton paused and considered before carefully phrasing his next statement. "And if I shared that I know a member of your team is affiliated with the group known as the Thickbloods?"

"I would be concerned if you didn't know," said Kavi. "Basic information on competitors, political landscape and existing threats are imperative for a worthwhile venture."

"Why would we entertain an investment from someone who has ties to a group that is actively trying to scuttle the deal?" asked Wharton.

Kavi's eyes glittered. He was having fun with the role. "You know as well as I that employees can be bought, Minister."

Kwan snorted. "You treat your squad like *employees*? That's counter to all intelligence we have on you."

"Our public personas are rarely in line with our true purposes, wouldn't you agree?"

Wharton froze Kwan with a look. Then he turned those disturbing, beady eyes to Kavi. "Are you saying you can peacefully eliminate the threat posed by the Thickbloods?"

"It might not be *entirely* peaceful. But yes, provided the payoff is worth my time and energy," Kavi leaned back in his chair. "If we're past the foreplay, gentlemen, how about you fill us in on the details of the opportunity."

18

The interview

Everything about the lead reporter for the Harpstran Post was short. He had to sit on several cushions so he was eye-level with Kavi. His short brown hair fit his squat face and clipped manner of speaking. Famous quotes from literary elites were tattooed around his neck in a spidery script. "Don't focus on the recording crystals when we do the interview. It took me a while to get used to the damn things, but this is the new world we live in thanks to the League."

Kavi looked confused. "And you transcribe it for tomorrow's edition of the Post?"

Reuben didn't look up from his notes. "Yes, but that's secondary. This interview will be shown in all the major squares tonight. Since the League projected those recordings last year, that's all the people want. They want to see you, not just read about you."

"How many major squares does Harpstra have?"

"Twelve in Harpstra, but this will be seen in Krom, Brickolage and Vonderia too."

All the major squares?! He hadn't realized how rapidly the League's technology spread. Kavi rubbed suddenly sweaty palms together. He'd been too busy to be nervous until right now. He looked at the twelve crystals surrounding them from every angle and paled.

"Don't worry, it's mostly a puff piece," said Reuben, misinterpreting the look. "I will ask a couple difficult questions, but I'm not dumb enough to make the League look bad."

Reuben worked with his staff to seat the two Ministers behind Kavi. The staff coached the Ministers on couching facial expression during the recording.

Patrice saw something she didn't like in Kavi's face and made her way to him. She bent down and whispered in his ear. "This interview isn't half as intimidating as the Marked. Grendar needs to see the young Lion! Ignore the crystals. Tap into that confidence...arrogance, if you need it. Act like you're about to go in to battle."

Kavi nodded and took a deep breath. With his second breath he started his mantra. The crystals faded and his heartbeat slowed.

"Ready to begin?"

Kavi nodded.

Reuben looked at the central recording crystal and began his intro. "I'm Reuben Price with the Harpstran Post. With me today is Kavi Stonecrest, son of the famed Lioness of Valun and tactician for the Sugoroku Peacekeepers. Kavi joined Company Sugoroku after four years as a Silver Eagle."

Kavi had to fight to keep the sneer off his face at Reuben's use of the word joined.

"He and his team were generously deployed by Company

Sugoroku to help Harpstra with the infestation of Marked terrorizing our farmers to the East," continued Reuben. "They sally forth to face the creatures tomorrow morning. Kavi has been generous enough to share his time today to help us understand more about the Marked and the League's new Peacekeeping initiatives. As you can see by Ministers Kwan and Wharton, who graciously offered to join us today, the Sugoroku Peacekeepers have the full support of our government."

The two Ministers nodded at Reuben and Kavi.

Reuben stopped talking to the crystals in front of him and turned to Kavi. "Thank you for joining us, young Lion."

"My pleasure, Reuben," said Kavi.

"My first question is about the League. Is it true the League has been solving Quests for years without anyone's knowledge? Why wait until now to tell the people?"

His first challenge. Kavi had to bite the inside of his cheek *not* to answer the question with the anger which started him on this path. He kept his calm by mentally calculating the countdown until his contract was up. Seventeen months and two weeks. He would have the time and reputation to share the whole truth then. "Yes, it's true. The League has been completing Quests since Korbah's Conundrum, which most of us believed to be the last Quest. The organization understands how dangerous these Quests are to the untrained. They felt intercession was the easiest way to keep the most people safe."

"But why not tell people they were doing it?" asked Reuben. "Why let the public draw the conclusion there were no more Quests? That the Ancients abandoned us?"

Patrice had prepared him for this question so it was easy to toe the company line. "We didn't have the communication technologies we have today. The League decided staying quiet was better than sharing incomplete information that could be misunderstood or misinterpreted. These Quests are so dangerous that even a single rumor could lead to a lot of people dying."

"Plus, they got to keep the rewards for themselves."

"There is that," said Kavi with a smile. "However, those rewards were reinvested in research and training teams of warriors to take on ever more difficult Quests. A lot of those same teams are now giving back with these peacekeeping missions."

"Still, it sounds a little demeaning, doesn't it? As if the League knows what's better for people than the people themselves. I don't remember anyone appointing them to that role, or asking them to do it, do you?"

Kavi shook his head. "No, and I agree with you." He looked over at Patrice who gesticulated wildly for him to continue. "But you have to remember, Reuben, it was a different time. A time of kings and queens where rulers didn't value the concerns of the people as much. Not like today. Just as governments had to evolve with the will of the people, so too did the League."

"A noble sentiment. Let me ask you about your training with the League," said Reuben, squinting as he changed topics. "A lot of volunteers signed up to compete in this next series of Quests. You can understand why, of course. Who wouldn't want to become one of this generation's heroes..."

Kavi nodded, waiting for the question.

"How does one train to become a hero?" asked Reuben. "How can one prepare for the horrors of fighting one of the

Marked?"

Kavi let the question sink in. He looked at Reuben, then to Patrice, vigorously shaking her head, intuiting he would go off script. It was the head shake that pushed him to answer truthfully. "The real answer is: you can never be fully prepared for the horrors of a Quest. The League doesn't want me to say this because they don't want to scare off new volunteers, but I believe those volunteers should know what they're getting themselves into."

Reuben stopped shuffling the papers in front of him and looked at Kavi earnestly, compelling him to continue. It was obvious Kavi's answers until now had been prepared, canned. Honesty couldn't be faked. This is what people wanted to see.

He ignored Patrice who signaled for him to cut the answer by running a finger across her throat. In a split second, Kavi let the consequences run through his head. He continued anyway. "Before the call for volunteers, new members of the League were called Ghosts because more than half of us died anytime we went on a Quest. The only way we survived was by accepting we were going to die, maybe not on this Quest but certainly on the next or the one after that. That's why my team's called Ghost Squad. We embraced the death coming for us. To be fair, the League trained us how to fight these monsters far better than any military could. That's not a dig on the military, mind you. The Bastion taught me discipline and trained me well. But they taught me how to fight men, not monsters. Not Marked." He shook his head and looked straight into one of the recording crystals. "When you get thrown against the true horrors of this world, being a soldier is not enough. You need to become more."

Reuben raised an eyebrow. "And how does one become more?"

Kavi shrugged. "We don't fully understand it, but the biggest components are death and love. Every warrior, every soldier knows pain. That's what we're trained for. Death is different, permanent. The fear that you're going to die drives you to amazing things, but none of it matters unless you are doing it for something."

"For something or somebody?"

Kavi nodded. "That's the secret, Reuben. Purpose is about people."

"Not power?"

Kavi grimaced as he thought about the two Ministers sitting behind him. "Those that pursue power for the sake of power are, frankly, useless. Think of the heroes of the past. The best leaders. They used power to help people."

"You mentioned love..."

"When you accept that not only are you going to die, but those on either side of you are going to die as well—" said Kavi.

"We all die," said Reuben.

"Exactly, no matter how much we try to avoid it, facing death on a regular basis changes the urgency. It forces us to confront what's really important. That's where love comes in. When you embrace your mortality and realize you'll do anything for the people fighting next to you, nothing is impossible."

A beautiful woman Kavi had not seen in the room until now began to clap slowly. Sarcastically. She wore a bone white, spaghetti-strap gown, totally out of place in an interview setting. She stood up, and Kavi looked to Reuben to see how the man would react to the interruption. Reuben closed his eyes incredibly slowly. It took Kavi a second to realize the man was blinking. Strange, he didn't sense time slowing. He looked at the woman and realized she was the only one moving at the same speed as him.

She had an impish smile on a face that oozed sexuality. The curves of her body were exaggerated, her breasts impossibly large over a tiny waist that flared when it transitioned to her hips. She stood and walked towards Kavi, hips swaying like a rowboat in the ocean. She continued clapping as she moved, stopping just outside the circle of recording crystals.

"So, you are the best of this century's heroes," said the woman. She scanned him head to toe. "Not impressed."

She looked familiar to Kavi, but the familiarity was impersonal as if he knew her from a story or painting. Not a painting, a statue. Many statues. Combined with what the Ministers said earlier...Kavi had a really good idea who this woman was.

He looked at Reuben who was still completing his blink, then turned back to her. "You're the first person I've met that can slow—"

"Time?" The woman asked. "We don't actually slow it, we skip over the flow like a flat rock thrown, just so, across the surface of a lake." She pantomimed with a flick of her wrist which caused her enormous breasts to jiggle. "We stay above the water for what looks like an impossible period of time, when, in fact, it's only a trick of angular dynamics and lift."

Kavi averted his eyes to look at Patrice. She was stuck in the motion of turning her head. The publicist's beauty looked commonplace next to this beacon of femininity.

"Can anyone use the trick?" asked Kavi.

The woman shrugged and her curves rippled suggestively. "I wouldn't say that. It requires a certain amount of...what is it Theron calls it? Evolution."

"Theron?" Kavi whispered. "The god of death?"

She snorted. "There's no god of death. Theron just happens to like death a lot more than the rest of us. Something I've never understood. When sex is an option, why would one choose to pursue death?"

"So you *are* Harp," said Kavi.

"Harp, Anat, Brigid, Bantera, pick your favorite story. I've had many names over the years," she purred. Her eyes glinted. Her sexiness shifted from impossibly desirable to predatory and menacing.

In that moment, Kavi remembered Rose's aversion to the gods. The fifth Sage spoke about them as if they were petty children. Rose loathed the deities with a passion Kavi had to respect. He needed to be very careful with his words.

"You're wrong, you know," she said. She smoothed the silky fabric of her dress near her left hip.

Kavi refused to be distracted. He used all his willpower to keep his eyes on hers. "It wouldn't be the first time," he said. "About what?"

"Power," Harp said. "Power for power's sake is all that matters. When you live long enough, there is nothing else. People come and go. They flutter in and out of your life like pieces of clothing. They are so...impermanent. In the end, the *only* thing that matters is power."

"That sounds...sad," said Kavi, speaking honestly. He regretted the words as soon as they left his mouth. *So much for being cautious, idiot!*

Harp's face flared with anger before she schooled her features. "You would pity a god?"

He shook his head. "I wouldn't dare. I merely tried to put myself in your shoes for a moment and wondered how it would feel."

She looked down at her sandaled heels and giggled. "These would never fit you, little warrior. Yet I find myself loving the image it conjures." She snapped her fingers.

Kavi looked at his feet to see his boots had transformed to women's high heels.

"That is so much better," she said. "I think you could pull off the look. What if we were to replace that boring outfit with a toga? Why did this generation get rid of comfortable clothing?" She snapped again.

Kavi looked down at his toga. "Doesn't seem like a great outfit for...physical labor?"

She shrugged. "Can't beat it when it comes to orgies. It's as easy to get naked in a toga as it is for me to pull down this little strap," she pulled down the strap of her dress and exposed her breasts while keeping her eyes fixed on his face.

Kavi was glad for the toga as the folds of clothing hid the effectiveness of her display.

She gave him a sultry smile and looked to his crotch. "See what I mean?"

"Your beauty is an inspiration," said Kavi. "I now understand why men created the arches of Falinor and the domes of Arcidon."

She smiled. "Don't forget the women. The domes of Arcidon were designed by a woman. Of course a man took credit for her work, but that's the way of the world." Harp continued to disrobe slowly, eyes pinioned on Kavi's face. "It's okay to give in to desire. I won't mind."

Kavi bit the inside of his cheek hard. The offer was unbearably enticing. His thoughts turned to his team, reaching out for an anchor, a distraction from this divine temptation. Most of them had teased him for not getting with a woman. They thought his celibacy played the leading role in his grumpiness. He thought of Clara. Taking advantage of Harp's offer would be a betrayal to any romantic possibility with her.

The thought dispelled the goddess's charm, if only for a second. That second was enough for Kavi to take stock of what was actually happening. If he gave in to desire, he would be putting himself under her control. That control might be temporary or it might not be. Being beholden to a divine being would be terrible for his independence.

Harp caught the shift in expression as her dress fell to the floor. She stood, naked in front of him as the predatory look shifted to a pout. It was the pout which nearly did him in. The thought of disappointing the goddess of fertility by not giving her what she wanted rampaged all over his inherent need to please. And how fun it would be to please that divine body.

He almost gave in when the pout turned calculating. "Perhaps you don't prefer the female form. If it's boys you like, I can make that work." Her body began to shift, large breasts slowly reduced from melons to plums as if air had been let out of them. Her hips receded at the same time. The pubic hair surrounding her fleshy folds thinned, leaving nothing to the imagination.

Kavi squirmed uncomfortably, close to popping, as her

beauty shifted from something traditionally feminine to something just as feminine, but with lean angles instead of voluptuous curves.

She smiled as he saw his discomfort. "So you do like the boyish look without liking the boy parts. Or maybe you prefer those too." Those salacious folds transformed into a fully erect member pointed at Kavi.

This was far enough out of Kavi's comfort zone to dampen his desire. He sat up straighter in his chair. "I'm sorry, Lady Harp, as much as I would love to take advantage of your offer, I have other obligations."

Harp's eyes narrowed when she realized she overplayed her hand. Her body transformed back into its female form. "Your willpower is admirable," she said. Her gown appeared back on her body.

Kavi looked down and realized he was back in the clothing he started the interview with. Illusion? Was that her true power? He wondered what she really looked like.

"All it took to flip the ministers behind you was an extended look at my cleavage. Then again, their level of evolution is early caveman." She looked at Kavi pensively. "I might have even allowed you to touch me, do you know that? It's been over five hundred years since I've felt the touch of a man. That earnestness of yours is sexy. Not to mention, you turned me down. That hasn't happened in over a millennia."

"Why are you here?" Kavi asked.

"It's our time in the sun, dear hero. Every five hundred years my fellow Gods and I get let out to make this world a better place. Don't your people study history?"

"Histories get lost and stories get muddled over the years.

Most think the gods are myths."

She laughed. "That's what makes this so fun. I so love an atheist. They're so cute when we first show our faces."

"I'd be happy to introduce you to the world right now. A lot has changed with our technology. Take a minute and share your message and your face with all of Grendar. They will love you."

She looked at the recording crystals. Interesting. She knew exactly how to stay out of their recording radius. "Kind of you to say. While I love this new technology it would ruin the surprise. The Gods have our own way of getting our message out. Trust me, you're going to love it."

Based on what he had seen so far, Kavi was almost sure the opposite would be true. He wasn't dumb enough to say so. "But why are you *here*?" he repeated.

"Because I needed to see how advanced this new generation is and you're the new model of heroism. If I liked you, I was going to give you a boon. If I didn't, I would curse you and your team."

"How did I do?"

"You passed. If you accept, I will grant the Harpstrans on your team knowledge to assist in your fight with the Marked."

Kavi nodded. "And they don't have to swear fealty?"

"They don't *have* to, but if they want to, that's entirely up to them. The only thing I ask is you mention the boon I gave when we do reveal ourselves."

Kavi thought about his vision and how overwhelmed Clara and Jory were about having such a pivotal role in tomorrow's fight. "I think I can agree to that. I'd like to discuss with my team first. How do I get in touch with you?"

"I don't work with committees. This is your choice. Either tell me yes right now or I'll consider it a no."

Kavi thought hard. It never went well when he made decisions for his team by fiat, but how could knowledge be a bad thing? He would tell them about the decision and ask them to reject Harp's knowledge if they thought it was a bad idea. "Very well, I accept."

"I would wish you luck tomorrow young hero, but with my boon, you're not going to need it. Tell your team I will see them in their dreams," she said.

She winked and disappeared.

Kavi splashed back into the river of time's passage. He shifted in his seat to reorient. It took him a moment to realize Reuben had asked him another question. "Apologies Reuben, I got lost in a memory. Would you mind repeating the last question?"

The rest of the interview passed without incident, though Kavi felt he floated through it in a dream state. Luckily, the remaining questions were the softballs Reuben had promised and the interview finished on a high note. Reuben and the Ministers looked at him with something bordering on adulation as he reiterated Ghost Squad would do everything in their power to eliminate the threat of the Marked the following day.

"Can my team and I be on site with our recording crystals when you engage tomorrow?" asked Reuben.

Kavi looked to Patrice who nodded. "As long as I can review the footage before broadcast," said Patrice.

"And as long as you follow my orders to the letter," said Kavi.

Reuben nodded dismissively and gathered all of his notes from the interview.

"No, I will need your word on that. You do not come with us unless you give me your word. If I tell you to move or to retreat, you do not second guess my decision. When we're on the field, my word is law. Understand?"

Reuben stopped gathering his papers and looked at Kavi. "You have my word," he said.

"And we'll be there in the viewing pavilion," said Minister Kwan.

Kavi looked to Patrice and growled. "Viewing pavilion?"

She nodded. "Not my doing. The League agreed to let the nobility watch the battle tomorrow."

"These aren't men we're fighting," said Kavi. "If we lose, there's a good chance the Marked and his minions will eat everyone in that pavilion. Do they understand that?"

"They signed a waiver," said Patrice as if that explained everything. She caught the hard look in his eyes. "No, I don't think they understand that," she finally said.

"Just realize you're the one who's going to have to clean up the mess if we lose," he said loud enough for the Ministers to hear.

"Why is that?" she asked.

"Because the rest of us are going to be dead."

19

Peacekeeping

"Let me get this straight, Lord Stonecrest," said Clara, using his title as a curse. "The goddess of fertility seduces you, then offers you a boon and you accepted."

"She didn't seduce me," said Kavi, just as sharply. Clara still looked angry from his comments of the night before, but why was she accusing him of being seduced? Was she jealous? That didn't make sense, he rebuffed Harp's attempt. He wished he had Pip's ability to read women.

She rolled her eyes. "Right."

Jansen took that moment to shoot Sliver a not-so-subtle eyebrow raise. Everyone in the room knew the look was about the conversation about relationships in squads.

Clara caught it too. She pointed at Jansen. "Screw you." She turned back to Kavi. "And what do you think the goddess of fertility is going to ask from us, for that boon?"

Kavi sat back in his chair. He hadn't fully thought through it. He hadn't had the time. "She said she was giving me the boon, but could only give it to her Harpers."

Clara practically shook with rage. "You are so fucking

naïve. She's the goddess of fertility. Last night you called my mother a whore. Today, you pimped *me* out as one. You do *not* get to make those types of decisions for us," said Clara. She stood with her hands on her hips, anger making her body rigid.

Kavi felt his stomach drop. Holy shit. She was right. Would Harp demand sexual satisfaction? If he could resist her, maybe the others could too? "I didn't...I didn't realize," said Kavi softly.

"Hang on a second," said Boost into the quiet room. He looked at Clara. "I know you're angry Kavi didn't share the vision with the rest of the team. I also know you're angry about the lack of solution for you and Jory to know which skills to use in that vision." Boost shut his eyes for a moment in frustration when Clara talked over him.

"Don't you dare lay this on me—" Clara shouted.

"I'm not," interrupted Boost. "I just have one question. If the vision is true and we're facing impossible odds, and—" He held up a hand to stall her. "—*and* this goddess gives us a way out. If you were given the same choice, would you have made a different decision?"

Clara opened her mouth to respond, then shut it.

Boost continued. "It's a shitty situation. Kavi was forced to make a difficult decision for the team, even if he didn't understand all the ramifications. Isn't that what leaders do all the time? We agreed Kavi is our tactician because he's shown, again and again, he's willing to make the difficult decisions to keep us alive. If you don't want the boon, don't take it. Kavi resisted her, so it is possible. It's still your choice."

"I'm glad we're getting it on the table," said Pip. "I

honestly don't know what decision I would have made if I were in Kavi's shoes, even if I understood the cost, but I know he has our best interests in mind. Even if he sometimes makes choices we don't agree with. However, to the outside world we have to be one unit fighting with one mind. We do *not* air internal disagreement to the press, to the League, to the Ministers, to anyone. If you have other concerns get them out now. When we face the Marked tomorrow, we do it with a united front. Is that understood?"

Pip wrapped up the briefing and shared a look with the Harpstran members of the team. Jory, Stix, Crystal and Clara met his gaze one at a time. "Sweet dreams," Pip said as they walked to the door.

Kavi looked at Pip. "I fucked up. I don't know how to fix this."

"I don't know that you did," said Pip. "You were thinking like a Ghost. Survival first. I think you made the right choice."

"But how do I fix this with Clara?"

"I don't know that you can. Boost started bringing her around, but you were put in a terrible situation and had to go with your instincts. If she can't see that, is that on you?"

Kavi put his face in his hands and groaned.

Pip got up and put a hand on his shoulder. "If it was meant to be, you two will figure it out. Go. Get some sleep. We have to focus on surviving tomorrow."

Moments after Kavi left the briefing room, Clara walked back in.

Pip gave her a flat look. "You really laid in to Tack. I get that you're pissed, but do we want to go into this fight with you and Kavi butting heads? I'm afraid what it's going to do to the squad."

Clara gritted her teeth and held up a finger. "First, not my fault. But you're right, it's not really his fault either. I'll apologize to him and the Squad tomorrow, even though I had *every* right to be pissed."

"Oh I agree, but be mad at the situation. Not at him."

Clara nodded. "He's just so frustrating. He always does the right thing. It makes it so difficult to be angry at him."

"Then stop being angry at him," said Pip. "He screwed up. He knows he screwed up last night and he apologized. And I'm sure he'll apologize for making this decision without your input."

"That's exactly what I mean," said Clara. "He really hurt me when he called my mother a whore in front of the whole squad. I know he didn't mean it that way, but it still hurt. Then, he apologized immediately and I could tell he meant it, which then makes me the unreasonable one for feeling hurt. You know what I mean? Then...then he resists being seduced by the goddess of fertility. What man could do that? He's too perfect. Sometimes I *want* to see him screw up, you know? Then he does. Twice in two days, and I couldn't let it go because it was too personal."

Pip gave a heavy sigh. "I do know what you mean. His sincerity is his best and worst quality. But if you're still interested in him, let him off the hook. If you're not, let him go. You both deserve better than petty bickering."

Clara nodded and turned to leave the room.

"I wouldn't try to work it out tonight, you're both too charged up and you need rest. Talk in the morning," Pip said to her retreating back.

* * *

Kavi didn't sleep well, imagining what he forced Clara and the other Harpstrans to face. He didn't remember any of his dreams last night, which was a good thing. If Harp had visited him in his dreams, he doubted he could have pushed off her advances again.

He stretched on his huge bed and made his way out from under the covers then moved to the large bay window and pushed away the curtains to look on the city. Slate gray clouds hid the early dawn's light. The lights from the city bloomed a fake dawn and Kavi gave the world a naked stretch before hitting the shower.

A moment after he dressed, Pip came in to share breakfast. "Turns out, you weren't crazy after all."

"You heard from our Harper dreamers?" asked Kavi.

Pip nodded. "They were each visited by the goddess last night. Most of them looked ashamed when they told me about it."

"I'm not going to judge anyone for what happened in a dream," said Kavi.

"Still, if she is as mind-numbingly gorgeous as the legends say, I don't know how you resisted."

Kavi shook his head ruefully. "It was close, but even with time stilled, I wasn't comfortable having sex in front of recording crystals. With my luck, she would have resumed time right in the middle of it."

Pip laughed. "That wasn't what stopped you though, was it?"

Kavi took a bite of his eggs as he thought about the

question. "No. It was anger. I was pissed off at the Ministers for their greed. That led to being angry that yet another powerful being wanted to use us." He sopped up what was left of the yolk with a piece of toast. "They only have power over us if we give it to them. If I gave in to the desire, I would be hers. Just like Clara, I'm tired of people making decisions for me."

A soft knock at the door was followed by Clara poking her head in. She nodded to Pip.

Pip set his coffee down and stood. He looked first at Clara then to Kavi. "Ten minutes, then meet in the briefing room. You need to be focused on what's most important."

Clara gave him a half smile. "The giant Marked trying to kill us all?"

Pip didn't return the smile. "The giant Marked trying to kill us all." He shut the door behind him leaving Clara and Kavi in an awkward silence.

Kavi opened his palm to Pip's empty chair. Clara sat. Kavi poured the rest of Pip's coffee into his own, then poured Clara a new cup. She took a sip, and set the cup down. She looked at Kavi, then back down at the breakfast table. She rubbed at her forehead with her palm, partially obscuring her face. She looked at her coffee when she spoke. "Kavi, I don't know how to say this—"

"Don't worry about it. As I told Pip, I'm not judging anyone for what happened in a dream," said Kavi.

She scowled and smacked her knee as she looked up at him. "Damnit, Kavi! What if I want to be judged? What if, for once, you stop saying the right fucking thing, and get pissed at me! I wasn't able to resist Harp last night. Doesn't that bother you? At all?"

Kavi sat back, in stunned confusion. "Of course it bothers me! The thought of you with the goddess has been running through my head over and over all night! But how can I get mad at you for it? It's my fault."

Clara took the coffee again and Kavi couldn't help but notice her hand was shaking. She looked down and spoke. "When she showed up in my dream it was as a stunning, model of a man. He wasn't wearing a shirt and he was impossibly beautiful. I knew it was her, the minute she showed up, but the man kept saying all the right things. I felt drunk in his power. When he kissed me—"

"Stop! I don't want to...I can't hear this," Kavi said. "Every word is a shard of glass pushing into my face. Please."

Clara shuddered and finally looked up to meet his eyes. "I don't know how you resisted her."

Kavi shrugged. "My situation was different. I was already uncomfortable, in the middle of that ridiculous interview. If Harp had set the time and place, like in your dream...I would not have been able to resist."

"Why is this so hard?" asked Clara. "Me and you, I mean."

Kavi shook his head. "I don't know. Maybe it's because our lives are impossible. Every time something goes well with us, something horrible follows immediately after. We can't escape being Ghosts. I feel like I'm swimming in a fur coat. I try harder and harder to make everything work, but the harder I try the more I sink. I don't know how you think I always say the right thing. When I'm around you I can't say anything correctly. Maybe it's because all I want to do is grab your face and kiss those amazing lips until my problems go away, even for a second, but then I say something stupid and the chance—"

Clara stood up from her own chair. She navigated around the table and sat in his lap. "Fighting with you," Clara said, "when in a couple of hours, we could die fighting this giant Marked is stupid." She turned to him so their faces were millimeters away. "Take the coat off and swim," she whispered and Kavi could feel the air of her words against his lips.

Their lips met hungrily. Their tongues danced and Kavi felt the regret of drunken words and hasty decisions fall from his shoulders. Who cared about goddesses when he could have this wonderful creature, here. Now. The kiss was interrupted with a knock on the door.

Clara groaned and stood.

"Come in," said Kavi.

Sliver opened the door. She wore her armor and her normal, playful expression was gone. "Something happened. We have to go."

* * *

While they had slept, the Marked and his horde of hideously transformed farm animals had rampaged and razed two hamlets west of Harpstra. The smoke from the closer village, Gabor, could be seen from the city. When Ghost Squadron set out from the eastern gate, the festival atmosphere was replaced with grim determination.

Most of the nobility who planned to watch from the viewing pavilions had second thoughts after news of the casualties rolled in throughout the early morning hours. The

Marked didn't take prisoners. They ate them.

They lost contact with the harrying forces from the Harpstran military. The goal of that force was to drive the Marked to a field of battle of their choosing. Last contact was four hours ago. At Pip's order, Tess left to gather information with her bond, Feather. Pip kept a void channel open with her all morning.

Tess met them on the field where the battle was supposed to take place. Her catlike eyes flashed amber in the low light of gathering storm clouds. At her side stood a midnight black cat, his head nearly as tall as Tess's shoulder. She wasted no time on pleasantries.

"Some of the regulars might have survived the last attack, but it would have taken a miracle," Tess said. "The animals facing us are more intelligent than we gave them credit for. They set an ambush for the Harpstran skirmishers and wiped out most of the force. Feather barely made it out alive."

The Squad looked to the giant cat. Under the attention, the cat sat back on his haunches, lifted a leg over his shoulder and began to lick himself.

Boost grinned. "He's a Ghost alright."

The cat looked at Boost and growled. The small Bricker paled.

"Be nice," Tess growled back to the cat.

The cat ignored her.

"What do we know about the conditions on the field?" asked Kavi.

Tess turned to him. "Not enough. This could turn ugly quick. The skirmishers were supposed to keep us free of flanking threats, but since we haven't heard from them..."

"Assume the Marked has forces to the North and South,"

concluded Kavi.

Tess nodded.

"Do we know how strong they are?" asked Sliver.

"Too strong. Feather saw hundreds of these demon goats," she waited for a second as she processed images that Feather sent. "And too many mutated dogs and cows to count. He's not great with numbers, but from the images he sent it looks like there's probably over a hundred of each."

"We're going to have to hope this vision of yours was accurate, Tack," said Pip softly.

Kavi nodded. "We can't allow hope to be a strategy. Let's get those fortifications up. Send the Harpers to me first."

Pip started shouting orders and Kavi was soon surrounded by Stix, Jory, Crystal and Clara.

"Whaddya need, Tack?" asked Stix.

"You learn what you needed from Harp last night?" he asked.

They nodded as a group but no one would meet his eye. He smiled without judgment. "She's hard to resist, isn't she?"

Stix's cheeks were red. "After a moment, I didn't want to. We've all had wet dreams, boss. This one was just a little more vivid...and more fun."

"What did she teach you?"

"She said the only way to seal the boon was with sex," said Jory. Kavi was surprised to see the gregarious troubadour blushing. "After she had her way with me, she taught me the chords I need. You'd be shocked at how well she can play a lute."

Kavi turned to Clara. "Did she teach you the runes for the arrows?"

She nodded. Her eyes lingered on his lips for a moment

before she looked up. "She called it a steadfast rune. The projectiles will ignore environmental factors. Once Tess charges the rune, it will fly true."

Kavi clapped his hands. "Let's get to work. Tess, hand Clara your quiver please!"

The ranger complied and Ghost Squad went to work. Several recording crystals hovered around the fortifications and Kavi looked to the viewing pavilion. It was about a half kilometer behind them. If Ghost Squad was overrun, the observers *might* have a minute or two to flee. Kavi had done what he could to warn everyone in those seats. They made their choice.

Reuben, the reporter, worked with his own team to make sure the crystals transmitted. Kavi respected the man's courage and was surprised to realize he didn't want to disappoint the newsman.

He scowled when he saw Patrice running his way.

"One quick question, I promise," said their public relations liaison between the orders Kavi shouted. "Would it be possible to move the fortifications two hundred meters to the south? The Post assures me the light will be better and the pavilion will have a better view of the battle."

"Get off the field," snarled Kavi.

"So, that's a no?"

"One more question and so help me, I will hand you a weapon and put your ass on that wall," said Kavi. "When we're in front of the recording crystals, you have a voice. When we're in the field, you stay out of the way!"

She pointed at one of the recording crystals. "We're in a bit of a combination situation, wouldn't you say?"

"Pip!" roared Kavi. "Get Patrice a bow. She just became

an honorary Ghost."

"A simple no would have worked fine." Patrice's eyes pleaded with Pip, as she bit at her lower lip.

"If she shows her face on the field one more time, I want her muzzled and bound," said Kavi.

Pip grinned at Kavi as Patrice's walk from the fortifications turned into a jog. "Don't think she's used to being talked to that way."

He thrust a thumb behind his shoulder. "I can't believe the League agreed to recording crystals for an actual engagement. Especially after I ripped into Kwan about stealing our technology. Fighting these things is hard enough without the circus," said Kavi.

"Ignore it. Patrice will make sure nothing confidential makes the feed," said Pip. "Besides, why should we care? Let the people of Grendar know how good Ghost Squad really is."

"But then our enemies find out too," muttered Kavi.

Their conversation was interrupted by a shrill scream from behind. Kavi whipped around, but it was only a noblewoman in the stands pretending to faint.

Kavi turned back around to view the rows of planted vegetables and wheat at the end of the open field they chose. Horned heads began to poke through the wheat. Kavi held his hand out for the looking glass and Sliver slapped it into his palm. The transformed goats were horrifying, identical replicas of his vision in the Fuse. Their normally placid eyes were beet red and filled with unholy hatred. Mouths which normally held the flat teeth of an herbivore were sharpened such that every tooth was a canine.

"No, no, no!" echoed a scream from across the field.

"Shit," muttered Pip under his breath. Several soldiers in Harpstran gold and white were pushed into the open by the Marked. Even at four hundred paces, it was easy to read the terror on their faces. "Clara's painting of that devil thing was good," said Pip. "But the waves of hatred flowing from it are impossible to capture."

The scarlet Marked had the same goatee Kavi had seen in his vision. The only difference from this version of the beast, besides the grisly realism, was instead of a dark black goatee, the facial hair and the face around it was stained with blood. The Marked pointed at the Ghosts across the field and drew a thumb across its neck.

The four Harpstran soldiers were pushed to the front where all could see them. With a bark from the Marked they were set upon by rabid goats. They screamed and howled as horned beasts tore into them until the screams died out. Kavi heard someone in the viewing pavilion retching.

"Tell Tess to knock one of those arrows," Kavi said calmly. "Jory, you ready?"

Jory pulled his lute from his back and played a quick melody. "Yes, sir."

It took less than a minute for the goats to finish their meal of raw soldier. When they were through, not a single bone or piece of clothing remained. Only a dark patch on the long grass showed any evidence the four soldiers were ever there.

The Marked raised the huge club in his right hand and screamed. The transformed farm animals screamed along with him.

The animals charged.

"Now, Tess. Fire now!"

20

Grim

Grim rode past the monumental, transparent fragments of the dome surrounding Krom. He switched mounts when he found Blue in the Stonecrest stables. The enormous draft horse whickered like a colt when Grim saddled him up. Over the course of the twelve hour ride to Krom, he fed the massive horse a half bushel of apples.

It felt good to spoil an old friend.

Another half hour of riding took him to the walls surrounding the city. As he approached the eastern gate, Grim thought about the trap he was walking into. He didn't have Kavi's head for strategy so he wouldn't out-think his opponents. His only advantage was he didn't really care about what happened to him. He loathed the idea of being questioned and tortured into betraying his Liberator friends, but thanks to past crippling depression and drinking problems, they never trusted him with critical information anyway. With nothing left to lose, his best bet lay in triggering the trap and letting the dice fall.

Kavi would berate his lack of a plan, but Kavi wasn't here.

Grim whistled as he approached the gate, his fatalistic non-strategy lifted any anxiety around expectations. Grim was a doer, not a thinker. He already made the tough decision to face his father. All he had to do now was follow through. He wasn't looking forward to the next couple of days, but he wasn't dreading them either. That's what taking action did—it eliminated second guessing. He was still whistling when he approached the gate guard.

"What are you so cheery about?" asked the guard as he rode up. The man spat a brown liquid that barely missed Blue's front hoof.

"I wouldn't say cheery," replied Grim. "Just not as consumed with soul crushing depression."

The guard looked up, finally realizing the size of both mount and rider. The guard looked up at the towering Grim and his eyes widened. "Sorry, sir, but you're going to have to dismount before passing through the gate."

"It's sir now?" asked Grim with a smirk. He was happy to comply. When he dismounted, he put palms behind his lower back and stretched. Small pops ricocheted off the city wall.

"Riding for awhile," said the guard with a smile. "What's your name and business in Krom?"

"My name is Grim Broadblade and I'm here to see my father."

The guard visibly paled. "General Broadblade?" he squeaked.

"That's him—large man? Not quite as big as me. Head of the council." Grim gave the guard an innocent look. "You've heard of him?"

"Sorry to detain you, sir," said the guard.

Grim took pity on the man. "I'm messing with you. He's a right prick, my dad, so don't give in to the hero worship, okay?" Grim slipped him a copper.

The guard bobbed his head in thanks. "You want me to send someone to let him know you're coming to visit?"

"Don't bother, he knows I'm coming." Grim looked at the men on the wall whispering back and forth. "I'm sure someone up there has an order to let him know I've arrived."

The guard looked up to the wall where a small group of guards had gathered. The man seemed to feel the pressure to continue the conversation. "Most of us thought you were dead."

"Not yet," said Grim. He decided to give the gossips on the wall a juicy tidbit. "Even the League couldn't kill me."

The guard's face lit up. "You went on Quests?"

"That's classified soldier," Grim said as he looked up to the setting sun, "and I better get moving. Don't want to be late for an appointment with the boss."

The guard waved him through. Grim grabbed the lead rope and walked Blue into the city. It was late enough that Grim considered stopping at an inn and meeting with his father the next day. He laughed out loud at the idea. The General would send men to escort him if he didn't show up at the War College in the next hour or two. No need to draw this out any longer than needed.

Grim walked slowly through the wide, spartan boulevards. The buildings were built of adobe brick with red terracotta roofs, boring in their uniformity. Even the inns and taverns abided by strict building regulations imposed by military dictatorships of centuries past. The only loophole in the uniformity was in the signs hung from the buildings. Vendors made their signs overlarge and garishly painted which lent brilliant flashes of color along the commercial boulevards. Grim almost had to shield his eyes when he passed the Three Suns tavern from the brilliant yellow, reflective paint the proprietor used on the one-story tall sign hanging from the second floor.

The obvious exceptions to regulations were the government buildings. At the heart of the city stood a quartet of massive edifices, each with a wide avenue shaded by ancient oaks and elms which neatly segmented Krom into quarters. The streets were wide enough to allow the entire Krommian army to parade through, which they did whenever Krom went to war. Something that seemed to happen every year.

Along these avenues jutted smaller streets leading to commercial and cultural districts. For each street that led to a residential or commercial area was another dedicated to an open air theater or carefully tended agora. Most open spaces were filled with men and women practicing martial skills.

Grim hadn't been to the center of the city in over five years. The Bastion was on the northern edge of town so it was easy to avoid downtown. As he walked down the hot, sandy boulevards Grim remembered why he avoided the city.

An entire culture dedicated to war, to hurting people. He hated this place.

He sighed and led Blue down the eastern dromos, or avenue, towards the War College where his father waited for him. As he walked, he couldn't help but wonder how much the city had changed in these five years.

He looked back to the center of town and even from two kilometers away, Grim could see the large columns that made up the Temple of Krom. The setting sun blazed against the wide glass windows of the Palace, now run by the Council. The Colosseum was quiet, but that was to be expected on a non-feast day.

As Grim neared the War College, trees were replaced by statues of great generals of the past. The marble and metal effigies were brightly painted in lifelike depictions of warriors in their finest moments. The artists overused the color red, surrounding the silent leaders in detailed gore of defeated foes.

Grim hated all of it. He wondered, not for the first time, how a people had become so enamored with blood and pain. *Who would want to live a life devoted to hurting others?* Turns out, most Krommians. Even though he hated it, he understood it. A surge of power came from dominating another physically.

He handed Blue's reins to one of the valets standing outside the College. The man gave him a numbered wooden chit. Grim patted Blue once on the forelock before walking the broad stairs to the War College.

The building was originally built to train the most promising officers coming out of the Bastion. Once the Council expelled the king, bureaucracy spread like a weed. They still taught high-profile military classes at the College, but most post graduate academics had moved to a new wing in the Bastion. A wing currently undergoing massive upgrades thanks to generous donations from the League.

He shuddered as he remembered his time at the Bastion. *I can't believe I once bought in to all that shit.*

He walked through the broad double doors. These were tall enough that Grim would have had no problem walking through them with Kavi standing on his shoulders. An officious looking man in full uniform sat behind a wide, semi-circular, marble-topped desk not far from the entry.

The man gave a quick glance to Grim's travel-worn clothing before looking back down at his work. When Grim stepped up to the desk, the man said, without looking up, "Please write your name on the left, the time of your appointment and the person you are here to meet. Though, I can't imagine anybody holding appointments this late."

Grim looked at the large appointment book and grabbed a pen. It looked like a toothpick in his broad hands. The man's officious tone annoyed him, so rather than squint to fit his name on one line, he took up four, writing in big block letters. He pushed the book back to the attendant and waited.

The attendant gave a world-weary sigh and looked at what Grim wrote. His annoyance at taking up four lines was immediately obvious. Then he read what Grim wrote and his demeanor changed instantly.

"Apologies, Lord Broadblade, we were not expecting you," said the lieutenant.

It was Grim's turn to sigh. "First, I'm no lord. Haven't you heard the rumors, lieutenant? I'm a drunk. And second, you *have* been expecting me. Let me know if I should make myself comfortable to wait out the boring game of dominance my dad loves to play, or if I should stay standing because I'm actually on the priority list."

The man didn't know how to respond to someone so intent on flouting military decorum. He pointed to the large, uncomfortable wooden chairs cordoned off in a waiting area and said, "Um, please make yourself comfortable. I don't think you'll be waiting long." The lieutenant ran off to talk to one of his superiors.

Grim rolled his eyes and walked over to the waiting area. He wondered how anyone could get comfortable on chairs like these. That was the point, of course. Military officers had all the subtlety of a man walking in to a crowded room and yelling fire. He briefly considered pulling one of the tapestries off of the wall to use as a cushion to spite his father. It would only get one of these innocent soldiers in trouble, so he resisted the urge.

In the end, Grim only waited fifteen minutes before one of the attendant's superiors jogged into the room. He walked over to Grim and saluted.

Grim shook his head. "I'm not in the military anymore, Captain," he said.

"Sorry sir, force of habit. I'm Captain Farber. I'll lead you back to the General, he's been looking forward to seeing you."

"No need to lie, Captain," Grim said with a laugh then extended an open palm towards the back offices. "Lead the way."

Save for the large reception room, the interior of the War College was a warren of poorly lit, tight corridors that reminded Grim of his time on League airships. Grim could see where dormitory rooms had been converted to small offices and lecture halls transformed to conference and briefing rooms. He supposed the large blackboards were just as effective in a briefing as they would be in a class.

As they got closer to his father's office, Grim kept expecting to feel nervous. Instead, all he felt was the same icy calm which came over him when he met with the Lioness. Regardless of the torments his father was capable of, he doubted they could measure up to what Company Senet put him through. What Coach Torin put him through.

The Captain knocked on a broad door with "General Broadblade" stenciled on the front in black paint.

"Come in," came a familiar, deep voice that once turned Grim's legs to jelly.

Grim pushed past the Captain before the man could announce him and walked into his father's office. He looked at the trappings of the lifetime service of a decorated officer. His father cared little for comfort, but he did love his medals. The room was large enough to fit a small conference table and a desk facing the door. His father sat at the desk scribbling away at a document.

Grim approached the desk cautiously. He still feared the man, but the fear had faded and tattered into unpleasant memory. Grim had stockpiled so many unpleasant memories that even this tableau of fundamental, character shaping memories—manifest in the man in front of him—no longer held the power to paralyze him. He looked at his father now as he would any predator—dangerous, but only deadly if one showed fear.

Grim eased himself into one of the two wooden chairs. He hoped taking a seat before given permission would annoy his father into giving something away. He crossed one leg over the other, sat back, and waited.

His father finished writing and finally looked up. "Good to see you, boy," said the General. *Was that a smile on his face?*

Grim let out a laugh. "You've never been happy to see me, General. Let's skip the bullshit, shall we?"

The general nodded. "Let's." The fake smile disappeared, replaced with a familiar, disapproving stare. "Judging by the beard, the red nose and the gut, you've been drinking again. Doubt you could even fit in a uniform these days."

"The Elites don't wear uniforms."

"A shame you got kicked out then."

Grim shrugged. "Better than not being selected I suppose." He dug the barb in, knowing his father still resented being denied candidacy as an Elite when he graduated the Bastion.

The General looked surprised, a raw disbelief that someone still existed that might talk back to him. He looked to the Captain standing frozen at the door. The man looked everywhere but at the two men. "Dismissed Captain, please shut the door behind you."

Grim didn't need to look to know the man fled as quickly as possible.

The General set his pen down. "And you got kicked out of the League too."

"That's where your facts are wrong, General. I never joined the League. I was captured, made a slave, and escaped the moment I was given the chance."

"Being pressed into service is hardly the same thing as being sold into slavery," said the General.

"Pressed into service?" Grim felt his own rage building. He took a deep breath and held it for a couple of seconds, then breathed out and held the exhale. His eyes never left his father's. He knew the man was trying to goad him. He was pretty sure his father didn't understand what would happen if he was successful. If the berserker rage took over, only one of them would leave this office alive. He stared at those hateful, unblinking eyes across the desk when realization struck. "So that's how the League justified it. Must have made it a lot easier to take their gold."

"Every military on Grendar has pressed men into service when threatened with war."

"The League is *not* a military and they were not at war," said Grim. "It's a game. One played for the enjoyment of the ultra-rich. All they care about is power, and you gave it to them. You and the Council sold Krom out for the low cost of a couple military buildings."

The General shook his head. "That's always been your problem, boy. You could never see the big picture. You know firsthand what these League warriors can do. What do you think happens to our soldiers the next time they go into battle if the other side has League technology and training and we don't?"

It was Grim's turn to shake his head. "You underestimate the League. What do you think happens when their priorities no longer align with yours? What if they ask you to look the other way when the Astrans march on an allied city like Loam? They already know you can be bought. The Council—all of Krom—belongs to the League now."

The General barked a laugh that struck like a challenge. "And you underestimate Krom. Alliances can be broken. I will always do what's in the best interest of Krom."

"But you're not a king. Your voice and your vote is one of nine. Do you honestly believe the League can't buy five Council votes whenever they need them?"

"And do you believe I can't force at least one of those votes back into my favor? The League is far away. The Council has to see me every day."

Grim shrugged. "Maybe. If there's one thing you're good at, it's bullying, but force doesn't work on everybody. You know that."

The General leaned back and puffed out his chest. "Not in my experience. I challenge you to name one person, when threatened with bodily harm, who wouldn't submit to the person threatening them."

Grim grabbed a letter opener shaped like a dagger off his father's desk. He scraped at a pebble that had lodged in the heel of his boot. Then, he looked up at his father. "Mom."

The General's face turned red. "Your mother was a weak and troubled fool. And she did submit. Many times."

The rage built again. Grim rhythmically tapped the inside of his thigh with two fingers. Focusing on a rhythm sometimes worked. He wished Albin, his fellow ghost who taught him the value of laughter, survived. A little humor right now would help. "It's pathetic you still think she was weak. Mom possessed a strength you will never have. Strength of character. She was so much smaller than you and she undercut you at every turn. She protected me even when you beat her close to death."

The General clenched his jaw to bring his own features under control. "It amuses me how much the weak love that phrase—strength of character—no one with real power gives a damn about strength of character. You know why? We're too busy running the world." He snorted. "Strength of character, what does that even mean?"

Grim knew the question was rhetorical. He also knew answering it would piss his father off. "It means using your strength to help or protect others, not for your own gain. It means standing up for what's right, even if it costs you personally."

The General reached across his desk and pulled the letter opener from Grim's hands. "You justify my actions with every word! Who determines what's right? The strong. I don't know what poison your mother whispered to you all those years. I do know that if the Bastion couldn't clear you of those ridiculous notions, there weren't a lot of other places for me to turn."

Grim's heart dropped. "What do mean by that?"

"Captain!" The General yelled to the door. The captain walked back in flanked by four soldiers. The man held something that looked all too familiar.

"Lady Stonecrest was too lenient with you," said his father. "I don't know what happened to the Lioness, but I suspect that Bricker husband made her soft. I'd be damned if I was going to let you waste your potential and let the Broadblade name fizzle out with a line of smiths."

"What did you do?" asked Grim, his voice sharp.

His father nodded to the Captain. The man stepped behind Grim and snapped a suppression collar around his neck.

Grim waited for the collar to click before he shook his head. "It was you," said Grim. "You put me on the list for the League."

"You *and* your friend Kavi. From what I heard, unlike you, that smug little prat thrived when forced to face a real challenge."

21

The Pits

"Where are you taking me?" Grim finally asked.

"The Pits," said Captain Farber.

"The General wants me to become a gladiator?" asked Grim. "Let me be first to say that's a really bad idea. I'd be super boring to watch."

"That's not what I heard," said the Captain. "But no, the games are canceled for the foreseeable future. KARP took over the Pits and the Colosseum to test League technology."

"What does military research want with me?"

"Nobody in the Krommian military has ever used League tech," said the Captain.

"You could have asked me to consult," said Grim.

"Would you have said yes?"

Grim grunted, conceding the point. "No, but it doesn't cost anything to ask."

"Apologies sir, but I'm guessing they're going to want you to do more than consult."

"Test subject then?"

The Captain walking behind him held the League baton

which controlled the suppression collar. When he didn't respond, Grim assumed the man nodded.

"And how do you feel about KARP taking Suli Elite veterans as test subjects?" When neither the Captain or four soldiers flanking him answered, Grim pushed his luck. "They're testing with veterans now, but you know what the next step will be, right? Regular soldiers becoming test subjects. It'll start with those soldiers without family, or at least those who have families with no power."

"Why did the General choose his own son, then?" asked one of the soldiers.

Grim looked over his shoulder at the speaker. "That's exactly why he chose his own son, Sergeant."

"That doesn't make any sense, sir," said the Sergeant.

"Captain Farber, do you want to explain it to your men, or do you not understand it either?"

Captain Farber sighed. "Our orders are to escort you to the Pits sir, not discuss the morality of KARP projects."

"So, you do understand it," said Grim. He turned around and started walking backwards so he could face the sergeant. "What the Captain doesn't want to tell you is my father and I can't stand each other." He pointed to the collar around his neck. "If the necklace I'm wearing didn't drill that point home, I'm not sure what will. If the General says he volunteered his own son to KARP testing, then it *must* be safe for other soldiers. See where this is going?"

One of the men spat, and it hit Grim's boot. Grim stopped and looked at him for a long moment. He had to admit he was impressed when the man didn't break his gaze.

"Why should we care what they do to a bloody deserter?" asked the corporal. "You brought nothing but shame on the

Elites, your father, and the Broadblade name."

"You seem brave, Corporal," said Grim. "Let's test that courage." He turned back around when they left the warren of the War College and made their way across the College Dromos to the broader Colosseum Dromos. Grim pointed to several children playing in a park. "What would you do if Captain Farber asked you to kill those children over there?"

"I would say no," said the corporal.

"Of course you would, you don't look like a homicidal madman. What if he ordered you to do it?"

The man paused. "I would ask why."

Grim raised his eyebrows and looked at the captain. "Soldiers under your command are allowed to question orders, Captain?"

The captain refused to engage.

"Of course they're not," said Grim. "So, Corporal, who's the coward? The one who follows orders and kills children and unarmed women, or the person with the conviction to say no."

The remainder of the trip to the Pits passed in silence.

* * *

The Pits were underground chambers below the Colosseum. A clever series of pullies and winches allowed the Master of Games to raise or lower the platforms at the base of each pit. Gladiators entered the Colosseum through the Warrior's gate, but prisoners and dangerous predators couldn't be trusted to follow orders. Carefully crafted panels on the floor of the Colosseum would slide open and the pit platform would rise in its place depositing its inhabitants on the sands.

A skilled Game Master would use distraction and pyrotechnics to make these deliveries look like magic. The drunken masses watching the games were happy to be fooled.

Farber and his men led Grim past the barred cells which normally held gladiators waiting their turn on the sands. They passed the empty animal cages next. Grim noticed the sloped drainage which led away from the animal cages was exactly the same as that for the men. The smell of stale urine clung to the cages in a torpid cloud.

Near the center of the cages was a narrow set of stairs leading down.

"Are these stairs new?" asked Grim.

His escort ignored him.

Grim had to bend at the waist to avoid the ceiling as they descended. When they reached the bottom they walked out of the narrow hallway to another set of stairs. These were wide and blessedly short. They opened into a larger set of rooms. The subterranean rooms had precise lines, as if someone had used a paring knife to cut them out of clay. They were painted white and lit with bright, white magelights which eliminated shadows from every corner. The bottom half of each room was painted stone but the top half was made entirely of glass. The rooms were neatly segmented to allow a corridor down the middle. From their vantage point at the base of the stairs, they could see researchers and military personnel working away.

Grim stopped and stared. It reminded him a little of Kavi's dad's laboratory, but Tribar and his lab weren't nearly so organized. He turned to the Captain. "How long has the

Council been working with the League?"

The captain ignored him. Grim and his escort waited awkwardly on the small stair landing entrance to the labs. They watched the bustle of researchers moving from room to room carrying samples and small rodents they injected with solutions of various colors. Anytime a door opened, they could hear the plaintive whines and yips from animal test subjects.

The clacking of boots ricocheted down the center hall. A short woman with raven hair tied in a ponytail walked over to meet them. She wore specs with thick lenses. The magnification made her eyes look like they took up more of her face than they actually did. Her wide face had jowls which could easily hold a handful of walnuts if she decided to stockpile food for the winter. The sicari scars were there, but lost in the folds of her face. A toad in uniform. He looked at the pin on her breast and the lines embroidered on her shoulder. A toad with the rank of Colonel.

The soldiers in his escort saluted and Grim heard Captain Farber breathe a sigh of relief.

"At ease," said the woman. "What do you have for me today?"

"Delivering subject two two nine, Colonel Proust." He handed the baton to the woman.

"Ahh yes, two two nine, the General's son." She walked around Grim as if inspecting a horse. "He's a big one. Looks strong too, if a bit out of shape. He'll do. Thank you, Captain. I'll take it from here."

Grim's escort gave a final salute and retreated up the narrow stairs.

The Colonel looked up at him. "The answer to your

booming question rattling my windows, is that we have only been working with the League for three months. These rooms did not exist before then." Her large eyes watched his face for a reaction.

The answer was obvious. The Krommians had an engineer with the architect skill, like Nettie. It was the only way this was possible. Grim was here to gather information for the Liberators not share any of his own. He schooled his features. "I knew the Krommian Corps of Engineers was efficient, but I didn't realize they were *this* good."

Proust's strigine eyes blinked once as they stared at him. "Interesting. I would have expected more of a reaction. Your time in the League must have been filled with revelations of the improbable and outright impossible. I know my eyes have been opened." She made a deep, almost coughing noise from her throat.

Grim looked at her curiously then realized she was laughing. "Filled to the brim. You can't truly understand the depths of human depravity until you work with slavers and power brokers of the League."

Her eyes blinked again. "Quite," she said. "The pursuit of knowledge is not much different than the pursuit of power. Ethics are incongruous with progress, are they not?"

Grim sighed. *Why were the powerful always crazy?* "You'd fit right in. I bet I could get you an interview. We could start you as a Ghost."

Proust made the same choking, coughing laugh. "A similar sense of humor to your father. You look like him. Shave off the beard, lose several inches, add some lines to your face...the similarity would be uncanny."

"Why am I here?" asked Grim.

"To give Krom an edge in the coming conflicts," said the Colonel. "Now that the League has shared its technology, it's only a matter of time before the leaders of our nation will want to play with their new toys."

Grim raised an eyebrow. "Are the Astrans deploying already?" Surely Rose would have known about something so serious.

"No, nothing like that, but I can't imagine this uneasy peace will last. Once the novelty of the upcoming Quest season wears off, the Council will resent not being the center of attention. You know how this works."

He stared into her hauntingly intelligent eyes. "I do. What I don't understand is how you can support it. You have a clear understanding of the pettiness of our leaders, yet here you are."

She pursed her lips as if trying to decide if the conversation was worth continuing. Finally, she said, "The boys and their toys are a means to an end. Do you know how much we learn during wartime? While we are at peace, people get wrapped up in things like personal rights and freedoms. That noise gets in the way of the pursuit of knowledge. When we're at war, the nation becomes united in doing whatever has to be done as expeditiously as possible. All humanitarian issues fade into the background."

Grim's nose crinkled with disgust. Her character was uglier than her appearance and that was saying something. He did his best to hide his disgust. "What do you need from me?"

"Two things. First, I need to understand how your training with the League differs from our current training regimens. We have a series of tests that we will run you through to illustrate those differences. Second, I've been tasked to uncover information about the fifth Sage."

"The fifth Sage?" asked Grim innocently.

"Don't do that," said Proust.

"Do what?"

"Lie. You're terrible at it. You call her Rose, I believe, and she's in hiding because she's too much of a wildcard to be cavorting about the world right now. There are already too many variables to account for. We can't have an agent of chaos bouncing around ruining everything."

Grim nodded slowly. "A man I respect once told me—all great ideas come from chaos. Though maybe he used the word entropy. I never understood the difference."

"Ah yes, you were raised, in part, by the great Tribar." She shook her head. "He was wrong. Great ideas come from the methodical exploration of all variables in complex systems. Breakthroughs come from the rigorous pursuit of testing every iteration of each variable interacting with every other. It comes down to process, you see?"

"I bet you're fun at parties."

"You'd think so," she said. "But I rarely get invited to social gatherings. People must know how busy I am."

"I'm sure that's it. Why do you think I would give up information about the fifth Sage?"

Her smile was dark and foreboding. "You're going to give up everything you know about her. You don't have a choice."

* * *

The bleached rooms under the Colosseum went on for kilometers. They must have burrowed under the War College *and* the Temple. He harbored a fantasy that the engineers didn't properly support the buildings above and the whole thing would come crashing in on itself. But the place was solid. The engineers were competent.

Colonel Proust left him in a room without windows. It held a small bunk and a hole in a bench for waste. While relieving himself Grim realized he couldn't hear his urine hit the bottom of the hole. It must be a long way down. He couldn't get himself to think of the dark chute as an escape route. A man had limits.

His eyes darted back and forth, prowling for escape routes the entire walk with Proust. The opportunities were few. Everything was well lit and the lock on the door was solid. Before she ushered him into his room, he noticed the number 229 stenciled on the door. The room was down a nondescript hallway which split from the main hall with doors that started with the number two hundred and continued to at least two forty. With the maze of hallways the numbers could have gone far higher.

He banged on the walls on each side of his cell but didn't get a response. The adjoining rooms were empty or their inhabitants incapable or uninterested in communicating. Another possibility flitted through his head. His captor's used League technology to dampen sound. If they had an architect, that technology was within reach.

Grim turned his energy inward. He had warned the Sage, more than once, that he was the wrong person for the job. He was right. Here he was, a prisoner again. They should never have trusted him with responsibility. He was less than useless.

Self-pity spread over him like a balm until Nettie's words echoed in the giant cavern he called a head. *No more of your wallowing in self pity bullshit.*

He hit his head against the painted stone wall of his cell. Anything to dislodge that voice.

Do something about it.

Whack.

Bring justice to the monsters that did this to us.

Whack.

You will fight by helping this group that took you in.

Fine.

He wiped the blood from his head and waited for the rage to knit the wound closed. It didn't. Damn suppression collar. Another mistake to add to his tally. He was such a lost cause he might as well go down swinging.

Wait a second.

They were probably observing him right now and knew he was a lost cause.

He could use that. His entire life, he'd been lauded for his fighting prowess, but no one ever saw him as a thinker. He was the stereotypical dumb warrior. No one was surprised when he became a berserker.

Why not play it up?

Meet the expectations handed to him by his size.

Nobody thought about the ulterior motives of the berserker. It was a perfect way to gather information. Act dumb by asking the stupid questions.

He sat on his bunk, his back against the wall with his feet up. This could work. This was *going* to work. He giggled, knowing the sound bordered on madness, as his desperation wrestled with this new feeling of resolve.

He had them right where he wanted them.

22

Back on the sand

The door opened with a click and Grim sat up. When the magelight went out the previous night he'd been thrust into the type of inky darkness which only existed underground. The narrow vertical slice of light cut the room in two.

"Who's there?" asked Grim.

The door pushed open and Grim squinted at the onslaught of light. "Just me, Broadblade," said Colonel Proust. "Ready for your first day of testing?"

"How many days of testing will there be?"

"As many as it takes. Don't scowl, you should be happy to provide this service to your nation."

Grim folded his arms over his chest "Tests on military personnel who volunteered are one thing, but kidnapping me is no different than slavery. Shall I call you master?"

Proust shrugged and Grim could tell his words had no impact. "If you wish. But you will follow me or I'll use the collar. I see you haven't donned your testing uniform."

Grim stood and made his way over to the hole of a privy and began to relieve himself. He looked over his shoulder to see if Proust would look away. Her gaze never wavered. He shook himself then wiped his hands on his pants. Then he began to strip. He made sure to get totally naked before he donned the dark green uniform with the numbers 229 stamped on the chest and back. He looked back to Proust. "I'm ready."

The first round of tests were medical. Proust dropped him off with technicians who took his weight, looked at his teeth, in his ears and up his nose. They asked him questions about diet, sleeping and bathroom habits. Everything was recorded in a small book with the numbers 229 stamped on the front.

These same technicians had him do a series of physical tests. They had him jump, sprint, lift weights and run around a small track. These results were also written in the small book.

Shortly after the battery of tests, Proust came back in and scanned the results. She looked at Grim. "These results are below average. It almost appears like you are not trying."

Grim shrugged and said with wide eyes. "I'm giving it my all, master."

She looked to the technicians. "Clearly an issue of mis-matched incentives. Let's see how he does when properly motivated. We head up to the sands."

It was hot on the sands. It was only mid-morning but the sun beat on the Colosseum like it held a grudge. It surprised Grim to see a group of ten others wearing uniforms like his, each with a number in the two hundreds. The combination of heat and uniforms felt like his first days with Company Senet.

The men and women on the sands regarded Grim warily

as he walked to the center of the primary ring. None of them wore collars, but Grim noticed Captain Farber and the four soldiers of his escort standing nearby, hands on weapons. They watched all those in numbered uniforms. Interesting. Maybe the other test subjects weren't volunteers either.

Grim decided to find out. He walked over to the group when he felt a charge ripple through his suppression collar. He stopped and looked back at Proust. "I'm not allowed to talk with my fellow prisoners?"

"Most of them are volunteers, Master Broadblade," she said.

Most, so I'm not the only slave, thought Grim. "What exactly would you like me to do? If you explain it, I might agree."

"I doubt that very much," she said. "Though I suppose there's no harm in asking. I'd like you to demonstrate the skills you acquired during your time in the League. Many believe the incredible display the League warriors put on for us during their recruitment drive was fabricated."

He gave her a crooked smile. "You mean *you* believe it was fabricated. Haven't been able to figure out how to unlock a skill, have you?"

"Not yet," said Proust.

"I don't know how it works either."

"That is irrelevant to this test."

"You want me to beat on my fellow prisoners?" Grim asked loudly enough for those in the numbered uniforms to hear. "I can do that without tapping into my skills." He turned to the test subjects and shrugged. "Not that I'd want to."

The men and women shouted in challenge. Krommians were notoriously prickly about anyone taking shots at their fighting prowess.

Grim tugged at his suppression collar. "You realize what this thing does and why the League uses it?"

"I understand the theory," said the Colonel. "But we've never had empirical evidence of its power dampening properties. The controlling shock it produces has been a useful side benefit however."

Grim lifted the hair covering his forehead so Proust could see the broken skin from when he banged his head against the wall the previous evening. "Take off the collar and I can demonstrate very quickly without anyone getting hurt."

Colonel Proust looked to Farber and the man nodded. He picked up the crossbow at his feet and the four soldiers with him did the same. They turned them on Grim. Captain Farber nodded.

"I told you," said Grim. "I have no interest in hurting anybody."

"We have our protocols," said Proust. She pulled the control key from the top of the baton and unlocked the collar around Grim's throat.

The wound on Grim's forehead immediately stitched itself shut. Grim didn't need to get angry anymore for the healing to take effect. It's as if the rage beast who lived inside of him realized keeping Grim alive was the best way for it to have a chance at coming out again. *That's probably why I can drink so much booze without killing myself.* He shook his head to dislodge the stray thought. He looked around at the surprised faces and smiled.

"Interesting. So, the concept of skill wasn't all fabrication."

"Great. Now that we've proven skills exist, I don't have to

hurt anybody," said Grim.

"That conclusion is not yours to draw, two two nine. We know League berserkers have more abilities than self-healing. I intend to see them all."

Grim shook his head. "You don't understand. If I get angry enough to access all my skills, people will die. I can't control the bloody thing I become when the rage takes over. That's why my skills are worse than useless. I'm more a danger to my allies than to my enemies."

"Let me worry about that, Master Broadblade. That's what the protocols are for."

"No. I'm not going to have more deaths on my conscience!" shouted Grim. He wrestled to control his rage. He barely beat the beast back into the corner of his tattered mind. He took a breath and held it. He looked around to see everyone in the immediate vicinity holding their ears and cowering away. Everyone but Proust.

She pulled pieces of wax from her ears and looked at him. "Interesting. The berserker bellow is real too."

She looked over at Farber and his men. "Get a hold of yourself, Captain."

The man's face burned. He grabbed the crossbow he'd dropped. His men grumbled and did the same. They reoriented their crossbows and put Grim back in their sights.

The other test subjects looked deeply unsettled. Their previous bravado evaporated like sweat on the hot sands.

"Number two two four, are you ready to spar?"

"With him? I'm sorry ma'am, but...I don't think so," said the man tremulously.

Proust smiled. "That wasn't a request two two four, but you can use one of the wooden staffs if you like. Two two

255

nine will remain unarmed."

The man grabbed a staff from a weapon rack and walked to face Grim.

"Begin," said Proust.

The man swung the staff in a feint. Grim ignored it. Then he swung it hard to Grim's left side. Grim caught the staff and tore it from the man's hand and threw it to the sand.

"Stop," said Grim.

224 was happy to comply.

"Two three two, two three six, two three eight, please join two two four against two two nine," said Proust, her voice never raising in volume. She pulled out a pen and began taking notes.

The three men and one woman raced to attack. They had all been trained in the basics, which meant quite a bit in Krom. Every child learned to fight, male or female, at the tender age of five. These Krommians were a step above the average Krommian citizen. He observed the way they moved, and Grim was convinced they had additional military training.

They came at him from all directions.

Grim ducked and weaved. He blocked where he could but it wasn't possible to avoid all attacks. A kick from the woman caught him in the kidney and he grunted. His healing kicked in and the pain faded. He dodged without ever striking out. Grim knew he fought five opponents, the four warriors on the sands and his own anger. He was determined to let the warriors win long before the rage took over.

Grim started to tire until he saw the annoyance painted on Proust's face. It gave him the energy to continue.

She pointed to the rest of the test subjects and shouted.

"Go. All of you. Take him down and you will be rewarded with a flagon of ale with tonight's meal."

The six remaining test subjects attacked. There was such a mass of men and women grabbing at Grim that he eventually fell to one knee. A kick to the back of the head dropped him to his stomach and the test subjects pounced, lying or sitting on him until he was motionless.

"Good fight," said Grim. "I surrender."

"Not so tough now are you," said one of the men on top of him.

"Don't be an idiot, Krenzer, he was a Suli Elite. He could have killed every one of us if he wanted to," whispered the woman who kicked him in the kidney. She spoke just loud enough so the pile of bodies could hear, but not Proust.

When the test subjects piled off Grim he stood and wiped the sand off his body and face. He spat to clear his mouth of the remaining grains but had so little moisture left in his mouth, the sand dribbled down his chest and over his belly in gummy little balls. *Classy. I still know how to impress.*

"This doesn't end until I see you tap into that rage, two two nine," said Proust.

Grim shook his head, convincing her was a lost cause. Time to try a different approach. "Can you give me a tour of the facility?" asked Grim. "Show me the technology you are using and how you are using it. Maybe I can help. Even if I showed you my other skills, you're not going to know how to unlock them."

"I'd give you the tour if you weren't working with the fifth Sage," said Proust. "But you are, and we can't risk it."

"Ok, then let me square off against the General. He's a warrior and we've sparred together for most of my life. If

257

you want to see rage, let me fight him."

She gave him a stern look. "We both know why that is unacceptable, two two nine."

Keep playing dumb. "I have no quarrel with my fellow test subjects. They're victims, same as me. Nothing they can do will drive me to the type of display you're looking for. Can I spar against the guards in my escort?"

"Don't worry, we haven't come close to running out of ideas." The lack of passion in her statement made her words more sinister. She looked up at the sun which was directly overhead. "I have a meeting I must attend. Captain, please take our test subjects to be watered and fed. We continue at two bells."

* * *

"You volunteered for this?" asked Grim.

A woman with four diagonal scars across her face nodded. "Of course! A chance to be first to train like the League. We saw the recordings. How could you *not* want to learn to fight like that?"

Grim took a long drink of water, scratched once at his collar, and tucked into the pile of ribs in front of him. From her perspective, he supposed it made sense. When he was at the Bastion, he would have done anything to gain an edge over fellow cadets. The test subjects around him must be regulars. They didn't have the advantage of learning from the best at the Bastion. League training could be life changing. Promotions, a spot on an elite squad, even a chance to compete in a Quest. All possible for someone who unlocked a skill.

He inhaled another rib. The pile of gnawed rib bones was much larger than the ones that still had meat on them. Grim was just getting started. The rest of the test subjects were done or almost done with their meals and they sat back to watch as Grim finished rack after rack of ribs. He hadn't eaten like this since...since before being captured by the League.

"Were you lying to Proust? About not knowing how you unlocked those skills?"

Grim shook his head. He was sure he was being observed but the information he had wouldn't give Proust and KARP anything new. "No, we never figured it out. That's the truth."

One of the men who piled on him earlier snorted. "You expect us to believe that? Everyone in the League has unlocked skills. You're saying they don't know how? Bullshit."

Grim gnawed on the bone of the rib he just finished getting the last morsel of meat from it with his front teeth. He turned to the man. "Krenzer, was it? I don't care if you believe me. Everyone in the League has *not* unlocked skills. In Company Senet, it was maybe five or ten percent that ever got that far."

"No way," said the woman with the diagonal scars. "We all saw what they could do. There were at least fifty League warriors doing impossible shit."

"Fifty from five different teams. Company Senet, my company, had over five hundred members. You saw the best of the best."

Krenzer snorted. "You're the best of the best?"

"You didn't see me in that recording, did you?" asked Grim. "You also didn't see all the dead Ghosts. That's what they called new slaves in our first season, on the account so many of us died. Of the twenty-seven Ghosts I started with, seven survived."

Krenzer opened his mouth to speak, but the woman elbowed him in the ribs. "Stop, Krenzer." She turned back to Grim, eyes squinted as she calculated something in her head. "Seventy-five percent casualty rate, that's disaster level. Krommian commanders have been sacked for twenty percent casualty rates."

Grim nodded. He was about to respond when Farber walked into the room.

"Finish what's in front of you, we're back on the sands in five," said the Captain.

Proust waited for them as they returned to the heat. A group of her researchers stood around a large arena cage. The cage was covered with an enormous white sheet.

Grim was not the only test subject startled by the sounds coming from inside the cage. He assumed the sheet was there for two reasons - to keep whatever was in there placid and cool under the hot sun and to keep the creature a surprise from the test subjects. The second objective failed as anyone within a kilometer could hear the creature hooting and banging against the cage bars.

"Oh, hell no," said Krenzer. "Nobody said anything about banglors."

"Those are just an urban legend," said the woman with the diagonal scars.

"It wasn't an urban legend that wiped out my brother's troop twenty clicks from home, Marina," said Krenzer.

Proust turned to face them. "It appears some of you have guessed what awaits in the cage. I will not bore you with the creature's scientific classification. Two three eight is correct. We have captured a banglor."

Proust nodded to the researchers. They removed the cloth covering the cage. Grim had never seen one of the beasts in the flesh but had fought plenty in the Pool. The enormous ape-like creature in front of them looked like it had been kept in captivity for a while. It was malnourished, its dark gray fur fell out in chunks. It was missing several teeth, but its large fangs still looked sharp. Even so, it was nothing like the healthy, terrifying beasts Grim had fought.

He felt bad for it.

The one thing it hadn't lost was its rage. It banged on the bars with all its strength. The other test subjects stepped back in horror or fear. Grim couldn't help but see a kindred spirit in the abused animal. Regardless of their fearsome reputation, and the damage banglors had done to Krommian troops, it didn't deserve this.

Proust turned back to the creature after it made a particularly loud screech. She looked at it with the same detached indifference she looked at the test subjects. There was no pride or shame in her eyes, only curiosity. Surprisingly, the cold gaze caused the creature to pause its wild screams. It focused on her. It was almost like it realized who was responsible for its current situation.

After fighting hordes of banglors in the Pool, Grim knew the creatures were more intelligent than Proust credited them. He wouldn't be surprised if it understood exactly what was going on and was planning an escape. Kavi's friend, Grundle, mentioned banglors were capable of speech.

261

Once it calmed down, Proust turn to address the nervous test subjects. "Two two nine, this is your next opponent. You may pick three companions to face off against the banglor."

Grim shook his head. "Unnecessary Colonel, I've trained against monsters like this. My companions have not. I warn you, I will not kill the beast."

"The General will be upset with me if it takes your life, Sergeant."

Grim nodded. "Good," he said. "Maybe we can skip this nonsense then."

"You know that is impossible. Choose your weapon and we'll get started." She gestured to the weapons rack.

"No need," said Grim. "I told you, I'm not going to kill the creature." He started wind-milling his arms to get the blood flowing.

"Don't be an idiot, Broadblade," said Marina. "Take a weapon. That thing is going to rip you apart."

"Hang on to that optimism," Grim said with a smile.

"Clear the circle," said Proust.

The researchers moved quickly. They piled into one of the caged staging areas.

Captain Farber and his men ushered the test subjects into an adjoining cage. The bars would protect them from the banglor if the creature won the bout. Farber's squad could finish it quickly with those crossbows. Proust removed his collar and followed the others into the cage.

When the door shut, she looked to Grim. "You have one minute to arm yourself. When that minute is up, I pull the lever on the wall beside me, and the cage holding the banglor collapses."

Grim ignored her. He continued stretching and made eye

contact with the mangy banglor. It ceased the histrionics and stared at Grim with intelligent eyes.

Grim moved forward until he was just outside the giant beast's bars. "If you can understand me," whispered Grim. "I don't mean you harm. I'm a prisoner here. Like you."

The banglor's eyes narrowed.

From that reaction, Grim was certain it understood him. "We need to trick the evil lady in the cage behind me. After we fight, you need to play dead. Then I will make a big sound and you run away. Understand?"

The banglor's eyes narrowed further. It understood him, but it didn't trust him.

"Five, four, three, two....one," Proust counted down.

The bars of the cage fell.

The banglor charged the moment the bars fell.

Grim dove to the side and rolled. He sprang to his feet to see the creature whipping around to face him again.

The banglor released a blood curdling scream and banged its chest.

Grim felt his blood rise. He shouted back, expelling all his fury at the situation in that one scream.

The banglor rocked back and its eyes widened. The first sign of uncertainty colored its broad face. It screamed again and leapt.

Grim looked up, disappointed in his opponent. *Never leave your feet in a fight.* It was pounded into all of the cadets at the Bastion again and again. He ran forward and slid under the trajectory of the creature's leap. When it landed, he punched the banglor in the kidney, hard.

It yowled and struck back, clipping Grim in the shoulder with a glancing blow. If Grim had been armored, the strike would have only left a bruise. Without armor, Grim heard something pop. He screamed and his vision went red. *No! Damnit. None of this is worth a thing if you lose your humanity.* But the pain was too much.

My turn, came the voice of the bloody beast who lived within.

Grim began to laugh.

23

Bloody Grim

Bloody Grim rolled on to his shoulder and giggled as he felt the dislocated joint pop back into place. He jumped to his feet and felt that wonderful rage knit torn muscles together. He roared at the banglor and slammed his fists one after the other against his chest in rapid succession.

The banglor answered in kind, but when the beast advanced it did so with caution. It slapped the ground in front of it twice, eyes fixed on the berserker.

Bloody Grim laughed.

The banglor screamed in fury, the laughter enraging it. It swung a meaty fist at Grim.

Bloody Grim caught the fist and began to squeeze, the rage lending him superhuman strength.

The banglor's eyes widened as the bones in its hand began to pop. It screamed again, this time in pain.

No! yelled Grim, relegated to the sidelines, a mere observer as his psychotic doppelganger took control of the fight. *We cannot kill this beast.*

Why not? asked Bloody Grim.

Grim was so surprised by the question, he paused. Bloody Grim never acknowledged him before. He just took over while Grim watched in horror.

The pause cost him. The banglor swung his other fist and scored a strike on the same shoulder.

Bloody Grim laughed when the strike landed. *Quiet now, little man. There is battle to be won.* Bloody Grim pulled the banglor towards him and launched a vicious kick at the beast's side. The banglor flew through the air. He chased after the flying banglor to be there to meet it when it landed. Grim screamed, but Bloody Grim held the reins. He watched with horror as Bloody Grim rained blows on the banglor's head and neck.

The banglor put its arms up to protect its head but the blows kept coming. Finally, it looked up at Grim and whispered, "Please..." through bloody lips.

Damnit, Eleven! shouted Grim into the void, using Kavi's technique. *If we can't work together, I'll make sure you never see battle again.*

Bloody Grim laughed again, but the punches stopped. *No more battle? You jest little man. There is always more battle. Battle follows us like Krom's obedient wolf, Vendriss.*

Not if we're dead.

Don't worry, I won't let that happen. Especially against something so pathetic as this creature. Bloody Grim scowled at the banglor.

Not in battle, said Grim to his alter ego.

Bloody Grim stopped laughing as understanding passed through him in a paralyzing wave. *You'd do something so pathetic as to take our life? That...that is the coward's way.*

The coward's way is killing without consequence. Do you

know how many friends we've killed? You kill and you don't have to see their dead faces after the bloodlust fades. You leave that pain to me. You are the coward.

But that pain isn't real, said Bloody Grim, confused. Not like a sword wound. It's only in your head.

Grim realized his alter ego was little more than a child. Battle was his only context. He flooded Bloody Grim with all the memories. All the pain of hurting others. He sent wave after wave of images of mothers grieving over the lives of sons and daughters Bloody Grim killed in battle. He shared the hurt and shocked looks of Ghosts who'd fallen to his axes. The betrayal when they believed he was coming to save them, but instead cut them down. He shared the whispers he pretended not to hear when his brothers and sisters in arms talked about him when they thought he wasn't listening.

Stop! yelled Bloody Grim in their head. Please, stop! I don't know how to heal this type of pain.

You can't heal it. Not with our powers. But love and forgiveness from friends and family makes it hurt less.

Friends? asked Bloody Grim.

Grim shared images of good times with brothers and sisters in arms. The times with Kavi. The times Nettie and Carlin stepped in to help him. The times when Tribar held him like a child as he sobbed over the memories of the vacant eyes of people he killed.

I've never known friends, said Bloody Grim.

I know. I can change that if you promise to work with me when we're in battle.

How?

I will give you control during some of the good times, not just in battle.

What do you need me to do? asked Bloody Grim.

I need you to follow one rule. No killing. No killing of friends and allies. No killing of enemies. No killing, ever.

What if we have to kill to save our own life or the life of a friend?

We'll cross that bridge when we have to. For now, NO KILLING. Can you do that?

I think so. What about this pathetic little creature? It looks like it's planning to take advantage of our conversation.

No killing. Let it strike, then put it in a hold. I want to talk to it. Can we do that?

We can do that.

The banglor looked at Grim in confusion. Grim could tell it planned one last, desperate strike. Grim nodded to it.

The banglor pushed against him with both legs and Bloody Grim allowed himself to be pushed off. He quickly spun behind the creature and wrapped a burly arm around the banglor's neck to keep it motionless.

Ok, said Bloody Grim. *Your turn.*

"I'm going to throw you into the stands behind us," whispered Grim to the banglor. "Nod your head if you understand me."

The banglor nodded.

"When I throw you, those men over there are going to shoot at you. Stay low and make your way north to the Draydale. North means the sun will be on this shoulder." Grim tapped the banglor's left shoulder. "Nod again if you understand me."

The banglor nodded.

"You have to pretend to break free then charge. That is when I will throw you into the seats above. Nod if you understand me."

The banglor nodded.

"Ready?"

The banglor nodded.

"Now," whispered Grim.

The banglor broke free from the hold. It jumped backwards and Grim jumped to his feet. It charged at him. *I need your strength!* Grim yelled to his alter ego.

I am here.

When the banglor reached him, Grim used the momentum of the charge and all of Bloody Grim's strength to throw the creature through the air.

"I've never seen anything like that," said Krenzer from the cage, eyes wide with wonder.

The test subjects, researchers and soldiers watched the battle with rapt attention, caught up in the drama of an unarmed man wrestling and besting a monstrous banglor. Once it was clear Grim would be the victor, the soldiers lowered their crossbows and joined the test subjects enjoying the fight.

"He threw it twenty meters in the air," said Marina.

The banglor landed in the stands with a squeal of pain. A moment later, it stood and ran. It sprinted through the viewing benches and climbed over the wall that topped the northern edge of the Colosseum. Its arms and fingers easily gained purchase on the large rocks of the exterior of the Colosseum. The beast was built to climb.

Proust, Farber, and the researchers were so caught up in the drama of the battle, they didn't move until the banglor was over the wall.

Only then did Proust scream. "What are you doing, Captain. Go! Capture it!"

Grim smiled and Bloody Grim laughed. *Look how angry they are! You're right. Battle without killing can be fun.*

Grim laughed with him. He watched the soldiers discuss how best to capture the banglor. When Farber and his men finally got their cage open, Grim could hear the frightened screams of citizens outside as the banglor ran north. The guards ran towards the closest exit which faced west, giving the banglor a large lead.

If the banglor could stay clear of guards within the city and avoid the northern gate at the far edge of town, it would have a chance of escaping into the Draydale. Grim's belly warmed with the glow of accomplishment. He did at least one thing that would make the Liberators proud today, even if he only liberated a banglor.

Grim's maniacal laugh tapered into a chuckle as he watched the soldiers rush out the western exit of the Colosseum. He was still laughing when Proust and her researchers approached him with the collar.

"Don't look so proud of yourself," said Proust.

"I did what you asked without killing the creature. Pride's the wrong word. I'm satisfied with the outcome and happy the creature you tortured has a chance to make it home."

"To do what?" said Krenzer, anger muted by Grim's display but not extinguished. "Lie in wait and kill more of our countrymen?"

Grim shook his head. Before he could reply, Proust interrupted him.

"Enough two three eight. I doubt two two nine thought through the consequences of his actions. He has a history of acting without thinking," said Proust.

Grim nodded. "You're right, Colonel, I'm too dumb to think things through." He pointed his chin at the collar in her hand. "Take that collar for example. How do you think you're going to snap it around my neck without the threat of Farber and his crossbows? Who'd have thought releasing a beaten banglor would result in you not having the resources to make me a prisoner again?"

Proust stared down at the collar for a moment. "We have other options." She nodded to two of her researchers.

The researchers stayed behind the bars of their cage as they pulled out small blowguns. They shot darts tipped with a sedative into Grim's chest.

Grim laughed maniacally as the darts struck. He wasn't sure if it was him or Bloody Grim holding the reins, but his rage immediately counteracted the sedative. He stopped laughing and pretended to nod his head with drowsiness.

Proust grinned with satisfaction. She moved to put the collar around his neck.

When she got close enough, Grim ripped it from her hand. "No. It's time you understand what it feels like."

He clasped the collar around her neck and tore the baton from her hand. The researchers and test subjects froze, waiting for the drama to play out.

He looked at Proust in mock apology. "You'll have to forgive me, Colonel. I have no experience with using one of these. I've only been on the receiving end." He looked at the baton pretending he hadn't memorized every little nook and cranny as the coaches tortured him with it every day as a Ghost. "I know the batons are normally bonded to their users so I doubt this will work."

Proust seemed to sag with relief as she imagined an

opening. "That's right. Don't be foolish, Broadblade. This will go worse for you if you torture a Colonel." She glared at her researchers, willing them to take action. Two of them reached for blowguns, but Grim arrested their motion with a growl.

"Ah, you admit to torture. Interesting," Grim said in his best imitation of her voice. "I *would* have worried about the bonding if I hadn't seen you pass it between you and your staff fifteen times. I'm guessing you were too arrogant to think a situation like this could arise as long as you followed the proper processes. Am I right?"

"What are you doing, idiots! Go get help!" Proust yelled, her desperation reaching a crescendo. Most of her staff remained frozen, stuck in the nightmare of a berserker off his leash. One of them edged towards the cage door.

"I wouldn't do that if I were you," said Marina, looking over at the researcher. "He took down a banglor with his bare hands. Imagine what he could do to you."

Grim had been worried what the test subjects might do. Most were active military or recently retired. He wasn't worried about them stopping him, but he didn't want to have to hurt them. It appeared they were starting to come around in thinking Grim got a raw deal.

He turned his attention to Proust. "I *think* all I need to do is twist this part right here." He twisted the top part of the baton as had been done to him countless times.

Proust began to shake.

"And then I keep turning to turn it off? Is that right?" He turned a little further.

Proust convulsed more violently.

"Nope, that's wrong. I wish I weren't so simple-minded

or I'd have this figured out by now." He turned the rotating section of the baton back to neutral and Proust's convulsions ceased. "I think I understand it now. Do you?" he asked Proust. He bent down so his face was millimeters from hers. He could smell the fear on her breath.

"Of course I understand. I was trained on the device," she said, in a high pitched squeak.

Grim kept his eyes a finger length from hers. "Yet, you have so little understanding of people...or double meanings. I'll be clear. What you're doing here is wrong." He stood to his full height and turned to the rest of the researchers. "That holds for all of you. If people volunteer for your experiments, by all means, experiment away. If they don't, whether man or beast, what you're doing is evil. I'm done preaching and I'm out of time. We're being observed and there's another group of scary men with scarier weapons on the way, so I'll make this part quick."

He walked to the cage that held the researchers and opened the door. He stepped in and walked in front of a researcher who shot him with the blowgun. He grabbed the blowgun, still in the man's left hand, and snapped it in half. He looked down at the man quivering in fear. "You're going to tell me what I need to know before the men with bows show up. Every time you decide not to answer a question, I will hit you, then I will zap your boss. Do you understand?"

"Don't tell him anything, Conklin!" yelled Proust.

The researcher's eyes shifted to Proust and he nodded. Slowly.

Grim turned the top half of the baton. He didn't look as Proust seized in pain.

Conklin turned white, his eyes shifting back and forth

between Proust and Grim. "Please, stop. I'll tell you."

He turned the baton back to neutral. Grim held Conklin's eyes, refusing to look at Proust. "She won't interrupt again. I promise. I want to understand exactly what League technology you are researching."

"Where...where should I start?"

"At the beginning. Explain the full battery of tests you run the test subjects through. What are you looking for and what does the League get in return? I want you to list every bit of League technology you've received. Explain how you are using each one. Finally, I want to know who else observed your research who is not part of your current chain of command. Do this and I won't hit you. Do you understand?"

The man nodded.

"Start talking."

Grim got five minutes of answers before a squad of soldiers arrived with crossbows.

He smiled when Proust put the collar around his neck.

24

Krom

"I don't understand why you didn't leave," said Marina as they sat for dinner. "You could have had a five-minute head start."

"I'm here for a reason, Marina," said Grim. "I'm not leaving until I finish what I came here to do."

"What reason?" she asked.

"That's between me and the General."

"What was it like, growing up with him? The man's a legend, he must have taught you everything about being a warrior."

The expression of worship on her face nearly made Grim snap. He gave a rueful chuckle at the building rage. "Don't ever meet your heroes. You're guaranteed to be disappointed. The General is an asshole. He beat my mother nearly to death until she finally left. Then he beat me, every day, until I escaped to the Bastion."

"We all got the strap growing up," said Krenzer. "Sometimes it's the only way to impart a lesson. Are you one of those softies who doesn't believe in disciplining children?"

Grim took a bite of the cornbread and stared at Krenzer until he finished chewing. He swallowed noisily. "I agree with discipline. I'm even fine with the strap. But, beating someone physically smaller and weaker than you who depends on you for security, food, and shelter? That's the sign of a very disturbed person."

"You got beat, big deal. We all did, it's a Krommian tradition," said Krenzer.

"What lesson does it teach?" asked Grim.

"To listen and respect your elders."

Grim held up a finger. "At all costs. To listen and respect your elders at all costs. That's not respect, it's fear. It's small men pretending to be gods of their household. It teaches children not to question anything, that thinking for themselves is a bad thing. How competent is a nation that doesn't have citizens who think for themselves? You've seen Bricker and League tech. How do we compete with that if we don't have our own thinkers? We end up with demented psychopaths like Proust. I bet you she was beaten every time she asked a question until something snapped. Now, all our thinkers are broken."

Conversation around the table ceased as the test subjects listened.

"We still have the strongest military," said one of the test subjects. Others loudly agreed with him.

"For now," said Grim. "With League technology, everything changes. Battles will be won by the thinkers, not who's strongest."

The grumbles around the table got louder. Grim knew he was shaking a foundation of Krommian culture. He also knew how important it was to do so.

"I'd still bet on a Krommian over any other in a one-on-one fight," said another test subject.

"So would I," said Grim. "Even in the League I never met anyone who could take me one-on-one. The problem is, I never met a Krommian tactician. Sure, we teach strategy and tactics at the war college, but only after we teach kids not to think for themselves. We have to change or we're not going to survive."

Krenzer scowled. "And who's going to change us, you?"

Grim laughed. "I'm no visionary. I never learned to think, remember? No, not me. Who knows, maybe it will be one of you. All I know is if we don't make the change, somebody, probably the League, is going to do it for us. When that happens our culture, even the good parts, will be destroyed."

* * *

They were escorted to the sands the next morning by Proust. Her eyes were dark and her uniform hinted at wrinkles. She either went out last night and got blackout drunk or received a third degree reprimand. Maybe both.

Grim wanted to feel bad for her, but couldn't summon the empathy. He surveyed the sands and wondered what surprises today would bring. The first thing he noticed was a contingent of military personnel in the first two rows of the stands above where they would be testing.

Behind the soldiers was an audience. Front and center was his father. The general spoke with other military brass and pointedly ignored the test subjects the way a young man might pretend not to notice the woman he's interested in.

Grim followed the others to the center ring. He looked to the cage rising in front of him. Three wolf-like creatures paced the perimeter of the cage on all fours. Not until the cage stopped moving did Grim notice how large they were. Each outweighed him by half.

One of the creatures unfolded and stood on its back legs so its ears tickled the top rungs of the cage. Grim could see the wolfman had paws but its claws looked eerily like fingers retracting. It used those fingers to grip the cage and stare balefully at the test subjects. Its growl was deep and angry. The growl's pitch became more menacing when its eyes lit on Proust.

At the sound, the other two joined the first in staring down the Colonel. Proust ignored them with the same ease she ignored the banglor. The same ease she ignored Grim.

Proust faced the test subjects. "Today," she said, her voice projecting mightily for the larger audience. "You will be facing the next iteration of mutations."

"Just me, or the whole squad?" muttered Grim.

She subtly turned the knob on her baton. The current ran through him like a hive of insects moving under his skin and burrowing into his mind.

You with me?

I'm here, replied Bloody Grim. *It hurts but won't do any lasting damage.*

We know one thing at least.

What's that?

Proust is torturing us in full view of the Council. They've signed off on everything she's doing.

Grim rolled his head around a vertical axis. He refused

his body's need to convulse even as Proust turned up the intensity. After one rotation of stretching his neck he held Proust's gaze.

She looked down at the baton and turned it a little higher.

He held her gaze. "Don't worry, it's working," he said. His voice quavered with the pulse of the current. "You probably won't cause permanent damage until you turn it up to the highest setting." He shrugged. "But you never know. The coaches at Team Senet never went as high as you've got it now, but they were more creative in their incentives. Then again, the League is more insidious than you. It comes from being more intelligent."

She turned the dial up to maximum and this time Grim couldn't stop it. He convulsed then lost control of his bladder and pissed down the front of his uniform.

Proust's face filled with rage. He laughed as he convulsed. He knew it was dangerous, but it felt good to break her icy calm.

She turned the baton to neutral and her eyes flicked to the seats. She gave the hint of a cringe before her icy stare fixed on Grim. "What did we learn from that?" she asked imperiously.

"That I haven't pissed myself in over two weeks. I can't believe it's been that long. Have I really not had a drink in over two weeks?" He turned to Krenzer. "Do they serve booze at the cafeteria?"

"Cut it out, Broadblade. Your father's watching," whispered Krenzer.

Grim turned to the stands and waved. "Hi Dad. I pissed myself when the angry lady turned the thingy all the way up. Just like old times huh?"

"Proving again why disowning you was the wise decision," said his father in the world-weary voice disappointed fathers everywhere have perfected.

His father's statement drew several uncomfortable chuckles from the VIPs around him. The General gave a 'get on with it' lift of his chin to Proust.

Proust nodded. "Right then. No, you will fight with at least two other test subjects. You can choose to fight with the entire squad if you wish but we need to see how you fight with allies."

"You know exactly how I fight allies. I kill them. That's why I fight alone."

But we're past that aren't we? Bloody Grim growled.

Yes, but she doesn't know that.

Proust's eyes flicked back to the seats holding his father. "Unacceptable," she said. "You will fight the three Vendri with a squad backing you up."

"Vendri. I get it, like Krom's wolf, Vendriss," said Krenzer.

"How original," said Grim. "But the answer is no. If you don't like that answer, feel free to kill me." Grim sat on the ground. "Since I know my father is watching, I'll spill the beans. That's why I agreed to come here. I'm on a suicide mission. I accepted death long ago and if I die now, so be it. What I won't do is be responsible for the death of another ally."

Proust turned the baton on and Grim lay back. He let the convulsions take him. He looked to the sky and marveled at how little it would care if he died. A moment later the convulsions stopped. Grim sat up.

"Still want to see the monkey perform? You brought all the best and brightest in their Kromsday finest. It would be a shame to cancel the show," said Grim.

"Fine, if you want to die this day, you'll get your wish."

Grim stood. He faced the stand that held the spectators and gave an exaggerated, courtly bow.

His father and the Council members scowled back at him. Only one man smiled, a huge warrior who wore the canvas vest and battle kilt of a gladiator. He sat two rows behind the others so his enormous body could fit. He clapped to show his appreciation when Grim made eye contact. The others ignored him. Sitting that far back, he couldn't have been that important.

Proust pointed to areas on the periphery of the arena. "The others will get the chance to showcase their training with League technology against lesser foes. Those battles will take place in the smaller rings." As her voice raised, she regained her icy composure.

She looked up at a sound from the stands, then sighed. "It seems our esteemed guests would like us to get to the main event. Master Broadblade, you'll be in the center ring. I highly recommend arming yourself."

Me too, said Bloody Grim. *A single banglor is a joke but these Vendri look worthy. They're probably pack animals, which means they know how to fight together.*

Fine, but no edged weapons. We can knock two of them out quickly then negotiate.

"I bow to your years of experience in the field," said Grim.

He didn't wait to see if that got a rise from the Colonel. He wouldn't have much time before the match started so he walked to the weapons rack and grabbed a war staff. It was made of solid oak and capped with steel on each end. He spun it several times to get a sense of balance. It was

Krommian made so the balance was excellent.

He walked to the caged Vendri. They hadn't moved from their position, leaning against the bars of their cage. All three glared back at him.

"I assume you understand the common tongue," said Grim in a low voice. "I'm a prisoner like you. I don't want to hurt you but we will need to make this fight convincing. I was able to free the banglor I fought yesterday by throwing him into the stands. Today, I'd like to do the same for you. You have a choice, I can throw you into the stands to a place where you can escape. Or, I can throw you to a place where you can get vengeance on those who captured you."

The Vendri on the far left made a slow wheezing, barking noise which Grim recognized as laughter. "Youse is funny yuman, youse look strong, but not that strong. No. Us work together. Us yalready yave pack, no need more." It was intelligent enough to keep its voice low.

Grim looked back. Proust ushered the test subjects and researchers into the protective cages. There was no sign of Farber and his team. They'd been replaced with a line of crossbowmen that went all the way around the first row of stands, save for where the General and his councilors sat. Escape would be more difficult this time.

Grim smiled. He showed as much of his teeth as he could in what he hoped was aggressive. "Sorry to hear that," he said.

"Youse be more sorry when youse fight us," said the leader of the group.

"Think about it," said Grim. "If your pack starts to lose, know it's an option."

The creature made the low wheezing laugh again. "Youse

is funny yuman. Us almost sorry to kill youse."

Grim nodded and stepped back. He took a defensive stance, legs planted, staff held at the ready.

"The cage comes down in five, four, three, two....one," said Proust.

The three Vendri shot out of the cage on all fours the moment the bars dropped, just like the banglor. The leader, the one on Grim's left, sprinted further left in an effort to flank Grim. The one on the right sprinted right.

What the Vendri didn't expect was Grim to charge. His defensive stance was a feint to get the wolfmen to commit. Once the bars fell, Grim knew he had to eliminate one of the attackers as quickly as possible.

Remember, no killing.

I know. I still don't understand why you make things more *difficult when we're fighting to survive.*

Yeah, you do.

Bloody Grim gave a mental shrug. *Focus!*

The Vendri in front of him was not idle during Grim's charge. It overcame its surprise and charged to meet Grim, hackles raised. Grim watched as the fingers retracted, replaced with wicked looking claws. As Grim closed, it leapt to meet him.

Why do these things always jump? It doesn't make sense, mused Bloody Grim.

Stop thinking and fight!

Bloody Grim laughed.

The Vendri descended, claws extended and jaws open wide.

Grim neatly sidestepped. He swung the metal tipped staff and struck it in the temple hard enough to make a sickening hollow thump. The giant wolf fell to the ground, unconscious.

Grim looked over his shoulder to locate the other two Vendri, but they had committed to their flanking sprints and hadn't turned back yet. The first attack happened that fast.

By Krom, I hope we didn't kill it.

It breathes, now focus! shouted Bloody Grim.

Grim moved forward until he was in the center of the cage platform which held the Vendri when they were lifted to the sands. He spun to track the remaining two. Bloody Grim relished in the surprise painted on their faces when they saw their fallen companion. His manic laughter grew louder.

This enraged the Vendri. They charged from both sides, paying no heed to the pack strategy created before the fight.

Grim looked down at the four segments of cage which lay around him. It should affect their footing while on the ground, but maybe... He only had seconds before the wolfmen reached him. He grabbed for the middle of the cage segment on the side from which the leader approached. He tugged mightily with his right hand and prepared for the Vendri on his left to leap.

I hope this works.

With a final groan, the cage segment rose. Just in time. He could see the muscles of the Vendri bunching to spring. The muscles in his right arm swelled to monumental proportion and he put everything into lifting the cage segment. Then he heard it, a click. The segment locked in place.

Grim released the segment of the cage the same moment the leader of the Vendri crashed into it. It committed to its jumping attack and its forward momentum was too strong to do anything other than turn a shoulder and brace for impact.

It yipped in pain as it struck the bars then fell to the ground in a heap.

The other Vendri had a straight path to Grim. Pulling the segment of the cage left him off balance and unable to swing the staff as he had with the first Vendri. His strike, when it came, lacked leverage and power. The blow caught the wolfman in the abdomen but it was a glancing blow, not enough to redirect the creature's trajectory.

The wolfman scored a strike on Grim's shoulder with those vicious claws. Grim grunted when three deep furrows welled with crimson blood. The Vendri grinned in vindication and spun for another strike. "Youse is not so strong, not in beating tree Vendri."

Bloody Grim howled with laughter. While the Vendri spoke, Grim anchored his legs against his opponents and swiveled behind the creature. He put an arm around its neck and fell to the ground using gravity to bring it down with him. It was a simple grappling move all Krommians knew, but that's what made it so effective. The Vendri were not grapplers. The wolfman fell to its back with a whoosh of air exploding from it.

Grim locked eyes with the final Vendri, the leader, and began to squeeze. Blood pumped from his wound but the flow lessened as Bloody Grim's healing took effect. The wolf creature writhed and squirmed, but it lost most its breath when it fell to the ground. It didn't take more than a couple of seconds before the desperate motions weakened. Grim squeezed harder until no blood reached the creature's brain. When it fell unconscious he released his grip.

Bloody Grim continued laughing.

Not now, said Grim. *We need to give the leader another*

chance. Laughing is going to send it into a deeper fury.

Bloody Grim didn't reply, but he stopped laughing.

Grim moved to the bars to look at the Vendri leader, licking an injured paw. It leapt against the bars, snarling. The creature's spittle flew like angry rain.

"Stop," said Grim. "It doesn't have to end with three of you lying unconscious on the sand."

"They'se no dead?" said the Vendri, tilting its head to look.

"Look, they still breathe," said Grim. "Quickly, we need to keep fighting or men with arrows will shoot you."

I think I figured it out, said Bloody Grim. *Why these creatures jump during battle even though it puts them into a vulnerable position.*

Not the time, said Grim.

"I need you to charge from that side," said Grim, his eyes flickered to the far side of the cage. "Then I can throw you into the stands at the people who captured us."

It's because they're predators accustomed to attacking prey animals, Bloody Grim said. *Prey animals only flee, so when the predator jumps they can't hear it moving anymore.*

Fascinating, now focus! We have one shot at this, said Grim.

"Yes yuman, they will yave Vendri revenge." The Vendri stood tenderly on its hurt paw to test it. It sprinted to the far side of the sands. It wheeled in a wide turn then charged at Grim with a full head of steam. This time the creature didn't begin its leap until it reached Grim.

Grim fell to his back and pushed out his legs with all his strength. He launched the creature twenty meters into the air. It happened too quickly for the crossbowmen to react until the Vendri started down towards the VIP section of the stands.

Most of the soldiers armed with crossbows couldn't take a shot for fear of hitting the VIPs. A few of the crossbowmen on the side of the VIPs gathered their wits and fired. All but one of the bolts flew wide. The one that struck left a bloody furrow along the Vendri's shoulder, but it wasn't enough to arrest its motion.

Grim watched with a measure of satisfaction as the looks on the faces of the Councilors turned from joy to terror. They scrambled out of the way and over each other as the Vendri missile closed on them.

Grim felt a strange tinge of pride for his father who didn't flee. He unsheathed the sword at his waist and faced the danger barreling his way. The General leapt back as he calculated where the Vendri would land. He stood in a ready stance, footwork perfect as the creature crashed into the stands.

The other Councilors fled up the stairs. They flowed around the huge warrior in gladiator armor like turbulent river water around a boulder. The enormous man had a look of pure joy on his face as the Vendri landed in front of him. He clapped with glee, but no one seemed to notice him.

When the Vendri landed it took one look at the General with his sword and decided it could create more havoc by chasing down fleeing Councilors. It too avoided the large man and so did the General as he raced after the Vendri.

The Vendri swiped at the back of the slowest Councilor, a large man bordering on obese, who struggled to run up the broad tiers and benches of the Colosseum. The man screamed and fell when the Vendri struck, blood pouring from his back.

Two of the Councilors seemed to remember they were Krommian. They turned to face the creature pulling ornamental swords out of scabbards that looked brand new. The Vendri growled and swiped at the first sword with his right claw while following up with his left to disembowel the female Councilor in front of him. The woman shrieked and reached down to catch the innards spilling out.

The Vendri disarmed the other man with a contemptuous flick of its wrist before raking claws down the man's face and chest. It howled in triumph when the Councilor fell back, screaming in pain.

The howl abruptly ceased when the General plunged his sword into the Vendri's back. A moment later two crossbow bolts sunk into its side. The Vendri fell to a knee then slowly collapsed over one of the arena benches.

The General yelled for a healer.

Grim watched in horror at the mayhem he created. Then, his eye was drawn to the giant in the third row. He continued to applaud, and the applause was directed at Grim.

The man leapt from his perch, flying high in the air to land in front of Grim in an explosion of sand. When the sand cleared, the man gave a bow and Grim realized how large he really was. His arms and legs were twice the size of Grim's. Grim had to look up at him.

"Who are you?" asked Grim.

We have to get out of here, now! Bloody Grim screamed in panic in his head.

"Come now, you already know the answer to that question," said the man.

Grim looked around to see if anyone else noticed the two of them squaring off in the arena. The arena had gone silent.

Impossible. Not with the mayhem Grim had just created. His eye was drawn to a small sand wasp floating several paces away. Its wings were motionless. That didn't make sense. How could it just be floating there? Then he looked to Proust and the test subjects. They were frozen as well.

Grim flared his nostrils and took a breath. "You're Krom, aren't you?"

"Of course I am," said the god of battle. "And you are the finest warrior I've seen since awakening in this dusty place." He jutted his perfectly square chin behind him. "After the mayhem clears, would you mind telling those idiots on this 'war Council' to get water flowing through my city? It helps with the dust."

"Umm, okay," said Grim. "What are you doing here your divine battle-godness?" He had no idea how to address the god.

You sound like an idiot. He's going to kill us for sure, whined Bloody Grim.

Krom laughed, and the force of it made Grim want to cover his ears. "Tell your battle twin to rest easy. I'm not going to kill you for sounding like an idiot. I don't care for titles, only battle. Call me Krom."

"You can hear him?"

"Of course. I'm a god," said Krom as if that explained everything.

Ask him what a battle twin is, said Bloody Grim.

"Ask me yourself, battle twin," said Krom.

Ok, sir...Krom, said Bloody Grim without his usual confidence. *What am I?*

"You are the mental manifestation of pure battle. In that moment of blood and chaos with men fighting, killing and dying, you are the unmolested version of pure survival. You, my friend, live entirely in the moment. Your only role is to live until the next moment. You so embody this quality that it gives you an edge—strength, endurance, healing. Power. It's okay to find joy in this. Your peals of laughter echoed over the sands with a beauty no orchestra of Harp could ever match. It warmed my heart."

Krom laughed again and Grim feared his ears would burst. Hopefully Bloody Grim's healing would keep him from going deaf.

"Is a battle twin common?" asked Grim.

"Only in the greatest of warriors. Those that fully embrace battle while fighting, who also have the intelligence and moral code to question whether what they did was right. That's what causes the bifurcation, or split, in the consciousness. Taking the life of another creature is the ultimate expression of power. Weaker warriors get lost in that power. It becomes an aphrodisiac, then an addiction. They can't control it and become monsters. A true warrior questions every death, analyzes every fight, looks for how it could have gone better."

Grim cocked his head in surprise. "Bifurcation, aphrodisiac? You're different than I expected," said Grim.

Krom laughed uproariously and Grim felt blood leaking from his ears. "Yes, you expect Krom to be battle god. Battle god fight. Battle god kill. Battle god no think." He laughed again. "That's nonsense. You've studied war. The skilled warrior falls to the master strategist every time. A skilled warrior is not enough to compensate for inferior numbers or a battlefield carefully chosen by the enemy. I doubt there's another warrior who could beat you in a one-on-one fight, but when has battle ever been one-on-one? You must train your mind with the same discipline you train your body, young warrior."

Pretty similar to the philosophy he shared with the test subjects last night. Maybe Rose was wrong to loathe the gods?

Krom gave Grim a hard look and shook his head. "Huh. Well, I assume you trained your body once. Maybe it's time to train again?"

Grim nodded, but refused to feel ashamed. "Perhaps. It's been a rough couple of years."

Krom nodded. "A time of trials is necessary for every great warrior. I'm afraid there are trials yet to come. For that reason, I will give you a boon. Two actually. One will help you greatly in battle. The other, you will not enjoy, but I do it with your well-being in mind."

"I'm not worthy of boons, great Krom," said Grim. "I just want to live a quiet life. One without killing. The life of a craftsman."

Krom frowned. "I'm sorry young warrior, but that is not your path. As you know, sometimes killing is necessary. We shouldn't strive for it, but we shouldn't hide from it either. What you did with the Vendri was admirable—and hilarious—by the way."

Krom's booming laugh echoed across the sands.

"Your captors never expected to fight this day. Men and women of power often forget the skills of battle which brought them to that power. That is a mistake. Sending others to fight battles you wouldn't fight yourself is the coward's way. At least your father hasn't forgotten his will."

They both looked to the man, still standing above the

fallen Vendri, frozen in time.

"Your father will treat with you, provided you show him nothing but strength," said Krom softly. "He caused you irreparable harm, but he is nothing compared to the monsters in your future. Forgive him and move on, otherwise he will be the weight that drags you down."

Grim nodded. "Why am I the only one that can see you?"

"Because it's not time yet. The rest of the world will hear from us soon, but until then, warrior, only a chosen few will know we gods are here."

"Care to tell me about the boons you've given me?"

Krom laughed again. "And ruin the fun?"

Grim sighed.

"Go warrior, you have much to do and not much time to do it in. Make me proud."

The god's form became incorporeal. Then he waved and disappeared.

Grim felt a surge of energy sweep through him as the god vanished. He fell to one knee.

Time resumed and so did the screaming.

25

Nettie & Leesta

"Twenty thousand gold, a kilo of sulimite, and five grams of trunite per controller," said Bernard.

"Five grams? Are you kidding me? We have maybe ten milligrams!" Nettie shouted. "And I just figured out how to charge the capacitors." She slapped the conference table. Only then did she look around the table. Her face turned beet red. She didn't even remember standing up. She held a hand to her mouth in horror. "I'm so..." she said while sitting down.

"No, don't apologize," said Rose. "I love your passion. We know your anger is not directed at Bernard, but at the news he brings. It's not his terms, but the VNC's. Bernard, is there a chance they can be bargained with?"

Bernard pushed his chair back, looking slightly stunned. "Maybe...if you do the negotiating ma'am, but I doubt it. They claim they have more orders than staff to fulfill them."

"I'm sorry, Bernard," said Nettie. "What did they say about our request to license the technology so we can build our own?"

"They laughed at me. They're not going to license any neuro-tech."

Nettie bit down on her anger. "Why would they? They're the only supplier in Grendar. If we could buy just one...I'm sure we could reverse engineer the damn thing."

"You know what this means, don't you?" asked Promo.

White nodded. "We have to go on a Quest. It's the only way we're getting our hands on that much tru."

"Can we handle a Quest?" asked Gavin.

Promo shook her head. "Not even close."

"You said we have over forty professional level warriors who have unlocked at least one skill."

Promo stared at Gavin flatly. "That's true, but we've been building an army, not a Questing team. I've split our League warriors amongst the units that don't have experience in the Pool. I can't take a random group of warriors and expect them to work together like a tight Questing team. Only way this works is if we build a roster and train them together under intense circumstances."

"How long will that take?" asked Gavin.

"Six months to a year if we want most to survive. These Quests are only getting harder," said Promo.

"Six months?" asked Gavin. His eyes widened in shock. "Do we have that much time?"

"To a year," said Promo, not letting Gavin get away with that annoying thing every leader did when given a range of estimates. "We can cut that time significantly with access to a Pool."

"If you could use a Pool, how long would it take?" asked Gavin.

Promo looked to White. "Six weeks, a month. Maybe,"

she said.

White nodded. "If we train every day," said the big Guard. "But if we have access to a Pool, we don't need the trunite. Damned if we do, damned if we don't."

"Could we lease time in a Pool?" asked Nettie.

"How would we do that?" asked Promo.

"Rent it, pay for each day we use it," said Nettie.

"I know what lease means," said Promo with a scowl. "But none of the League teams are going to rent us that time, so who do we lease it from?"

Rose looked from Promo to Gavin. "It's a good idea. Didn't Carlin say the League used Pool technology in an attempt to bribe the leaders of the Garden Cities?"

"Meaning what?" said White. "Did they actually give them Pools?"

Gavin nodded. "I think so, but only the holdouts. It didn't take much to bribe Krom, Brickolage and Harpstra. There's rumors Harpstra might have one, but Carlin could find no evidence of it. Vonderia already had the technology."

"Which leaves Astra or Loam," said Rose.

"I can't imagine the Astrans will work with us," said White.

"Not unless we have someone who can out-devout them," said Bernard. The man bent his head and silently mouthed the words out-devout to himself several times as the others pretended not to notice.

"Which leaves Loam," said Promo. "Grundle is already down there meeting with the Keepers. Can you use your Sage powers," Promo waggled her fingers, "to add Pool usage to his list of asks?"

The leadership team stared, wide-eyed as Rose closed her

eyes and moved her fingers about in a hypnotic dance. No one at the table had ever seen her use her powers. She always just *knew* stuff. She opened her eyes and smiled. "Nope. Wiggling my fingers still doesn't bring visions of the future or project me to the astral to communicate with Loamian shape-shifters. It's a shame, I was hoping it would work this time."

A laugh exploded from Nettie. She had never seen the playful side of Rose before. The rest of the team joined a moment later.

"We can send a delegation," said Gavin. "What was Grundle's friend's name?"

"Leesta was the other Loamian on Ghost Squad," said White. "I wouldn't call her a diplomat though."

"This is important enough for me to go in person," said Rose. "The Loamians are our best chance for an alliance against the Collective. Maybe I can add a little gravitas to Grundle's conversations with the Keepers."

Gavin frowned. "Won't the Collective expect that? Carlin's eyes and ears believe the Collective has written off the Loamians. It would be the perfect site for an ambush."

Rose nodded, face all business. "I have divined nothing to indicate that level of planning, but I'll attempt to scry this evening before we commit to a plan."

"I'd like to lead your escort," said Gavin. "Could I borrow several candidates to analyze the Pool before we commit to a lease?"

Promo nodded.

"I could go," said Nettie. "I have almost as much experience with the Pool as Ghost Squad. It would give me a chance to peek at the technology."

"No offense, Miss Patching, but I was hoping for Ghosts with skills that were more...battle-centric," said Gavin tactfully.

Nettie scowled. "You want brawn, not brains. I get it, but I can hold my own in a fight."

"Why not take both?" said Promo. "White and I can't take a break from training the troops, but there's no reason Nettie can't join a larger contingent of League-trained warriors."

"What about the trunite capacitors?" asked Bernard. "They're critical to our nomadic defense turrets."

"I passed the plans to Quon'Ji. She knows what she's doing," said Nettie. "If I can get a head start on reverse engineering the Pool we may be able to bypass the VNC and not need to go on a Quest at all."

All eyes turned to Rose.

Rose folded her hands on the table. "Having Nettie with us will increase our chances of success. I want her there."

Nettie swallowed a celebratory whoop and nodded. The smile on her face ruined the solemn look she was going for.

"Can you divine a Quest that gives us the reward we need?" asked Promo. She caught Rose's head shake and continued. "Or nudge us towards one divined by another Sage that gets us the trunite?"

Rose frowned. "Shared Quest knowledge results in paradox. If you know the reward, it changes the outcomes. Does that make sense?"

"Not at all," said Promo. "But I stopped trying to figure this out a long time ago. It feels like a waste that we can't use your abilities to help our cause. Is there a work around?"

"What do you mean by that?" asked Rose.

"Could you 'accidentally' leave a note lying around which

happens to reveal which Quest has the reward we need? Then one of us 'accidentally' finds it?" asked Promo.

Gavin grinned as his gaze shifted from Rose to Promo. "I can't tell you how many times I tried something like that," said Gavin. "I'll save us a lot of time by saying, it doesn't work that way. Shortcut the process, change the result."

A collective groan rose from those around the table looking to sidestep fate, but it was lighthearted. They knew it was a losing proposition.

"Any other topics before we wrap the leadership meeting?" asked Gavin.

"Any word from Grim or Flask?" asked Nettie.

Rose shook her head. "Nothing yet, but Carlin is due to return in the next several days. He should have new information."

Nettie picked at a loose thread on her pants. "And you haven't *seen* anything about either of them?"

Rose shook her head. "Nothing I can share, except to say they're both alive and making progress on what we tasked them."

Nettie gave a sigh of relief. "Thank you. That helps."

Rose gave her a sad smile before turning to Gavin. "How long will it take us to travel to Loam?"

"Five days if we take Grundle's route, passing through the outskirts of Krom. Three days if we take the southern ferry across the Rhune. Faster, but more dangerous," said Gavin.

Rose nodded to Gavin then turned to Promo. "Can you handpick a League-trained escort for us?"

"When do you need them?" asked Promo.

"Tomorrow morning," said Rose.

* * *

The day dawned dark and rainy at the Liberator camp. Nettie packed her gear with the expectation she might be in Loam for weeks. If Rose was successful in negotiating a lease for the Pool, Nettie hoped to stay until the Quest team arrived. With any luck, she'd have access to a Pool controller the entire time.

She packed her tools and tried to think of what she was missing when Leesta walked into her room.

"You're late," said the tall, scowling Loamian. "Rose sent me to fetch you. She said you remembered everything but the multi spanner. Find it and let's go."

Nettie smacked her forehead. Of course! She lent it to Quon'Ji yesterday. That woman was notorious for stealing tools. "Fine, I know exactly where it is. I'll be out in two minutes."

"Take your time," said Leesta. "We're all just waiting in the rain...getting wet."

Nettie ignored her. They were going to be in the rain for a lot longer than two minutes today. She slipped an oilskin duster over her shoulders, pulled up the hood, and ran to Quon'Ji's room.

"Sorry, sorry," said the young woman when Nettie came running in. "I meant to bring it back last night."

"Sure you did. Now the Loamian sasquatch is angry with me." Nettie took a deep breath, steeled herself and walked into the rain.

* * *

They'd been traveling for three hours. The rain grew steadily stronger. Leesta led the group south on an overgrown road leading from the Liberator camp. The foliage overtaking the road hungrily absorbed most of the downpour, but what was left of the road turned to mud.

When the mud got bad enough, the Liberators were forced to dismount and lead the horses so as not to risk a broken leg. After an hour slogging through the muck, even the hardiest Liberators questioned why they joined the cause.

Leesta looked to Rose every ten minutes or so as if expecting her to divine a way out of the rain. "Will this stop any time soon?" she finally asked the Sage.

Rose looked up to the sky, letting the rain fall directly into her face. She shrugged. "Even Sages can't predict the weather."

Leesta grunted and moved to the front of their small column. She reached out to the foliage in front of them on several occasions, tapping into her nature affinity. The plants responded with nothing but their version of joy at the bounty of rain. Their enthusiasm was as bad as the annoying Bricker's. Leesta couldn't understand how such a distasteful person like Nettie could keep such a high level of enthusiasm as they sloshed through another small river of rainwater.

If she was being honest with herself, Leesta knew her bad mood had more to do with their destination than the rain, or the company she kept. Leesta dreaded returning to Loam, the city of her birth. She did not leave on good terms.

Leesta stomped down hard on what looked like a piece of

dry earth. The earth crumbled and tumbled down the slope of the river bank and into the rising Rhune. The road(*more like path, but whatever*) followed the Rhune on its passage south. The river was higher than she had seen it in years.

Leesta looked back down the path. They had been hiking upwards for the past half hour or so, and the toll showed on the non-warriors in the group. The Rhune was a good twenty paces below so a crumbling path wasn't cause for worry, but Leesta didn't fully trust any of the group who weren't part of Ghost Squad.

"Stay on the far side of the path," she shouted to those following her. If she was going to guide this group, she was going to take the role seriously.

She surveyed the team as they caught up to her. She had no concerns about the ex-Ghosts. Pyre complained softly to Piety and Rice as they trudged at the front of the group. The two Astrans had the patience of saints. Leesta told Pyre to bugger off three times already this morning. How a man that powerful in elemental magic could be such a wimp when it came to rain confounded her.

She looked at the skinny man babbling away to the silent Astrans and realized, in a shocking moment of self aware-ness, that what she really hated was how negative the man was all the time. *Kind of like me.* One might have thought it would make them companions in shared misery, but they loathed each other. Apparently, there was only room for one negative Nettie in the group. She smiled as she thought of how the name would annoy the young Bricker.

Following the first trio came Nettie, Rose and Gavin. The three of them were in heated discussion. Rather, Nettie and Gavin were in heated discussion while Rose interjected something which made no sense every once in a while. *Why did it seem like anything Nettie was involved in was heated? Some people had opinions on everything.*

Taking up the rear were four Liberators she didn't know well. And Reaver. She remembered what Promo said when she asked her why the ranged Striker was going with them. "Reaver needs to keep moving or he gets antsy. Besides, you couldn't ask for someone better to watch your tail."

Leesta couldn't argue with that. She'd seen Reaver train. He claimed he could shoot the wings off a dragonfly at fifty meters and no one had the guts to dispute him.

As the rain dripped over the brim of her hood, she realized she felt something else as she looked at the group. Something she hadn't expected. Pride. She spent so much of her time annoyed, feeling underutilized and resentful that she forgot how impressive the company she kept was. Every one of them had unlocked skills once believed to be fairy tales. Rose was a bloody Sage! And Leesta was a part of this group. Screw her family. She was a member of Ghost Squadron and now a Liberator. Not one of *them* could claim such titles. So what if she never qualified for the Keeper trials like her six siblings. Leesta was a member of Ghost Squad.

"Any chance we can stop for a midday meal soon, dear?" asked Rose when they caught up.

Leesta jumped, caught up in her musings, surprised to see most of the group standing around her. Only Reaver still walked up the trail.

Leesta dropped to a knee and sunk her fingers into the wet earth. She tapped into the fungal network below the surface and surveyed the immediate area. The Rhune was a blank spot as the water moved too quickly, but she sensed three giant oaks a half kilometer away just off the trail. Their large canopies would give them a chance for a dry meal.

Leesta nodded. "Ten minutes ahead is a copse of oaks. It should give us the chance to get dry before moving on."

"Sounds lovely, dear," said Rose. She put a hand on Leesta's arm in gratitude. The simple gesture made the young Loamian feel powerful and protective.

Leesta put her own hand over Rose's. "I'll move ahead and see if I can't convince the oaks to keep us dry."

"Mind if I join her?" asked Pyre. "A fire could raise spirits."

"You think you can find dry wood?" asked Nettie.

"Who do you think you're talking to?" said Pyre with a cocky grin. His eyes shifted to bright orange for a moment and his skin took on that tanned look. "Leesta, wait up!"

She ignored him and trudged forward.

"Why does it feel like I'm always chasing after you when we're on patrol?"

She smiled at the memory. "At least this time we don't have ants trying to eat us."

"*Yet.* We don't have ants trying to eat us yet," said Pyre. "Our last Quest was only a hundred clicks that way." He pointed vaguely southwest. "I'm surprised we haven't seen any red rock yet."

"We should see the rock by tonight," said Leesta.

"Once we hit the desert, maybe this bloody rain will stop."

"Or maybe not," said Leesta darkly, thinking about the flash flood that took Lodin, Mouse and Rhaine.

Pyre kicked at one of the rocks on the road then cursed when it didn't move. Leesta knew he blamed himself for Mouse and Rhaine's deaths. Pyre was an asshole, but he was a Ghost. Ghosts looked after each other. "Maybe not," he muttered.

They walked in silence until the oaks came into view. Leesta looked at the unusually quiet Vonderian. It was obvious he was torturing himself. She was surprised how that affected her. "You know that wasn't your fault," she said. "I wasn't bringing it up to make you feel bad."

"Forget it," said Pyre. "That's what I try to do. Can you sense any dead wood lying around?" he said in a desperate attempt to change the subject.

She shook her head, wanting to draw him out, wanting to help. Not knowing how. "You can talk to me you know," she tried.

His eyes flashed red. "And say what Leesta? You can't stand me. I get it. I'm annoying. I've always been annoying. We went through awful shit together but we're never going to be friends. I accept that."

Leesta couldn't believe how much the words hurt. He was right. She couldn't stand him, but they were members of Ghost Squad. "Maybe not, you prick, but Ghost Squad runs deeper than family. I've seen you die a hundred times and you've done the same with me. We've seen each other at our darkest and our proudest. Don't you dare brush me off as if that didn't mean anything."

His eyes lost their fiery orange color, fading to a solemn gray. "You're right. I'm sorry. I'm just so screwed up, I don't know where to start. Nobody deserves to deal with my crap when they have so much of their own, you know? Let me go find some firewood so I can burn some shit." He said the last with an almost convincing smile.

"Alright, but this conversation isn't over," said Leesta.

She closed her eyes and made contact with the earth. "Head that way twenty paces and you'll come to a dead pine."

Pyre followed her directions without looking back. She heard loud cracking noises from his direction as the others filed in to the small sanctuary offered by the oaks.

A moment later, a smiling Pyre walked back with a handful of firewood. "Piety, Rice, I could use your help taking down the rest of that dead pine. A big fire is what we need to dry my Vonn's damned socks! Now, back up."

Pyre's skin went dark orange as he tapped into his elemental power. The wood sizzled and popped for several seconds before bursting into flames.

"Bow down to the great fire-starter," said Piety, pushing her arms out in mock worshipful homage.

"That's better," said Pyre. "That's the reaction I expect anytime you see me from now on."

"You're an idiot," said Rice. "Can you dry the rest of the wood we brought so us lowly humans can feed the fire?"

"I'll do you one better," said Pyre. His eyes turned a brownish orange this time.

Leesta stuck a hand in the dirt and felt it as Pyre's earth and fire magic went to work, simultaneously warming the earth around them until the water on the ground began to softly steam.

"Careful, or you're going to kill the roots of these oaks," said Leesta.

"How much should I take it down?" asked Pyre.

"Two, maybe three degrees. The fungi are fine but the young roots are in pain."

Pyre began to sweat, that level of temperature modulation was incredibly advanced magic. "How's that?"

"Not bad Twenty-six," she said. "We can comfortably sit on the ground without getting any wetter, and you didn't kill anything."

Leesta looked up and saw a break in the clouds. "Would you look at that," she said. "We might even get a sunny afternoon. Things are looking up."

That's when she saw it. "Everybody get close to the trunks of the oaks," she hissed. "Now! Pyre, can you kill the fire?"

He nodded, knowing when to play and when to keep his mouth shut. "What'd you see?" he whispered.

"Ach'Su," she whispered back loudly enough for the group to hear.

The travelers sank into absolute silence.

26

A dip in the Rhune

"But I thought Kavi killed the Ach'Su," whispered Nettie.

"Shh," hissed Leesta. "Be quiet for *once* in your life."

Leesta pushed her awareness into the earth for signs of the Ach'Su's passing but found none. She ignored the Bricker woman's glare and continued to probe. Then she nodded to Rose.

"It was flying south," said Leesta. "Frankly, I was surprised to see it this far north."

"Don't be," spat Nettie. "We first ran into it when we were all the way up in Stonecrest."

"He did kill an Ach'Su," said Leesta. "With Pip's help, but there was more than one of them."

"Just so," said Rose before Nettie could respond. "I don't see an encounter with the Ach'Su in our immediate future as long as we're near the river. Pyre, please light the fire again, it's safe now."

Leesta raised an eyebrow at Rose. Who was she to doubt a Sage? She lowered her guard and did her best to get comfortable. The good mood caused by the anticipation of a hot and relatively dry meal had vanished with the arrival of the Ach'Su. Even worse, the break in the clouds proved only a short reprieve. By the time they finished lunch, it started raining again.

Leesta grabbed her dry duster and headed back on the road. Things could have been worse. They could have had to fight the Ach'Su.

Maybe a little rain wasn't so bad after all.

* * *

Nettie hated the rain. When she was at University, she loved rainy days because it was nice to sit and study while the rain pattered on the sloped roof of the library. It soothed and enhanced the coziness of the book lined rooms.

She hadn't felt cozy in years. Ever since her brother Pick died, her life jumped from one emergency to the next. She hadn't slowed in what felt like ten years but, in reality, hadn't been ten months. In that time, she hadn't paused once to read a book which wasn't used to solve a specific engineering problem. She hadn't taken a break to look at a piece of art or stopped to listen to music. Ever since she became a Ghost, every waking hour was spent trying to survive or keep others alive.

A busy life of survival and purpose filled her with passion. Yet, she always had that nagging thought she was missing something. It wasn't until right now, when she thought of being cozy in the University library, that she understood what. She missed spending time letting her brain roam free, letting it daydream and travel along the wild roads of imagination.

As she traveled through the rain with this amazing group of people, she realized she wasn't actively solving a problem. Her brain was free to flit over whatever ideas it wanted. Suddenly, the rain hitting her oiled gear wasn't so bad. The sighting of the Ach'Su not so ominous. For the next three days, she had nothing to do but get from one place to the next. She had nothing but time to think.

Coziness wasn't dictated by place or weather. Coziness was a state of mind afforded to those with enough time they could waste it in the pursuit of daydreaming. Suddenly, Nettie wished this wet, dreary journey along the side of the Rhune would never end.

Her mind turned to what she would do after all of this was over. What did she actually want? A small Bricker home with all the amenities, a couple of children running around? No, that was not the life for her.

She saw herself returning to the University, a conquering hero, lauded for the amazing architectural developments she invented as a Liberator. That felt hollow too. She didn't want fame, she hated being the center of attention. She thought about Tribar—a lab where she could invent and build anything she wanted while some warrior husband or wife, maybe Kavi...oooh or how about Promo, governed the people in their community. *That* was the life of a happy Amelie Nettie Patching.

She grinned at the thought and it struck her. That's what she already had with the Liberators. Well, sans husband or wife. What really made her happy was solving problems. She thrived on learning and the Liberators went out of their way to make sure she did nothing but. At that moment, she was so grateful to Rose for the life she had that she moved her horse up to tell her so.

She was only paces away when the road collapsed beneath Rose. It fell into the river, taking the Sage with it.

Nettie screamed, but her shock lasted only a microsecond as her brain turned to solving this new problem. "Leesta! Any greenery on the banks that can bring Rose to safety?"

The tall Loamian rushed over and sunk her hands into the riverbank. "I'm sorry. The river is moving too fast. No! Her head went under!"

"We're sure as hell not going to let her drown," said Nettie. "I need wood and fiber for ropes. Can you get them for me?"

"We don't have time to build a damned raft!" shouted Gavin.

"I do," said Nettie. "Stop wasting it panicking and get me the material. Pyre, if you have water magic that can help stabilize Rose until we get there, use it."

Pyre nodded. His skin turned an opalescent blue and his eyes filled with a watery film. "I'm not as skilled with water, but I can skate."

"Go," said Nettie. "We're right behind you."

Pyre jumped towards the river. He fell several meters and landed on a small disc of condensed water. He stabilized himself as the current grabbed the disc. He put another disc in front of that and stepped tentatively towards it. Then another in front of that. He stepped again. After a shaky start, his motions took on a skating tempo and he began to move faster than the current. The observers on the bank saw him gaining on the flailing and bobbing form of Rose.

Leesta called in every favor she'd ever done the earth,

asking trees and surrounding foliage for wood, vines and fresh bark.

Rice took a different approach. His fists glowed with holy light and he punched through trunks of nearby trees until they collapsed in a cloud of splinters and sawdust. In under a minute, they had an impressive pile of vines, logs, and branches at Nettie's feet.

Nettie closed her eyes. She'd never built a boat or even a raft. She'd never needed to, but come on, it was just a raft! Nettie looked down at the growing pile of raw materials. "That will work," she said softly. The others couldn't hear her over the desperate noises of producing more materials. "That's good!" she yelled. "Stand back!"

Nettie spun and the raft coalesced around her. She purposefully built it next to the fallen section of road so they could slide it down the slope into the river.

The eyes of her companions widened as the raft appeared in front of them. It was far bigger than anyone expected. It could easily fit all the Liberators and have room left over for a horse. Nettie squatted back, exhausted.

From the time Rose fell in, to finishing the raft, less than ninety seconds had passed. Too much time! Nettie looked downriver to see Pyre closing in on Rose's floating form. She wasn't flailing anymore, and Nettie imagined she could see slightly darker water around Rose's moving form that looked like blood.

"Go, go, go! She's not going to make it," yelled Gavin, eyes wide with fear and panic.

"We're going to need everyone's help to get the raft in the water," said Nettie. "One. Two. Three. Heave."

The raft slid to the water where Leesta caught it. Piety,

Nettie and Gavin joined Leesta on the raft. Nettie grabbed the rudder while Leesta and Piety grabbed the two poles Nettie crafted. "Stay up front and be ready to pull her out when we reach her," said Nettie.

The raft edged into the current and the women pushed for greater speed. Nettie steered them past rocks and floating obstacles in their mad chase to catch Pyre and Rose.

Pyre finally reached Rose. He created a large disc of condensed water next to her, grabbed her cloak and pulled. He flipped her on her back so her upper body lay on the disc. Her face was white and it didn't look like she was breathing. *How did she not see this coming?* thought Nettie. Pyre looked upriver to see Nettie's raft navigating the rapids.

"Hurry!" he yelled. "She's not breathing and I don't know how much longer I can hold her up!"

The women on the raft poled faster as they closed on the floundering mage and inert Sage. When they were five meters away, Pyre's platform struck an exposed rock. It popped like a soap bubble and mage and Sage dropped into the water.

"No!" yelled Gavin.

"Take this," said Leesta, handing Gavin her pole. She shrugged out of her cloak and dove into the water.

* * *

The icy river shocked her system. Leesta's head broke the surface and she took a surprised breath. Then she dove under. "Help me!" she screamed into the water sending out a blast

312

of desperate images, hoping beyond hope that any creature might catch the call and help.

She had no time to be shocked when a school of brown river trout surrounded her with concern. She'd never been able to communicate with animals before. It mattered little now. She knew the theory, so she sent images of Pyre and Rose feeding the trout plump mayflies if the fish could swim under them and buoy them to the surface.

The fish complied and within moments a carpet of fins and scales lifted Pyre and Rose to the surface.

She sighed in relief as Piety and Gavin lifted first Rose then Pyre to the raft. Nettie sighted Leesta and reached a hand off the stern of the boat. Leesta swam towards the small woman and gratefully took the extended arm, pulling herself on to the lashed logs.

"Anybody see any mayflies?" was all she could think to say as she flipped over on her back and took a long deep breath.

Piety pushed Rose's chin back then pushed on her chest twice. She put her mouth over Rose's and breathed deeply into the Sage's mouth. She pushed twice more on her chest and repeated the breathing motion.

When Rose finally coughed up water Gavin cried in relief.

Piety moved her to her side so she could drain the rest of the water from her lungs. She prayed for healing and a soft white light engulfed Piety and Rose. Rose's color shifted from pale white to her normal pinkish, yellow hue.

Rose's eyes blinked a moment later. She caressed the side of Gavin's face, still wet from tears, rain and river water. "Thank you," she whispered.

She turned her head to look at each of the Liberators who

313

saved her and thanked them individually. "All of you are amazing. Remember what you're capable of," she said and closed her eyes.

Piety kept her hand on Rose's chest. "She'll be fine, we need to let her rest."

Nettie looked at Leesta still lying on her back. "You were incredible Leesta! I didn't know you could communicate with fish!"

"It wouldn't have mattered if Pyre hadn't stabilized Rose before we got there."

Pyre brushed wet hair from his face. "Thank you for saving us. I thought we were goners until I felt that ripple of scales. Rose is right, you're amazing Leesta. You saved my life. Again."

Leesta smiled at him. "That's what we do isn't it?" She turned to Nettie. "I'm sorry I've been such a grumpy bitch. The raft you built, in all of three seconds, is something the Tinkerer himself couldn't have done. Rose wouldn't have made it without you."

"Water under the raft," said Nettie with a smile. "Let's see if we can't pole this thing over to that eddy. The bank looks low enough, we might be able to pull it up."

"With Rose unconscious, the raft may be the best way to get her to the ferry," said Gavin.

"Hmmm," said Nettie. Leesta recognized that look on Nettie's face. She knew, that in her mind, she was already building a safer raft. "It would be more comfortable than lashing her to her horse."

Gavin looked uncertain. "Fine, we'll have Reaver and Pyre lead the rest of the group on horseback. Unless you think you could build us a bigger raft to fit us and the horses?"

Nettie shook her head. "Too tired, and I don't think I could pull it off if I tried, but this will hold the five of us. As long as we scout the river ahead, no reason why the Rhune can't take us all the way south."

27

Derkin's Ferry

With their reckless pace, they made it to the ferry a day ahead of schedule. A small village had built up around the crossing, which the locals dubbed Derkin's Ferry. With the recent traffic from the Southern Market, there was plenty of coin to be made for enterprising ferrymen and stevedores. Where there were ferrymen, there was call for drink and women.

When the Liberators arrived in the small settlement, Gavin gladly handed over a gold talon for four rooms in the shabby riverside inn. It was a fortune for the rundown rooms, but after traveling through the previous night, they were ready to drop. It felt like a bargain.

Gavin negotiated passage across the Rhune for dawn the next morning. The hired ferry was more than large enough to get the Liberators, their gear, and horses across with room left for other passengers.

A small, gnomish looking Bricker helped Piety, Rose and Nettie pull the raft from the water. "Interesting craftsmanship. Have you considered selling her?" he said. His eyes roved from Piety to Nettie to Rose. They widened slightly as he looked at the tired, bedraggled Sage. He soon fixed on Nettie as the most likely creator of the raft.

"I'm not sure how you did the lashings but it appears you left room for a propulsion device on the stern. What did you have in mind for propulsion?"

Nettie helped Rose from the raft until Gavin scooped her up, then looked at the small man studying her raft. "I'm sorry, it's been a harrowing journey. Can we discuss this in the morning? What was your name, stranger?"

He waved away her apology. "Oh, no need for us to be strangers, the name is Rin Keter."

"Okay Rin," said Nettie. "Yes, I am interested in selling and I'd be happy to discuss my thoughts on propulsion as long as you're up before dawn."

The odd man smiled. Nettie's eyes were drawn to the gap between his front teeth. "I'd be happy to buy you an ale after you get settled," he said.

"Perhaps," said Nettie. "Right now, I need to get out of these wet clothes and get some food in me."

"Oh my," said Rin.

Nettie blushed. "*After* I put on some dry clothes."

"That does seem more reasonable than the alternative," said Rin. "Tell you what. Leave the raft with me and I will lash it to an empty slip. I will talk to some of the ferrymen to see if there's interest in a purchase. After you change and eat, I'll meet you in the common room of the Jaunty Rapid and we can discuss proposed terms, your plans for propulsion and any other engineering topics you find interesting. How does that sound?"

Nettie sluiced water from her forehead and gave a tired sigh. "Frankly, it sounds too good to be true. What's the catch?"

Rin shrugged. "A small finder's fee if there's interest. My rate will be fair and will become more so when you talk me through your propulsion ideas."

"Very well, I accept. See you in the Jaunty Rapid in an hour."

Rin smiled, spat on his hand and pushed it her way.

She looked at the hand in disgust.

He blushed. "Sorry, that's how the river folk around here seal a deal. They're very particular about binding everything with some form of water."

"That's disgusting."

"I suppose it is." Rin wiped his hand on his pants and nodded to her. "No spit shaking then. I'll see you in an hour."

Piety waited for Nettie several paces from the river. "What a strange man," said Nettie to the Astran Guard.

"Huh, hadn't noticed. Then again, I think all Brickers are crazy," Piety said, tempering the words with a grin.

Nettie smiled back. "And I thought all Astrans had no sense of humor."

The rooms in the Jaunty Rapid were small, drafty and smelled like tar. At least they were dry, thought Nettie, as the drizzle outside turned to a downpour. The owner must continue to add tar to the roof anytime they discovered a leak. Which had to be often, considering the shoddy workmanship. Nettie couldn't help passing judgment on any building she walked into these days.

There were two small beds per room. Gavin convinced the owner to bring an extra pallet into each. Nettie split her room with Piety and Leesta. The three of them changed out of their wet clothes and draped them over the foot boards of the two beds. There was a small fireplace that didn't look usable. There were no ashes and no grate for firewood. Luckily, there was plenty of blankets.

The smell of food and sound of men drinking bled through the floors and wafted up the narrow staircase. It was motivation enough for the three women to dress quickly. The aroma of a hearty stew won the war between appetite and exhaustion.

They descended the stairs into a tavern filled with formidable men of disrepute. Stevedores prided themselves on their base nature.

The women ignored the catcalls and surveyed the room. With relieved sighs, they saw Gavin had beat them to the common room and secured several tables in the back.

On the way to the back, one of the larger men slapped Leesta's bottom. She turned and leveled a punch that knocked the man off his chair. The other three men laughed uproariously at their fallen companion.

He looked up at Leesta with love in his eyes. She shook her head and kept moving. They made it back to the tables and gratefully grabbed chairs.

"Is Rose strong enough to join us?" asked Nettie.

Gavin shook his head. "She needs rest. She muttered something about needing her strength for the next couple of days."

"And I was hoping we were past the hard part of the journey," said Nettie.

"I'm sure she meant for the upcoming negotiations," said Gavin.

The rest of the Liberators slowly filed down the stairs and

joined the growing party at the back of the common room. The moment Pyre sat down, the innkeeper walked over with heaping platters of lamb, freshly baked rolls and an entire cook-pot of stew. It was enough to feed three times their number. Eyes slowly turned to Reaver.

The man shrugged. "What? I told him we hadn't eaten in days. Can you honestly tell me we're not going to finish all that?"

The Liberators took the statement as a challenge and conversation was replaced by the sounds of chewing and cutlery clinking against crockery.

With her stomach full, Nettie was disappointed she hadn't seen Rin yet. He was an odd one, no doubt. Not a single augmentation enhanced his body, but those eyes hinted at a knowledge far greater than his years.

As if the thought summoned the man, he burst through the front door of the inn. "Gather arms, we're under attack!" he shouted into the busy common room.

The ferrymen and dockworkers ignored him.

Nettie jumped up and rushed over to him, surprised no one reacted. "What do you mean we're under attack?"

"Just that. I heard screaming and smelled smoke blowing from the east."

She looked around, yet no one took action. "Why are they ignoring you?"

Rin looked just as puzzled. "I don't know. Brickers don't get much respect this far south."

Rin and Nettie jumped back as the door to the inn flew open. A large man with a huge red beard and unruly hair stepped into the common room. He had an arrow with a black shaft and black fletching sticking out of his chest. Rain and wind raged behind him making him look like a storm god.

"Move, you fools!" said the man in a booming voice that matched his stature. "We're under attack from the...from the...," blood began to bubble into his words and he fell to a knee. "Go. We're. Under. Siege," he croaked. He slumped back against the open door and collapsed into the night.

This time, the reaction was pandemonium. These were hard men but none of them soldiers. "Who's attacking?" asked one man. "And why now?"

"Something strong enough to down Red John! Quit talking and arm yourselves," shouted the innkeeper.

Most of the men fled into the night. Others grabbed rusty weapons or made makeshift clubs from the inn's chairs and tables. The big man Leesta flattened looked at his fellow stevedores and said, "Finish your ales, it's time to earn some hazard pay." He grabbed his club and walked into the night with half the men following him.

Nettie rushed back to the table of Liberators. They looked to her for direction. She took a breath. "Leesta, Reaver, scout to the east and report back when you know what we're facing. Gavin, get Rose to the ferry. No, scratch that, the ferry will be chaos, get her to the raft. Rin, is the raft still docked to one of the slips?"

The gnomish Bricker nodded. "It's docked at the northern-most slip. Farthest upriver."

"Gavin, did you hear that?" asked Nettie.

Gavin blinked. "What?"

"Look at me," said Nettie. "Get Rose and take her to the raft, it's in the farthest slip upriver. You see any signs of danger and you go. You leave us, you understand? Rose must survive. I will send news when we have more information, but you need to go now!"

Gavin snapped out of whatever inaction had taken him. He stood, grabbed his long spear and darted for the stairs.

She shook her head in surprise, wondering what had taken over Gavin. He wasn't the same since the river experience. She turned back to Rin. "Does this town have a wall or gates? Any defenses?"

Rin shook his head. "None to speak of. The town posts a sentry with a swinging gate so they can take a tariff on goods from the Southern Market, but it only blocks the roads. People can and do get around the sentry all the time. There's holes everywhere."

Nettie nodded grimly. Not what she wanted to hear.

"Pyre, find high ground facing east. Whether that's a second story or a roof, I don't care. We're going to need ranged support. Make sure it's something you can abandon quickly if we have to run. If you see anything chasing Leesta or Reaver when they return, light it up."

Pyre nodded and ran into the night.

"Piety, Rice, I want you outside setting up a defense of the inn if it comes to that. Rice, I know you're a Striker but that fist of yours can be used for protection."

"I think you're the only Fort in the Group, Net," said Piety.

The League designation of Fort still fit, Nettie had built a lot of fortifications since she joined the Liberators. "I know. I'll be out there momentarily," Nettie said.

Piety and Rice followed after the dockworkers. Piety pulled her mace from her belt as she stepped over the fallen Red John.

Nettie turned to the remaining four Liberators. "None of

you are League trained, do I have that right?"

"Yes ma'am," said Colson, one of the men she met for the first time on this trip. "We're diplomats and traders."

"You may need to become warriors before this is done," said Nettie darkly. "Grab some sort of weapon, even if it is just a table leg. I want you to escort Rose and Gavin to the raft. Oscar and Henna, grab the gear from our rooms, pack it into wherever it fits and bring it to the raft. Colson and Gar, lead the horses to the river. We're not going to be able to get all of them on the raft but they'll have a far better chance on the riverbank then they will tied up in the stable."

Oscar and Henna ran up the stairs. Colson and Gar left by the side door nearest the stable.

"Rin, do you know anything about defensive structures?"

He gave her a crooked grin. "A little."

"Good, let's do what we can to save this town."

* * *

It was chaos outside the inn. Men lit torches but they were fireflies compared to the bonfires of two warehouses to the east. The first familiar faces belonged to Piety and Rice. They did their best to get the more sober dockworkers in a defensive line across the eastern road, though they were mostly being ignored.

"What do you see of the attackers?" asked Nettie.

"Nothing yet," said Piety, "but this stretch here is the most defensible. We have the smithy to the north and the wainwright to the south. If you can put up a couple of palisades to narrow the area into a kill zone, we can hold against a large group for a while. What I wouldn't give to have a Dancer toss some surprises on the road."

"If wishes were rainbows," said Nettie. "Did you see any materials I can use for fortifications?"

"Wainwright," said Piety, pointing. "That entire back section is probably filled with lumber long and sturdy enough to make a wagon."

Nettie put a hand on Piety's shoulder in gratitude and ran to the building. She looked inside and smiled. Piety was right, lumber and logs were stacked almost to the ceiling. She had the materials she needed.

"What are you thinking?" asked Rin.

"I'm thinking with this much wood, I can build two towers and a wall spanning the road."

"We don't have that much time."

"I do," said Nettie. "Help me drag some of this out."

Rice and Piety rushed to help and some of the dock workers joined them. They quickly had a large stack of wood lying in front of them. Before she started building, Nettie saw a familiar figure slowly walking their way during a particularly bright lightning strike.

"Rose! What are you doing here? We need you on the raft, ready to flee!" said Nettie.

Rose's haggard eyes found Nettie's. Rose shouted to be heard over the rain, but Nettie could barely make out her weak voice. "And I will be, but I have to warn you. This is not a fight you can win. You and your team can give these people a chance, but don't be heroes. Be ready to retreat."

Nettie nodded. "Okay, now head to the raft. Please! We'll be there soon."

Rose turned to go then her eyes settled on Rin. Her face darkened. "You!" she said pointing at him.

"Me?" said Rin, eyes wide with surprise.

"Don't play coy with me, don't you dare endanger my—"

Gavin grabbed her by the arm and Nettie shooed them off. "Take her! We're right behind you!" yelled Nettie after them.

The small group ran north and east to the water. Nettie looked after them and felt her stomach drop as a group of beasts—the shape of which she couldn't make out in the darkness—rounded one of the northern buildings to close on Rose's position. Nettie screamed after them, but they didn't hear her.

Gavin set his feet and hoisted his spear as the beasts closed on them. Rose stood next to Gavin and faced their attackers. The Sage wagged a finger and yelled at the beasts as if admonishing naughty pets.

Nettie's eyes widened as the creatures turned long tails and ran the other way. How? Rose and her group continued towards the raft. Nettie shook her head and turned back to the task at hand.

She turned to Rin. "Why is Rose upset with you?"

"I have no idea. I've never seen her before last night."

Nettie looked at him sideways. "We'll get to the bottom of Rose's reaction, I promise you. Right now, we have defenses to place. I'll start with the tower on the right. Watch my motions, who knows, maybe you'll be able to see what I'm doing."

Nettie stood over the raw materials and began to spin. The tower appeared as if out of thin air. It was tall enough to provide advantage and strong enough to withstand damage.

The dockworkers whispered and pointed at her in awe.

She looked to Rin about to ask if he saw what she had done. Instead of Rin, she saw an identical tower finishing where he stood moments before. She blinked to make sure her eyes didn't deceive her.

She pointed at him in mimicry of Rose's motion moments before. "You! You're an architect too?"

He nodded. "Of a sort."

"What aren't you telling me?" she asked.

He pointed to the east and Nettie could barely make out the worried faces of Reaver and Leesta running their way. She couldn't tell what they were running from until a column of flame rose behind them to take the shape of a rampaging bull. Pyre. His flames revealed a horde of deformed and distorted animals rushing after their scouts. The monstrous army made almost no noise other than the squeals from those Pyre ignited.

It reminded Nettie of the jungle scenario in the Pool that all Ghosts suffered through. Except these lizards looked sentient. Some chose to run on back legs. They were joined by feral monkeys. Not the great apes turned Banglor, but small balls of fury. Nettie searched, but Pyre's column of flame sputtered before she could locate the Irborra she knew to be driving the creatures. How the Irborra kept the horde silent was a mystery.

"Lo's breath," whispered one of the dockworkers standing at the wall Nettie erected in front of the towers. "We're all going to die." The man dropped his club and turned to run.

"Don't you dare," growled Rice, his fist glowing with power. "We hold here until the children and wounded make it to the boats. Only then do we retreat."

Nettie searched frantically for Pyre until she saw the silhouette of the Vonderian atop the roof of the building in front of the smithy.

"Get out of there!" she yelled.

She needn't have bothered, Pyre was already moving. He used a gust of air to propel himself atop the roof of the smithy. From there he used another gust to land on the squat tower Nettie built.

"What's the one thing you can make without materials?" asked Rin from over her shoulder.

"Not now," said Nettie. She gauged the distance to their scouts. "We're out of time."

"No, we're not," said Rin. "Think."

"A hole, a trench," said Nettie.

"With the two of us working together, the seconds it takes will give minutes to those fleeing to the boats."

Nettie nodded. "Especially if we trap the trench." She pointed to the large man who smacked Leesta in the common room. "You, get some tar. The innkeeper has loads of it. Bring it back as fast as you can."

The man nodded and darted towards the inn.

Nettie and Rin moved in front of the wall. "Leave a path for Leesta and Reaver to retreat through."

The two Brickers spun and dirt flew. Not only did they build a trench between the two buildings but the dirt and cobbles they removed made a makeshift rampart in front of the trench. Leesta and Reaver made it through and Rin eliminated the small path.

The horde stopped in front of the rampart, waiting for something. Pyre summoned flame within the tightly bunched enemy in the shape of a massive snake that slithered through their opponents, igniting any it came into contact with. He had to duck behind the tower wall as the acidic spit of lizards careened towards him.

With the light from the flames, the defenders could see the inky pelts of the Irborra behind the enemy lines.

Leesta and Reaver moved into either tower as the bulky stevedore returned from the inn with two of his buddies. All held pails filled with tar.

Nettie pointed her chin. They climbed the towers and splashed the thick liquid into the trench. The Irborra saw them doing it and, surely, understood why. Nettie hoped they didn't care if they lost the lesser creatures of the horde. The Irborra were eventually going to direct the creatures around their defenses to the north and south, but for now, the defenders held the horde's attention.

With the light from the flames, Leesta and Reaver had clear lines of sight. They used it. The first arrow took an Irborra in the throat and the crack from Reaver's weapon registered a hit that turned the head of the largest Irborra into a gory, inverted horseshoe. The two ranged Strikers didn't wait to admire their work and two more midnight catmen dropped before the rest took cover by dropping below the line of the horde.

The second largest cat growled an attack as the other Irborra called on their foul brand of magic. Tiny, amethyst spheres appeared around them. The lizard and monkey creatures knew the bite of that dark magic and charged over the rampart and into the pit, hoping to reach the defenders before the purple globes struck them from behind.

With the tar in place, a single dart of flame from Pyre was enough to set the entire mass of creatures within the trench alight. Their screams filled the air. Yet, more and more lizards and monkeys ran towards them. Some of the purplish black balls of magic made it over the walls to find defenders. Nettie watched in horror as two of the dock workers disintegrated into ash.

The tar began to harden and the flames flickered their last when Nettie called for a retreat. There were too many of them. The walls wouldn't hold much longer but the bodies of the dead creatures should be enough of an obstacle to give the defenders the time they needed to make it to the river.

As the defenders leapt from the towers and retreated to the inn, Nettie heard a noise which chilled her to the bone. Two enormous lizards, five times the size of a horse, stomped their way to the walls. They stopped to screech in earsplitting harmony. Each screech sent a current of energy at the towers. When the energy struck, the towers exploded. The thunder lizards cared not for the tiny creatures they stepped on and over as they made their inevitable way to the wall.

Nettie paled. "Those things will demolish the ferries. We need to move!" she yelled to her squad of Liberators. "If we're not across the Rhune before they arrive, everybody dies."

Nettie glanced back to the thunder lizards. They were too fast. She knew the defenders weren't going to make it. It would be up to her to build something to give the rest of them time.

She looked fondly at her companions and wished them luck as she turned to face the horde.

28

An architect's prayer

Gavin smacked each horse hard on the flank so they'd flee north along the riverbank. They *might* have a chance if they kept running. With the horrible sounds drifting from the eastern side of the town, the chance was good they would keep running until they found safety. It was a small measure of comfort.

It was Leesta who first noticed Nettie was missing. "Where's Nettie? She didn't...No!" she yelled as the Liberators piled on the raft.

Piety grabbed the tall Loamian by the arm. "She made her choice to give *us* a chance. Help me push the raft, Sixteen!"

Leesta wanted to strike her. She almost did. She doubted Piety would have blamed her. Instead, she shifted and looked at Rose. "You know damn well Nettie is worth more than the rest of us combined. We need an architect. Even if we can convince the Keepers to give us access the Pool it doesn't matter without her. I need to go back. Let me go back."

Rose smiled and tears welled in her eyes. "Your passion does you credit. Hang on to it. It will make you great. I've seen nothing to make me believe Nettie's story ends here. Not tonight. Please, help Piety with the raft. Have faith we'll see her again."

Pyre fired darts of flame into the horde closing on their position. Whatever Nettie was doing slowed the central force, but the outliers were uncomfortably close. "We go now or we're not going to make it," said Pyre. He summoned another column of flame that morphed into a fiery thunderbird. The bright light from the flame beast outlined the threat better than his words.

"You better live. I just started not hating you," said Leesta into the air where she last saw Nettie. She pushed with all her strength and hopped on the raft as it caught the current.

* * *

Nettie built trench after trench as she backed up to the Rhune. Each trench slowed the horde, but she was exhausted. *If I build one more, my friends should survive. See you soon, Pick.*

The trenches slowed the smaller creatures, but not the thunder lizards. They were large enough to step over them. If one of them summoned storm energy again, it could take out the Liberator raft and her friends with it. She couldn't let that happen, but had no idea what to do about it. Maybe draw their attention so their strikes would focus on her and not the boats in the river.

If she was to be a sacrifice, she would make it a spectacular one.

She yelled at the lizards in a bid to divert their path. She

331

was so invested in catching their attention that when Rin put his hand on her shoulder she jumped. She looked at the small Bricker in shock.

"You're supposed to be on one of those boats!"

"And miss the fun?" The small Bricker looked at her with ancient eyes. "What you've done here is nothing short of miraculous Amelie Nettie Patching. I'm impressed and I don't impress easy."

"How do you know my full name? Who are you?"

"You haven't figured it out?"

She paused and stared at the small man. As she did, the chaos around her seemed to slow, then pause altogether. The giant lizards froze mid-step on the far side of her final trench. It was so disconcerting and she was so exhausted. She had to put both hands on her knees to prevent herself from toppling over. "What is...," she looked up at Rin then to the frozen horde. "How are you..." Another deep breath reengaged her mind and she shook her head. "Rin Keter. An anagram for Tinkerer." She chuckled. "I'm standing here with the gods damned Tinkerer himself."

"Careful young lady, some would call that blasphemy."

"Why tell me now, when I'm about to die?"

It was the Tinkerer's turn to chuckle. "That's *not* going to happen, at least not today. Now watch me, as I watched you."

The Tinkerer began to spin. As he spun, Nettie's head filled with ideas, engineering concepts, equations detailing the progression of the heavenly bodies, time at a cosmic level. She felt it as magic and science combined to create something new, the origins of life on Grendar. It was so much. Too much.

The Tinkerer kept spinning and Nettie got caught in the whirlwind. "Please stop...can't...process...any...more." Each word pulled from her overwrought brain and reconfigured at her lips to bring meaning forth.

No need for verbality. Rin's soft voice echoed in her mind. His soothing tone cut through the noise of ideas like a lighthouse beacon above stormy seas. *Anchor to me and watch.*

Nettie clung to his words like a life raft. *It's too much, I can't hold for long.*

You can hold for long enough, sent Rin. *If anyone can understand, it's Amelie Nettie Patching. Now watch.*

Rin pulled at the earth, at the buildings around him. The buildings fractured then crumpled. Raw materials flew in their direction. A map of a clockwork automaton of tremendous proportion blinked in front of Nettie's eyes. The image flashed then three copies materialized in front of them. No way could these giant golems operate independently, but Nettie knew the thought unworthy. This was the Tinkerer, a being without limitation.

Not true, said Rin in her mind. *I operate within the same fundamental laws of the universe as everyone else. The difference between me and other engineers is I never stopped looking for answers and I've been around for millennia. Imagine how many answers you would find if you didn't die. Every so often we discover something that changes how we think about everything else. When that happens, we create a knowledge gap between those that have it and those that don't. That gap makes the results of those ideas look fantastical, unrealistic, impossible. In reality, it's just new. Different.*

Yes, but knowledge must be built over time, thought Nettie back, *each piece of knowledge attained by understanding the steps that came before. You can't learn advanced engineering without knowing addition and subtraction.*

True, but once the knowledge is gained by one person, it spreads. Your mind picks up ideas faster than anyone I've met. You remind me of a younger me. You already have a large enough base of knowledge to cross the gap. So, watch.

But why are you teaching me? asked Nettie.

Because not only do you have the aptitude, you have what too many engineers lack on the path to knowledge.

A moral compass. You care about people. That's why you're worthy of my boon.

Boon?

Of knowledge. NOW WATCH!

The whirlwind continued. The Tinkerer armed the three golems with devices capable of immense destruction.

Time resumed.

The golems sprang into action. They pinned the thunder lizards to the ground with massive feet, so their next energy charges surged into the ground. The lizards fell victim to their own energy pulses. The energy which wasn't absorbed by the ground splashed back into their open maws. They slumped to their bellies as their heads turned to smoking husks. The energy disintegrated everything but their hides.

Nettie observed as the Tinkerer gave subtle commands to his clockwork guards. They turned their weapons on the masses of smaller creatures. Lizards and monkeys burned and exploded in the hundreds.

I'm not allowed to interfere directly in the affairs of mortals, said Rin. *But I am allowed to give boons and my boons come in the form of knowledge. This was the only way I could teach a matter of such magnitude. The final lesson I hope to impart:* there's always another way. *Now go. Search your mind for another way across the river. I'm sure you'll find something interesting, especially in regards to propulsion.* He winked at her.

What about you? Will I see you again?

That remains a mystery. At least to me. Perhaps you could ask your friend Rose. Go now while I clean up the rest of Theron's mess.

Theron? The god of death?

He's more the god of making a mess. He plays by no rules, so I must find another way within the fundamental laws. Enjoy your boon, young Bricker. Stay ever curious.

Rin blinked out of existence, but his golems rampaged through the distorted creatures like a trio of children stomping ants on a summer day. Purple spheres of energy splashed off the golems like rain on leaded windows. It wasn't long before the Irborra called a retreat.

Nettie stumbled to the vacant docks to find a pile of wood, metal and fiber lying on the northernmost dock. A final gift from the Tinkerer. She plumbed the depth of her mind and found a myriad of new blueprints. Watercraft she didn't have names for flittered from one side of her consciousness to the next. She picked a simple one and, for hopefully the last time of the evening, she began to spin.

The boat took shape quickly and Nettie knew a small sulimite core, placed just there, would power the craft to high speeds. She knew that once the boat planed it would dramatically increase in speed but didn't know how she knew. *Yes, you do. Don't start lying to yourself now.* She did know. She sent a Bricker prayer Rin's way, one she hadn't given since she was a child.

After all, logic dictated gods couldn't be real.

*By the angle of the sun and the orbit of the planets...*she started. She could hear Pick's voice in her mind as they spoke the prayer together as children. For the first time in a long time, she thought of her younger brother fondly instead of with heart-rending sadness. *Please provide us with the insight of the cosmos. We'll ask the questions if you provide the inspiration to find the answers. May the Tinkerer check our work...and find us worthy.*

She bowed her head in gratitude and hopped on the boat. She didn't have the sulimite to propel the small engine so she grabbed an oar from the dock and pushed into the current.

* * *

"You've got to be kidding me," said Leesta as the small boat pushed to the far side of the Rhune. "I'm sorry I doubted you, Rose."

"Could you ever have imagined you would have felt this strongly about her before my little dip into the river?" asked the Sage.

Leesta gave Rose a sharp look. "You planned that?"

The Sage gave her a mysterious smile. "Give our savior some assistance. She looks exhausted."

Leesta pulled Nettie's boat to the shore and gave her a fierce hug. "Thank you for saving us. I'm sorry I doubted you."

Leesta looked at the group of Liberators with the pride and

protectiveness of a mother bear. They didn't lose a single one of their party, despite all odds. Leesta knew that was due to whatever clockwork mysticism Nettie summoned in the waning moments of their flight from Derkin's Ferry.

There was no settlement on this side of the Rhune, only the road to Loam. Wet and bedraggled refugees littered the road. Small camps were erected. The cries of the wounded mixed with the sobs of those missing loved ones.

Piety and Rice set up a healing tent and word traveled through the camp. Those injured in the fight lined up and Rose and Gavin ushered the survivors through. Rose had a kind word and often slipped a coin into the hands of the most desperate.

One of the healthier stevedores approached the tent with murder in his eyes. "You!" said the man, pointing at Leesta. "This trouble started when you and your lot came into town. How do we know you're not behind the attack?"

Leesta looked at the waterlogged dockworker and bit down an angry reply. "I'm sorry for what you lost tonight. We all lost something. You have to believe the attack was coming whether we were there or not," she said.

"Oh yeah, and what did you lose?"

"Our horses, most of our supplies and if it wasn't for the grace of our companions, we would have lost our lives," said Leesta.

"She's not wrong, Clem," said the man who smacked Leesta on the ass hours ago. Leesta was surprised to realize she was happy he survived. "They didn't need to save us, but most of us live only because they showed up."

The first man growled but lowered his club.

The second man nodded to Leesta. "I apologize for how I

treated you earlier, miss."

Leesta nodded back. "No grudges with comrades-in-arms," she said, repeating the Krommian phrase she heard Jansen mutter more than once.

The man held a fist to his chest in a symbol of Krommian gratitude. He nodded once then left to help others move their belongings into makeshift tents.

Leesta walked towards the Liberators who held a heated discussion around a small fire pit. The rain finally stopped and small fires dotted the refugee camp in at least a dozen places.

"We have a target painted on us, Rose," said Gavin. "I don't know who's painting it, but we risk the lives of all here if we linger."

Rose put a hand on the man's shoulder, more to support herself than to offer comfort. "I believe you're right, but I don't know if I can go farther tonight. Look at poor Nettie. She fell asleep sitting up. We can do much for these people simply by staying the night. Piety and Rice have patched up the serious wounds, but there's scratches and breaks they haven't started to look at yet."

"Not to mention every person we help becomes a supporter of the Liberators," said Colson.

Gavin snorted.

"What?" said Colson. The man narrowed his eyebrows. "I know we're not supposed to care about our reputation, but this is what we do. We help people. The more people who trust the Liberators, the more people we can help."

"And your support has nothing to do with that bedroll you've been eyeing for the past hour?" said Gavin.

"A night's sleep would be good for all of us," said Rose.

She turned to Leesta. "I haven't seen further threats to us here, but something changed tonight. There are new players on the field. Players who can pull the threads of time and fate causing disruption and distortion in my Sight. Can you whisper with the earth to make sure the immediate threat has passed, at least for the night?"

Leesta nodded. "I'll do you one better. After I check with the life around us I'll set up a perimeter and we'll set a watch. Get some sleep, Rose. We need you rested and feeling better for the upcoming negotiations."

Rose gave her a grateful hug. "I don't know what we'd do without you, Leesta. All of you," she said. She looked fondly at her band of Liberators. "A night's sleep sounds wonderful. Can you make sure Nettie rests undisturbed?"

Leesta smiled. "If anyone's earned it, it's her."

29

Caster

Caster moved seven milliliters of the dark liquid from the flask to her sample dish using a glass pipet. She was no closer to solving the second stage of evolution the Thin Man constantly nagged her for, but she was close to mastering the first. The secret turned out to be trunite and a tiny bit of salt. Salt, of all things! Unbelievable. In retrospect it was obvious with the dire warnings coming from the Salt Wastes. Yet, the idea that salt was the missing component was such an inelegant solution. Pedestrian.

Why salt? She didn't have an answer for that yet, but she was making progress.

Progress wasn't enough. The Thin Man understood general research took as long as it took. Understanding didn't mean patience. Caster's slow progress meant independent teams had been brought in. Her lack of progress lost her influence. Loss of influence meant loss of resources.

Even her assistant, and sometimes lover, Drew, had been promoted to another research team who focused exclusively on the second stage of evolution.

Caster remembered the conversation with Drew vividly. "Advancing the investigation on the second stage of evolution before we understand the mechanisms of the first is incredibly dangerous," she had said.

"Aren't you all about taking big risks?" Drew had asked.

"Yes! Which is why you should pay attention when I warn you off. I'm all about taking big, calculated risks, but there is nothing calculated about this. The team you're joining is throwing the dice and hoping to get lucky. That's a recipe for disaster," said Caster.

"It's the only way I'll be able to make my own name as a tinkerer," Drew had said. "Our relationship isn't nearly as discrete as we hoped. Elspeth made a comment to Rhianne yesterday where she was sure I could hear it."

Caster had smiled. "Sleeping your way to the top?"

Drew hadn't smiled back. "I believe the actual term used was fuck slave."

Caster choked back a laugh. "Since when do you care about what Elspeth and Rhianne think?"

"Don't do that, Cas. I can see you trying not to laugh. This is my life. My career. I can't keep doing this."

"Fine, you don't have to wear the collar tonight," said Caster, trying to lighten the mood.

"No. I don't," said Drew. He stood and stomped to the door of her bunker apartment. He looked back over his shoulder. "I'm taking the new position," he had said then slammed the door behind him.

Caster sighed and looked around the lab. Half her evolution team left with Drew. Even Elspeth. New tinkerers were added to the team daily, but they had to be trained and the team felt like it was constantly in transition. When she looked over at the lab bench where Drew used to do his work, she couldn't remember the name of the man who replaced him. Stefan or Stewart, something that started with an S.

Then Rhianne moved over to the man's bench and said, "I told you yesterday, Richard, you need to use the micro pipettes for this new solution."

Richard. Huh. Why did she think Stefan or Stewart? Oh right, because she had been thinking about salt. Drew's ending of the relationship hit her harder than she expected. She hadn't been able to form a coherent thought all morning. Caster prided herself on not letting emotion impact her work. If the end of the relationship affected *her* brain patterns this much?

No...it couldn't be that simple. Could it?

Her muddled thoughts were nowhere near definitive proof that emotion had an impact on pathways in the brain, but it was enough to build a theory.

Using trunite diluted with a weak saline solution, she could catalyze evolution in every human subject she worked with. That evolution persisted regardless of whether or not she added hybrid components to her test subjects. Caster got over her squeamishness of merging human test subjects with big cats long ago. She had to admit that using avian hybrids still felt unethical, even to her.

Survival of the test subjects was no longer the goal. Figuring out a way to eliminate the rage and hatred of the evolved test subjects was paramount to new advancement. Sure, the Collective could create an army of Marked, human or hybrid, but they couldn't control them. What use was an army of superhuman creatures if they would just as easily attack their creators as they would an enemy of the Collective.

Could emotion change that?

The data the Collective received from the League strongly suggested accepting death was the primary catalyst for evolution. Trunite filled that gap. Whether the component forced the test subject to accept their own death or whether it created a chemical replacement for that acceptance was unknown. The process was grisly. The moment the trunite solution was introduced, the test subject went through immense amounts of pain. That could very well be what caused the rage, but it also caused the transformation.

How to counter the rage without destroying the evolution?

League candidates operated in an incredibly challenging environment. They were asked to push, to train, to better themselves every single day. Not so with the Collective's test subjects. Caster's test subjects had it easy in comparison. The only thing they were asked to do was go through a series of injections and a battery of surgeries.

Maybe that was the problem. Maybe the test subject needed to earn the evolution.

That didn't sound right. If that were the case, the Garden City militaries would see more natural evolutions. There was something more. *Think!*

Back to emotion. Bonds were built under extreme circumstances. Bonds caused people to take selfless actions.

Tribar's brat Kavi led the charge when it came to pushing evolutionary boundaries. He was an obnoxious child of the worst sort. An idealist. From the reports Caster read, he inspired others. He pushed them to be more than what they were. What was Kavi's underlying ideal? Commitment to the survival of the team. Kavi fought for the people around him. Not his captors. Not his coaches.

Kavi and his team fought to protect those they cared for. Those they loved.

Love. Caster shuddered at the word. The whole concept sickened her. Why someone would ever give that much power to another was moronic. For years she believed it all a lie, a scam. Ever since Uncle Cam touched her. No way could the emotion be real.

Yet...there was something there. She couldn't argue with Stonecrest's results.

She looked around the lab and realized she hired researchers who held similar opinions about love. About emotions in general. The Collective drew a certain type of thinker.

If anything, it made her more certain. That's why it hadn't occurred to her team yet. They discounted emotion.

The real question now, how to test it? How to put test subjects in a situation where they would not only accept their own deaths, but make a selfless act for another? Was it time to bring their families in?

* * *

Caster forced herself to ignore the successes of the neuro-bath team. Rumors in the hallways said they had their first successful advancement to the second stage of evolution. As the Collective's research director, she had access to their data and methods of action. She didn't have the power to approve or deny research anymore.

Their experiment was clever. They submerged two subjects in a carefully diluted solution of trunite, salt, and sulimite. They removed the top of the subjects' skulls so a bit of brain matter was directly exposed to the solution and the other subject's brain. They had a Vonderian neuro-mage listen for signals from the subjects' minds.

Over the past two months, the neuro-bath team tweaked the compounds in the solution, the amount of brain matter to expose, the number of test subjects submerged in the bath, the number of neuro-mages massaging the signals and the types of test subjects to expose to the test.

They basically changed every variable of the test every day. Reckless and dangerous. Caster would have shut them down a long time ago.

All they accomplished thus far was increased levels of rage in their test subjects. After they were pulled from the bath and sewn back up, they would howl and bang their heads against the bars in their cages until knocking themselves unconscious. The test was a complete failure.

Until yesterday.

It was Drew's idea to run a weak current through the solution while the test subjects lay dormant within it. Saline is a good enough conductor that the insulating properties of the heavily diluted trunite and sulimite weren't enough to prevent the effectiveness of the charge. Seconds after the current was introduced, chaotic neuro-signals exploded from the test subjects. The two neuro-mages appointed to proctor the test were quickly overwhelmed. They stopped the current after a minute to analyze the signals.

Just this morning Caster fielded three requests from members of her own team to transfer to "Drew's team". One of the requests came from Rhianne who despised Drew. Maybe

Caster *was* stymieing his innovation.

She quashed the requests for transfer.

Their own experiments were ramping up and she didn't have time to train new people. She developed a test where a test subject who had not evolved would go through the first transformation at the same time a child was under a simulated attack from a savannah lion. The neuro-mage she worked with assured her the test subject would believe the attack was real. The child *was* real, in case the test subject accidentally bumped into the kid during the experiment.

The test subject and the child were sedated and ready for the experiment to begin. Rhianne laid the injections on the operating cart and the rest of the team took their positions.

Caster looked over at Rhianne who was staring at the door. "Rhianne!" she snapped. "Focus. I need you here now, not thinking about what other teams are doing."

"Do you hear that? Is that screaming?" asked Rhianne.

Caster leaned back and allowed her senses to expand. It *was* screaming. Not the usual feral howls coming from the recently transformed either. Those were screams of terror.

Caster stripped off her gloves and ran to the door of her lab. She turned and looked back to her team. "If I'm not back in three minutes, lock this door."

Rhianne nodded and took her place in front of the door.

When Caster stepped into the hall, nothing seemed different except for the screams echoing down the halls from the direction of the Neuro-bath team. Drew. Before she had time to think, Caster rushed towards the screams.

When she arrived at the Neuro-bath lab, the doors were locked. The screaming was coming from inside. She knocked on the glass door and screamed, "Drew! Open up! Let me help."

She reached for the keys at her belt, ignoring the loud voice in the back of her head that yelled it was a very bad idea. She turned the key and looked in on a nightmare.

The two test subjects flickered in and out of sight in perfect synchronization. Two research techs lay at the base of the bath in expanding pools of blood. The two neuro-mages stood back-to-back on the far side of the large room. They each held a finger to their temples as they tapped into the mental energy of the room.

Drew sat in the segregated observation booth with the three lead researchers on the project. Drew saw her enter the lab and gestured in a shooing motion for her to leave.

She moved back towards the door just as the test subjects converged on the observation booth. Moving in perfect harmony, they struck the glass of the booth with hardened fists.

The glass held.

Caster saw blood well on their knuckles. She looked down at her own knuckles. The scabs from just before she asked the Thin Man for help had finally flaked off. The fresh skin beneath beckoned invitingly. As her stress level rose, her eyes fixated on the skin like a writer in front of an empty piece of paper.

The test subjects struck the glass of the booth again, in perfect synch. A small crack appeared on the glass.

Caster edged towards a research bench and grabbed two small syringes. She quietly reached for a flask and a scalpel.

The test subjects struck again. Two fists one motion. The glass spiderwebbed with cracks.

Caster knocked over a stand holding rows of volumetric

pipettes. It landed in a crash of glass splinters. Caster breathed in as the test subjects turned their heads at the same time to look at her. They labeled her as non-threatening and continued their assault on the thick glass of the booth.

Caster rolled the freshly healed skin of her knuckles into the shards of glass. The pain brought clarity. She knew she should flee. The Collective would send men and women capable of dealing with the threat at any moment. What kept her here? She knew the answer, but her analytical mind denied it. If she left now, Drew would die.

The twice evolved subjects struck again and this time chunks of the hardened glass clattered to the inside of the booth. Two more strikes and they would pull their prey out of that booth like a minx pulling a stoat from its den.

Run! screamed her analytical mind.

No, answered a part of Caster which had lain dormant for twenty years.

But we'll die, argued her analytical mind.

We all die.

We still have so much work left to do! So many weapons left to craft.

I'm not leaving Drew to die like a rat in a hole.

Caster shuddered, and a perfect moment of clarity struck. She looked at the bench. Neatly labeled components stared back at her from multi-tiered shelves. Flasks lined the back of the shelf at eye level. The exact combinations of explosive mixtures marched through her mind. She ground her knuckles into the shards of glass a final time and began to mix.

She eyeballed every amount, but had no doubt each solution was perfect. It only took moments for Caster Ada Vigner to finish the two explosive mixtures. She spun, a flask in each hand.

She threw the flasks at the base of each test subject's feet. With the flasks in the air, two heads moved as one to look at this new threat. It was too late. The flasks struck the floor and exploded.

The test subjects burst into flames. One hate-filled scream came from two mouths as flesh bubbled. Then, they collapsed to the ground.

A dark mist surrounded them and coalesced moments later into the form of the Thin Man. "Over these last two months I wondered where the Caster I hired had gone. It's good to see you back."

Caster nodded at the Thin Man in exhaustion then began to convulse.

"Caster!" yelled Drew.

The world went black.

* * *

The Thin Man materialized back in his office after supervising the transformation of Caster. He looked down at his hands, recently covered in the sticky, reddish-black liquid of evolution. It reminded him of the disgusting mess of amniotic fluid that came from natural childbirth. He had no idea how women could go through that process. Thankfully, the fluid didn't stick to him as he traveled in his gaseous form.

349

Regardless, he wiped imaginary residue on his cloak. Blood was as natural as water to the Thin Man, but that goo disgusted him.

He sat at his desk and rubbed a finger over one of the small crystals set into its surface and imagined the face of the Majordomo of the League.

Moments later, she appeared on the large wall screen in front of him.

"What can I do for you, milord?" asked the wizened woman. Her tone was respectful without being obsequious.

"They're here."

Majordomo raised an eyebrow. "By they, I assume you mean your brethren?"

The Thin Man nodded.

"Interesting. My network caught no wind of their arrival, which means they're masking their presence."

"Yes, but they can't help themselves. Be assured, they're already meddling," said the Thin Man. Irritation caused his darkened authority to expand behind him.

"Would you like us to accelerate the execution of the Divine Will Project?" asked the Majordomo.

The Thin Man drummed partially substantial fingers against his desk. "No. We proceed according to plan, but maybe we can nudge the dice."

The Majordomo smiled and waited.

"Perhaps if we release a bit more technology..."

"So soon after we released recording crystals? That was less than a year ago."

"True, but maybe we take the governor off the recording and broadcasting technology."

The Majordomo frowned but nodded.

"As the residents of Grendar evolve, so must the pace of their technology," said the Thin Man.

"You've asked me to push back in situations like this milord..."

The Thin Man nodded even as his authority continued to expand behind him in frustration.

"So I find it imperative to ask...won't this capture the attention of the Adjudicators?" asked the Majordomo.

"Not if we do it as a Boon."

"I see, but won't that raise the ire of the Tinkerer?"

"Like I would care about the anger of that sniveling little... nerd. You do yourself a disservice domo."

The majordomo gulped but asked, "Nerd, milord?"

"A term from a different age. Nothing you need be concerned about. Please give the League owners the recording crystals with the power to record things not visible to the human eye."

"Yes, milord."

The Thin Man ended the transmission and stared at the wall of images of Grendar as his brethren wreaked havoc upon the world he called home.

30

Kavi

"Now, Tess. Fire now!"

Tess took a deep breath and released the sigil-inscribed arrow. She looked back at Clara already inscribing another just in case.

The moment she fired, Jory played power chords on his lute. The sound chased, then caught the arrow, pushing it to greater speed than Tess' ropy muscled arms could create on her own. The chords didn't impact her aim.

Ghost Squad watched with satisfaction as the arrow crested its trajectory and screamed towards the Marked.

With a critical eye, Kavi gauged the arrow's flight. He knew it would strike the creature's throat. Hopefully, the devil's death would demoralize the army of demented farm animals into panic. Ghost Squadron was good, but they were hopelessly outnumbered.

The arrow plunged towards the Marked, picking up speed as it fell. Kavi waited for the satisfying thunk of its tapered point penetrating through the beast's windpipe.

Quicker than a greased ferret, the horned Marked reached

up and plucked the runic arrow from the air.

Kavi's eyes widened in shock.

Tess knocked another runic arrow and loosed. The entire process was repeated, Jory striking power chords to push the arrow for more speed.

It ended with the same result.

"I thought Harp granted a boon," said Jansen.

"Me too," whispered Pip.

"Cut the chatter," said Kavi. "Clara, tell me exactly what Harp said in the dream when she granted you the Boon."

"She said we would have to work in perfect harmony," said Clara. "If we did, nothing could stop Trueshot's arrow."

"Trueshot?" asked Pip.

"Questions later," said Kavi. "We're out of time. Perfect harmony she said. Ghost Squad is good, but the only way to achieve perfection is a fuse."

"We've never successfully fused outside the Pool," said Pip.

"I know," said Kavi. "But we're out of options. Elana, you know the theory. We're going to need Jory, Tess and Clara in the fuse."

Tess and Jory stared at Kavi in disbelief.

Kavi held their gaze. "I wouldn't give the order if we had another choice."

Elana paled but nodded. "I've never done more than two."

"I know," said Kavi. "I also know how good you are. You never would have been chosen for Ghost Squad if you weren't the best."

Elana stood up straighter. "I need the three of you to link hands. Clara, take my left hand. Tess, take my right. No time to ease our way into this, so here we go. Close your eyes and focus on my voice in your mind."

The four Ghosts arched back, mouths open in a silent scream. Then, they breathed as one. Four sets of eyes opened at once.

"I'll start," all four said together. Clara grabbed a blank arrow from Tess' quiver. Her fingers blurred as she etched perfect runes along the length of the arrow and its tip.

"My turn," they said together. Tess knocked arrow to string and pulled back until the wood of the bow creaked under the strain. "Loose!" four mouths chanted as one.

The arrow took to the air, the hopes of Ghost Squad and the remaining spectators pinned to it as it flew.

"Major chords only," they said together as Jory's fingers found the frets of his lute. He strummed twice with such volume that two of the strings snapped with a metal twang as he played the final chord.

The arrow raced into the sky and the powerful sounds of the lute strained to reach it. When the wave of sound hit the arrow, it took on a silver glow as it reached its apex. The arrow streaked towards its target, glowing like a tiny sun.

"Here they come!" yelled Pip. "Sliver, get Herman in front," said Pip. "Guards, anchor the line around him. Ten seconds until this horror show reaches us."

Kavi let Pip's words wash over him, his focus on the arrow streaking through the air. The Ghosts moved to execute Pip's orders, the big golem, Herman, lumbering to the front. Their defense was in place. Kavi didn't think it would matter. There were too many even for Ghost Squad.

The arrow streaked faster and faster towards the Marked. The devilish creature squinted as it tracked the runic missile. It never lost its confident smile, sure it would catch this arrow too.

Kavi held his breath.

The Marked reached out its lightning quick hand, but this time the super-heated arrow parted the flesh and bone of the hand and plunged into, then through, the beast's throat. The Marked stood for a moment, blood fountaining from its throat. Its body couldn't accept the loss of executive function. It toppled slowly, goat hooves a poorly balanced platform for the massive, dying body.

The horde of charging animals slowed. They were ten meters away when the timbre of snarling hate shifted. The largest sheep at the front of the pack stopped. It put its face to the ground and nibbled at a tuft of grass. It raised its head, looked at Ghost Squadron and let out a plaintive "baa." Its eyes returned to a watery brown.

Its brethren joined it in grazing.

None of the placid farm animals questioned their fate as they milled around looking for food.

Kavi's eyes scanned the horizon for more threats. Was that it? A single Marked mutated and controlled all of those beasts? The thought chilled him, but the threat was gone for now.

Kavi breathed a sigh of relief and walked over to congratulate their fused members.

The four fused Ghosts nodded in synch and collapsed.

"Healer!" yelled Kavi.

* * *

"It's just strange," said Jansen. "To go on a League mission and not have to fight for our lives, it's like—"

"Tell that to Clara, Tess, Jory and Elana," said Sliver.

"I know, I know" said Jansen. "But that's not my point, what I was going—"

"Oh, here we go," said Stonez. "You all ready for the philosophic musings of a shield bearing eggplant?"

Jansen stood up and pushed Stonez. "Let me finish my thought!"

"Enough," said Pip. "We're all on edge."

"No," said Jansen, "not until I ask my question."

The argument twanged Kavi's last nerve. Amity and Felicity did everything they could, but none of the fused Ghosts had wounds. They were stuck in their own heads. Completely unresponsive. It was like they couldn't break the fuse. Kavi had no idea what to do. He spun and rounded on the bickering Guards.

"What? What brilliant thing do you have to add to this conversation, Twenty-two?" Kavi said, getting up in Jansen's face.

Jansen's head reeled back as if slapped, but he held his ground. "Easy, Kavi. What I was going to say was, is it possible that the Marked was fused with those animals just like we fuse when we're in the Pool? You saw the animals change back when he died. If he was fused, then aren't we facing a new level of Marked?"

"That's a *really* good question," said Boost. He nodded to the big man with respect.

They all stood for a second, stunned at the implications of Jansen's insight.

"Sorry I snapped at you," said Kavi. "Pip, can you check if

the League has received reports of other Marked behaving like this?"

Kavi barely heard Pip as he issued orders. He knuckled his forehead as the events of the last hour replayed in his mind. "I can't believe I had to order them to fuse like that!"

Stix walked over to him and put a hand on his shoulder. "If you didn't, we'd all be dead, mate."

"We'll figure it out, Tack," said Boost.

"That's what we do," said Sliver. "All we need is some time with a neuro-mage. I'm sure there are some in the city. Ask your Minister friends and they'll have one waiting for us when we get back to the Vondam."

Pip caught Kavi's eye and jutted his chin over Kavi's left shoulder. Kavi glanced back and saw Patrice rushing their way. "Damn that woman," muttered Kavi.

"Want me to intercept her?" asked Pip.

"Thanks, but no," said Kavi. "I knew I was going to have to do a post action interview. Sliver and Boost are right, there isn't much we can do for those stuck in the fuse until we talk to a neuro-mage. Might as well get it over with. Want to join me to provide color?"

Pip nodded and they walked towards Patrice.

To her credit, the first thing Patrice asked was, "Are they going to be okay?"

"We don't know yet," said Pip. "We need a neuro-mage to examine them. Immediately. Does the League keep any on staff?"

"I don't know, but I'll ask," said Patrice. "I hope they pull through. Everyone in the world is going to want to hear from Tess Trueshot after that phenomenal performance."

Kavi turned away in disgust.

"Of course that's all you care about," said Pip. "Whatever makes the League look good."

"No!" said Patrice with heat. "I'm sorry they're in danger, but the League needs women heroes. She's an inspiration and I want to share that with the world!"

"Can we push the interviews until after they recover?" asked Kavi.

Patrice shrugged. "I'm sure I can get Reuben to agree to push the in-depth interview until tomorrow, but he's going to want a quick word about what you think happened here today. If you give five minutes now, I'll do everything in my power to push the follow-up interviews to tomorrow."

Kavi sighed and nodded. He and Pip made their way over to the news crew.

They were intercepted by Ministers Kwan and Wharton before they reached Reuben.

"Good show," said Kwan, smacking Kavi on the back.

"Not only did you kill the Marked, you did it in a way that the livestock could be recovered. That's going to make the crown and treasury very happy, young man," said Wharton.

Kavi wanted to strangle both of them, but he'd seen his mother navigate such hurdles many times, even when he knew she boiled with rage on the inside. He swallowed his murderous instincts. "Glad we could help. Do you know any quality neuro-mages in the city? My companions are lost and that's the only thing that might help them find their way back."

"Of course," said Kwan. "I will send Madam Protengara to the Vondam. She'll be waiting for you when you arrive. She is the neuro-mage to the crown and the House of Royals."

Kwan whispered to one of his aides. The man nodded and

rushed off.

"I've heard of her," said Pip. "She's a legend in Vonderia." He looked at Kavi. "There may not be a more qualified neuro-mage in all of Grendar."

Kavi breathed a sigh of relief and, for the first time, felt gratitude towards the Ministers before him. "Thank you, milords."

"You've proven your worth, young man, consider it a return of favor," said Kwan with a bow. He moved aside to let the tacticians continue towards the news tent.

"I'm still not taking back all the horrible things I said about those two," said Pip, just loud enough for Kavi to hear.

Kavi grinned for the first time all day. "They're still awful, but even awful people can do good things every once in a while."

Reuben walked from under the tent to greet Kavi and Pip. "Thank you for agreeing to do this," said the short newsman. He rubbed a hand over the back of his neck, obscuring the tattooed quote on integrity from Traston. "I'm sure it's difficult with the fate of your companions still unknown. I promise to make it short so you can get back to them. If it were up to me, I'd push the whole thing to tomorrow, but I've learned disappointing the League is a great way to get fired."

"Or killed," said Pip.

Reuben let out a nervous laugh. Pip and Kavi didn't join him and the laughter died on his lips. "Right, then," said Reuben. "We best not disappoint."

Reuben lined them up to sit just outside the tent. Bright yellow magelight shone from inside the tent, flattering faces for the crystal. Their backs to the battlefield, Kavi could hear the sheep mewling as they grazed.

Kavi caught a glimpse of the divine Harp, standing behind and to the left of Reuben, just out of view of the recording crystals. No, he couldn't deal with her too, not now. But she did deserve his gratitude. He nodded to her. She smiled, blew him a kiss and disappeared.

Reuben looked over his shoulder then back at Kavi, confused.

Kavi waved off the man's unasked question and said, "We're ready when you are."

Reuben looked directly into the crystal floating between them and gave his regular intro. He turned to Pip and Kavi. "That was quite the performance. Most of us have heard the rumors of Marked and monsters roaming the land. Few have seen them. Most consider them myths and fairytales. Not after tonight's broadcast. Kavi Stonecrest and Pip Tern are tacticians for the Sugoroku keepers. Tell me gentleman, is this typical of Marked incursions?"

Reuben shuddered, but continued before Pip or Kavi could respond. "We saw what those things did to those brave soldiers. What should, no...what *can* normal people do in the face of a Marked incursion?"

"Run," said Kavi. "If you face the Marked and you haven't been through League training, your chances of survival are almost zero. Please, get far, far away and seek out a League office and report the incursion."

"A hard pill to swallow for people forced to leave their homes and their lives due to these incursions," said Reuben.

Kavi shrugged. "Would you rather leave your home, or lose your life?"

"Back to my first question. Is this standard for a Marked

incursion?"

"I'll take this one," said Pip, and Kavi gratefully passed him the spotlight.

"This was different," said Pip. "Most our encounters with the Marked happened during Quests. It's common for Marked to be surrounded by lesser creatures similar in nature. Not so with our opponent today. This Marked was powerful and seemed to have the ability to turn creatures into monsters. If this is a trend, it's a troubling one."

As Pip spoke, Kavi saw Harp appear once more. She flitted between equipment and hangers-on in the crowd. Nobody else saw her. If they had, they would certainly notice the transparent shift which covered absolutely nothing. Harpstra was a lenient society, but even they drew the line at total nudity.

"Thank Harp the League sent you and your team," said Reuben.

The goddess blew a kiss to the newsman and gave a little wave. Since no one else reacted, Kavi assumed it was just him who could see her.

"How did you know Tess would make the shot? Especially after the Marked caught the first two arrows?"

Kavi looked at Harp when he answered. "Faith. We should all thank Harp for how Tess and our Harpstran team members performed today. They're amazing warriors and amazing people. They never stop training, never stop improving. They took that coordination and communication to a new level that could only be called divinely inspired."

Harp took a regal bow that caused her unconcealed breasts to bounce and jiggle.

"Will they be okay, your squad mates?"

"We don't know yet, Reuben," said Pip, taking the open door the newsman offered. "Which is why we need to get back to the Vondam to see if there is anything we can do to help."

Reuben nodded. "Best of luck. Thank you both for taking this time. I look forward to our extended interview tomorrow. Until then, we'll all pray for their swift recovery."

* * *

That night, when Reuben was back in the office preparing for the morning interviews, he heard a yelp from his editor. The man was reviewing the crystal recordings before broadcast to clear any dead air.

"Reuben...come in here and look at this," said his editor.

Reuben finished revising the question list he was working for the interview tomorrow then walked into the editing booth. "What's the matter?"

"Watch this clip with you and the Sugoroku tacticians."

Reuben did, it only took two minutes. "Looks good," he said. "What's the problem."

"Look what happens when I turn on the new setting the League gave us last week." Uriah fiddled a knob. "Wide beam, high definition."

They watched the recording again and this time a gorgeous, naked woman danced through the set as if no one was watching. Reuben was there. He knew no one *was* watching.

"Now watch Stonecrest's eyes as he thanks Harp."

"Holy shit! Has anyone else seen this?" asked Reuben.

"Not yet. I came to you first."

"Don't show anybody. We can still broadcast the low definition version right?"

"Of course, but why not push it up the chain? We could be the ones who break the story of Harp appearing on Grendar!" said Uriah, eyes wide with incredulity.

"Think, Uriah!" Reuben growled. "What do you think happens to us if the Goddess doesn't want us to break this story? If you value your life, swear to me you won't tell a soul about this until I've had the chance to speak with Kavi Stonecrest."

31

Lighthouse in a storm

She looked so small as she slept. Innocent. Kavi realized he had no idea how old Clara actually was. When you didn't know if you were going to survive the next day, years already lived was irrelevant.

Clara slept next to Tess. Jory and Elana lay side by side on an adjoining bed. Pip cleared the room of concerned Ghost Squad members to give the professional neuro-mage room to work.

"Are you going to participate in the exercise or not, Lord Stonecrest?" asked Madam Protengara. She was dressed in the formal robes of her order and she wore a practiced scowl.

Kavi tore his gaze from Clara's face to look at the neuro-mage. "It's Kavi. Yes, I'm going to participate."

Her features softened when she caught the pain in Kavi's eyes. "I acknowledge I don't understand what life and death decisions you're forced to make while under attack. That said, merging consciousness is incredibly dangerous. I can't believe young Elana Starsight took such a grievous risk. It was irresponsible at best and deadly at worst."

"You're right," said Kavi. "You will never understand what decisions we're forced to make when fighting for our lives against the Marked. She didn't take the risk. I did. I ordered her to do it." Kavi met the older woman's eyes with an authority that was quickly losing patience.

She arched an eyebrow in question, then nodded.

"That said," continued Kavi. "I don't mean to be rude. My squad desperately needs your help. *I* desperately need your help." Kavi dug his fingernails into his palm.

She pulled a chair between the two beds and sat. "What your Brickers call a strong bond is what we call a neuro-channel. It goes beyond mind reading, which only catches errant thoughts floating close to the surface. A neuro-channel is an invitation into all aspects of the mind."

Kavi rubbed his temples to ease the mounting headache. He wished the wizened neuro-mage would get on with it, but didn't want to risk offending her again.

She must have picked up on his impatience, as she said. "We're getting there, but it's important you understand what we're up against before we begin. All research of neuro-channels was discontinued at the Academ after losing three pairs of promising neuro-mages."

"The Costica Trials," whispered Pip.

Mage Protengara nodded. "Alfonse Costica posited that if a mental connection was strong enough, two minds could act like a single, super mind. He believed mind-to-mind communication took place over neural waves. When those neural waves were in synch, just as ocean waves can combine during a storm, the combination becomes a force multiplier, creating power we can only imagine. He never figured out how to get the waves in synch. You've done a simulated fuse, so you understand a bit of what's involved in sharing the shame and fear of the darkest corners in your mind. Costica believed that only by baring everything—not only with the other person, but with yourself—could we find alignment. Costica failed. Most neuro-mages believe it's impossible. The cost of failure is that when those waves combine, then remain out of synch for too long, the sources creating them break down."

"By sources, you mean each individual mind?" asked Kavi. "That's how his test subjects died, isn't it?" His face reddened in desperation and fear. "Then we have no time to waste! Let's get started!"

She stood and reached out one hand to Pip, the other to Kavi. "Let me show you what you're facing."

When their fingers touched Kavi was thrown into something resembling one of his visions. This time he had a guide.

He and Pip stood side by side with the neuro-mage atop an impossibly tall lighthouse in the middle of the Whisper Sea. From it they could see all of Grendar. Four tempests swirled towards the lighthouse, each centered around an individual eye. Where the storms overlapped, huge waves whipped up from the sea. The storms battered against each other in tempestuous combat.

"Do you see now?" asked Madam Protengara without moving her lips. "They're caught in their own nightmares. When their signals overlap, their turmoil increases. They don't know whose fear, whose shame is whose. When the mind dips in despair, everything is fear and shame. There's no kindness. No joy. No hope."

"What can I do?" asked Kavi.

"You need to stabilize each of them individually. You

have to show them there's something worth coming back to. The intervention has to be precise. While working with one, you must avoid the other three. It may be impossible, but I believe if you give substance to one, they will become an ally in bringing the others back. To rebuild them, you must help them face their darkest secrets. They've been in there long enough that it's likely their fears will manifest as something substantial when they hit the Pool. You may have *fused* before, but not like this. The level of despair is going to be four times as powerful as anything you've faced."

"Can we limit the power by putting only one of them in the Pool at a time with Kavi?" asked Pip.

Mage Protengara shook her head. "It's a good idea, but it won't work. The signals in their minds are already tangled. If you free Elana first, she'll be your strongest ally. She, at least, understands neuromantic theory."

* * *

Minister Kwan was happy to escort them to the bunker which housed the Pool the League had gifted the Harpstrans. His only request was the opportunity to observe.

"Apologies, Minister," said Madam Protengara, "but I fear we already have too many neural signals in the room. Even with the booth, another signal could result in catastrophic outcomes for our wounded peacekeepers. We may only have one shot at this. I'm sure you understand."

The Minister looked at the wizened neuro-mage as if trying to decide if she was telling him the truth or trying to get rid of him. "Of course, Madam Protengara. I only want what's best for the League."

Sliver and Boost immediately went to work rewiring the neuro-transmitter to allow for strong bonds. After weeks of working with Hiram at the Nest, it took only minutes.

"Ready to load them into the Pool, Tack?" asked Stix.

All of Ghost Squadron escorted their lost team members. Stix and Stonez had Jory on a stretcher between them while the others carried Elana, Clara and Tess.

It was Madam Protengara who answered Stix. "Not yet." She looked to Kavi. "I wasn't *only* trying to get rid of the Minister." She smiled. "Though I admit, it was a happy side effect. If you insist on going through with this, you'll need everyone else out of the chamber."

"What if something happens with the Pool?" said Sliver. "Me or Boost need to be on hand to monitor from the booth."

Kavi looked from Sliver to Madam Protengara. Equally stubborn visages stared back. They both had valid concerns. There had to be a third way.

"Is there a way you can shield neural signals from within the booth, ma'am?" asked Pip. "Having you there, observing, offering advice, could be the difference between success and failure."

Madam Protengara frowned as she thought through the idea. "Perhaps. Let me run a quick test before we activate the Pool."

"While she runs the test," said Stix, "can I have a second? Regarding our other operation."

Kavi barely restrained himself from snapping at his Harpstran Guard and part-time mentor. He didn't want to think about anything until his downed Ghosts were safe, but Stix and his family had deadlines of his own. If they weren't ready to help the Thickbloods by tomorrow, Stix's father and a lot of others would be executed.

Stix led Kavi to a secluded corner of the room. "I saw Red ten minutes ago. Our victory over the Marked hasn't slowed the Ministers' project. If anything, they want to use our victory to promote their 'grand initiative.'" Stix clenched his fists in an uncharacteristic show of constrained rage. "I can't stand that snake Kwan. The idea of him using our victory to promote his agenda...we have to stop these pricks, Kavi."

"We will," said Kavi. "I wonder if there's any chance we can get Harp to make an appearance at the ceremony. Maybe a god can convince them that oppressing an entire group of people is wrong."

"Do you know how to contact her?" asked Stix.

"Not exactly," said Kavi. "But I saw her today when Pip and I were doing the post-fight interview. If you pray, she might answer."

Stix thought about that for a second, then looked to the other Harpstrans in their group. "We can try. If you see her again, can you ask her?"

"I'll do what I can, but she normally appears when I'm in no position to ask her anything," said Kavi. "It's a power thing. She distracts me and I can't do anything about it."

"Sounds childish," said Stix. "I expected better. Think she'll support what we're doing?"

"She's your god, but I'd assume she'd want to protect as many Harpers as possible."

"We'll treat it as a bonus if she shows, but we won't plan on it. For now, the plan stays the same," said Stix.

369

"When we figure this out," Kavi pointed at the pool, "you'll have the full Squad scouting the square first thing in the morning, but if—"

"Get our people out of there," said Pip, walking over and interrupting Kavi's thought. We'll be waiting with a big steak dinner to celebrate."

Madam Protengara stared at Pip and Kavi from the top step of the stairs into the observation booth. "I can shield our signals, which means I may be able to whisper into your ear as Sliver, oh for Vonn's sake, is that your real name?"

"Yes'm," said Sliver meeting her eyes with a steely gaze.

The neuro-mage rolled her eyes. "As Sliver here monitors the Pool."

She walked the rest of the way down the stairs and grasped Kavi's arm. "Good luck in there young man. I'll help where I can."

Kavi thanked her and the conscious Ghosts undressed and loaded their catatonic companions into the Pool. They were careful to keep their heads above water as they strapped them in.

Jansen looked at Kavi and flashed him the Ghost Squad sign with his left hand. The large Guard twisted his fingers into the symbol he carved into his face when he became leader of the Guards. The hand gesture never caught on.

Kavi returned the signal now. He felt a flush of warmth as all the Ghosts made the same gesture and filed out of the room.

The glowing sphere from the ceiling descended.

32

A tangle of thread

Before the light completed its descent, Kavi pulled his left arm from its strap and entwined it with Elana's right. Just like a fuse. Maybe the physical contact would help.

The light blinded, and he closed his eyes.

He opened them to the morning's battlefield. Demented farm animals raced towards their position, red eyes above snarling muzzles. Kavi watched as the devil Marked caught the second arrow.

He stepped into his role smoothly. The feeling of déjà vu was multi-layered. He just experienced all of it this morning, but he was reminded of when he turned back time at the end of their last Quest with Team Sugoroku.

This time was different.

He wasn't in control of the temporal stream

* * *

"I know," said Kavi, again. "But we're out of options. Elana, you know the theory. We're going to need Jory, Tess and Clara in the fuse. I wouldn't make this call if we had another choice."

Elana paled but nodded. "I've never done more than two. Even in the Pool."

"I know," said Kavi. "I also know how good you are. You never would have been picked for Ghost Squad if you weren't the best."

Elana stood up straighter. "I need the three of you to link hands. Clara, take my left hand. Tess, take my right. No time to ease our way into this, so here we go. Close your eyes and focus on my voice in your mind."

He cheered them on, again, as the four began to operate with one mind. The shot went out. It burned through the Marked's hands and into it's throat. He sagged in relief as the beast fell to the earth.

He turned back to Elana. "I knew you could do it."

Her horrified look told a different story.

He whipped his head around and scanned for the Marked. The sheep in the vanguard still charged. The left leg of the fallen devil twitched. It rolled to an elbow and pointed at them. It gave a gurgling scream and the tormented sheep closed on their front line.

Pip shouted orders and Jansen, Trsitan, Stix and Stonez closed around Herman. Sliver placed a suli core into Herman's back. The first wave of sheep impaled themselves on Boost-upgraded spikes in front of the palisades set by the Forts.

"We have to hit it again," said Elana, through four mouths. "Harp said one perfect shot. Right?"

The fused Ghosts began the process anew.

Kavi drew his swords and decapitated a sheep that managed to sneak around the barriers. There were so many of the damned things. Their front line was powerful but pitifully small against so many. He slashed twice more and two more sheep fell.

Wait. Why was he letting himself get pulled in? They'd already won this fight. The Pool was valuable for training and team cohesion, but he had different goals now.

He flexed that muscle in his mind and slowed time. The sheep advanced, slower now. Not enough. He focused and flexed again. It required a third time until the battlefield shuddered and came to a stop.

"Elana," he said. He walked to her. She and the other fused Ghosts were the only things moving.

"Elana," he repeated, louder now.

"Not now, Kavi," she said. Her voice came out of only her mouth.

Progress.

"Elana, stop."

The mind mage never shifted focus from the Marked. "Not a chance. Not until that thing falls."

"Elana, stop!" yelled Kavi. "We already won this fight."

"You're slipping, Tack," said Elana. She pointed. "Look at *it*, look at the things charging us. I don't know how you do your little time thingy, but when it snaps back to its regular flow, this problem isn't going away unless we take down the Marked."

Kavi grabbed her arm and squeezed. "Elana, *stop*. Talk to me, we have time."

Her eyes widened at the contact. "No, this is wrong. Kavi

Stonecrest never stops, and never in a fight."

"Exactly! What does that tell you?"

"Not the time for tests, Tack," said Elana. Anger caused her cheeks to splotch, the pale yellow hue of her neuromancy caused a leopard pattern against her dark skin. "If I can't keep all four threads aligned, none of us walk out of this fight alive. Whether the Marked falls or not."

"You're right," said Kavi.

"I know," she growled. "So, leave me alone so I can focus."

"I can't do that. I need your help."

"Of course you do," she said, skin shining with anger. "You always need more! You ask and you ask and you ask even though you know I'm not good enough for this. Pitiful Elana, the girl with the voice as horrible as the person inside."

Kavi frowned, surprised. "I like your voice. It's unique."

"Stop it!" she shouted. "Stop always knowing the right thing to say to get people to do what you want. You may be able to stop time, but that's not your real skill. Your real skill is manipulation."

Kavi stepped closer in a bid to gain her full attention. "A little harsh, but fair."

Her face began to lose its whitish yellow hue and her eye color faded from yellow to her normal brown. A tear of frustration clung to her right eye. "See! That's what I mean. You're accommodating when you should be screaming at me for my failures."

"What failure?"

She looked up to the sky. "What failure he says." She pointed at the Marked. "Look at it! We didn't kill it. We tried, but we weren't perfect enough. Just like my life, imperfect in every way. You could have had your pick of neuro-mages. For Vonn's sake, you could have had Yantzy, a true professional. Why did you pick me?"

"I didn't want Yantzy. I wanted the best."

"Stop doing that and *stop* lying to me," she drove a finger at his chest, frustrated tears freely rolling down her face.

"The first criticism was fair. That one's not," said Kavi. "I'm not lying and I *never* settle when it comes to my team. The stakes are too high."

She threw her hands in the air. "More manipulation. Fine. What do you need my help with?"

"Sense the neural waves around us," said Kavi. "Tell me what you feel."

She focused and her skin and eyes snapped back to that shortbread hue, all other pigments fading away as she called on her power. "Odd," she said after a moment. "That signal is strikingly similar to what I feel when we fuse in the Pool."

"Exactly," said Kavi. "We're in the Harpstran military's Pool. You were successful, Elana. The four of you killed the Marked. Those psychotic sheep went back to being...sheep. However, you're stuck in the fuse and I need your help to get all four of you out."

She drew a shuddering breath of relief as she processed the news. Then, the red splotches on her face came back. "See, it *is* all my fault. I'm in charge of the fuse and I can't even hold that together. That's what I do. I fail. Did you know I never got invited to compete in the Suli Trials? My parents were so ashamed. *I* was so ashamed. I got captured by the League's slavers because I was running away from home. Can you believe that? I ran away from home. Like a child."

Kavi shook his head. "This is not your fault. I gave the order. I knew it was untested. I knew the risks and I ordered it anyway. This is not your fault, Elana, but mine."

"But—"

"No," he cut her off quickly. "That's my burden to carry. Not yours. We're all running away for one reason or another. That's the story of every Ghost. I ran from responsibility and the death of my brother. Jansen ran from the shame of desertion. Pick any member of our team and you'll find a runaway story. We stopped running when we became Ghosts. We make our own destiny as peacekeepers. Help me fulfill that destiny."

She shook her head sadly. "I'm the wrong person. I'm the weakest member of this team and everyone knows it. I'm useless and I should be dropped if we make it out of this alive."

Kavi slapped her across the face. Hard.

She reared back in shock.

"That's enough," he said. "I will not tolerate anyone badmouthing another member of Ghost Squad. That includes members of Ghost Squad, even if they're badmouthing themselves. This is the first time in my life I've had a team without a weak spot. I do not enlist useless people. I've made my share of mistakes, but when it comes to recruiting, my track record is flawless. Cut the negative self-talk. We have work to do."

"He's right, Mage Starsight," came a voice from the sky above. "The strides you've made with neural communication outstripped even Alfonse Costica. I've never seen such flawless weaving of so many channels at once."

Elana looked to the sky. She turned to Kavi. "Who's that?"

"I know you recognize my voice, girl. I was still teaching when you were at the Academ."

"Madam Protengara?"

"I always saw great potential in you. All you lacked was confidence. Are you ready to drop the self-pity and get to work?"

Elana curtsied to the sky. She smoothed her hair back and with a twist of her wrist had it in a ponytail. She turned to Kavi. "Tell me what to do."

* * *

With gentle guidance from Mage Protengara, Kavi and Elana navigated their way into the closest storm.

Like anything in the Pool, reality was indistinguishable from simulation. They summoned rain gear and leaned into the squall. Driving rain pounded as they trudged forward at a sloth's pace.

The transition was instant, like walking through a beaded curtain. One moment they were soaked to the bone, the next they walked through a cobblestone square under the heat of the noonday sun.

A stone fountain with delicately carved statues sat in the center of the square. Playful stone fish spat water on dancing nymphs and angelic cherubs. Church bells tolled in the distance like tired mothers calling children home for dinner. The heat of the sun magnified an aroma of stale sweat and the sharper, metallic scent of freshly spilled blood.

A cadre of robed monks walked circles about the square,

heads bowed, muttering prayers. Every fourth step, they stopped and pointed at the figures in the center of the square. They chanted 'repent' in perfect unison.

In the center of the square stood Jory. He was bare chested. He flagellated himself with a spiked cat-o-nine tails. Each strike drew bloody weals in a tapestry across his back. Each time the monks pointed and chanted 'repent,' the wounds stitched together, replaced with freshly healed skin. Four figures, hoods on wool habits raised, walked a tighter circle around him whispering a litany of his sins.

"I've heard of this place," whispered Elana. "I think this is Penitent Square. We're in Astra."

"Where else?" muttered Kavi darkly.

"Be careful, Mage Starsight," boomed the voice from the sky.

Kavi and Elana winced and shrank back at its volume. They glanced furtively around the square, but no one reacted to the voice.

"About what?" whispered Elana.

"Don't grasp the neural threads so tightly. It'll cause tension on the line and expose you before he's ready. That could cause the thread to snap, which would be very bad. Give him as much slack as he needs until you get to the root cause of his turmoil."

"I'll assume you know what that means," said Kavi.

Elana gave a tight nod. Her face and hands turned a soft buttermilk as she tapped into her power. "It means we don't have much time. Let's figure out how to get him out of here."

Kavi flexed the muscle in his mind and time slowed. He weaved through the outer circle of monks without drawing attention. He held Elana's hand and led her through the revolving circle with him. She followed limply, like an old rag doll missing too many threads. Kavi felt the energy coursing through her as she juggled neural pathways.

When they closed on Jory, his piercing blue eyes stared into nothing as the four figures circled around him spewed bloody vitriol. Kavi peeked into one of the drawn hoods to see the face of the devil Marked they fought early that morning. He looked into the next hood and the one after that. Same face.

"You're the laughingstock of your family. You'll never create anything worthwhile of your own," hissed the first devil, face a hairsbreadth from Jory's. "You only landed a place on the Squad because they couldn't find anyone dumb enough to volunteer."

Thwack, crack, crack, crack. The cat-o-nine tails struck flesh with a savage blow. Jory believed every hateful word.

"You're not worthy of love. You'll never be worthy of it. You're an abomination," said the second.

Thwack, crack, crack, crack.

"It should have been you. The last thing the world needs is another, pointless artist," said the third.

Thwack, crack, crack, crack.

"They never trusted you. Why would they? You break their trust with every breath you take," said the fourth.

Thwack, crack, crack, crack.

This last strike was followed by 'REPENT!" from the surrounding monks. All fingers pointed in Jory's direction. The look on his face was of a man who felt lower than the dirt staining the cobbles below. A man who accepted his fate. One who believed he deserved every bit of it.

The hopelessness was too much for Kavi. With all his

strength he pushed the first of the demonic Marked. His hands and arms passed through its incorporeal form.

"You're more useless than balls on a priest. You're a waste of good air. They keep you around because they feel sorry for you," said the first.

Thwack, crack, crack, crack.

"That one sounds familiar," said Kavi.

"Because it's mine," said Elana.

Elana summoned a dagger into her hand and thrust it up through the first devil's chin and into its brain. She pulled back the hood to expose the devil's face. "You no longer have power over me," she said.

The demon popped like a balloon, red motes of dust scattered into the wind. A quarter of the monks in the outermost circle vanished along with it. Elana summoned another dagger in her left hand and stabbed at the second tormenting devil. Her blade sliced through it like a tern's wing through early morning mist. The devil reformed and continued its hateful tirade.

Jory paused before his next strike. The eternal rhythm had changed. Something had shifted. He turned his head. "Elana? What are you doing here?"

"Jory, we're here to hel—"

"An abomination," interrupted the second devil. "They knew. Even when you were a small child. All children love to sing, but it was more for you. You also liked to play dress up and hang around the baths."

Thwack, crack, crack, crack.

"Jory, listen to me," said Elana. "None of this is real. You're in the Pool and we're here to help."

"Easy girl," boomed the voice from above. "Pull too hard

and the whole skein will fray."

"Two of these don't belong to him," said Elana. "I don't know which two, but even if I did, what can I do about them?"

"You can't dissipate the fears until you deal with the source," thundered Protengara, "just like you did with your own fear. Look around, you may be able to anchor the other fears to something until you isolate Jory's."

The rotation continued for two more cycles.

"Watch his reaction when the second devil spews his hate," said Kavi.

Elana nodded. "That's got to be it. How do we anchor these other two fears?"

Kavi looked around. "The statues in the fountain."

"That should work," thrummed the sky. "You need a physical representation of the neural thread to link to the statues."

Kavi slowed time again. He pulled his swords and sliced two tails off Jory's whip. "Will these work?"

Elana grabbed the spiked ropes and her dark skin turned the color of summer sand. She closed her eyes and the length of both tails increased ten-fold. She threw the two ends to Kavi who hurriedly tied them around stone fish.

"I hope this works," Elana said. She fashioned the other side of one of the extended whip ropes into a wide lasso and spun it around her head.

"It will," boomed the voice from the sky. "The physical manifestation of the neural path is irrelevant. All that matters is what's inside."

Elana threw. Unlike the other weapons they used to strike Jory's tormentors, this one landed around the third devil's throat and stuck. The devil whipped its head to look at her in surprise.

They faced off for a moment before the voice boomed again causing Elana and Kavi to jump. "Do it, girl. Don't toy with these things."

Elana concentrated and the whip-rope contracted back to its regular size pulling the devil along with it. The devil dangled from the mouth of the fish in an odd, ornamental role reversal.

Jory paused again in his self-flagellation. Only two devils remained to torture him.

Elana repeated the motion, more confident now. The lariat swung and entrapped the fourth devil. The rope pulled tight and reeled the demon in to hang from the other fish's mouth.

Jory stopped hitting himself with what was left of his whip. He sank to a knee under the weight of the scorn of the remaining devil. "Abhorrent. You bring *such* shame to your family. All your mother ever wanted was grandchildren. Tiny children to brighten her day with merry, little laughs. She'll never have that now, will she? You'll never seed the garden if you keep sticking your hoe into unfertile earth."

Kavi caught Elana's eye. "I didn't know Jory preferred men."

"Men like you are always the last to know," said Elana. "Does it matter?"

"Of course not. What do you mean men like me?"

"Traditionalists. You can't imagine anyone being different from your own cultural norms so you don't look."

Kavi stepped back. "Ow. That was harsh." He thought about it for a second. "But true. That's kind of your thing."

This brought a half smile, the first he'd seen from her since he entered the Pool.

"I didn't think men liking men was a big deal in Harpstra," said Kavi.

"Of course it's a big deal," said Jory. He turned to Kavi and his face was tight, skin pulled thin like parchment. He looked down at the ground. "It's always a big deal. Everywhere. To disappoint expectations of society. Of family. No one has a child and thinks, 'Please Harp, bless my child to be different. Make him an outcast.'"

He looked everywhere but at Kavi then drew a shuddering breath. "I'll tender my resignation when we're done here."

"Like hell you will. Believe me, Jory, I had reservations when I heard we would have a troubadour on our team, but that was because I didn't know what you could do. Now? Now, I can't imagine Ghost Squad without you. As Elana said, our squad is a group of runaways. We *are* the outcasts. That's what makes us special. Not only do I not care that you like men, your difference *adds* to who we are. We're going to destroy the societal norms which cause harm. To anyone. Those shitty traditions belong in the past. They deserve to die before the generations that brought them to us. With Ghost Squad, you can own it. Own what makes you different. You have my support and I will cross swords with any bigoted bastard who says otherwise."

The devil continued to spew its vile hatred over their conversation. Kavi sliced another tail off Jory's whip and threw it to Elana. "Can you gag that thing?"

Elana's skin shifted but no matter what she did to the neural channels, nothing could muffle the final devil. It taunted and spewed as she fumbled about.

"It's a nice speech, Tack, but we have Astrans and Krommians on the team. They will not be so forgiving. Most of them won't work with me once they know. You have the gift of knowing the right thing to say, but I saw how you looked at me when you figured it out. You couldn't hid your disgust."

"Because you are disgusting!" said the devil. "You are the lowliest of low, the sodomizer of dreams."

"That's really annoying," said Kavi. "Look, physically I may be one of the fastest people in the world. Mentally, emotionally...not so much. It takes a minute to get things through this thick skull, but eventually...I do learn. Jory, we've died so many times together now. How could something that makes you...*you*, ever be disgusting? Ghosts don't do petty bullshit. We accept the things that make us unique."

"Kind words, Kavi." said Jory. "I know you mean well, but you'll never know this pain. This shame."

"Yes, I will. When we're out of this mess, fuse with me. I already see it, Jory, I already accept it. Do you think I would give up someone with your unique blend of skills because you prefer men instead of women? Now who's being ridiculous?"

Jory shook his head as if he wanted to believe, but couldn't.

Kavi walked towards Jory. He grabbed the troubadour on either side of his face and planted a kiss on Jory's lips.

Jory pushed him back. "You should have asked!" he said with wide eyes. Then he laughed. "But I appreciate the gesture. You are *so* not my type."

"Hurtful, but I was out of ideas to show I meant it," said Kavi. "Can we go now? We're running out of time. We have to pull Clara and Tess out of this mess before it's too late."

Elana had her face in her hands. "That was so awkward and embarrassing. If only I could die of shame for you."

384

"Thanks for the support," said Kavi. He cocked his head. "Wait a second, you've done fuses with Jory, how has this not already come up?"

"I've been discrete with my choice of partners," said Jory.

Kavi pointed at the devil still spouting hate. "I think it's time you let that particular disgusting partner go."

Jory twirled the whip around his head and struck at the devil spewing poison. It popped and vanished in a cloud of dust.

"Where to next?" said Kavi.

33

Love & betrayal

They plunged back into the storm. The crosswinds were so strong they were forced to dodge branches that careened their way.

"Does this one seem stronger than the last storm?" asked Kavi, yelling to be heard.

Elana's answer was lost in the wind.

Like walking through a waterfall, the storm abruptly ceased, and the three Ghosts found themselves in the tanner's district of Harpstra.

Jory wrinkled his nose. "This place normally stinks worse than a beggar on a bender, but this smell...this is unnaturally rancid."

Kavi climbed atop a large vat of cleaning solution and surveyed the area. He recognized it from his fuse with Clara, but there were two striking differences from his last visit. Everything was slate gray as if someone had covered the area with stone dust, and the normally noisy square was devoid of people.

"I've always wondered how the world looks when you're

colorblind," said Jory. "I don't like it."

"This is how I imagine Astra, all grim and blocky. Never how I'd think of Harpstra," said Elana.

"You'd be surprised," said Jory. "Astra's beautiful. They take all that repressed emotion and put it into their architecture. I got the chance to visit once as a child during a lull in one of their wars. Wonderful kebabs. They also serve this sweet iced concoction with noodles in it. Strangest thing I've ever tasted, but delicious."

Kavi let the chatter wash over him as he imagined where they might find Clara. He pointed. "I think Clara and Trixie used to live in a small apartment down that alley."

"Want me to scout ahead?" asked Jory.

"No need. This isn't a Pool scenario, but keep your eyes peeled for whatever might be tormenting Clara."

They walked down the eerily quiet alley and came to the same back door Kavi remembered Clara and Trixie walking through on their way to the Harvest Ball. The door was locked, so Kavi broke through it with his shoulder.

They walked up the back stairs to the third floor. Kavi couldn't remember which apartment was Clara's so they systematically opened or broke through the locks of each door on the floor. All were empty. When they came to a door with a small rune carved into the front, Jory looked at Kavi. Kavi nodded and the troubadour flung the door open.

It looked exactly as it had when he fused with Clara. A pauper's room, lovingly decorated by young women with no money, but plenty of taste and talent.

"Who knew it could be possible to make a dump like this look good. Clara has—"

Kavi held up a fist to cut Jory off. He pointed to his ears

then to the door of Clara's tiny bedroom. Kavi had picked up a hushed conversation.

Jory nodded and drew his short sword.

Elana called on her power. "That's her neural signature," she whispered. "I can't tell who's in there with her though."

"Ease up, you're gripping the connection too tight again," rumbled Protengara.

Jory jumped at the voice and dropped his short sword in a clatter. He bared his teeth in a grimace.

"Who's there?" came Clara's voice from behind the door.

"It's Kavi. Can I come in?"

Clara let out a strangled sob loud enough to be heard from behind the closed door. "Not again," she said. "Please, not again."

Kavi gritted his teeth and looked at Elana. She shrugged and motioned him forward.

Kavi knocked on the door. "I'm coming in, okay?"

The door swung open and Kavi took a step back. The face which met him was one he thought he'd never see again. "Oh, look who's here," said Trixie. "It's the hero. Come to rescue us again."

Kavi stepped back in surprise. "Trixie, what are you doing here?" He longed to pull her into a hug. He looked her up and down and noticed dimpled knees and cloven hooves.

"Well," she drawled. "I'm having a conversation with my best friend. The real question is, what are you doing here?"

Kavi looked over the imposter's shoulder at Clara. She lay curled on her bed. "Clara, this is not Trixie. You know that, don't you?"

"No! Get him out of here, Trish," Clara said. "Call Rake or Boost if you have to. I'll gladly take a beating over another condescending lecture from Kavi."

Kavi walked right through the devil Trixie, blatantly exposing the illusion for what it was. Clara's eyes widened as he sat on the bed next to her.

"Kavi, is that really you?"

"Of course not," said evil Trixie. She leaned against the wall. "Even if it was, why would you want him? What kind of simpering fool encourages his girl to fuck a god? Maybe he's into the whole divine cuckolding thing. Or...he isn't your boyfriend, but your pimp."

Evil Trixie reached around Kavi to grab and lift Clara's chin until Clara's eyes met hers. "You like it that way, don't you? Being with someone who's honest about your worth, up front." She roughly pawed at Clara's breasts. "These gams are pay to play." Trixie barked a cruel laugh and dropped Clara's breasts. "Lean into girl, you would have made an amazing whore."

Kavi wanted to strike back, defend himself. Defend her! But he knew it would do no good. If Trixie was torturing Clara, it wasn't about what Kavi had foolishly said. It was an older, deeper pain. "It's not your fault, you know," said Kavi.

"What's not?" whispered Clara, staring at the wall.

"Surviving."

"You're wrong," said Clara. "I was supposed to keep an eye on her. We were supposed to keep an eye on each other, like sisters. I didn't hold up my end. I failed and she died. It should have been me."

"That's right, you entitled little trollop," said the Trixie doppelganger. "You're a waste of space. Another boring artist in a rotting city filled with them. I had real value. I was the first to unlock a skill. But you? All you did was play the pretty, helpless artist. The only reason you're still on the Squad is it gives Kavi an outlet for his hero complex. A helpless princess to his prince in shining armor."

Jory laughed, like he couldn't help it. "You? Helpless? Are you kidding me? You've kicked my ass up and down the sparring circle. You've saved my life...all of our lives, more times than I can count."

Kavi looked at Jory, annoyed at him for laughing. Then he noticed Elana smiling too.

"And you stand up to *him*," said Elana. She pointed at Kavi. "And he's terrifying—especially when he's in tactician mode and thinking we're out of time. Which is pretty much always."

"Me?" protested Kavi. He never considered his team might find him frightening.

Jory nodded. "She's not wrong. You can be downright scary. Especially when something gets between you and your target."

"I had no idea people saw me that way. I'm sorry," said Kavi.

"Don't be," said Jory. "We need a tactician who can be terrifying. Ghost Squad wouldn't be what we are without it. My point, however, was Clara isn't afraid of you. Even when you're at your most terrifying. Because she's just as intimidating. I never knew Trixie," he jilted his head in evil Trixie's direction. "But I heard she was as fearless as she was kind. This...thing," he looked at evil Trixie with disdain, "couldn't hold a candle to the legend of Trixie. You're letting yourself be bamboozled, Clara. Seriously, can't you see her legs?"

Clara frowned then looked at Trixie's cloven hooves. "How did I not notice those?"

"Because you don't want to let her go," said Elana. "And it's torturing you because you think you deserve it. You have to make peace with her being gone."

Clara's face twisted with pain. "I don't know how."

"Maybe this is a chance to say all the things you wished you said to Trixie before she died," said Elana. "Ignore the hateful nonsense this thing spits back. Better, do what Trixie would do, use that hate and turn it. Remember how she flipped Boost?"

Clara sat up then stood to face the Trixie beast. "I'm so sorry, Trixie. I'm so sorry you died and I couldn't stop it."

"No, you're not, you ungrateful bitch. You always hated me. You were always jealous of me," said evil Trixie.

Clara ignored her. "I love you. I'll always love you as the sister you were."

Trixie devolved into a series of uncreative, meaningless cursing—completely off brand for the real Trixie.

"I wish you could forgive me for surviving when you died and didn't get to see all of this. Didn't get to be a part of this world." Clara gave the cursing Trixie devil a sad look.

Clara moved to her and pulled her into a tight hug. "I forgive you for dying," she whispered into her ear. "I forgive you for everything."

Evil Trixie stopped struggling and leaned into the hug.

Clara hugged tighter.

After a moment, Trixie faded into a cloud of hazy particles that dissipated into nothing.

Clara wept.

* * *

"What do you say we get Tess out of here so we can head back to the Vondam and get some rest," said Kavi.

Elana, Clara and Jory looked exhausted, but they nodded with grim determination.

They donned their rain gear and headed into the storm. The driving rain was less intense, less intimidating than their other trips through the storm. Kavi had companions behind him and the threat ahead didn't seem so bad. After all, this was Tess, the most reliable member of Ghost Squad.

How bad could it be?

The driving sleet of the storm transitioned to a gentle rain as they walked into a lush forest. The tall trees seemed to climb forever into the sky. Maybe they did in this version of the forest which lived in Tess' mind.

"How are we going to find her in this?" Clara asked. "You know how good she is. She could lose anybody in an open field if she wanted to—except maybe Leesta."

Kavi scanned the area. "Elana, can you sense her neural signature?"

Elana squinted eyes that turned the color of shortbread as she focused. She pointed. "Up there, half a click. She knows we're coming."

Clara looked at the neuro-mage, impressed. "I stand corrected. Let's get moving. I could use some sleep."

As they closed on Tess' position, the trees got denser, like they were being pushed on from above, forced to curl in on themselves. Kavi wondered what could exert that type of force on a tree when he ran face first into an invisible barrier.

"Ow," he said.

Clara followed right behind. She managed to stop before running into him. She walked around him and placed her hands against the barrier. "Feels like the dome that surrounds Harpstra. It's got the same energy pulsing through it, like it was sewn together using millions of invisible, squirming ants."

Jory crinkled his nose at her. "Eww. I always thought the dome felt like the strings of a lute after playing a low note." He put his hand on the barrier in front of them. "No, you're right. This is definitely more ants than strings."

Kavi felt a growing pressure on his right foot. He looked down, puzzled until he realized what caused it. "The barrier's shrinking. The dome is moving inward."

There was a rending crack high above them. "Back!" yelled Kavi as a series of thundering crashes came from above. Several large branches fell on the spot they stood moments ago.

When the barrier reached the fallen branches it ate away at the wood, consuming it, like Clara's million invisible ants might break down a crumb falling from a picnic table. Moments later the branch was gone, as if it never existed. No sawdust, no broken leaves. Nothing remained.

"Can you still sense her signal, Elana?" Kavi asked. "I don't think we want to be near the dome."

Elana focused then pointed. "She's close. She moved that way when we came to the barrier. She's got to be in the trees."

"Double time," said Kavi. "I don't know how big the dome is or how much time we have before it collapses, but I know we don't want to be here when it happens. I haven't seen another living thing besides the trees since we got here. I think it's time we call to her. Tess!"

His shout echoed through the forest, ricocheting from tree to tree. It sounded hollow and weak. The other Ghosts winced, waiting for the other shoe to drop. One thing they all learned early in the Pool: never draw attention. They always died when they went in to the Pool, but there was no reason to bring death faster than necessary.

They kept moving. Kavi looked to Elana who pointed in the same direction. "She's moving, but we're closing on her."

They picked up the pace to a brisk jog. No way could Tess move this fast jumping from branch to branch, even if the trees were helping her.

"Stop," said Elana.

Four arrows, one for each of them, planted themselves in the ground at their feet faster than they could process how they got there.

"Not another step," said Tess from a perch high above. Feather prowled around the huge tree trunk, growling and moving from branch to branch in a tight circle around the ranger.

"What are you doing, Tess?" asked Kavi. "What do you say we head back to the Vondam and get some rest?"

She scowled and knocked another arrow to her string. "That's a new one. You have a new story every time, right before you go speedy and try to kill me. Good thing my cat moves almost as fast."

"And how is Feather? Did he get locked in the fuse with you or have you finally been able to figure out how to summon him in the Pool?" asked Kavi.

Tess arched an eyebrow. "That's new too. None of the other versions of you knew his name. I'm listening." She drew her bow, the arrow aimed at his heart.

Kavi held his hands out and explained their tangled fuse situation.

"So, if we're in a Pool, I can kill Jory and he'll just wake up, right?" Tess released her arrow and it flew unerringly into Jory's chest.

Jory looked at Kavi then Tess, surprise painted on his face. "Why did you...why me?" he mumbled then sank to the ground.

When he fell, Tess, Clara and Elana screamed in unison, grabbing their heads in pain.

"Cease fire, Seventeen!" yelled Kavi.

"That was a very bad idea," boomed the voice from above.

"Who in the hell is that?" said Tess. She recovered faster than the rest of them and had already knocked another arrow.

"This is Mage Protengara. I am the neuro-mage your tactician went to for help," her voice reverberated off the trees and the dome. "Jory should be okay, but he's going to have horrible neural whiplash. He'll have headaches for weeks. That pain you felt? That was the last of his neural thread being forcefully yanked from your fuse. If you had killed Elana, all four of you would have been lost to the fuse."

Elena was still on the ground, writhing in pain.

Kavi ran over to her. "Tell me what I can do."

"The threads are jumping all over the place, like I'm wrestling three giant snakes at once," Elana managed to get out.

"Deep breaths, Mage Starsight," echoed Protengara. "If

you're calm, the threads will calm with you. That's it...
.if you can weave them around yourself or Kavi, it should
anchor them. Well done. You'll be happy to know Jory is
unconscious, but stable. I was able to buttress his neural
patterns with some of my own. Thank Vonn you untangled
most of the threads. He should pull through."

Kavi looked back to the ranger. "Tess, please lower the
bow. I'll stay down here. I will have Clara bind my hands if
it makes you feel better."

Tess nodded and Clara summoned some rope.

"Tighter," said Tess. "Convince me."

Tess spun and fired three arrows in rapid succession. She
hit everything she aimed at. Jansen, Stix and Crystal fell to
the earth with wet crunching sounds. They didn't utter a
word when they attacked or when they fell.

"You and Pip are always the hardest to kill," said Tess.
"You almost got me last time."

"Why is the Squad trying to kill you?" asked Kavi.

She scowled at him. "Don't act like you don't know."

Kavi looked to Clara and Elana, confused. The confusion
was mirrored on their faces.

"We each had to face an unpleasant truth before Elana was
able to untangle us from the fuse," said Clara. "I had to face
Trixie and Rake over and over again for months."

"What don't I know, Tess?" asked Kavi.

She loosed two more arrows and Stonez and Sliver fell
from the trees. She draped an arm around Feather's neck
then looked back down at Kavi. "It was me, Kavi. It was
always me. I betrayed Ghost Squad and fed information to
Sugoroku. I've been doing it since we arrived at the Nest the
first time."

Kavi fell to a knee, poleaxed. Not Tess. He trusted her as much as he trusted Pip. He trusted her with his life. With the Squad's life. It would have been kinder to shoot him through the heart then share this news. He stared at her with such pain and heartbreak etched on his face that Tess buried her face in Feather's fur to avoid the look.

"Why?" whispered Clara.

"The League has Mikkel. My cousin. I'm good at communing with nature but Mikkel is in another class entirely. He's what we call green-borne. The Loamians get one green-borne every three generations. My whole family, my whole civilization is counting on me to protect him. I kept thinking I was biding my time until I could figure out how to save him. They have him in one of those labs, Kavi. They're experimenting on him. They told me experimentation would cease if I informed on my team. I know now that's a lie. I think I knew it then. They're never going to let him go."

"But I fused with you, Tess. No way could you have hidden this from me," said Kavi.

"You keep telling yourself a story long enough, you start to believe it as fact. That's the only way I could live with it."

"What story could possibly justify...this?" growled Kavi.

"A simple one," said Tess, voice cracking. "I was doing it *for* Ghost Squad. And I still think it's kind of true. Anytime they interviewed me, anytime they showed me recordings of Mikkel in that little room with all those tubes sticking out of him...I told myself I was gathering as much information on them as they were gathering on us. I never hid it in the fuse, but I always looked on those meetings and interviews as espionage training. All of us who can move silently or disappear get that training, so it wasn't out of the ordinary."

Tess spun and fired two more arrows. This time it was Boost and a different Clara who fell.

"But why not tell us? Or tell just me...or Pip," said Kavi. "We could have helped."

"Because that's not how the story went," said Tess. Her amber eyes were moist with regret. "The story was always justified by finding out something so important it saved Ghost Squad. And...I knew. No matter how many times I told myself the story, it didn't matter. I always felt dirty. You don't feel dirty after doing something heroic. The first time I betrayed you, I knew there was no way back. I'm a cheat. I'm a filthy fucking rat and you should slit my throat before I wake up in the Pool."

"You're right about that," spat Kavi. The ice of initial betrayal turned to liquid heat inside his chest. Kavi wanted to kill something. He wanted Tess dead. Every exposure, every plan the Ghosts put into play to find autonomy from the League. Every conversation with Rose. She probably sold out the Liberators too. She didn't deserve to live. He stomped on the small voice in the back of his head. *If Rake deserved to live...*

No. This was too personal, too close. It had to have been her that sold them out when they planned to steal the sulimite off the ship. Krom...she could be the reason Trixie died. She could have fed bad information to the Ghosts, weakening them just enough for Rake to take the moment to strike. Who could know? Anything Tess said was suspect now. She always acted so distracted. Kavi blamed it on her communing with her bond, but now, she was probably sharing information with the enemy the whole fucking time.

Kavi flexed and time slowed. He broke the bonds which

398

held his hands. He dodged the first arrow Tess shot at him and caught the second. She needed to pay.

"Stop!" yelled Clara. The word was slow and drawn out like it was caught in molasses.

Kavi batted away another arrow and looked back at Clara. She waved madly at him so he breathed out and time resumed.

"What, what can you say, Clara? Tess could be the reason Trixie is dead!" said Kavi.

Clara sat back on her haunches, stunned. Then she shook her head. "No. I don't believe that. I just forgave myself and Trixie. I'm done blaming people for Trixie's death. Tess did what she had to do to survive."

Kavi's rage wasn't satisfied. "No! You can't compare what she went through to what any of you went through. Trixie's death happened *to* you. You didn't choose that path. Jory and Elana, they can't control what they are. They didn't have a choice. But Tess?"

Kavi turned and pointed at Tess. "You chose this. You decided to betray us. Willingly." He turned back to Clara and shouted. "There's no defense for that. So, what, Clara?"

Clara didn't back down, looking disappointed rather than scared at him raising his voice. "You're being given the same choice the Lioness was given. The difference is, you know why Tess betrayed us. Your mother never knew." She folded her arms over her chest. "This is your moment, Kavi. Your unpleasant truth to face. Are you going to wield the executioner's sword yourself? I bet the League would be impressed. I'm sure your mother would be proud."

The words hit so hard that Kavi fell back and sat on the leafy ground.

"Was it a choice?" Clara asked. "What if it was your brother, or Grim in the same situation as Tess' cousin? Can you call that a choice?"

Kavi grabbed his knees and fought for breath. He rocked back and forth like a lost child, hoping motion would give him clarity. "We're all under the same threat. We know the League will go after our families if we step out of line. None of us betrayed Ghost Squad."

"A hypothetical threat is different than seeing it happen," whispered Elana. "It's impossible to predict how any of us would react when it's our family being tortured."

"But why not tell somebody? Why not let us help?" asked Kavi.

"Just like you told us about reversing time?" said Clara. "Or like you told us about those visions you had?"

They were right. He hated to admit it, but Elana and Clara were right. They all had secrets. He put his face in his hands for a moment. He stood and looked at Elana and Clara, eyes pleading. "How could you possibly forgive her? What if she had something to do with Trixie's death?"

Clara eyes softened and she embraced him. "Because it's in the past," she whispered. "There's already too much hate. I can't pile more on."

Kavi pulled away and took a deep breath. "Okay, but I can't see a way forward where Tess stays on the Squad."

"We tell them tonight," said Tess. Her voice floated down through the branches like a gentle breeze. "*I* tell them tonight. I leave out nothing. Then I leave and the Squad decides what to do with me."

She shot an arrow at Pip as he emerged from a void gate, but he vanished into tiny motes of black and white sparks before the arrow reached him.

Kavi nodded. "I can live with that."

"I've got her thread and all three are stable," said Elana.

"Get them out of there, Mage Starsight," boomed the voice from above.

34

Thickbloods

Tess' confession went about as well as expected. Even after Clara put up a solid defense for the ranger, Ghost Squad was furious. Kavi and Pip agreed not to call a vote that night. People needed to think through the betrayal. They needed to put themselves in her shoes, if even for a minute.

Would sentiment change by morning? Kavi doubted it. It was a sad, angry group that left the common room on their shared floor of the Vondam. Clara and Elana offered to stay with Tess that night. They did it under the pretense of setting a guard, but Clara wanted to make sure Tess didn't hurt herself. Kavi and Pip stayed behind with a few others after everyone else left.

"We were so happy when you woke up in the Pool," said Pip. "I could tell by your face it was bad when you opened your eyes. I never would have expected this. Not Tess."

Kavi scowled and shook his head, still processing.

"She's been in all the strategy meetings for tomorrow, Kavi. You can bet your ass the League knows exactly what we're planning with the Thickbloods."

"We drop her and do damage control," said Stonez. "We come up with something tonight that'll pull your Da out of the fire tomorrow, Stix. We can do this!"

Jansen took a deep breath before he spoke. "Or we forgive her and do what Ghosts do best, let her redeem herself."

Stonez stared at him, incredulous. "That's the stupidest thing I have ever heard you—"

"Let him speak," interrupted Boost.

Stonez turned his look on Boost. "And who the hell are you—"

Boost stood and looked down at Stonez. "A Ghost. I *said*, let him speak." The augments in his legs and arm whirred, anticipating a fight.

"Easy," said Stix. "Both of you. Jansen, say your piece."

Jansen nodded. "I'm personally responsible for five Ghosts dying. I wouldn't train in the Pool, and that stubbornness prevented those Ghosts from reaching their potential. That's on me. I accepted it and wanted to kill myself. Kavi gave me another chance."

"True," said Pip, "but you weren't working with the League against Ghost Squad."

"Maybe not working *with* them, but I was doing their bidding. Causing discord, keeping us from uniting. And, I *was* working against Ghost Squad. I did what I did for the exact same reason Tess did what she did. Fear. Not being able to face it. Not able to think of another way. Kavi, you gave me another way. You let me prove myself. Why doesn't Tess get another chance?"

"Different circumstances," muttered Kavi, anger building.

Jansen saw the anger and asked, calmly. "How so?"

"Because I needed you, Jansen! I needed you to convert

the rest of them. And you did! You helped make Ghost Squad what it is today," said Kavi. "But Tess...we can find another Striker. Her replacement may not be as good, but at least we can trust them to watch our back."

Jansen looked at him, mimicking Stonez incredulous look from moments ago. "I can't believe I'm the only one seeing this," he said. "You're letting your rage run your brains. All of you. I'm disappointed in you, Kavi. I'm especially disappointed in you, Pip."

"What? What is that thick skull dreaming up that the rest of us can't see," said Pip. He stood up so he could glare down at Jansen. He stopped, his lips made the shape of an O.

"Get it now?" he asked. "And I'm the one with the thick skull..."

Pip dropped back in his chair, gears turning. "Counter-intelligence. You get one, maybe two shots at it before they know the source has been compromised." Pip was nodding in agreement now. "That first time though...especially if the source has been feeding reliable information for a year." Pip turned to Kavi. "They'll believe anything Tess tells them."

Pip shook his head ruefully when he looked back at Jansen. "I'm sorry I doubted you. You always surprise me. I know exactly how we can use this..."

* * *

Patrice made it clear, regardless of the Squad's decision, that Tess Trueshot (as everyone in the stands that day—now all of Harpstra—was calling her) was going to give her firsthand account of what happened on the field. The League wouldn't have it any other way.

None of Ghost Squad was happy about it. Least of all Tess. She was never one for the limelight. With all the Ghosts furious with her, she looked moments from fleeing.

Ghost Squad reluctantly agreed to the new plan. If Tess could help them and the Thickbloods, she would be allowed to stay on the squad for a probationary period which lasted until they got back to the Nest. The next time she was to report back to her League handler was an hour after the interview.

The timing couldn't be better. It was four hours before the executions, plenty of time for the League to communicate with the corrupt ministers. Plenty of time for them to make the necessary changes for the Ghosts and Thickbloods to pull off their plan.

Kavi and Pip escorted Tess and Patrice to the studio. The interview would focus on Tess, but Patrice was sure Reuben would ask follow up questions of the tacticians.

Kavi and Pip took advantage of the free refreshments as Tess had her hair done by a professional in the next room. Kavi took a bite of something that looked like a teacake. It had a unique blend of spices he'd never tasted. He sniffed at it before taking a second bite. Definitely cinnamon and cardamom, but what gave it that spicy punch? He took another bite when he saw Reuben signal him from a partially opened door down the hall.

Kavi touched Pip on the shoulder and walked down the hall. Reuben ushered them in the room and shut the door behind them. Kavi looked at the man expectantly.

"We found something yesterday and have no idea what to

do with it," said Reuben. "I feel compelled to tell the story, but I'm afraid it's going to get us all killed."

"What? Is it something we did?" Pip asked. "Are the ministers leaning on you?"

The man shook his head and gestured to the other man in the room who fiddled with some dials while looking at a view screen in front of him. "I don't know how to explain this. Uriah, show them what we picked up in that first interview with Lord Stonecrest."

Uriah ran the recording and they watched, transfixed.

"Who's the smoke show?" asked Pip. "Nooo...is that Harp?"

"Look what happens when we slow the recording to a single image at a time," said Uriah. "The upgraded equipment we got from the League allows us to capture all of it."

"Now I get why you were so distracted during the second half of that interview," said Reuben.

"Have you done any interviews or run any stories about the disappearances on the east side?" asked Kavi.

"What does that have to do with Harp?" asked Reuben.

"Stick with me for a second," said Kavi. "I'm starting to understand why Rose doesn't trust the gods. The way Harp helped us felt off. Dirty."

"She is the goddess of fertility," said Pip.

Kavi nodded. "Yes, but what if Harp and this Eastside project are linked? Kwan and Wharton have a ridiculous amount of resources. From the questions Pip's been asking, that financial backing is not coming from the League or the Harpstran government. So, where's it coming from?"

"You think Harp is funding them?" asked Pip.

Kavi shrugged. "You read their proposal, they want to build a business and cultural district. At the center of it is a temple dedicated to the fertility goddess."

"Why would a goddess care about an investment, or money at all?" asked Reuben.

"Money and power are tightly linked. She told me herself that power is the only important thing." Kavi shrugged again. "Plus, another temple feeds her vanity. Who knows, maybe the temple will be the site of her grand entrance back to Grendar."

"You think she could be linked to these disappearances?" asked Pip.

"No idea," said Kavi. "But she's way too interested in us. It's almost like she's following us around, trying to determine if we're enemies or potential partners. My guess is she's not affiliated with the League, but she's trying to figure out whether or not the League will poke their noses in her business." Kavi looked at Reuben. "So, have you done any interviews about those Eastie disappearances?"

"Not my beat," said Reuben. "We always give the east side to rookie reporters. It's a test to see if they can hack the job. If they can get stories on that side of town, they can handle anything we throw at them."

Reuben frowned at their disappointed faces. "That said, I've heard the rumors like everybody else. We lost a promising young journalist down there three weeks ago. Jackson was chasing a story about the disappearances in Eastie. Something spooked him bad. Next day, the studio gets a letter, Jackson went home to help his sick mother. Not an uncommon excuse for reporters that don't make it, but it surprised me. I thought he had what it took."

"What spooked him?" asked Pip.

Reuben shrugged.

It was Uriah who answered. "I caught him before he skipped town. He said he interviewed an old woman down by the docks who claimed she knew who was responsible. The biggest problem with her story? She claimed she was only eighteen-years-old. Two of her eighteen-year-old friends were right there next to the old woman, corroborating what she said. The woman was convinced that whatever aged her was also responsible for the disappearances. Jackson saw something when he was interviewing those girls. That's what freaked him out."

"What if she's behind all of it?" asked Pip.

Kavi and Reuben gave the same slow nod as the pieces started to fall into place.

* * *

"Now we see if they take the bait," said Stix. He pulled Sliver's zoom goggles from his head and handed them to Stonez so he could get a closer look.

Most of Ghost Squad and a collection of Thickbloods lay on the flat roof of the Harpstran Post building, heads poking over the roof's protective wall. They faced the gallows erected on the south side of Independence Square. The five story Post building was two blocks away. It was far enough and high enough not to draw attention while affording a great view.

"There we go," said Red. The man had an old spyglass he

leaned against the rim of the roof wall. "They just moved another guard to Milken. See, he's walking through Hero's Gate right now. They're doing it in ones and twos. Every ten minutes. I can't see them past Hero's gate but I'd bet every copper in my pocket they're gathering at Milken and Main." The currant haired man snapped the glass together and handed it to Mamma Esther.

"I think you're right, Bernie. Sorry...Stix," Esther said. She looked him dead in the eyes. "You best be sure you can trap them in that corridor. They get free, for any reason, and that square will be soaked in blood."

There were only fifteen guards left protecting the gallows. More were leaving every ten minutes. Easy picking for Ghost Squad, but it would be the Thickbloods doing the risky work. Mamma Esther insisted.

"This is a Harper battle for the soul of the city. If it's won by folks who don't live here, why would they listen to us?" she had said.

Ghost Squad was a diversion and an escort if it came to it. That was fine with Kavi. If he was right about Harp and the Ministers, Ghost Squad had bigger fish to fry.

Third bell chimed and people started to file in to the Square. Stands had been erected on the north side so anyone who wanted could come enjoy the grisly festivities.

Kavi met with the Ghosts in the middle of the roof, where there was no chance of being seen. Pip swept the area before they climbed the roof. Tess was noticeably absent.

"Take your suli allotment at fifth bell," said Kavi. "Exactly. We move five minutes after, those of you with timepieces make sure they synch with the Harpstran bells. You know what you need to do." Kavi shook his head as he caught

Stix's eye. "Don't even ask again. I know what role you want to play, but it was your mother who shot it down. I need you, Stonez and Jansen covering Reuben. None of it means a damn thing if he's not there to record it. Remember, the minute anyone has eyes, make sure Pip knows."

They filed off the roof a couple at a time. Pip opened a void gate and Kavi followed him through it. They stepped off the roof of the Post building and on to the roof of the Vondam. The Vondam was a kilometer from Independence Square, but it had the best views in the city. They couldn't see into the Square but they had a great view of Hero's Gate.

They watched Boost and Tess take their perches a block from the Gate when fourth bell struck.

Pip's finger moved to his ear as he managed five different void channels. A half hour past fourth bell, he nodded to Kavi. "Everyone's in place."

"No time like the present," said Kavi.

Pip opened a void gate and motioned to it. "Well then, Lord Stonecrest, put on your fancy shirt. It's time for you to be belle of the ball."

35

Independence Square

They walked through the void gate in to Reuben's office.

The reporter gave them a disappointed look. "Don't you two *ever* dress up? Here, take this." He handed Kavi a blue sports coat with shiny brass buttons.

"Uriah!" He shouted down the hall. Uriah poked his head out. "You have an extra jacket Pip could wear? Seriously guys, we're going into the ministers' box."

"I don't care about any of this nonsense," said Kavi, tugging at one of the lapels.

"Which is exactly why it will throw them off guard," said Reuben. "You're known for not playing by the rules, so if this time you show up in a jacket? It will keep eyes on you. They'll try to figure out why you're playing by the rules, instead of looking around and noticing things you don't want them to notice. The ministers are corrupt, but they're not stupid. They're some of the most observant people in the city, especially Wharton. He doesn't miss anything."

"You think the king will be there?" asked Pip.

"He's not one for executions. When one is actively and

intentionally losing power, shows of force are counter to the agenda. That's my theory anyway," said Reuben. "Plus...I think he's actually a good person."

The ministers had rented the whole second floor of the large inn on the south side of the square. It had a wide balcony which stood above the stands erected in the Square this morning. Someone Kavi's size could reach up and touch the underside of the balcony if he stood on the top seat of the stands.

Kavi and Pip glad-handed their way through the crowd of VIPs. They were the talk of the town. Especially after Tess' deadpan delivery of the events of yesterday morning.

"That Trueshot has ice in her veins," said a bulky soldier to two other men in uniform.

"Those eyes, I heard she's green-borne," said a tall woman in yellow satin to the three elegant women standing around her.

Every conversation they passed seemed to be talking about Tess and Ghost Squad.

Everyone had seen the recordings. Kavi hated the recognition. Pip, on the other hand, soaked it up like a sunflower on a beautiful day. He accepted the praise, cracked jokes, and let the smoky glances from the women in the room linger.

Kavi felt like a plus one as Pip worked the crowd.

The glances the VIPs sent Kavi were ignored. No one took offense. They knew real power when they saw it. They'd seen him fight. They knew his title. What Kavi didn't realize is power recognized power, and it never confronted equal or greater power directly. Pip was the intermediary to Kavi. Everyone in the room knew it but Kavi.

Fifth bell struck and Pip took his leave to ink himself in

the inn's facilities. Kavi pulled a pinch of suli root from his breast pocket and surreptitiously tucked it into his bottom lip as he stared at one of the paintings on the wall. He spread it out across his lower teeth so the bulge wouldn't show. He took a couple deep breaths as the aggression and wave of power gripped him. *It's about damn time I get to take some action that wasn't dealing with my emotional bullshit or that of my team!*

He knew it was the suli talking, but a stand-up fight sounded amazing in its simplicity.

He made his way to the seats at the center of the balcony and gave Ministers Kwan and Wharton a genuine smile. Yesterday was a preview. Today they would see what he and his team were capable of. He wondered if the two ministers would live through the demonstration.

He looked on the gallows. Four nooses hung over four collapsible platforms. Kavi shook his head at the arrogance of the guards. Only eight remained in the square. Kavi hoped the bait they provided hadn't worked too well.

Too late to change anything now.

The guards made a big show of opening the small door on the northeast corner of the square. The prisoners were led by six well-armed guards holding their chains. They walked down a path protected by a squat wall so only those at the top of the stands and in the balcony could see them. Fourteen guards in total then. Kavi was sure the Thickbloods could take them.

He strained to find Stix's father, but all twelve of the prisoners were dirty. Long, filthy hair covered necks and faces. Even the most vibrant tattoos were masked by the filth. They looked defeated as they trudged to the gallows. Kavi

413

was reminded of the slaves who walked outside his caged cart when he was captured those many months ago. He clenched his fists as the suli-enhanced anger burned through him.

It got worse when they came out from behind the wall. The crowd jeered and threw rotten fruit and vegetables at the prisoners.

"Easy," whispered Pip. "Act before we're ready and a lot of people are going to die."

Kavi gave him a tight nod. Thank Krom for Pip. Kavi recognized some of the men throwing rotten tomatoes and heads of lettuce. They were Thickbloods! They had to sell it and they did a hell of a job. If these men could keep their cool, Kavi would too.

The six new guards walked the first four prisoners up to their places behind the collapsible platforms. The men manning the levers to drop the prisoners wore black hoods with small eye holes to protect their identities. Kavi was pretty sure the one left of center was a Thickblood plant. The executioners placed similar black hoods over the heads of the four prisoners. The prisoners' hoods didn't have eye holes. Kavi couldn't imagine their fear as vision faded to black wool and angry shadows.

An imperious looking judge in formal black robes took his place on a platform on the far side of the gallows. He raised a hand and the jeers and chatters from the crowd stilled. The silence was complete as the gravity of the moment sunk in.

"These twelve men were found guilty of the crimes of sedition and treason against the crown and council of the Garden City of Harpstra."

As the man spoke, Kavi caught movement out of the corner of his eye. When he turned his head to look at the prisoners standing farthest from the judge, the movement vanished. He looked back to the judge and caught movement again in his periphery.

He flexed that muscle and time slowed. This time when he looked at the prisoner, he saw her. He sighed in relief. At the same time, butterflies fluttered in his belly. No turning back now. He guessed right. She wouldn't stay away from something where emotion ran so high. She *couldn't* stay away from an event like this.

Harp was flimsily dressed in gossamer silk. The design was arachnid—three webs spread outward, one from each breast and one from her nethers. The web lines shimmered where they overlapped, accentuating each voluptuous curve. The center of each web covered just enough to toe the line of pornography without walking over it. Downright staid for Harp.

She moved around the first hooded prisoner, her hands millimeters from his skin without touching him. The caresses taunted as they brushed achingly close. Her hot breath tickled the edges of the hood until the man's head moved side to side to figure out what force would tease him in such a way in the last moments of his life.

Kavi looked to the press platform and nodded very slowly to Reuben who was the only one of the observers looking at Kavi. The press was not allowed to record the hangings, but they could record the judge before the execution began.

Reuben nodded back and whispered to Uriah. Uriah fiddled with the knobs on his equipment. The man's eyes widened and he gulped.

Good, Harp's performance was being recorded.

Kavi relaxed that muscle and time resumed.

The judge finished reading the charges and started a sermon on morality. The crowd grew restless. Some of the VIPs sighed in disappointment. Self-important men loved to hear themselves speak, but didn't feel the same when other self-important men spoke.

Harp moved from hooded prisoner to hooded prisoner, acting out the same perverted dance. Each time she moved from one to the next, the man she left sagged, as if she had scraped the last vestiges of hope from the pan of the man's soul. When she was through with the four of them, she moved over to the judge who continued to drone on. She rolled her eyes when the judge invoked her name in a call for higher ideals.

She'd finally had enough and began a similar dance with the judge. Kavi stifled a smile when he saw the man cough and shift his pelvis to conceal his growing desire. It wouldn't do for a judge to get that kind of excited before a hanging.

The stomp of giant feet echoed from outside Hero's Gate. Right on time. Raised voices followed. The mass of guards outside the gate expected this. They would not be taken unawares.

The sound pulled the attention of the crowd from the judge to the gate. Who would dare interrupt justice being carried out? No matter, with so many guards stationed outside the gate, the proceedings continued. The mutters from the VIPs behind Kavi grew, but they were annoyed, not anxious.

That would change soon.

"You know who I am. Everybody in the city knows who I am. I know the guard is not known for intelligence but - 'who goes there?' Y'all need some new material." Sliver's voice rang across the square. Her unnatural drawl turned the regular sharp corners of her speech into lazy, drawn out arcs.

Even the judge stopped speaking. He looked to the distraction at the gate. An angry scowl took residence on his face at the gall of someone disrupting his big moment.

Kavi only had eyes for the goddess. Harp's head moved like a bird, rapidly shifting focus from judge to gate, to the prisoners then up to the balcony to find Kavi's eyes. She winked at him, supremely confident. Eager to see what would happen next.

* * *

Outside the gate, Sliver rode on Herman's left shoulder as the giant golem clump clumped up to the guard captain. Tristan walked at the golem's left side, each stride smooth and measured like that of the giant cat he turned into. Elana walked at the golem's right side, her new confidence majestic as her robes of office fluttered behind her. Following the golem were Crystal and Clara pulling a cart filled with fortification materials.

The guard captain wore gold epaulets that looked buffed for at least an hour each morning. He didn't look happy by the interruption, but knew he had to treat the heroes of Harpstra judiciously. If he didn't, those pretty shoulder decorations might be stripped from him.

"Yes ma'am, of course I recognize you, but what are you doing *here?*" he asked in the most reasonable tone he could summon.

"Well...my boss heard there might be some trouble from those...Stickybloods, I think they're called?" said Sliver, loud enough so everyone in the square could hear her. "He wanted to offer our help to secure the area. Clara, Crystal, y'all go ahead and put fortifications facing out. If those Stickies come at us, I want them to hit those chevals so hard their spit flies back three blocks, you hear?"

Clara and Crystal went to work installing cheval traps facing out.

"Wait! If you do that, we're not going to have any mobility," said the guard captain.

"Oh don't mind that Cap'n, you've seen us fight. What mobility you gonna need anyhow with Herman here anchoring yer line?" Sliver said, each word drawn out, totally uncharacteristic of the fast-talking Bricker.

"No, no fortifications! We're not sure they're coming this way. If we need to move, we need to move quickly," said the guard captain. "Wait, why is her skin going all sand-like?"

"Oh Cap'n," said Sliver in her new, slow drawl. "It's far too late for that kinda question, wouldn't you say?"

The guard captain's mouth pulled into a moue one might see on an angsty teen. His men collapsed behind him. "Why? You're supposed to be on our side," he said right before Elana's whisper brushed his mind. The last thing he would remember was that gentle, beautiful voice say, "Sleeeep, we've got this. Everything will be okay."

* * *

Inside the Square, the mutters shifted. It was anxiety now. Many looked to the ministers or Kavi and Pip to tell them it was going to be okay.

Harp looked out the gate. She rubbed her hands gleefully when the guards collapsed.

Two of the guards inside the square went to check on the guard captain.

That's when the Thickbloods attacked. Nearly half the crowd in the bleachers joined the attack. The rest screamed in horror and rushed to the other exit out of the square. That exit was protected by only four guards who were quickly overrun by the fleeing mob.

Kavi nodded to Stix. He led Jansen and Stonez through the gate before the mob overwhelmed them. They vaulted to the press podium and took flanking positions around Reuben and Uriah. Stonez had to pull Stix back twice when the man looked like he was about to jump into the fray.

The Thickbloods quickly overwhelmed the remaining guards in the square. The VIPs shouted in anger and fear. They retreated from the balcony and into the second floor of the inn. They tripped over each other in a rush to make it down the stairs and out the back door.

Mamma Esther's orders held. Not one of the Thickbloods pulled an edged weapon. They subdued the guards with clubs, cudgels, and the weight of numbers.

During the chaos of the riot, Kavi made his move. He'd watched Harp the entire time. She showed no signs of leaving, drawn to chaos like a bee to a flower. She reveled in the melee, deftly avoiding blows as she stopped to caress the face of a guard here, reach for the crotch of a Thickblood there.

Kavi jumped from his place on the balcony, bounced off the third step of the bleachers and sprung to the gallows. He flexed and time slowed. He grabbed Harp by her left arm and wrenched it behind her back.

She looked over her shoulder at him fiercely then bit him, impishly, on the side of his neck. "Yes!" she yelled. "Now *smack* that ass!"

Not what he expected. He pulled back and rubbed his neck against the side of his jacket. She hadn't drawn blood. She thought it was a playful attempt at rough sex. He looked down at her as she brushed her ass against his crotch.

"Take me now," she said. "Right here in front of all these people. They'll never know. Join with me. Give me your seed. You're the only one worthy of taking me on this whole damn world."

He smacked her hard on the ass, playing her game, drawing it out. Anything to keep her speaking. She kept rubbing against him and it had the intended effect. He grew harder than pig iron as he pushed himself against her.

She squealed with delight.

He took his other hand and wrapped it around her neck. "Now tell me how you stay so fucking gorgeous after all these centuries. Is it something you can teach?"

"Only after you throw that hog inside me." She squirmed.

He squeezed tighter than he wanted, sulimite mixing with adrenaline. He took a deep breath and forced himself back to the plan. He had his suspicions, but he needed to be sure. "No, tell me now. You get nothing until I know it's not my seed that gives you long life. I'm not stupid enough to let you drain me into a shriveled raisin."

She laughed, deep and sultry. It turned to a purr as he

twisted her arm even harder. "Yes!" she cried again. "Give it to me now."

"Not until you answer me."

"I know the brain shuts down when all the blood fuels your little soldier, but I know you saw me." She smiled at him over her shoulder. "Wasn't it obvious?"

"When you were walking around the prisoners? You were sucking the life force out of them, weren't you? Like some grotesque mosquito."

"And what of it?" Harp asked. "That's all mortals are. Food. Cattle." She rammed back hard and this time when her backside struck, it was done in anger. "You mortals have such infinitesimal lifespans. You might as well be bugs. Who cares if I suck a life here or there. Few will remember in a year. Everyone will have forgotten in ten. I'm over eleven thousand years old, boy. Ten years to you is a blink of an eye to me."

He ground himself against her. Keep her talking. "These people worship you! Don't you owe them protection?"

"People worship the sun and the moon too. You want to know why? Because they're stupid. Besides, I *am* offering protection. That's why the good ministers are building me a temple! Hence the fracas." She waved her free hand at the riot dismissively. "In only five hundred years, these people converted all my old temples to something no respectable goddess of fertility would be caught dead in."

"And how does a temple protect them?" hissed Kavi.

"Rather than die to the rot, or addicted to hazeweed, they can come to my temple and live their last moments in pure bliss. It's a gift I give freely."

"Free? The cost is their soul."

She rubbed back against him hard. She laughed that sultry laugh. "The soul! That's the biggest myth of all. It's all just energy. Live long enough and you'll figure it out. Now, I've been more than patient, it's time you give me what I need."

"Agreed," said Kavi. He pulled the rope off his belt and bound her hands behind her back.

She arched her neck and looked at him incredulously. "Oh ho, you mean to capture me young man? Have you thought this plan through? There isn't a cell on Grendar that can hold me."

"Maybe not, but someone needs to hold you to account. Your games have caused a lot of pain, a lot of death. It has to stop."

"You have no idea what you're dealing with, boy," she hissed. "Life is pain, and it *always* ends in death. Unless you're me. If that doesn't scare you, you're an idiot! You want to see games, I'll show you games."

Harp broke the rope binding her wrists contemptuously. She spun and pushed Kavi so hard he flew off the platform and in to the bleachers with a painful clatter. She raised her hands and liquid silver ran through her fingers. Her fingers moved in a blur and she spun the silvery firmaments into an immense web. She tossed it over the crowd.

Harp winked at him and time resumed.

Jansen and Stonez locked shields in front of Reuben, Stix and Uriah, but it wouldn't be enough. Jansen invoked shield wall. When the web struck, it bounced harmlessly off the golden patina of the summoned barrier.

Kavi ran to the wall of the inn and took shelter under the balcony. The web struck the balcony above, and he remained free of the strands.

Pip had the wherewithal to summon a void gate, his eyes and skin dark as the midnight sky. He walked through the gate and on to the wall atop Hero's gate. He held a finger to his ear and shouted loud enough to echo across the square. "Ghosts to me!"

Those who remained in the Square or on the balcony were not so lucky. When the web expanded and struck, they convulsed. They looked, as one, to Harp.

She closed her eyes and raised her hands in exultation. Those struck by the web mimicked her motions.

Kavi flexed and time slowed. He gained his bearings and charged the goddess. Kavi bounced off a guard's shoulder, arms raised in the air. Then off the shoulder of a Thickblood, synchronized in motion, enemies united in divine purpose.

Kavi launched a kick at the goddess as he gained the platform. Even at his extreme speed, she easily dodged. Her power interfered with his. Time moved jerkily, slow then fast.

The crowd turned as one to point at Kavi. "Heretic!" they yelled with one voice. "How dare you strike our goddess? Heretic!"

Kavi pressed the attack. Harp dodged without expending any effort.

As the web took over his people, Stix boiled with rage, no longer able to contain the suli aggression. He jumped from the press platform and charged the goddess. When he reached the steps, he drew steel and invoked his dervish spin. A tornado of steel whistled towards the goddess.

Harp looked at him and laughed. "You can't use skills I invented against me!"

As Stix closed, she grabbed one of his hands and led the

spinning Guard around the platform in a graceful dance at a speed only Kavi could recognize. She released Stix and sent him spinning like a top towards Hero's Gate where Ghost Squad gathered.

Jory pulled the lute from his back and played two power chords. The music arrested Stix's movement. The Guard fell like a spinning coin hitting a wall. The wave of power from the chords swept forward, mowing down the converted. Harp turned her attention to Jory.

"What did I just say?" she scolded. "Music is *my* thing." She raised her voice in a beautiful, haunting melody that picked up the converted as it clashed against the discordance of Jory's composition. Her melody spun around Jory's playing, taking his notes and deflecting them back at the Ghosts. When the wave of sound struck, it scattered Ghost Squad out the gate like autumn leaves before a winter gale.

Pip made a split-second decision from high on the wall above Hero's gate. He stepped through a rip in the void to land behind Harp. Taking inspiration from her web, he left the rip open and pulled at the void, black and silvery celestial goo stretched towards his hand like taffy. He cut the strands by closing the gate then formed them into a crude net which he tossed at Harp.

Kavi and Harp continued to trade blows. Kavi was the mouse being toyed with by the cat. Harp fought at least five battles at once while a suli-enhanced Kavi could barely keep up with one.

Harp had seen Pip's sloppy net whirling her way. She summoned a spidery shield above her head. What she didn't expect was for the void net to pass through her shield and land over her head and shoulders.

She screamed.

The crowd of converted Harpers continued to point at Kavi and Pip and yell, "Heretic! Heretic!"

Kavi drew back when the void mesh dispelled her illusion. The goddess was hideous. Her gray skin looked like melted rubber, pulling tight in some places, hanging in wrinkled masses in others. Her breasts sagged to a protruding belly and that wizened face, littered with boils, would give Kavi nightmares for weeks. She had wisps of white and avocado green hair poking from her mottled skull.

Kavi fought the urge to vomit.

"Heretic! Heretic! Heretic!" The screams from the crowd grew frenzied. The mob moved for the first time, towards the platform.

Kavi looked to the press booth and saw Reuben gesturing to him. "Speak!" the newsman yelled over the din.

Kavi faced the recording crystals. "You call me heretic!" he yelled. "And I say, if this," he pointed to the obscenity that was Harp, "is what we're asked to worship, then call me heretic! I wear the name proudly. The gods are not what we thought. They are not here to help. They are here to increase their own power by feeding on us. We can't give in to these parasites. Join me, for I am heretic!"

The void net faded from around Harp's shoulders and she transformed back into the impossibly beautiful woman. Pip readied another net. Harp took a last look at him. She shook her head and wagged her finger at Pip. With a pop, she disappeared.

Pip walked to Kavi and stood beside him above the crowd, his eyes on the recording crystal. "If you're a heretic, so am I."

"Heretic Squad, report!" bellowed Sliver, from atop Herman. The rest of Ghost Squad picked themselves up and marched through Hero's Gate. Jory played a militant tune that fit the mood, bedraggled but triumphant.

"Heretic Squad reporting," yelled Clara in Kavi's direction. She beamed at him.

Kavi wanted to go down there and sweep her up in his arms, but he resisted the urge. No reason to paint an even bigger target on her back.

The crowd stopped their chanting when Harp disappeared. They looked about as if waking from a dream.

"We got it," said Reuben after a nod from Uriah. "Though it will likely mean our heads if we broadcast."

"Heretic Squad is your personal escort until all of Grendar sees what's on that crystal," said Kavi.

"I'm a little more worried about what happens *after* they see what's on it," said Reuben with a wry smile.

36

Grim

Grim stood, eyes drawn to the mayhem in the stands. On the sands. Everywhere he went. He was a bringer of chaos. He felt sad for the death of the Vendri, guilt for the death of the Councilors and confused about what just happened with Krom.

More than anything, Grim felt tired.

Enough! We have work to do, said Bloody Grim.

He looked to his father and nodded. Fatigue turned to anger. Anger lent energy. It wasn't the crazed anger brought by battle lust. This was a slow burn, a pilot light lit when he was a lad. Now the boiler was ready to burst. He tapped into it, used it, but didn't hand Bloody Grim the reins.

He dropped his staff and charged the stands where his father knelt over the obese, still screaming, male councilor. The woman councilor had bled out. Her face was waxy and pale, open eyes unblinking.

When Grim reached the wall, he leapt. He cleared the five-meter barrier to land in the stands. He moved at a sprint, taking several wide steps with each stride. Stealth was counter to his purpose. He wanted his father to hear him.

He burned for this confrontation.

His father spun, naked steel held in front of him, like a priest with a holy relic warding off evil. His eyes widened when he saw Grim. For the first time, Grim saw fear in his father's eyes. The general knew how to control his emotions, and that fear transformed to rage.

"Look what you've done! This is all your fault!"

"NO!" roared Grim in his face. The fear sidled back in to his father's eyes.

The remaining councilors covered their ears at Grim's booming denial. They resumed their sprint for the exits atop the coliseum. Several had started to walk back to help their colleagues when the General killed the Vendri. Now, they ran from Grim.

Grim stayed inches from his father's face. "None of this is my fault. You orchestrated my capture, my time at the League. You put me in that psychopath's hands for experimentation. No longer. I will no longer tolerate you taking credit for every accomplishment. I will no longer tolerate you pointing the finger of blame for anything that goes wrong. I will no longer tolerate that nothing is *ever* your fault!"

The general flinched, eyes wide, as if surprised by Grim's accusations. "That's ridiculous, you know damned well I've never played the victim!"

"No, you're so much worse. You're an egomaniacal hypocrite who truly believes everything you do is right. Simply because, it's you who did it. You've never once apologized for anything in your life, have you? Do you know how pathetic that is? You could never consider anyone else has a valid reason for doing anything! Mentally, you're a seven-year-old who hasn't realized other people feel things too. You're a worm of a man."

The rage grew with each word, and General Broadblade finally swung his sword. The blade moved towards Grim lazily, like a spoon through honey. Grim looked at his father in confusion. Then he looked for Krom, but there was no sign of the god. Everyone around them moved at regular speeds. The councilors made it to the exits and were high-tailing through them.

Tired of waiting, Grim plucked the slow-moving sword from his father's hands and examined it. Mizrak was the name of the sword. After fourteen generations, it still had the clean lines it was famed for. Not a single scar or blemish on its edge. His ancestors replaced the hilt three times that Grim knew of, but the blade itself remained pristine after generations of battle.

He held the blade with one hand on the hilt and the other near the point. As a child, he dreamed of when the sword would pass to him. No longer. He slammed it down on his knee with all his berserker strength, snapping it in two, then tossed the pieces over his shoulder disdainfully. It was a legacy of abuse and subjugation that no longer belonged in Grendar.

His father looked at Grim in horror, then fell to his knees over the broken pieces. He looked as old and broken as the sword. He whispered, "Fourteen generations...ruined, destroyed because of a...a temper tantrum?"

"You have ten minutes to explain why you didn't take the League's money. The others jumped at the chance to line their pockets. They then claimed to their constituents that they strengthened the army and brought glory to Krom. But not you. Why?"

His father continued to stare at their broken legacy. "Mizrak was over four hundred years old...the Broadblade name is nothing without it."

Grim grabbed his father by the back of his collar and lifted him to stand. "Pay attention. If you answer my question truthfully, you might live through this."

His father finally looked up, resignation in his eyes. "You never did learn to respect your elders."

"My *elder* sold me into slavery. Nine minutes." Grim dug thumb and forefinger into the hollow between his father's neck and shoulder.

His father held a hand up. "Okay. I'll tell you." The general looked around for a wine skin in the ruin of supplies the councilors brought for the afternoon review. He found one and took a long pull.

"You're stalling."

The general ignored his son and took another sip. He sat in silence for a long enough moment that Grim contemplated slapping him. Finally, he spoke. "I worked too hard to get to where I am today. I couldn't live with the idea of slipping a yoke around my neck."

Grim snorted. "Yet, you had no problem slipping a slave collar around mine."

"Do you want an answer to your question or not?"

Grim gritted his teeth but nodded.

"Our name guarantees a spot at the Bastion. That's it. Broadblades work their way through the ranks. We don't request cushy commissions, no gallivanting through the countryside as Eagles. We fight on the ground. With the men. We sling mud next to them, listen to their stories, swap blood, and shed tears over the fallen. That's why they respect us." He looked at Grim to see if he understood.

Grim gave him a tight nod. He'd heard it again and again as a child. The words often accompanied a beating. He held his tongue because the honesty in his father's delivery begged for an attention Grim never gave when he was younger.

His father took another pull from the wine skin. "Most Councilors got to where they are today because they mastered the art of kissing ass. Not all. There's still a couple of warriors on the bench, but most. When they kissed the right asses, they got promoted. They got paid more, they gained more influence, gained access to greater asses to kiss. When they got to the top, they realized there are always more asses to kiss: allies, the obscenely wealthy, other councilors. Our leaders are groomed to be obsequious. The League shows up and puts on such a display of power that the councilors fell over themselves to be the first to kiss their asses. The League made extraordinary donations of buildings, arms and technology. All the Council needed to do was show support for their recruiting efforts. Our answer was obvious. The Council knew it, the League knew it, all the citizens knew it. Of course we would take the money."

"But you said no," said Grim.

The general nodded. "It bothered me that everyone assumed we would take the bribes. Make no mistake...that's what they were. No one even asked why the League would give us so much for so little in return. When I asked why, I found the Council didn't want to know. They wanted the money. Money is a powerful aphrodisiac, gather enough of it and you forget where you came from. You stop caring about everything *but* the money. That didn't sit right. When I asked the next logical question - what happens when the money's spent and they ask for the next thing? Nobody had an answer."

"And Krom falls to the League with a jingle of coins." Grim shook his head in disgust. He had held out hope that his father's denial was noble, a stand against tyranny. But no, it was only another symptom of the man's enormous ego. What a disappointment. "What about the research? Was that the council's idea or the League's?"

"Mine. We have to unlock some of these secrets ourselves or we fall deeper under their sway," said the General. "The Council is already discussing what they can give the League for more access. Somebody has to speak for the people of Krom. To do that we need leverage."

It made a sick sort of sense. "So you exploit the men under your command before the League can."

His father ran his fingers over his short gray hair. He looked up at Grim as if seeing him for the first time, and was still not impressed. "Look at you, talking down to me. It's the same decision commanders of men have made since the dawn of civilization. Sacrifice the few to save the many. When there are no good choices, you make the one that does the least harm to the men. If you had lasted more than a couple of months you might have learned that."

Grim shook his head. "I will never lead men. Leadership requires trust, a man who can't tell the difference between friend and foe on the field will never earn trust."

"Wrong!" said his father sharply. "Men don't follow because of trust. Men follow strength. You have more strength in one finger than most have in their whole bodies. Every street in Krom has been buzzing about what happened with the banglor. The General's giant of a son, nine-foot-tall behemoth of solid muscle who eats rocks for breakfast so he can shit diamonds for dinner. Apparently, you drink so much that you piss the finest Krommian whiskey. Wait until they hear about the Vendri. Any man, woman or child in this city will follow you if you ask."

Grim clapped the man on the shoulder, hard. "Don't worry Dad, I'd never threaten your position. Can you imagine me with that type of responsibility?" Grim barked a short, bitter laugh.

His father winced at the blow. "No," he said honestly. "It'd be the purest form of disaster, like an earthquake during a hurricane. But people need heroes. People also love to hear about someone sticking it to those with power. That stunt with the Vendri will be even more popular than the one with the banglor. You might be exactly what this city needs to show we're more than servants of the League."

"Too bad I can't stay."

"I could have Proust lock you back up."

Grim looked to where Proust and the test subjects squared off on the sands. The technicians remained locked in their cage waiting to see what would happen next. Proust faced the men and women in the numbered uniforms without a tremble. Grim admired her courage, even if it came from lunacy.

"We're long past that," said Grim, "but I do have one more question before I go."

His father looked at him and nodded. "Go on then."

"If the League ends up being as bad as we think, can I call

on you to stand against them? Can I call on the people of Krom to stand against them?"

His father blew out his cheeks and looked to sky. "It depends on how strong you are when you ask. Yes, I know all about the Liberators and the fifth Sage. The League is doing a good job framing her as a coward. They won't follow her but they might follow you."

Grim looked down at his father, not realizing how small the man looked until this moment. He had always been larger than life but now he looked old and worried. Even his scars had started to fade to wrinkles.

"Maybe it won't come to that," said Grim. He started to walk away then looked back. "But don't be surprised if it does."

Grim walked up the stairs to the second-floor exit and left the coliseum.

* * *

Blue was still in the stable outside the War College. The stable hand looked at Grim with wide eyes and retrieved the monstrous horse. The stable hand bowed and gladly passed over an apple from the bushel outside the row of stalls. Grim fished for a coin from one of the two councilor's purses he picked up on the way out of the coliseum. The dead woman wasn't going to use hers and the other, well, let's just say the grossly rotund man could skip a few meals anyway. He found a copper and tossed it to the lad.

"Thought you'd be bigger," said the boy. "The stories

says you is a giant."

"Never believe the stories," said Grim with a wink.

Grim grabbed the lead rope and bit into the apple. Blue gave an annoyed whinny. Grim laughed and fed the rest of the apple to the big horse. As they walked down the large boulevards, people stopped to look at him in his numbered uniform. Others pointed and whispered. He looked around, expecting to see Farber trailing him to the city walls, but his father hadn't sent an escort.

How did so many people know about him? Why hadn't the general locked the story down?

It must have something to do with the banglor escaping. The Council was probably looking for a scapegoat.

Grim shook his head wryly when he figured it out. They weren't looking for a scapegoat. They were using him as a recruitment tool. Glory to the Broadblade name and a horde of new volunteers for their research.

He reminded himself to never underestimate his father.

The contemplation took him halfway out of the city towards the eastern gate. He hadn't formed a plan yet but realized he didn't have supplies to get him and Blue to Stonecrest much less a Liberator camp. He looked for a tavern or an inn.

He passed up the Rusty Axe and the Mournful Raven. Their windows were dusted and the interiors looked sad and lonely.

He finally stopped at the Oaken Shield. It was a clean establishment a stone's throw from the city wall and a quick walk to the eastern gate. He hitched Blue to the post outside, hoping to get in and out quickly. The common room was bright and clean. High top tables near the bar were made from flat tower shields which had been flipped over and mounted to a stand. These tables were empty. The low tables near the fireplaces sat several merchants conducting business in boisterous tones and solemn whispers.

Grim walked up to the bar and caught the eye of the squat, matronly woman coming from the kitchen.

"Don't think the kitchen's big enough to feed the likes of ye," she said in a soft, lilting voice. She had no scars and her accent pinned her as an implant.

Grim gave her a crooked smile. "You should see the size of my horse. Can I buy travel supplies for three days for me and my mount?"

She snorted. "So, ten days of supplies for a normal person and if yer beast is big enough to hold ye, let's count on ten days for him as well. Will that do it, love? How about an ale while ye wait?"

Grim considered for less than a second before agreeing. *Just one to warm the belly.*

It's never just one, is it? asked Bloody Grim. *Remember what Krom said about getting in shape.*

Grim ignored his battle twin and smacked his lips as the woman laid the mug on the bar. The foamy deliciousness of the head bubbled over the rim of the cup. He took a long pull and burped happily as it hit his stomach. A sense of well-being crept up on him. This was what he'd been missing. In one gigantic gulp he drained the rest of the ale and ordered another. *What's the big rush anyway.*

Don't do this, said Bloody Grim.

The no-nonsense innkeeper approached with the second mug and Grim licked his lips in anticipation. Before he could pick up the mug, a burble muttered in his belly. He felt the anticipatory saliva of impending vomit wet the sides of his tongue. He tried to hold the explosion back but there was no stopping the disgusting flood. He looked around in panic, face turning green. Grim settled on retching on the floor below him. The yellow and brown chunks spattered his boots and the base of the bar.

"Krom's Grace!" shouted the innkeeper. "When did ye start drinking—this morning? Yer gonna have to clean that up ye know."

Grim looked down at the mess he made then back at the innkeeper. "This was my first ale in weeks. Are you sure there's nothing wrong with the keg?"

The woman pointed towards the merchants. "They're drinking the same stuff. Don't ye be blaming yer weak stomach on the beer or I'll kick you out on yer ear."

Grim had been kicked out of so many taverns in the last five years he could tell she wasn't serious. He couldn't understand it. He could down a bottle of moonshine without vomiting and a single beer laid him low? He reached for the new mug but the innkeeper pulled it away.

"Not until ye clean up the mess ye already made." She grabbed a half-filled bucket from under the bar and threw a washcloth at him.

He didn't have a full stomach to begin with, so the clean up took only seconds. He passed the bucket back to the woman who now wore a full faced scowl.

"My apologies, Goodwoman. I don't understand what happened. Can you pass me that second mug? I'd like to test a theory."

She frowned mightily but handed him the mug.

Grim sniffed at the ale. It smelled alright. He wet his lips on the foam. Still no issues. He took the smallest sip and felt the pre-vomit saliva well up in his cheeks.

Oh, that divine son of a bitch.

Could this be one of the boons? asked Bloody Grim.

And exactly what am I supposed to learn from this? shouted Grim in his own head. *I haven't overcome anything. I haven't beat it on my own. This is a divine shortcut. A cheat.*

So what? said Bloody Grim. *You heard Krom, we don't have the time for you to crawl back in a bottle. And we definitely don't have time for you to find your own way out of it again. Take it like the boon it is and move on.*

Taking away my right to choose is evil. Even if I make the wrong choice, it's my choice.

Grim heard the sound of booming laughter in the back of his mind. This time it sounded ominous. Just what had he gotten himself into?

"Sergeant Broadblade!" called a female voice from the open door of the inn.

Grim reached to his belt for a weapon, but he was unarmed. In his rush from the coliseum, he'd left his weapons behind. He spun to face the voice.

"Marina?" he asked.

37

New heroes

"You forget us already?" asked Marina, eyebrows arched in mock condemnation.

"I was trying my best," said Grim looking down at the full ale in front of him. "What are you doing here? Did Proust send you after me?"

Marina snorted and walked to the bar. Five test subjects trailed behind her.

Krenzer, the most cantankerous of the five, shut the door to the inn and joined them. He looked slightly confused, as if he wasn't sure what he was doing there.

"Once you walked out, it was like the air was pulled from the arena," said Marina. "The general and Proust wilted. That's when we decided we were done with the trials. We weren't learning what they promised and they treated us like shit. We knew we'd be branded deserters, so we decided to find you. We heard your conversation with the General."

Grim scanned the others then looked at Marina. "How?"

She gave a half chuckle. "Everybody in the coliseum heard your conversation. I wouldn't be surprised if half of Krom heard you yelling at each other. What I took from it is that sides are about to be taken. We want to take yours."

Grim shook his head. "I'm no leader, Marina."

"Maybe not," said Krenzer, laying his elbows on the bar. "But you're the strongest warrior I've ever seen and you don't fear authority. I like that. That's why I'm here."

"He's an idiot," said Marina, "but he's not wrong. Krommians follow strength and you're the strongest warrior in generations."

The innkeeper walked out of the kitchen dragging several bags filled with bread, cheese, hardtack, grain and oats for the ride ahead. She leaned them against the bar. "Two talons and four copper for the lot," she said to Grim.

"Where we going?" asked Marina.

"*We're* not going anywhere," said Grim. "I haven't agreed to take you on." He couldn't babysit this crew. What would he do with six Krommian regulars?

The Liberators need more warriors, said Bloody Grim.

Grim took a deep breath. His battle twin was right. The Liberators had taken on too many civilians in the past six months. Promo was constantly complaining about not having enough trained soldiers.

"The life of a deserter is a dark one," said Marina. "Don't think you'd do that to us."

"Should have thought of that before you left," said Grim. He looked away from Marina and down at the supplies.

Marina smacked the bar to regain his attention. "We *did*! We came anyway."

Grim looked to the full mug of ale in front of him. Getting drunk would make things so much easier. No, not easier, simpler, but only for as long as it lasted. Maybe Krom did do him a favor. "Augh! Fine, do you have mounts?"

Marina shook her head.

"Any of your own supplies, weapons, anything?"

She shook her head again. "We were test subjects, like you."

Grim looked through the purses he nabbed when leaving the arena. The woman councilor only had one golden crown and four silver talons in her purse but the obese man had over fifteen crowns. "Fine, let's see what we can do."

Grim turned to the innkeeper again. "Can you get me five times the supply and set us up with three more mounts?"

"Three?" asked Krenzer.

"You're doubling up until I'm sure you're worth the effort," said Grim.

The innkeeper looked the six Krommian regulars over, noting they all had the same uniforms as Grim. "Those outfits are horrible. What regiment did you say you were from?"

"We didn't," said Grim.

The Goodwoman harrumphed. "I can get the supplies, but not until tomorrow. I'll have to send out for some of it."

The innkeeper turned back to Grim. "Now, how many rooms will ye be needing for the night?"

* * *

Grim knew it was a dream the moment it started, something rarely true of his vivid dreams. This one was different. It had an urgency which transcended the dream world. It also had Rose in it.

They stood alone in the canyon where they met all those months ago. She wore the same flowing black silk that had become her hallmark look. He wore his ratty Ghost armor and full helm.

Shame filled Grim as he looked down at her. "I'm sorry, Rose. I failed again. I didn't...I *couldn't* get Krom to join the cause. You sent the wrong person. I blew it."

Rose flipped the veil over her head so he had a full view of those mysterious, almond eyes. "Only you could see your trip to Krom as a failure. You faced your father and the psychopath he put in charge of research. You conquered massively powered beasts without killing them. You faced a god and made peace with your rage. You shifted the attitude of an entire platoon of die-hard Krommian nationalists, so committed they agreed to have research done on them. And you convinced that stubborn, stubborn man of a father to concede he might throw his support behind you."

"He never said that," said Grim.

Rose dropped the hand. "Not in those words, but he would. When he said the city would stand behind you if you were strong enough, that's what he meant."

Grim appreciated her confidence in him, but it felt off. "So why doesn't it feel like a victory?"

Rose shrugged. "Most things don't. The hard work we put in every day doesn't have a scoreboard with wins and losses. As long as you take the next step, every day, it's a victory. Failure only comes when we give up."

She placed a comforting hand on his elbow. "But you're not one to give up. You can't see victory because you look at yourself through your father's eyes, where nothing is ever

442

good enough. That's silly. I just listed your accomplish-
ments over the last several weeks and you shrugged them
off. If I told you someone else did those things, would you
admire them?"

Grim looked down at the red sandstone. "Probably," he
muttered.

She smacked him on the arm. "You need to learn to
appreciate yourself. You're a complex, amazing, behemoth
of a man, Grimstance Broadblade. Even the *gods* have taken
notice." She spit on the ground as she said gods.

He looked back into her eyes. "Why do you hate them so
much?" Krom wasn't all that bad—except for the no alcohol
thing.

"A story for another day, young man. That's not why I'm
here."

"Why are you here, Rose?"

"Because I need your help again."

* * *

"I know we're going south but where south are we going?"
asked Marina.

Grim tried to ignore her. She was like a small child.
Questions poured out of her mouth in an endless deluge
of curiosity. After they stopped to look at the remains
of the broken, translucent dome which once surrounded
Krom, Grim started to suspect Marina had never left Krom.
Sure, the material which made up the dome was fascinating.
Nothing stuck to it, for as long as it had existed. It was

as pristinely clear of debris as expertly blown glass. Years of running to the rock from the Bastion had stripped the mystique for him. Not so for Marina. Grim got the sense she could have spent days playing around the ruins.

Grim clapped his hands together. "New plan. Instead of continuing to torture those poor horses with you fat slobs, we're going to train the whole way to our destination. Every ten clicks one of you is going to ride and one of you is going to run. Maybe that will cut down on the questions for a little while."

When the grumbling started it was directed at Marina.

"Not her fault," said Grim. "I need to understand what you're capable of. Quit your whining or pack your gear and head back to Krom, or wherever the hell else you want to go. If you're going to stay, you're going to run." He held up a hand. "Besides, we used to run double that distance every day at the Bastion."

"They really used to make you officer types run the rock every day?" asked Krenzer. "I thought that was bullshit to make the officers sound tough."

Grim laughed. "Does the General seem soft to you?"

It might do us good to run with them, said Bloody Grim.

Fine, but you're doing the running while I daydream.

The complaining stopped when Grim dismounted and began to jog. He set a quick pace that had him breathing hard within the first two minutes. He knew he just needed to run those first three kilometers before his body would acknowledge the torture was intentional and self-directed. Grim checked out and let Bloody Grim take over. Let him deal with the pain. Krom knows, he put Grim through enough to last a lifetime.

The King's road was surprisingly empty for the first two days of the trip. A few traders had passed, but for the most part they had the road to themselves. Which is why it took Grim a moment to recognize the threat for what it was when he crested the next hill. He stopped jogging.

"Move to the side of the road," he hissed. "Don't arm yourselves but make sure your weapons are within reach. No one talks but me."

Coming toward them was a group of eleven men and women dressed in gold and black. They rode sleek black warhorses trimmed in the same colors. They moved at an easy canter and Grim hoped with every fiber of his being they would ride past. He didn't fear much, but he recognized Mehen colors. Grim knew he wasn't good enough to take on a professional League team on his own. Nobody was that good.

No such luck. The small woman in front put up a hand and the eleven stopped at the same time, executing the move better than a trained cavalry squad.

Grim cursed.

"What was that?" asked the woman with flaxen hair. The symbol of a snake biting its own tail was prominent on the chest of her gambeson.

"Nothing, ma'am. Clearing my throat," said Grim, offering her a meek look.

"The seven of you look like you're up to no good. Who are you and what are you doing on the King's Road?" Her tone was imperious. She expected immediate obedience.

"We're a small merc outfit on our way to Loam to look for a contract," said Grim. He sent a quick prayer to Krom that the improvisational cover would work.

445

"Really?" She tilted her head giving him the same incredulous look his father had so many times.

Grim clenched his fists. He hated that look.

"You look more like bandits. If you're a merc company, where's your standard?"

"We're new. The standard isn't finished yet. The name's Grim's Blades and we registered in Krom three nights ago. Our guild number is four two seven three." He gave her a courtly bow. "Perhaps there is something we can do for you and your company milady? Provided there is some coin in it of course."

"Grim Blades, not very unique." She interlaced her fingers and cracked them in front of her. It was a move Grim had seen too many warriors do when readying for a fight.

"No ma'am, it's Grim's Blades. You see, my name is Grim. It's the play on words that makes our company name unique." He cast his eyes downward in respect while he surreptitiously looked at the hands of the other League warriors. No one had reached for a weapon yet—not even the ranged folks in the back.

That was something.

The ruse appeared to be working. They didn't see the seven of them as a threat.

"Is that so?" she said. "And what makes you qualified to start a guild sanctioned mercenary squad?"

He looked back up at her and noticed that her posture had become slightly more relaxed. It was working.

"I did two tours in the Fourteenth Shield and one as a suli elite," said Grim, puffing out his chest in pride.

She snorted as she looked at his middle. "That's not the gut of a suli elite."

He summoned the haunted look he wore when living in a bottle. "No ma'am, but most of us turned to drink after a tour in the elites. We saw some awful shit. I started the company as a way of giving myself a second chance. Better than being a bandit."

The woman nodded slowly. "I can understand that. We've seen some dark shit in the League, too."

"What our modest leader didn't mention is he's League trained too!" offered Marina in her peppiest voice.

For fuck's sake! The damned woman was going to get them all killed.

The woman's eyes narrowed, and all eleven Mehens reached for weapons. Grim held his hands up. "We don't want any trouble."

"Are you deserter or Liberator?" she snapped.

"Neither. I did my thirty Q and retired. Crispix was Mehen's Tack when I was with Senet. He'll vouch for me. Is he still there?"

She stared hard at him. "Why didn't you start with that?"

"Because I knew it would get this reaction." He scrambled to find common ground. "How do you like being relegated to peacekeeping?"

The large man to her right snorted. "Peacekeepers...a convenient way of putting you old timers out to pasture."

"Oh ho, so you're the new volunteers!" said Grim in surprise. "You're crazy to sign up for this stuff." He looked at the man quizzically. "I thought the season didn't start until next month. They sending you out early?"

The woman, who Grim surmised to be the new Mehen Tack, gave her second a furious glare. "Keep your mouth shut, Argus." She turned to Grim and pointed. "I'm asking the questions. How do I know you weren't a first-year deserter? A lot of you got sprung by the Liberators last season, or so we're told."

Grim looked into the air to put on a show of how to prove his worth. "You can check my league name with Crispix when you get back. It's Bloody Edge. If you don't like what you hear, you can round us up in Loam."

"Crispix is dead," she said.

Grim lowered his head again. "I'm sorry to hear that, he was a good man."

"He was a ruthless prick."

Grim smiled. "He *was* a ruthless prick, but so were most of us. Had to be to survive."

Her expression didn't change. "I'm not buying it, and we're not gonna ride all the way back to the Pit while you roam free. They sent us out here to get non-Pool experience before our first Quest. Taking out bandits like you is a great way to do that."

"Can't say I miss the Pool," said Grim with an exaggerated shake of his head. He watched as three of the volunteers gave commiserating nods. Some of them believed his story. "But maybe there's another way which doesn't end in blood?"

"Like what?"

"A demonstration of skill which proves I'm not a first-year deserter. Most first years don't unlock a single skill—I've unlocked three."

She raised her eyebrows but Grim watched her team. Most looked downright impressed. They might walk out of this after all. "Okay, you piqued my interest. What's your categorization and order."

Grim took a deep breath. "Order?" he asked innocently,

playing for time. He'd have to ease into this.

"Designation, we're calling it Order now."

"I was a Striker," said Grim.

"But you're Krommian," said the tactician.

"That's right."

"Oh shit," said Argus behind her. "You're a berserker?"

He nodded.

"Not sure this is worth it, Koda," Argus said.

The tactician ignored him. "How do you propose we test your skills without a lot of people dying?" She made a gesture with her left hand and Grim watched as two of their ranged warriors backed their horses up.

Grim clamped down on the laugh Bloody Grim was about to release. *Not helping!* he shouted into the recess of his mind. "I needed you to understand the stakes," said Grim calmly. "We both know your ranged strikers will likely take me down, but not until at least four of you are dead."

"You're that good?"

"He took down—," started Marina.

"Silence!" yelled Grim at the woman behind him. He used his berserker's howl which left the six test subjects covering their ears and shivering in fear.

He turned back to the Mehen Tack. She looked shaken. "I survived thirty Quests as a berserker, what do you think?"

Koda gripped the reins tighter but didn't draw steel. That said a lot for her courage. And her intelligence. "So, that's one skill, but you didn't follow it up with an attack. Berserkers are supposed to go insane when they tap into their rage."

"I've learned to control it."

She shook her head. "That's not possible."

"A lot of people died before I figured it out. A lot of friends." Grim pointed at the ranged warriors who continued to back up, looking for space. "You need to tell them to stop before people start dying. I'm sick of killing innocent people, but I'll do it to protect my own."

She held up her hand and the two women stopped their retreat. "I'm almost convinced," she said. Her voice held only a small quaver.

Grim was again impressed.

"Demonstrate your berserker strength without hurting anyone and we'll let you go."

Grim looked around. "Where's your fort and gear cart?"

"We're training without it."

"That's a terrible idea," said Grim before he could help himself. He held his hands up again before Mehen's Tack could take offense. "No shot at you. I only meant it would have been the easiest way to demonstrate my strength."

Koda looked at Argus, still angry at him for speaking out of turn. "Argus, he's the heaviest member of the team."

Grim raised an eyebrow at her. "You want me to throw him?"

"No, just lift him. He's wearing full armor, so he's got to weigh close to two hundred kilos, that ought to do it."

Grim laughed then but it wasn't his berserker laugh. "You want me to lift your second. Fine."

Argus started to swing his leg over his mount but Grim waved him off.

"No, stay mounted," he said. "Can you keep your mount calm?"

Argus' feet found the stirrups and he nodded.

Grim put both of his long arms under the belly of Argus'

horse and bent his knees. *Your turn.* Bloody Grim laughed and they straightened their legs. The horse lifted off the ground and gave a terrified whinny. Grim put him down quickly and jumped to avoid the splash of urine aimed his way.

"Satisfied?" he asked the tactician.

She nodded. "I'm glad we didn't cross blades today, Bloody Edge."

"Me too," said Grim, quickly hiding his confusion as he remembered the fake name he gave her.

The Mehen team got back in formation.

"Koda," said Grim. "Be careful out there. These Quests are no joke. Use your Forts and Dancers more than your Strikers and most of you will walk out alive."

She nodded and kicked the sides of her mount.

"They were a cheerful group," said Marina, moving to stand next to him.

He put all his anger and pain into the stare he directed at Marina. "You almost got us all killed. If you ever disobey a direct order again, I will kill you. Do you understand me?"

She gulped and nodded.

"Say it. Tell me you understand me, Marina."

"I understand. If I ever disobey a direct order again you will kill me."

Grim nodded and looked at the rest of the group. "Everybody who was jogging, keep jogging. We still have four clicks left in our circuit. Except for Marina. She runs the rest of the day."

451

38

Loam

"Where've you been? When Rose sent me the dream, I expected you in a day or two, not three weeks!" said Grundle. When he got mad or annoyed, his ears rounded and hair popped out around them.

"Don't you pull that bear shit on me," said Leesta. She broke into a grin and gave him a hug. She grabbed one of his ears and rubbed it. "When it's just the ears, you don't look ferocious, you look adorable," she whispered to him

He hugged her tight before breaking the embrace. "Never expected a hug from Leesta the Ranger. You look different. Happy." He gave her an appraising look. "It suits you."

She blushed.

"Well, what happened? Where were you?" Grundle said.

Leesta looked over at Nettie, Pyre, and Rice then to the huge redwoods of the Northern Grove. She breathed in the scent that prickled and cooled at the same time. It smelled like a well kept closet, like her grandmother when she dressed for a holiday. It smelled like home.

"Quit torturing him," said Pyre. The tall Vonderian

gave Grundle a masculine hug with large amounts of back slapping.

Rice stuck out a hand which Grundle shook.

Grundle eyed the Astran and the stubble on his head. "Nice hair."

Rice smiled ruefully. "Got tired of fighting it. These evolutions really do remake us."

"It's nice to see you again, Grundle," said Nettie. "As to what we've been doing...well, we've been building good will with the people of the southern reaches. We got into a spot of trouble with the Marked. The people of Derkin's Ferry and the surrounding villages had to flee. There were so many injured. We couldn't just leave them to their fates. That's not who the Liberators are." She looked over at Rose who spoke with Grundle's mother, Keeper of the Northern Grove. Gavin and Reaver trailed behind Rose like well-trained hunting dogs.

Leesta looked at Nettie with raised eyebrows. "A spot of trouble! Nettie here faced Irborra, thunder lizards and waves of angry jungle creatures. On her own! Except, of course, for some help from the gods damned Tinkerer himself. Then," she threw her hands in the air. "Then she built several new villages for the refugees. She can put up a house like that." She snapped her fingers.

"I thought you two couldn't stand each other," said Grundle.

"Oh, she's still a bossy pain in the ass," said Leesta. "But she's our bossy pain in the ass."

"How about you?" asked Pyre. "Any luck with the Keepers?"

Grundle nodded. "They'll give us access to the Pool. My

mother convinced the governing Bosque to hear Rose." He lowered his voice. "To be honest, I think they may give us the Pool. The Loamians don't use it. The Keepers don't trust the League, and they find the technology of the Pool abhorrent. If Rose can convince the Bosque she's not going to use it for evil, it's as good as ours."

"The Bosque," said Pyre. "I've read about it, but never understood it. Do the trees actually vote on issues?"

Leesta laughed. "Trees don't vote, they commune."

Pyre spread his hands. "What the hell does that mean?"

Grundle smiled. "Once I explained to my mother how we use the Pool, she was convinced the VNC stole the idea of linking people together from the Bosque. From the Groves." Grundle looked at Pyre then pointed to the Grove. "Look at those trees and tell me what you see."

"Oooh, I love trick questions!" said Pyre with mock enthusiasm. "Trees. Leaves and needles. Sticks on the ground. Mushrooms, bugs. You know, a forest."

Grundle ignored him and looked at the other Ghosts. "You ever wonder how Leesta and Tess *talk* to the plants?"

"Not really," said Pyre, refusing to be ignored. "I assumed it was some form of nature ether, like what I call on when I summon fire or wind." His eyes flashed vermillion and a flame danced a jig across his fingers.

Grundle gave him a hearty smack on the back causing the pirouetting flame to sputter. "Not even close. The trees are interconnected. They constantly communicate through wisps of wind and fungal channels in the ground. Every tree in the forest knows everything that happens under the forest's branches within a matter of minutes. The forest has grown to fear men. All creatures that chop or burn. Except for the Keepers. The Keepers have grown alongside the trees since the beginning."

"The trees have to be older than the Keepers," said Pyre.

"The Groves are older than any individual Keeper, sure," said Grundle. He looked over at his mother walking barefoot through the Grove, hand in hand with Rose. They looked like children skipping through the woods.

Grundle turned back to Pyre. "Our oldest legend tells the story of the very first Keeper, Brook Greenborn. She was stillborn. Her distraught mother laid her tiny body at the base of Mother Silva, the oldest Cyprus in the Northern Grove. Her mother poured out her heart that night. She told Silva her hopes and dreams for a child who would never be. The broken woman finally collapsed into exhausted slumber. She was awoken by a timid cry. The baby's pale blue skin transformed to an emerald sheen. Her eyes were open and her fingers and toes wriggled in the ground like tiny grubs hunting for food."

Leesta slung her arm around Grundle's shoulder and took up the story. "Her eyes were the milky white of a troubled sea. She would never see as we did, but as the Grove saw. Brook learned the language of the trees—sun, wind, and rain—long before she learned to speak the language of men. One morning when she was eight-years-old, Brook made a horrible keening noise that burned through the small village. Her parents and several village elders followed as she ran into the Grove, wailing the entire way."

Grundle pointed. "It was this Grove, the oldest. Brook found a man who had crafted a new tool, one sharp enough to cut down a tree. The villager had chopped a third of the way through a young Cypress. Brook pointed at the man and shrieked. Roots whipped around him and held him fast. Fungi crawled up the tool and cracked then broke the sharpened black rock of the axe head. Brook ran to the man and screamed in his face. As she did, one of the roots slipped through his clothing and into his side. Blood poured on the ground."

"Intense," said Pyre. He smiled at Leesta with that cocky grin. "Like you."

"Cute," said Leesta. "But true. The elders pleaded with Brook. Nothing got through to the small girl. Until her mother wrapped her in a hug. 'This is how it feels. This is how it feels,' cried Brook over and over."

"Those were the first words she ever spoke," said Grundle. "'I didn't know,' said the man. Brook shook her head and wagged a finger at him. 'Never again.' Then the small, eight-year-old girl cut her own hand with a piece of the same, sharpened rock. She rubbed her reddish, white blood against the wound on the tree until new growth covered the gash in the wood."

"From that point forward, Brook was consulted by village elders on all important matters," said Leesta. "She became the first Keeper to speak for the trees. For all living things in the Grove. Over time, she trained others to commune with the world around us. The Keepers learned to sing songs of earth and sun which taught the trees to take new forms, ones to protect themselves from men and protect men from the elements. That's how the first of the tree villages were formed."

"What happened to Brook?" asked Rice.

"Legend says she lived for over two hundred years," said Grundle. "But she never had children. The forest was her family. When she passed, the Keepers brought her body to the southern tip of the area enclosed within the dome and buried her," said Grundle.

"Planted her is more accurate," said Leesta.

"Planted her," corrected Grundle. "New growth sprung up within a year to become our famed Southern Grove. Since then, all major decisions in Loam have been made by the Bosque—a group of Keepers, city leaders and the groves around us."

"So much better than a bunch of crusty, old men on the Mage Council deciding everything. They're always three decades behind what the people actually want," said Pyre.

Rice snorted. "Better than three centuries. Try growing up in a theocracy. We're ruled by a book which was written a thousand years ago. I hope the rumors of gods coming back are true. Astra's going to be pissed at those greedy bastards who rule in his name."

They stared at Rice. He never said much and he never, ever, talked poorly about his home city.

Piety caught Rice's explosion in her periphery and quickly finished her conversation with Colson, the last of their non-warrior Liberators. They lost three of them during their aid mission with the refugees, each new village needing someone to stay behind to help administer the fledgling communities. Rose planned to pick them up on the way home.

Piety walked over and gave Grundle a hug. "Good to see you, Grun."

She turned to Rice and he winced, as if expecting her to react poorly to his comments about their home city. "It hurts me to say it Rice, but you're right. When I first met you, you were just another zealot. The more time you spend away from Astra, the kinder you've become. Why do you think that is?"

"Still testing me, Twenty-one?" asked Rice with a smile. "The answer's obvious now. I met all of you. I used to see you as worthless heathens. At some point you became people, then friends. We've died for each other so many times now you're more like family."

"Aww, look at him. He's cute when he's sincere," said Pyre. He rubbed the stubble on Rice's head until the man growled and his hand began to glow.

"Except Twenty-six," said Rice. "He might still be family, but he's definitely the slow cousin." He turned back to Piety. "The only reason the zealots still hold power is they don't let our people interact with other cultures. If they did, they know exactly what would happen. That's why they need to be removed."

Before Piety could respond, Rose walked over. "Liberators, I'd like you to meet Willow, Keeper of the Northern Grove. She's going to take us to the Pool the League gave the city. If you didn't already know, Keeper Willow is also Grundle's Mom."

She gave a beaming smile. "I was so proud to hear my boy is a shifter!"

* * *

They took bets on how many hours it would take Nettie to figure out the technology of the Pool. They were all wrong.

It took under twenty minutes.

She laid her hands on the controller devices and could feel the blueprints and specifications of each piece. Every advance which had been painstakingly created by the Vonderians over decades were laid bare to Nettie's critical eye. She flipped through each layered script with the ease of a professor reading a picture book.

No secret was safe from an architect.

Nettie nodded to Rose, then to Keeper Willow. "You were right, they stole the idea from how Groves communicate. It's a form of networking that uses ether instead of fungal pathways."

Pyre passed the silver talons he collected from the group to Leesta. She was the only one who bet it would take her under an hour.

Nettie felt a warm flush when she caught Leesta's smile. "You bet I could do it under an hour?"

"I told you weeks ago I was done underestimating you." Leesta flipped her one of the talons. "That one's yours by right, I bet it for you." She winked at Nettie.

Nettie's flush deepened. "Thank you," she said softly.

"Don't act shy," said Leesta. "I like you better when you're bossy."

"Ooh, are we flirting now?" said Pyre with that cocky grin. He turned to Rose. "What's the next move?"

Rose gasped and her eyes went white.

Gavin rushed over to her as she sank to her knees. He took off his jacket and pillowed it under her head. "Give her space."

All but Piety moved back. "Is she in pain?" asked the Astran healer.

"I don't think so," said Gavin, his wide face a portrait of worry. "At least physically. I've only seen her surprised by the Sight twice. Each time it was something momentous."

Rose opened her eyes and sat up. She looked around frantically until she found Keeper Willow's eyes. "Oh Willow, I'm so sorry. I fear we've brought mortal danger to your Grove."

39

Kavi

"It's amazing that you've managed to piss off this many people in one month," said Sugoroku. "Not only people! No...Kavi Stonecrest aims higher than mere mortals. You've even managed to draw the anger of a god."

Kavi pointed to the suppression collar the guards had put on him.

Sugoroku nodded and her assistant Tom unlocked the device and set it on the conference table.

Kavi sat in the plush chair in the owner's conference room and looked at his boss. He was surprised to receive a summons so soon after their last meeting. Not even two months had passed. He hadn't expected to see her again, ever.

He learned a long time ago, from his mother and his superiors in the military, that when you were pretty sure you were in trouble, you only spoke when asked a direct question. That training kept his mouth shut now.

"A week in Harpstra, and you changed the city's entire power dynamic," continued Sugoroku. "Ministers Kwan and

Wharton fled the city which lost the League some powerful influence, by the way. Then, that reporter slipped Harp's embarrassing performance into the nightly broadcast. Now the entire city is experiencing a crisis of faith. Luckily, the Harpstrans aren't that religious. Thank the gods we didn't send you to Astra."

Tom scribbled notes in his journal as Sugoroku spoke.

Kavi waited for a question.

"Where is Mister Price, by the way?"

He shrugged. "We were never close. I only did the interviews because they were in my contract. I never wanted the attention." He knew exactly where Reuben was. Hiding, under the protection of the Thickbloods. He was pretty sure Sugoroku knew that, too. *She's testing me again. It must be lonely for every interaction to be a form of mental warfare.* Kavi felt bad for her.

Sugoroku eyes narrowed as if she could sense his pity. "Then, we send you on a simple mission on the outskirts of the Scorch, and you and your team embarrass two of the Grandmasters on Vonderia's Mage Council."

Kavi shifted in his seat, but kept his mouth shut. That was more Pip's fault than Kavi's, but he was the Tack of Heretic Squad.

She held out her hands. "Tell me why I shouldn't dissolve your Peacekeeping Squad and get rid of the lot of you along with it."

Pip prepared him for this question with a rigor that would have made Patrice proud. He answered calmly. "Because we completed our last two contracts without losing a single member of Heretic Squad. More importantly, we've brought an endless amount of good press to you and the League.

According to Patrice, the League is seen in almost as positive a light as the Liberators. Respectfully ma'am, that's not because of Sugoroku's B Team, or any other peacekeeping squad in the League."

She leaned towards Tom. "Tell that fucking woman to stop sharing data with the Peacekeepers."

Tom wrote it down.

Sugoroku turned back to Kavi. "And you think good press makes up for the loss of political capital in two of the wealthiest Garden Cities?"

Kavi nodded.

"Why?"

Kavi leaned back in his chair and put one leg over the other. "You know why."

She leaned forward. "Indulge me."

He leaned back even further. "Okay. We are winning the public to the League's side. If something is popular with the public, it's popular with politicians. The political capital we lost was of the shadiest sort—that which could be bought."

"All politicians can be bought."

Kavi shook his head. "Not all. Mostly all, but politicians that are bought through initiatives which support their constituents become long term supporters. If those initiatives line their pockets at the same time, like the upcoming Quest broadcasts, all the better. Now that my team and I have created a positive persona for the League, these politicians can throw their support behind you with a clear conscience. That builds lasting loyalty. Kwan and Wharton would have sold the League out the first time a better offer came along."

The scratching of Tom's pen drew Kavi's attention for a moment. He looked at the book and asked, "Why am I here, ma'am?"

She sighed. "One of these days, you will piss the wrong person or god off, young Lion. I just hope I'm not here to see it. As for your question?" She paused, looking for something in his eyes. "You're here because I got you your meeting with the Collective. The Thin Man arrives tomorrow."

Kavi's eyes widened. That was the last thing he expected when he was summoned to this conversation.

Before he had a chance to respond, three pounded knocks rattled the conference room door.

Sugoroku looked to Tom who looked just as surprised as her.

"Enter," said Sugoroku.

The burly boxer of a guard stepped forward into the doorway. His face was deathly pale. "Ma'am, the Nest is under attack."

* * *

Kavi ran to the Aerie and was surprised to find Lady Sugoroku running alongside him. She had to be thirty to forty years his senior, but she took the stairs two at a time. The black and green gown she wore was tailored with sensible splits that allowed her to sprint. They lost the guards at the first landing. They lost Tom at the second.

When they reached the doors to the Aerie, she said. "Open the damn door and let's figure out who has the audacity to attack a League installation." She wasn't even out of breath.

Kavi threw open the double doors to see Coach Sug standing in conference with the other professional coaches, Pip, Yantzy, the leader of the other peacekeeping squad, and Stonez. The recently renovated Aerie easily held this group with room to spare for the Snoops and Rooks who filed in and out with new information.

"Who?" asked Sugoroku, her voice a whip-crack.

The leadership team stood straight and turned to her.

"We don't know yet, ma'am," said Coach Sug.

Sugoroku raised her eyebrows in challenge. "Come now," she said, voice low and deadly. "Who but a god would have the gall to attack the League?"

"Harp is the most likely aggressor, ma'am," said Coach Sug. "We haven't ruled out other options yet, because Heretic Squad intel states she prefers to work from the shadows. A direct attack is more Krom or Astra's style."

The owner looked at Kavi. "I told you—I didn't want to be here to see it when you pissed off the wrong person." She directed that fearsome gaze back to the leadership team. "I'm assuming all exits from the Nest are being watched."

Coach Sug nodded. "Yes ma'am, the Aerie is the safest place in the Nest right now."

Sugoroku gave Kavi a small push. "Get to work. If we have to sacrifice you and your team to save the rest of my company, I'll do it in a second. Impress me, young Lion."

Kavi gave her a lopsided grin. "Your warmth is legendary, ma'am." He bounded towards the others and turned to Pip. "Give me the thirty second version?"

Pip nodded. "As you were being escorted to your meeting, two events happened simultaneously. A beautiful woman approached the intake building in a horse drawn carriage and demanded to see you. At the same time, another gorgeous woman approached the docks in a flying carriage propelled by technology we've never seen. Each woman was accompanied by a single footman. When they made contact with the double As manning the intake areas, the double As immediately moved to do their bidding."

Kavi puffed out his cheeks as he thought. "Sounds like Harp."

"I don't disagree," said Yantzy, "except that I recognized one of the women."

Kavi analyzed the woman who led the other peacekeeping squad. She had grown into her role. The pettiness she expressed as an alternate for the professional team was gone. She spoke with the confidence and weariness of someone carrying the same burden as Kavi. "From where?" asked Kavi.

"She's a neuro-mage I trained with at the Academy," said Yantzy. "There's a good chance the Grandmasters you pissed off on your last mission are involved."

"Is she any good?" asked Kavi.

"She's a world class bitch, but she's very good," said Yantzy. "She *used* to be better than me. Her specialty at the Academy was mind dominance. If you took one look at her, you'd know why she had a long list of willing subjects to experiment on."

"It's got to be Harp," said Kavi. "Two neuro-mages won't attack a League base to fulfill the vendetta of some crockety Grandmaster. The most likely scenario is Harp is working with the Grandmasters."

"Damnit, Pip," said Stonez. "We told you to stay away from his daughter. Then, you embarrass the man in front of the entire city?"

"Hold on a second," said Pip. "She came on to me."

Kavi stepped between the two. "Not the time. This is just a convenient excuse for Harp to take a shot at Heretic Squad. The only things that matter to Harp are power and influence. We stole both from her. She's not going to quit until we're dead." He paused. "Or she is."

"Is it possible to kill a god?" asked Stonez.

"We could give her what she wants," offered Sugoroku. She found Kavi's eyes. "You."

Kavi smiled. "And I thought you were made of stronger stuff, ma'am. We hurt her in Harpstra. We can do it again. You want to give the League credibility? Watch what happens when we kill a god. If we can't kill her," Kavi pointed at Pip. "I know a certain void mage who can capture her, especially if both peacekeeping squads are working together."

"No sighting of Harp herself?" asked Sugoroku.

"No, ma'am," said Couch Sug. "We are being extra cautious bec—"

"Stop, Coach," said Sugoroku, pinning him with a glare. "Are you telling me that, as far as we know, we are being attacked by only two neuro-mages? Two women have my entire Company buzzing with fear? Why the fuck haven't we sent you," she pointed at Yantzy, "and Mage Starsight to take care of this problem? Two peacekeeping squads should make quick work of two mages that haven't been League trained."

"We're doing exactly that, ma'am," said Coach Sug. "Mage Starsight is with the rest of Heretic Squad holding the passageway outside of the intake building. Yantzy's team holds the stairway leading up to the dock. We wanted Kavi's sign off, and yours, before we wrest back control of our double As minds."

Kavi nodded. "You think it's a feint."

Coach Sug nodded.

"Explain," demanded Sugoroku.

"We believe Harp is waiting for us to expose our neuro-mages, once we do—"

"She takes down our neuro defenses with her little time warp trick," said Sugoroku, "All while Stonecrest was locked in a meeting with me." She looked impressed. "She's clever. I'll give her that. It also means we have a spy in our midst feeding her information."

The thought had occurred to Kavi, but he shook his head. "Not necessarily, ma'am. If Harp can enter our dreams, she can probably riffle through our heads to pull whatever information she wants. I'd bet every penny I own she's watching this meeting right now. She *wants* us to fight amongst ourselves. She wants us to expose our neuro-mages. They have some level of protection against her. Yantzy, Pip, can you give us a privacy dome?"

"I can't sense any traditional listening channels," said Pip.

Yantzy struggled in her efforts to summon a screen. "Four neural channels in this room alone."

"Who!" shouted Sugoroku.

Yantzy shrugged. "Coach Sug, Stonez, your assistant Tom and you, ma'am."

Sugoroku's face twisted with fury. "Oh, that little skank. You have my permission to do whatever it takes to eliminate the bitch."

"Yes, ma'am," said Kavi. He turned to Pip. "Pull Elana back now. Send the word to our new Quest teams and any double A with neuro skills. We need them here, now. They are our most important assets until we know where the real attack is."

Six Rooks fled the room at a sprint, orders in hand. The messenger runners for Sugoroku had highly developed Dancer skills.

Pip opened a channel to Sliver. "Send Elana up to the Aerie. Have Boost escort her. No." He paused. "Because I don't trust her, Sliver." Another pause as Kavi listened in on the one-sided conversation. "I'm not arguing about this, get it done."

Good, thought Kavi. *I don't trust Tess either. We promised a second chance, but that doesn't mean she gets the same responsibility and access she had before she betrayed us.*

Pip pulled his two fingers from his temple and addressed the leadership team. "Sliver has Herman blocking the stairway. He's been instructed not to hurt anyone from Sugoroku. Even without lethal force he's an effective barrier on those stairs, and he's immune to mind magic. Elana has already fended off three neural attacks, each one stronger than the last. They're probing our defenses."

"Once we pull Elana," said Kavi, "make sure the rest of Heretic Squad, besides Herman, pulls back far enough they're out of range from mental attacks." Kavi looked to Yantzy. "The rock in the mountain should be enough protection, right?"

Yantzy shrugged. "From the neuro-mages, yes. From Harp, I have no idea. If she can listen to our conversation in here, everything is in range for her."

"If it is a feint," said Coach Sug. "The primary attack is going to hit somewhere else. The question is where."

The whole room shook. One of the Rooks ran back in to the Aerie. Her hair was dusty and matted with blood oozing from her skull. "The battle cavern is under attack," she said breathlessly. "I don't know from what, but I saw what looked like a tentacle?" She gratefully took a sip from the glass of water one of the professional coaches handed her. "Our Quest teams are getting torn apart."

Sugoroku's scowl grew with every word the woman spoke. "Handle this," she hissed to Kavi. "Now."

Kavi looked to Pip who held up a finger. A moment later Boost and Elana burst through the door.

Stonez directed two pairs of double As carrying suli application chests from the treasury. They placed them on the conference table. Stonez popped the clasps and extended the collapsible shelves within. He popped a suli root into his lower lip and tossed Kavi another.

Boost grabbed the clockwork neck brace fitted with three syringes and put it around his neck. All three pierced his skin at the same time and slowly released the accelerant into his bloodstream. A buzzing clicking noise accompanied the syringes at precise intervals as they engineered the timed release. Pip and Elana stood face-to-face tattooing suli ink in practiced designs.

As the aggression of the accelerator sunk in, Kavi took a deep breath and let the familiar mantra wash over him. *Move like wind, strike like fire, defend like earth, parry like water.*

Kavi turned to Boost. "What did you see in your run through the cavern?"

Boost winced as the three syringes pumped the last of the cloudy liquid into his neck. "Chaos. The Quest teams are doing their best, but they're outmatched. I don't know what the hell we're up against. A saw a tentacle and maybe a naked woman? Varseid called it a vuori kraken, but I'm pretty sure he made that up."

Kavi wasn't surprised. The tactician of the new Quest team was as arrogant as they came, but he was intelligent and creative. Kavi couldn't stand Varseid, but he respected how hard he trained and how he treated his people.

Kavi turned back to Boost when the man's words finally registered. "Did you say naked woman?"

Kavi turned to Yantzy. "Can you keep this privacy screen up while we're moving?"

Yantzy nodded. "Yes, but so can Mage Starsight. I need to get back to my team."

Kavi grimaced. "I understand, but I need one of you protecting us while the other identifies the source of these neural attacks."

"Do it," said Sugoroku. "Quit screwing around and neutralize the threat."

The buzz in his ears caused by the suli drove him to action. "Let's move!" he shouted.

Boost ran through the double doors of the Aerie with Stonez and Pip a step behind. Kavi took the rear, putting the neuro-mages in the center of the group. They zipped down the stairs and through the large hallway to the battle cavern at the speed of mounted warriors at full gallop. When they arrived at the massive entrance to the battle cavern, Kavi took in the scene before him. Tentacles jerked spasmodically about the room striking and grasping anything wearing black and green. Naked and scantily clad women danced through the fray.

"Pip!" yelled Kavi. "Describe what you see." Illusion

471

didn't work on the void mage, and this had to be illusion.

Pip's eyes and skin darkened as he called his ether. "It's layered," Pip said. "Illusions tucked into truth, hard to tell what's real. Let me try something." Pip's eyes screwed shut for a moment. He took a gasping breath. "I pushed my consciousness out and it's not getting better. The kraken thing is real and so are those naked women!"

"Elana, where's the brain of this vuori kraken?" asked Kavi.

"Below us. Can't tell how far," said Elana, her dark skin lightening to a jaunty alfalfa as she called the ether. "The creature is enormous. It's almost as big as the battle cavern." She pointed. "Watch the tentacle with the polyp at the end."

Kavi tracked the tentacle waving about and noticed a large growth near the tip of the suctioned feeler. It looked like a cyst about to burst. The cyst pulsed several times then fell off the tentacle to hit the ground. When it struck the cavern floor, it burst like an egg dropped from a roof. A naked woman rose from the pool of slime the exploded cyst left behind.

"Eww," said Elana, caught up in the birth of the creature. "I can't sense real thought coming from that thing. It's alive but...empty. It's not even animalistic, it's more like Sliver's creations, a golem following a script."

Another of the naked women lurched in their direction. Elana sent a pulse of neural energy towards it. She spoke the directives she heard aloud. "Confuse, distract. If close enough, attack."

Stonez drew his weapon. He screamed and decapitated the lascivious automaton with a single blow. The naked woman's body flopped on the ground like a fish out of water for several moments before lying still.

Kavi grabbed the creature's head and handed it to Yantzy. "Take this to the Crackers and Spooks. Maybe they can give us a strategy to defeat this vuori kraken."

Yantzy blanched, but gingerly took the head.

"Go," said Kavi. "I'll recall my team to the lower entrance of the cavern and fight them from there. You and your team fight them from this side and we meet in the middle?"

Yantzy nodded and took off at a run.

Pip held two fingers to his temple and started speaking. "No, move now." A pause. "Damnit Silver, do it! Tack wants everyone at the entrance to the battle cavern. Everyone but Herman. I'll open a gate to the lower entrance and seal that stairway once I get back, *then* we can have Herman join us."

"Boost, find us a path," said Kavi. "We move at suli sprint until we get to the other side. I'll cover the flanks. Only engage if you have no choice."

Kavi flexed that muscle in his mind and time slowed to a crawl. The cavern was filled with stone dust so it was hard to make out details, but with time slowed he might see a pattern to the kraken's movement, maybe even catch sight of Harp.

Kavi drew both swords. He spun, swords out, turning his momentum and speed into torque. Both blades struck the tentacle at the same time. The swords struck in a shower of sparks. Rock crust around the giant appendage created a form of armor. Even with his speed, he couldn't cleanly cut through the thick limb. The contact of both swords jolted his arms and rattled his teeth. He had to swing twice more to fully sever the suction-cupped atrocity. He moved on to the next threat, leaving the severed tentacle flopping on the ground.

On two different occasions across the cavern, Kavi ran into squad members on the new Quest team. Varseid split his team into groups of four, one from each discipline. The Fort of each group fixed or built defensive structures as the Guard held off the stronger attacks, giving the Striker and Dancer a chance to whittle the tentacles down or slay naked drones.

Boost only fired his hand cannons twice, both times obliterating a drone. Kavi severed two more tentacles in their dash across the cavern. At his suli-enhanced speed, he doubted the others even knew he struck.

The lower exit came into view and Kavi breathed a sigh of relief as he saw Tess running their way. He was sure Heretic Squad could take down this vuori kraken if they were fighting together. Boost lowered his hand cannons cautiously as Tess closed on them. The bricker slowed and smiled at the ranger.

That's when Tess struck, her blade severing Boost's arm at the elbow.

40

Harp's Revenge

"It's not Tess!" yelled Elana.

Boost screamed and passed out.

"Healer!" yelled Stonez.

The tip of an arrow exploded out of Tess' throat and she slumped to the ground.

Kavi blinked twice when Tess walked up with her giant cat, Feather, loping alongside her. She pulled another arrow from her quiver and knocked it. "Damn right it's not me. Healer's on the way." She looked at Kavi and her eyes flashed at his expression. Tess prided herself on keeping her emotions in check, but the hurt on her face was clear to everyone in the area. "But you thought it was me. You thought I was capable of killing someone on Ghost Squad."

Kavi nodded.

"Good to know I'm the only one that doesn't get a second chance from his holiness, Lord Stonecrest," said Tess. "If we make it out of this, I want to be transferred to Yantzy's squad."

"*When*...we make it out of this," said Kavi. "You and I need to have a long sit down and figure this out."

"Fuck you, Tack," said Tess. "I earned my spot. I fucked up because I faced an impossible choice. I owned it. I'm not going to be a charity case. I'll play my role today, but no more conversation. I'm done."

She was the one who betrayed me! Who betrayed all of us. Now, she has the gall to take the high ground? The familiar anger rose and Kavi couldn't tell if it was the suli or if he just couldn't let go of the betrayal.

He'd deal with it later. They had to survive this first. He turned and went back to work.

The squad, besides Amity and Felicity who were busy reattaching Boost's arm, had watched the entire exchange with Tess. Most of the men were stone-faced. Jansen, Clara, Crystal and Sliver gave Kavi the disappointed look his father gave him when they disagreed on something important.

Kavi scowled. *Screw them too.*

A memory flashed through his mind. He and Grim were in the briefing room with the Lioness. Grim had said, "When almost everyone around you is acting stupid, sometimes you're the problem." His mother had snorted. "Spoken like a man of weak conviction. Most of the time, they're just wrong." That killed the conversation, but Kavi remembered when they walked out the door, Grim said, under his breath. "Case in point." Kavi had pretended not to hear his friend.

Focus! He reached for his familiar mantra. Kavi looked to Boost who had woken up. The Bricker was pale and shivering, but he gave Kavi a single thumbs up as the bone and tendons on his arm knitted together under the ministration of their healers.

Kavi shook his head and faced his squad. "Does anybody

476

understand how to control the battle cavern biomes?"

"The Coaches," said Sliver.

"Good," said Kavi. "Because we need to see this kraken eye-to-eye. " Kavi looked around. "Where's Pip?"

A slight pop preceded Pip walking through a void gate. "What?" he asked as he saw their expressions. "What happened?" He handed an open suli chest to Sliver.

"Later," said Kavi. "Right now, I need to know if the Coaches can create a giant pit in the cavern. Get us most of the way to where we can hurt this thing."

Pip nodded and held two fingers to his temple. "Yes, a giant pit. The creature is submerged," Pip looked over at Elana who shrugged. Pip grunted and said, "Call it thirty meters. Can we go that deep?" A long pause. "I guess it's going to have to do, isn't it?"

Pip mouthed, *twenty meters*, to Kavi.

Kavi turned to his Guards who had just finished applying the suli Pip brought. Stix, Jansen and Tristan opened their mouths wide in an effort to acclimate to the strength of the accelerant. "You four find Varseid. Tell him to get his people out of the cavern. You've got three minutes."

"Give us three minutes then make the shift," said Pip into his void channel. "We have to clear the cavern of the Quest teams."

The Guards sprinted in opposite directions. Tristan shifted to cat form and sprinted to the far end, as Stix, Stonez and Jansen headed for the other three quadrants.

Kavi moved into the cavern and looked for targets. He needed an outlet for his suli rage. The first drone to close looked enough like Sliver that he hesitated. He looked over his shoulder to confirm Sliver still knelt by Boost. *Fool me once...* He took all of his anger at Tess, at Sugoroku, at his situation, and turned it on the drone. His blades cut once, twice, five times and the fake Sliver died naked and confused.

Kavi went hunting for a tentacle.

One obligingly burst through the ground at his feet. Kavi waited until enough of its length made its way above ground before he struck the outer rocky carapace of the wiggling limb with a spin that ended with both swords cutting a slice out of the widest point. He spun once more and his swords passed through his previous divot and out the other side, only slowing when they hit the rocky armor of the far side. Kavi screamed in savage triumph. He moved on to the next tentacle and repeated the process.

He gritted his teeth when he saw Varseid trailing Stix. He had told Stix in no uncertain terms to clear the volunteers out of the fucking cavern! He slid under another tentacle, jumped up and hacked at the rocky exterior until he found flesh beneath. When he did, he came down on it with both swords in an overhand chop. The tentacle writhed on the ground unmoored from the kraken.

Kavi looked for more to kill, but Stix stood before him with a thumb pointed back at Varseid. The Questing tack's severe face was hard lines and pointy surfaces. His eyes danced with flame. Kavi grabbed a long sleeve of the man's robe. *Only a special brand of idiot wears battle robes. Might as well wear a cape.* He wiped his blades on Varseid's billowing sleeve.

"Get out of my battle cavern," growled Kavi. He turned back to Pip. "Line them up and let's kill this thing!"

Varseid whined about not being included in the attack and Kavi throttled the urge to choke him.

Pip opened a portal to push the man through, but Varseid

summoned a line of fire between them and ran back to his team.

Their funeral. Kavi sensed Jansen, Tristan, Stix and Stonez forming a line around him. Tess and Boost moved to the ends of each line, Boost holding his right cannon gingerly. The man was pale, but Kavi knew there was no way the Bricker would sit this one out. Jory joined Kavi in a utility role. He stood next to Boost to cover the wounded Bricker when it got thick. Their healers and other Dancers found their spots behind the lines. Kavi breathed in deep as Heretic Squad readied themselves around him like a single organism. One pissed off organism. How dare this goddess attack their home? It could be the suli, but their fury towards the kraken was red hot.

Four drones struck at once. Tess filled the first with arrows while Boost turned a second to paste. Kavi moved in to take the third but Stonez and Jansen beat him to it. They moved in perfect harmony, both swords entering the drone's body from opposite sides. As they withdrew their swords their momentum took them around each other to take the other's spot on the line.

Kavi sprinted to the other side to take the fourth drone, but Tristan and Stix had it in hand. Stix's right saber cut through the drone's neck as Tristan's clawed paw batted the drone's head off the body like a grisly ball of yarn. The disgusting missile flew towards the kraken.

Kavi screamed in frustration at not getting to engage. He looked around for more enemies. He felt a hand on his shoulder and spun. Pip.

"Take it down a notch, Tack," said Pip. "Tell me what you see"

479

Kavi took a shaky breath. "The drones are starting to work together."

Pip nodded and said. "Two minutes and the floor drops."

"Press!" shouted Kavi.

Their Guards moved forward with Kavi, Tess, Boost and Jory on the back side of the wedge. Three giant tentacles—the biggest Kavi had seen yet—crashed towards the line. Stix and Stonez shifted position. As the tentacles fell Jansen shouted, "I got shield wall!" The giant Krommian invoked the skill and a golden, transparent wall sprung up at a forty five degree angle arresting the motion of the tentacles.

"Dropping in three, two, one!" shouted Jansen just as they had practiced. The barrier dropped. Kavi slowed time and leapt with all his suli-enhanced might. Both swords pointed towards the nearest tentacle falling back to earth. An arrow whizzed over his head, creating a chip in the rocky armor. That's where his swords slid in. With his momentum, Kavi exploded through the tentacle in a shower of blood and gore.

It was their Dancers, Sliver and Crystal, who destroyed the middle tentacle. They threw perfectly timed exploding traps to hit the tentacle the moment it began to fall. The stone armor surrounding it cracked and rained pebbles on the Guards. Giant blisters appeared on the revealed skin. The appendage thrashed backwards, but not before Stix and Stones cut into the exposed area. Their synchronized strike easily severed the unarmored limb. It lay twitching at their feet.

Kavi quickly scanned the cavern to see Yantzy and her team having similar successes by the entrance closest to the Aerie. Varseid's team struggled. Two of their front line down. The idiot hadn't pulled his team back, deciding instead to

480

make their stand on the Rim, halfway between Kavi and Yantzy's teams. Kavi checked on his Forts and Dancers. Clara rapidly painted tranquility runes on two of their large palisade sections.

Interesting idea.

More drones assaulted their line. They were working together now. A large group of at least thirty charged. More than half split when they reached their line in an effort to flank them. Were they trying to flee for the stairs?

Tess invoked her fungal rot and three of the closest drones began to decompose in front of Kavi. Kavi and Feather struck out in disgust and the rotting flesh turned to dust. The drones toppled.

On the other side of the line Jory and Boost worked in practiced tandem. Jory loudly strummed and sang a ballad which slowed the drones on his side. They became target practice for Boost's hand cannons.

The fighting was heaviest in the middle. The Guards met the challenge. Jansen and Stonez angled their shields in a wedge while Tristan and Stix invoked their skills. Stix spun and his tornado of steel diced every drone he made contact with. Tristan pounced and slashed and drones fell like wheat before the reaper.

Kavi's mental countdown dropped to zero and the cavern floor in front of them disappeared, just as the coaches promised. Kavi signaled and Heretic Squad reassembled in formation.

Kavi peeked over the edge of the rim and looked down upon a squirming mass of tentacles and drones. He scanned the pit but couldn't find a head. "Elana, can you sense intelligence?"

Her skin softened to the color of shortbread as she tapped into the ether. She walked to the lip of the giant pit and stared. "There's intelligence, but it's not centralized, it's like it has a hundred minds all spread out."

"How're those rune coming?" asked Kavi.

"Just finished two of them," said Clara. "Tess, can you communicate with it, let me know where to place them?"

Tess stuck her hands under the lip of the pit and focused. After a moment, she shook her head. "Too much turmoil. It's not like the plant we encountered. It's not just tainted, it feels like it's being controlled. Doesn't matter how many tranquility runes we use. This thing won't be pacified."

Kavi frowned and pointed at two drones trying to sneak behind them to get to the stairs. Boost brought down one, Tess the other. Something wasn't right. Kavi felt like he and his team could easily whittle this thing down, no matter the number of drones it threw at them.

"Why don't we just light it up, Tack?" asked Boost. He stared into the pit and muttered. "Wouldn't mind having Pyre with us right now."

Pip held two fingers to his ear. "Yantzy asked the same question. What are we waiting for?"

Kavi shook his head, trying to work it out. Harp worked from the shadows, she wasn't one for direct attacks. The goddess had them holed up inside the Nest, fighting this creature. Yet, for all of its strength, it had done very little damage to Kavi and his team. Except to anger and bring confusion. *Harp wanted them to attack. The goddess wanted them to destroy this beast. Why?*

"It's a trap," Kavi whispered. *The drones weren't trying to escape for the stairs, they were trying to keep Heretic Squad from retreating!*

Varseid must have grown tired of waiting. The Vonderian launched an assault in the form of a giant column of fire in the center of the squirming mass of tentacles. Yantzy and her team joined in, raining fire on the beast. Then Kavi heard the rumble of Boost loosing his hand cannons into the mass below.

Kavi flexed and time slowed. He watched as drones popped in fleshy explosions. The kraken itself began to glow under the onslaught. *She played us. We have to get out of here!*

"Sound the retreat!" Kavi shouted to Pip.

"What, why?" Pip asked. "We have a bead on this thing."

Kavi grabbed him by the arm and spun him around. "No, we're doing exactly what she wants us to do. Think! Sound the general retreat and open a portal to get us out of here!"

Pip held his hand to his ear and called for the retreat. A moment later, his skin still ebony from the communication, he summoned a giant, suli-enhanced, portal.

"Heretic Squad, retreat!" yelled Kavi at the top of his lungs. He wished he had Grim's berserker shout to boost the order.

Kavi waved furiously towards the portal and his squad began to move. They weren't going to be quick enough. He began to run, pulling and throwing his team towards the void gate Pip created.

Kavi felt the pressure in the cavern building. He glanced to the other entrance to see Yantzy and her team running towards the exit. As he ran towards Crystal and Clara, he caught site of Varseid and his team. They continued their onslaught on the kraken below.

Idiots!

Kavi's speed allowed him to hurl Sliver and Crystal

through the gate with what felt like a small push. He banked and went back for Clara and Tess. They were the only ones not running towards the gate on their own.

Then the monstrous explosion began. He would only make it to one of them.

He made his choice and bodily hurled the woman towards the gate.

The explosion caught up to him and the wave of heat struck him in the back.

The force was tremendous.

Kavi flew through the air, through the portal, and lost consciousness.

41

The League

"What do you mean the Nest has fallen?" asked Wari.

The other League owners had the same sick look on their faces at the emergency summons arriving in the middle of the night. They gathered in the opulent palatial suite high above Castari Fountain, the crown jewel of the Vonderian Trading District. When the Thin Man sent a personal void portal, nobody was dumb enough to ignore it.

"It was Stonecrest, wasn't it?" asked Ch'es, jowls quivering "I never trusted that little creep."

The Majordomo gave the Thin Man a moment to answer, but if he was still in the room after summoning that last portal, he remained silent. "No, at least not directly," she said. She ignored the urge to wipe the sleep from her eyes. It had been a long several days. "In fact, we're almost certain he died in the attack, along with Sugoroku."

The looks of consternation deepened. Senet removed his spectacles and cleared his throat.

The Majordomo looked at him and nodded, impressed at his impeccably pressed three-piece ivory suit, especially after being woken in the middle of the night.

"We've all heard the rumors," said Senet. "Only a god has the power to take down a stronghold like the Nest. If that is the case, are we next? Has the League angered the gods?"

Just like Senet to get to the heart of the matter without preamble. Majordomo paused for another second, hoping the Thin Man would step in. She hadn't been privy to all the details of the Divine Will Project, but she knew enough. What she didn't know was how much she was allowed to disclose to the League owners. It would be a subtle dance with Senet. He would see through any bending of the truth. None of the owners would be happy with the standard Collective non-answer—not after losing one of their own. She cringed and rolled the dice. If the Thin Man was unhappy with what she disclosed, he could deliver the news himself.

"No," said the Majordomo. "At least I don't believe the gods are specifically targeting the League. You saw the broadcast of Heretic Squad embarrassing Harp. We believe the goddess targeted Stonecrest and his team. He just happened to be at the Nest when she attacked."

Mehen loosed a shrill laugh that sounded like a miniature poodle barking. "So, the downfall of one of our League Fortresses is...what? Collateral damage?"

Lord Go stroked his long, wispy moustache with trembling hands. The man looked even more ancient in the wee hours of the morning. "I'm afraid the divine scale of power is different than what we're used to dealing with, my dear."

Mehen scowled at him. "Don't talk down to me, old man. Divine power scale, my ass. The gods have shown their hand. If they can level the Nest, none of us are safe."

Risk put a hand on Mehen's arm. The two owners bickered

constantly, but everyone around the table knew Risk had feelings for the fiery owner of Mehen Company. "We've never been safe from the gods, Mehen. What's changed?"

She pulled her arm away and gave him an incredulous look. "What's changed?! Are you serious? What's changed is that they are *here*. Now. In person. Or godhood. Whatever you want to call it." Her eyes were wide as she looked around the table. "They're not abstract heads of ancient religions. They're live, divine killing machines. What do you think happens to the people at the top when a new breed of more powerful beings shows up?"

The owners squirmed uncomfortably in their chairs.

Wari broke the silence. "Maybe they can be bargained with." The man's normally perfect hair was tousled, but Majordomo thought it merely made him look more handsome with his devil-may-care nonchalance.

Ur stroked his chin. "How would we contact them?"

"Talk to a priest?" offered Wari.

"We could pray," said Risk.

All the owners but Ch'es laughed.

Mehen speared the obese man with a glare. "You tried, didn't you?" She continued to stare at him. "Did it work?"

Ch'es shook his head sharply once, though his jowls continued to move back and forth like curtains in a breeze. "No. At least not with Lord Astra."

"You didn't stop there, did you?" asked Mehen.

"Of course not," said Ch'es. "And no, none of the gods answered my prayers. Frankly, I'm shocked none of you tried communing with them. You saw the broadcast. If Harp is back, the rest are too."

Senet looked to the Majordomo. "Is the Collective in

contact with the gods?"

Majordomo sighed. *If they only knew.* She believed Senet suspected, but suspecting and knowing were very different. "Not to my knowledge. The Collective and the Thin Man are aware of their presence and have been for some time, but a dialog has not yet been opened."

Senet finished wiping his spectacles and put them back on. "I'll assume the information you're omitting is because you don't have permission to disclose it. Will our benefactor from the Collective be shedding more light on the gods this evening?"

Majordomo looked to the dark corners of the room and waited again. "It appears unlikely."

Senet pursed his lips. "Then let's cover what you do have permission to discuss. Are the rumors of Sage Knute's escape true?"

That caught her by surprise. She had only heard of his escape last night. She must have let the surprise show on her face because Senet nodded.

"How?" he asked.

The Majordomo shrugged. "He's a Sage. Ever since the fifth Sage came into her power, the remaining four became more lucid. Knute is the youngest and most mobile of the four. All we know is that he had outside help. How do you know about his escape?" As the question left her lips, she knew she shouldn't have asked it. Might as well hand him control of this damn meeting.

Senet gave her the same smug smile she normally gave the group. *Damn the man.* "One of the gods? Or help of a non-divine nature?" Senet asked.

"Unknown," said the Majordomo. "But he's a Sage, and

keeping them contained is always risky. Doors happened to be left open, guards happened to not be paying attention when he made his move. That's never been an issue before because at our facility, there's nowhere to escape *to*. That's where the outside help came in."

Ch'es slapped a meaty hand on the table. "What's Knute's escape going to do to the season? The preseason demo was a huge success! The Vig on that one Quest paid off all my expenses for the disaster of last season. We can't afford to miss the upcoming events."

"What's *his escape* going to do?" screeched Mehen. "What does losing an entire Company do? How do we have a season without Sugoroku? The schedules have been published. It's not like we can hide the loss of an entire Quest team."

The Majordomo wanted to hug the two explosive owners. They turned the discussion towards something she could manage: making money. She pounced before Senet could shine the light back on the Collective's failings. "You all know we still have an impressive backlog of Quests which will take us through the entirety of this first season."

Senet arched an eyebrow. "Were the Quests in the backlog given before we made the move to volunteers? If we share old Quests, we run the risk of the difficulty destroying entire teams. I doubt that will make for quality entertainment."

She wondered how it would feel to wring his throat. His neck was small enough. "I assure you, the season will continue as planned," said Majordomo.

This time when Senet spoke, he addressed the owners. "The assurances of the Collective don't have the same weight they once had, in light of recent events."

The Majordomo opened her mouth to protest but Senet

held up a hand in her direction to stop her. *How dare he? And where was the Thin Man?*

Senet continued. "Renegotiating a deal with the Collective in the midst of this chaos is impossible. However, there is no exclusivity clause in the deal we signed with them. I propose we discuss what we're willing to give up to the gods in return for their blessing that the League continue to operate without divine interference."

The other owners leaned forward in their seats. Senet offered a plan of action, something the Majordomo hadn't been able to do. It was a struggle, but she didn't let her annoyance reach her face as she spoke. "There may not be a clause in the contract, but violate the spirit of the agreement and there will be consequences."

Senet leaned back and looked at her through steepled fingers. "I wondered when the threats would begin. Before they get terribly nasty, I have one important question. Can the Collective offer protection from these gods?"

Majordomo tapped her fingers on the table, stalling for time. "I'm afraid that's not a question I can answer," she finally said.

Senet nodded as if expecting her response. "Then I'm afraid your usefulness in this meeting has ended. We are going to have to ask you to leave."

The other owners watched the exchange, wide-eyed. Taunting the Collective was never a good idea, especially when it was the Thin Man and his portals who personally brought them here tonight.

Wari's expression changed first, before Majordomo could respond. "What do you know, Senet?" asked Wari.

Before Senet could answer, Majordomo finally dropped her

mask of serenity. She pointed at Senet and growled. "You can bet the Thin Man will hear about this!"

Senet's poker face remained. "See that he does. Until then, I'll have to ask that you leave the room while we figure out how best to negotiate with the gods."

Majordomo pushed her chair back noisily and stood. Only then did she wonder how she would get back to the Collective base. The Thin Man brought her without explaining how she would get back. She might have to book lodging in Vonderia. How embarrassing. If the Thin Man wasn't responding to Senet's outright defiance, something must be wrong. He must be occupied with his "brethren".

Then she felt the temperature of the room drop. The magelights dimmed, and black clouds formed behind her. She smiled and slowly sat back down. She almost felt bad for Senet.

The other owners scooted away from Senet, not wanting to be painted with the same defiant brush. To his credit, Senet's expression never changed. He waited patiently for the Thin Man to coalesce from the darkness, looking bored. She no longer felt bad for him.

The Thin Man stared at Senet when he took shape behind Majordomo. "You dare renege on your deal with the Collective?" His voice held the menace of a room filled with iron maidens.

"No, milord," said Senet calmly. "As I pointed out to your assistant—"

"Silence!" bellowed the Thin Man, clouds of inky black surrounding his now billowing cloak.

"As I pointed out to your assistant," repeated Senet, ignoring the Thin Man's outbreak. "Unless you can offer protection from the gods, we will need to make other arrangements. I'm sure you understand."

The Thin Man's malevolence was ruined by the confused expression on his pinched face. His order of silence was never disobeyed. Majordomo knew mortals didn't have the strength to resist his authority. *Senet did know something. Something that would change the entire power dynamic in the group.*

"Who...?" asked the Thin Man softly, voice laden with poison. "Who gave you their boon?"

Senet shook his head. "Answer my question first. Can you offer that protection?"

The darkness around the Thin Man fled. "Have you truly thought this through? You may be protected, but what about your family, your friends?"

Senet looked at him quizzically. "Do I strike you as someone that doesn't think things through? My family is protected and I don't have any friends."

The Thin Man nodded. "This generation is protected perhaps, but what about those to come?"

"I could care less about future generations," said Senet. "Now answer the question."

The Thin Man held his gaze for an uncomfortable period of time, but Senet didn't flinch. "No, the Collective cannot protect you from the gods. Now, who gave you the boon?"

Senet smiled and leaned back. "He's not a big fan of yours. I can tell you that."

The Thin Man scowled and disappeared with a pop that shattered two of the magelights in the room.

The Majordomo sighed. It looked like she was going to have to find lodging in Vonderia for the rest of the evening after all.

42

The Gods

"Why do you keep disappearing like that?" said Vonn. "It's incredibly annoying. You're the one who called the meeting!"

"Seriously Theron, you are committing the most grievous sin of all," said Harp, with a mischievous smile. "You're beginning to *bore* us."

Theron took a deep breath and spared a glance at their surroundings. It had been centuries since he'd been up here. The view was magnificent.

The gods sat in the open-aired, golden cathedral of Meritopolis, high atop Mount Ominous, the largest peak in Grendar. The Tinkerer installed a dome around the expansive buildings the group of divinities had designed. The dome was keyed to their ether signatures so that the deities were the only beings who could ever enter, unless access for another was approved by all seven gods—something which would never happen.

That's how Theron knew the naked naiads frolicking in the fountains and the equally naked dryads playing a game

494

of tag around an ancient oak preserved in this land of eternal summer, were illusions. Illusion had always been Harp's specialty, but the detail of these creatures was impressive. Must be her way of compensating for the embarrassing broadcast at the hands of Stonecrest and his Heretic Squad.

The Thin Man grinned inwardly. He was thrilled that his technology was responsible for forcing the promiscuous bitch to show a little humility. Well, maybe not humility. She wasn't capable of such a thing. Maybe caution was more appropriate. Then again, she threw caution to the wind when she attacked the Nest.

More likely, she learned nothing. She seemed to lose her ability to learn shortly after the seven of them completed their own trials. Just like the other fools who called themselves gods, whom he was forced to share this world with every five hundred years.

Theron carefully transformed the sneer forcing its way to his face into a beatific smile aimed at the goddess. "That will be my last interruption. I would *hate* to bore any of you at such a momentous time." He put a mask of sympathy over the smile. "One thing that may not bore you, Harp, is that I've discovered some amazing skin care products in this century. Please send me a raven if you'd like to speak with my beautician."

Krom's laughter washed out Harp's angry reply, the sound a jovial thunder that rattled the table and chairs. "Sweet Burn! Do me next!" boomed the god. He clapped with enthusiasm.

Theron knew the stupidity of the warrior god was an act, but it was a good one. It got under his nerves more than anything and Krom knew it. "Sadly, you're too easy a target, old friend," said Theron. He leaned over and patted the enormous god on his enormous shoulder in an attempt to soothe Krom's disappointment. "I'm afraid it would be wasted on you."

"How do you have so many interruptions?" asked Vonn. "We've only been here a month and you're busier than a seventh-year mage training for the Suli Trials."

The other gods leaned in to listen to his response. Harp and Lo dropped the pretense of watching the frolicking illusions—though Lo was probably admiring the oak instead. The Tinkerer set his book down.

Theron was prepared for the question. It was the obvious one. Vonn was smart, but not as smart as he made himself out to be. The one Theron had to watch out for was the Tinkerer. The small prodigy played four-dimensional chess while the rest played checkers. The Tinkerer would be the most powerful of them all if he didn't have such a strict moral code.

The other one to watch was Lo. Reading the earthen goddess was nigh impossible. Theron would have better luck playing poker against a sycamore. She rarely spoke, but when she did it was with a wisdom that rivaled the Ancients. She was patience incarnate, but she brooked no fools, especially those who threatened her world.

If Theron was being honest, he knew he couldn't under-estimate any of the gods—even Astra. They all earned their way here. That's part of what made the game Theron played so dangerous. And so fun.

"You put the right people in place before you leave only to find their descendants are morons," said Theron with a shake of his head.

Krom laughed again and the others winced at the volume. "You got that straight, big T. The idiots in my city decided to reroute all the water running through the city to have more room for sparring. Then they wonder why it's hot and dusty."

Astra looked up from pondering his reflection in one of the small pools in the pavilion. The man was beautiful—always had been. His orator voice could charm the clothes off a monk sworn to celibacy. Charisma oozed from him, so much that it masked the arrogance behind his perfect eyes. He was always the most beautiful in the room, and he knew it. "The rest of you give these savages too much credit," Astra said. The words bubbled from his mouth like silken honey.

"By savages, you mean followers?" asked Vonn, matching Astra word for word in arrogance.

Astra ignored him. "They *only* thrive under simple rules. It took one day for me to get my house in order. Orthodoxy does wonders for compliance."

Theron wasn't the only one who viewed Astra with disdain. Only a narcissistic megalomaniac could build a restrictive religion around the worship of ego and call it purity.

Harp snorted. "And how are your pack of zealots stacking up against the new technology?"

Astra lent her a dazzling smile. "With numbers of course. That's rule number one for my followers—make lots and lots of babies. Not only is it fun, it's incredibly effective. I thought of all of us, you'd appreciate that most, you magnificent strumpet."

Harp playfully swatted in his direction and offered a look so steamy it could iron clothing.

"You two are disgusting," said Vonn.

"And you're in dire need of a good screw," said Harp. She shook her head. "And no, that is not an offer."

"Why did you call the meeting, Theron?" asked the Tinkerer.

Theron nodded to the small man in thanks for getting them back on track. He moved over to the wide table and sat. "This world's technology has advanced enough that we do not have access to the same...discretion we enjoyed in previous visits." He nodded to Harp. "Our good friend and colleague witnessed how quickly our indiscretions can ripple through this world."

Harp scowled.

"And you're afraid we'll draw the attention of the Adjudicators," said the Tinkerer. "Maybe that's exactly what we—and this world—need."

All heads whipped towards the small god, except for Lo, who sighed and nodded.

"Hold on a second," said Vonn, pulling nervously at his long gray beard. "The Ads play for keeps. We have all...*bent* the rules on occasion, but they wouldn't see it that way. If they see our minor indiscretions as more than...minor, they might decide we are no longer fit to rule over this world."

Lo stared at the god of magic with world-weary eyes. "Are we?"

"Are we what?" Vonn asked, voice shrill.

"Fit," said Lo.

"*I* am," said Vonn. "I'm not ready to give up this sweet gig. Why would you, or the Tinkerer, consider something so drastic like bringing the Adjudicators in?"

"Because this world is falling into the same trap our own did," said the Tinkerer. "And I tire of the strong preying on the weak."

"Then *help* them!" shouted Vonn. "You get the same number of boons as the rest of us. Do something good with it."

Theron's form began to swell before remembering where he was. Time to move quickly. If the Tinkerer and Lo were already aligned, things had moved farther than he feared. He held up a hand in the Tinkerer's direction. "That's actually why I brought you together today. Rin, do you mind if I use your informal name?"

The Tinkerer shrugged and shook his head.

"Rin makes a good point. I'd like to offer an alternative to calling the Adjudicators." The six gods stared at him, even Lo. He had their attention. *Time to make the most of it.* "I agree with Rin *and* Lo. We've been doing a poor job of shepherding this world towards the trials. Instead of tattling to the Ads, I propose we take the eleven months we have left to police ourselves."

Rin shook his head.

"I'm not finished," said Theron. "We do a review of the rules and punish those of us who violated said rules. We then write a report for the Adjudicators that not only shares what we've done, but presents a plan of what we will do next. How we will bring this world to a state of transcendence. This comes across as proactive instead of reactive. We share the report with the Adjudicators in the five hundred year span between this visit and the next. It gives us ample time to decide whether we actually are *fit* to preside over this world's transformation."

Harp and Astra began to laugh. Krom joined in while pretending he didn't know why. "But you're the worst of us when it comes to following rules!" brayed Astra through a snorted laugh that made him look ridiculous.

Theron frowned and looked hurt. "Oh, come on, that's not true."

"You're just better at hiding it than the rest of us," said Harp, as she wiped away tears of laughter. "Your best quality is your sneakiness. Who's going to police you?"

Theron gritted his teeth and thought hard about breaking the rule that stated gods weren't allowed to attack each other. Instead, he smoothed his features and looked to the Tinkerer. "If anyone can see through my...stealth, it's the Tinkerer. What do you say, Rin?"

Rin's eyes never left Theron as he explained his plan. Theron had to hope the multiple layers of obfuscation he put in place would slip past the small god's massive intellect. "I believe your many *indiscretions* would be a simple thing to uncover which means..." The Tinkerer looked at each of the other gods in turn. Confused looks met him until he finally landed on Lo.

"Theron believes the matter of this world's transcendence could be decided in this session," said Lo.

"Exactly," said Rin. "And I must admit I find myself intrigued."

How? How could that little prick have figured it out that *quickly?* Did it matter? Theron didn't think so. His preparations should be enough. He had a two millennia head start after all, but it *was* disconcerting.

"I haven't agreed to any of this," said Vonn.

"Doesn't matter," said Krom. All hints of the happy moron vanished. "Any one of us can call an Adjudicator to settle a dispute or get a ruling on a violation. None of us have been dumb enough to do that..." He pointed his chin towards Rin and Lo, "until these sanctimonious jackwagons decided they tired of the game. If Theron believes he has us in mate, then it's time the rest of us make nice and stop his sneaky ass."

Theron nodded. "And that, my not-so-dumb friend, is what I recommend we do next. A rule review followed by a commitment to follow those rules for the next eleven months. Then, I recommend we confess which rules we have already broken and offer a fitting punishment for each."

None of the other gods saw that one coming. Not even Rin. Maybe the man was beatable after all. "As persuasive as Rin's guess was," said Theron. "I don't believe we are in the end game. I *do* believe we need a reset, a realignment with opening principles."

"I don't need a rule review," said Krom to the other gods. He looked at Theron. "What I need is to squash this little turd in front of us."

Theron smiled. "I'd argue you do need a review, because that's against the rules."

Vonn held up his hand. "I could use a review. It's been an extraordinarily long time. Keep it high level, none of that legalese bullshit."

Theron looked to the Tinkerer who shrugged.

"I'll make it quick," said Rin. "One—no attacking other gods. Two—we are not allowed to directly interact with the world of men except in these four ways. We can issue edicts to an inner circle of followers that number no more than ten. We can grant up to one boon a month to champions of our choice. We can select a champion to represent us and do our bidding. We *cannot* raise a finger to the mortals of this world except in self-defense. Three—we are commanded to spend the five hundredth year of every half millennia on Grendar. After that year concludes, we must leave this world." Rin stared at Theron as he said this last before continuing. "The rest of the time can be spent anywhere we choose within this universe or any other."

Harp raised her eyebrows. "That is certainly the abridged version. What you failed to mention is that the bending of the rules happens within the interpretation of the subtext."

The Tinkerer shrugged. "Vonn wanted high-level, I gave high-level. We all have access to the full set of rules. I recommend you read them again."

"So, what are you going to confess to first, Theron?" asked Astra. "It was your suggestion after all."

He was prepared for this, too. It had to be grievous enough that he drew the others out, but not so grievous that they decided to band together and call the Adjudicators on just him. For example, they could *never* find out he hadn't left this world, after their year was up, for the past four sessions. He nodded slowly as he juggled the list in his head. "I suppose that's fair."

"Get on with it already," said Harp. "You're terrible at building suspense."

That decided it. "I am responsible for releasing some of our technology into this world, specifically...recording crystals."

Harp stared at him, so angry she let her illusion drop for a fraction of a second. The misshapen hag jumped towards him, reverting back to beautiful woman mid-flight.

Krom stepped in front of her, gently placing a restraining hand on her chest. "Rule One, Harpy. Don't worry, we'll get our chance for revenge."

The Tinkerer nodded. "I had wondered how a magical realm like this would have access to video technology. How did you release the tech?"

"Time release capsules buried deep below Brickolage," said Theron. "I made it look like a Quest reward."

The Tinkerer summoned a clockwork horse that pranced its way across the table. "Clever, and what do you think a fitting punishment would be?"

Black smoke swirled around Theron's head. If Rin was going to show off, why shouldn't he? "Perhaps we should wait until we have each confessed something, then compare the gravity of each before deciding on fitting punishment."

"I fucked one of my inner circle," said Astra.

Harp raised an eyebrow. "Really? You're telling me that's as far as you went?"

"Fine," said Astra. "I fucked all my inner circle, in my inner sanctum."

Harp's eyebrow remained raised.

Astra sighed. "Multiple times. Often two or three at the same time."

"I still don't understand how you get hard for bald women," said Harp.

Astra settled himself in his heavily cushioned chair and smiled. "Well, it helps that they're bald *everywhere*. And who said it was just women?"

"You're such a bigger slut than I am," said Harp. "I don't understand why you put such strict rules against sex in place."

"You've never understood," said Astra. "It's so much hotter when it's forbidden."

Theron cleared his throat and looked at Harp next. "And

the whole world knows of Harp's indiscretion."

Harp daintily held up a hand covered in lace and filigree. "Hold on a second, I didn't technically break any rules. The vuori kraken *was* my champion."

"And the Harpstran Ministers were in your inner circle?" asked Theron.

Harp shrugged.

"Feel free to confess to another indiscretion," said Theron.

Her face contorted in anger before she caught hold of it. "My public indiscretion will be enough."

Krom cleared his throat. "What if we have no indiscretions to admit to?"

"We've spent enough time together by now," said Harp with a smug smile, "to know no one here farts rose petals." She looked back to the dryads frolicking about the big oak. "Except for maybe Lo. That's kind of her thing."

"The only indiscretion I care about is who created the League," said Lo. "Who is responsible for the group actively defying the will of the Ancients? Getting in the way of true evolution? Come now, it must be one of us. Someone with the hubris to name each Company after one of the ancient games of our world."

They all looked at Theron.

It was the Tinkerer who broke the silence. "If we are in the end game, perhaps we should ask ourselves: why is the Ancients' will sacrosanct?"

The gods looked at him in shock.

"Don't tell me, after all these years," said Krom, "that *you* believe the rules should be questioned? Now? At the end? You've always been such a stickler." The warrior god's voice rose in volume with each question.

"I don't have issue with the rules," said Rin. "Every world needs structure, as do the people that live on it. It's the game itself that I have a problem with."

43

Nettie & Leesta

"Quickly!" said Willow, circling her arm to usher them out of the Pool sub-basement. They ran up stairs made from roots that smoothed to polished wood at the Keeper's unspoken request.

Nettie churned her legs as she chased Gavin and Leesta upwards. When they burst into the open of a city glade, the first thing she heard was the screech of a cockatoo. She looked up to the branches of the stout redwoods in the northern side of Loam. Hundreds of cockatoos chirped an alarm so loud Nettie had to cover her ears.

Men, women, and children fled south. Some took cover below ground. Passages opened in front of them as the lucky few with power to commune willed the trees to create an escape route. Most on the ground fled upward.

The majority of Loamians ran about the city barefoot. They were able to scale trees with the ease of a Bricker walking stairs. Those that wore shoes, wore a split toe design with a grippy sole reminiscent of League footwear. Once in the branches, the Loamians sprinted from tree to tree on byways which had provided safe passage for millennia.

Others ran north. Most of these wore the uniform of the city guard. Loam never had an army. They never needed one. Their far southern location and complete disinterest in collecting trinkets and baubles others considered valuable made them unlikely targets.

The guards moved in packs, emulating the movement of the wild wolves who took shelter in the groves during the winter. Another group of five sprinted past her and her group of Liberators. They knew the terrain, but Nettie believed only Kavi, or maybe Leesta on a good day, could hold their pace for more than a minute. Yet the members of these packs hardly looked winded.

While the wolf packs ran on the ground, Nettie caught sight of two Rangers running north at top speed in the branches above. There had to be many more. Though she couldn't see them, she could hear them, even over the shrill alarms of the cockatoos. They communicated to each other through whistles and hoots which sounded like a troop of monkeys.

"Where are we going?" Nettie asked breathlessly. "I need to catch my breath."

Leesta stopped and held her hand against a tree. "The Northern Grove, that's where I feel the most pain."

Gavin dropped back to look after Rose so Leesta led the group alone. Nettie stood with hands on knees and sucked deep lungfuls of air.

Leesta tapped her on the back to get her attention. "Not like that. Hands behind your head, like this." Leesta laced her fingers behind her upper neck. "It helps open your lungs to get more air."

Pyre and Rice reached them first. The rest of the old Ghost Squad were moments behind. "Do we know anything yet?" asked Rice, shouting to be heard over the cockatoos.

Nettie shook her head. She pointed to Rose and Gavin, acting as guardrails to a distraught Willow. The Keeper rode propped on grizzly Grundle's back. Willow moaned in pain into his dark brown fur.

"How much further to the grove?" asked Rose.

"Five minutes if we run," said Leesta. "At this pace, it'll take fifteen."

Rose shook her head. "This will be over in ten minutes. We need to run."

Rose moved to stand in front of Willow. The Keeper turned her head the other way. "No, Willow," said Rose. "We can help, but you need to show us how."

"They're burning," moaned Willow. "All my friends are burning." She sobbed into Grundle's back.

Pyre looked on in confusion. "The city guard is on fire? Could it be Vonderians?"

"No, you idiot," said Leesta. "She's talking about the trees. Her friends, her sacred charges, are the ancient trees of the Northern Grove." She looked to Willow for a moment before turning back to Pyre. "It could be Vonderians. It's something strong. Powerful enchantments protect the ancient Groves from fire."

"Willow!" shouted Rose with the authority of the fifth Sage. All the cockatoos in their immediate area ceased their chirping and an unnatural silence fell.

Willow lifted her head up to look at Rose. "You did this," she hissed. Viney tendrils wrapped around Rose's legs.

"No," said Rose, the command echoed through the forest

like a thunderclap. The vines retreated. "Blame me later. Right now, you need to help us stop this attack."

Willow flopped from Grundle's back and sunk her fingers into the earth. Her face paled when she looked up at Rose. "They're headed for Mother Silva."

"Who?" said Rose. "Willow, who is heading for Mother Silva!?" she repeated with Sage authority.

"Winged beasts. Horrible, ugly winged beasts. They spew flames of darkness that rot and burn. Unnatural darkness snuffing out life. Who would create such a thing?" She sobbed and got back on Grundle's back. The contact with the warmth of her son's enormous bulk stiffened her resolve. "We must stop them, Sage. These abominations cannot be allowed to roam free or they will end all life on Grendar."

"How are we going to fight an Ach'Su without a void mage?" asked Pyre.

"Sounds like there's more than one," said Nettie. She turned to her fellow Ghosts. "We'll find a way. I'm not about to let these bastards burn down Loam, are you?"

"Hell no," said Leesta.

Pyre puffed out his cheeks in a long exhale. "Here we go again."

"Again!" said Rice with a nostalgic smile. "*That* sounds like Ghost Squad."

"We move now," said Rose. She grabbed Grundle by the snout. "Have your mom lead us to where the pain of the forest is greatest. We'll follow you."

Grundle nodded and took off through the forest, the Liberators hot on his triangular tail.

* * *

Chaos and destruction replaced the tranquility of the glade from the day before. The smoke made it hard to see and breathe. The stressful chirping of the cockatoo alarm was replaced with the screams and moans of dying guards and rangers.

Nettie looked to the sky but saw nothing. Where were they? If it wasn't Ach'Su, who was attacking? Until she knew what they were facing, constructing defenses was a waste of time. And what would she use? Even with her new skills and massive mental library of engineering templates, she would need materials. One thing she was sure of: Willow wouldn't take kindly to chopping the trees of the sacred grove.

Nettie looked back to Rose who had stopped just inside the grove. Rose stood like a statue, the unnatural stillness a giveaway she was receiving or sending a calling. After a moment that seemed an eternity, the Sage opened her eyes and gasped.

"What? What did you see?" asked Gavin.

"Is it the Ach'Su? Are we facing something else?" asked Nettie.

Rose shuddered and held up an open hand. "Five Ach'Su," she whispered.

"Not good," said Rice.

"We were barely able to kill one and that was with Kavi, Pip, and Grim doing the heavy lifting," said Pyre. His eyes were wild. "We're going to die today, aren't we?"

Rose shook her head. "It's worse than that. They've evolved. They're working together and they're no longer stuck in beast form. And...," she sighed, "and I think they might have the boon of a god making them even stronger."

"Which god?" asked Piety.

Rose shook her head, unknowing or unwilling to share the information.

"Does it matter?" asked Rice.

Most of the Liberators sagged, defeated before they entered the fray.

"They're not the only ones," said Nettie. She straightened and faced the deflated group. "I'm a hell of an architect, but I didn't win the battle of Derkin's Ferry on my own. The Tinkerer helped. He gave me a boon which will help us now. I can build damn near anything if I have the resources and the ideas." She caught Rose's eye. "And I've got plenty of ideas."

Piety hefted her mace and stood next to Nettie. "We're not done here. I for one am looking forward to a little payback on these Ach'Su. Ghost Squad, we've faced worse odds and come out on top. At least it's only a god trying to kill us and not the Ancients through some Quest."

Leesta laughed. "*Only* a god. I love you guys." She adjusted the bow strapped to her back and addressed Nettie. "You have the ideas. How do we get you resources?"

Nettie tilted her head to the side indicating the grove over her shoulder. "It's all going to burn if we can't defend it. Let's sacrifice some of these trees to save the rest."

Leesta shook her head. "Logical, but you'll never convince Willow. Maybe there's another way. Let me see what I can do."

Leesta walked to Willow who stood with her hands pressed against a large oak, tears streaming down her face. Grundle, back in man form, helped keep her upright. Leesta gently cupped a hand on Willow's face. She put her other hand on the oak.

All three Loamians went rigid. Their backs arched then slowly relaxed.

With a huge breath Leesta opened her eyes and pulled her hand off the oak. Her eyes found Nettie's. "The grove is going to help."

The sounds of battle grew closer. Rice barked orders and the remains of Ghost Squad formed a wedge with Piety at the center.

Willows' eyes snapped open a moment later. The sadness was replaced with white hot rage. "You'll have what you need, but you'll need to commune with the glade and with Mother Silva."

Nettie blinked. "I don't know how to commune with nature."

"I know you don't, but she does," said Willow, putting a hand on the small of Leesta's back and pushing her towards Nettie. "You two have to do this together."

Leesta cocked her head like a dog trying to understand an unfamiliar command. "I'm sorry Keeper, I don't know what you mean."

Two brightly colored mushrooms sprouted at the Keeper's feet. "You will." She plucked the mushrooms and handed one to Nettie and the other to Leesta. "Quickly, link hands and eat these. Mother Silva will show you the way."

Piety caught Nettie's eye as she popped the mushroom in her mouth. "What do you need from us?"

"Time," whispered Nettie.

Then, the colors of the world shifted into impossible hues

before narrowing to a small pinprick of light.

* * *

"You heard her, Ghost Squad!" yelled Piety. "On me!"

The smoke thickened. A ranger flew from the sky to land at Piety's feet. She leaned down to check the woman's pulse, but her throat had been ripped out. She stood and gripped her mace tighter as she looked into the smoky glade.

A pack of Loamian guards fought something that could only be seen in silhouette through the smoke. The guards were losing. Badly. Three of the six fell in seconds. Arrows flew from the branches above into the menacing man-like shapes advancing on Ghost Squad. The shapes flickered when the arrows made contact. The arrows continued their trajectories to stick harmlessly into the ground.

What in the hell?

One of the shapes transformed into a beastly form all of Ghost Squad recognized. It shrieked.

Piety looked back to Nettie and Leesta. Both women had fallen to the ground. Willow knelt over them with a hand on each of their foreheads. Piety shifted the grip on her shield and turned to face the threat of the charging Ach'Su. She sent Leesta and Nettie a silent entreaty. *Hurry, please! We're not going to last long against these things.*

Grundle roared. Ghost Squad roared with him.

* * *

Nettie blinked. Then again. She couldn't see! She panicked. She tried to run, but couldn't move. She tried to scream, but made no noise. No! This wasn't an answer, this was a nightmare.

A soothing whisper rippled over her, gently caressing her branches. Was that wind? It felt so...real. She had access to none of her other senses. Only touch. What she felt was, quite literally, breathtaking. Her sense of touch,or was it taste, was infinitely layered. She felt the warmth from the sun above, the malevolent heat of the fire as it burned her appendages to the north. She didn't feel pain, just a profound sense of loss. Hundreds of millions of years of collective experience turned to ash in a single cycle of the sun.

That was the problem with these two legged beasts. They were always in such a hurry.

Where did that thought come from? That's when Nettie felt a new layer. Vast awareness. She felt every living creature around her. Not just the squirrels in her branches, but the earthworms aerating the soil, the insects feeding on the body of a hare who died a week ago. The awareness wasn't limited to creatures that run and wriggle. She felt a flower shift its petals to salute the sun. She felt when the seed of an old friend, the poplar, received just the right amount of water and nutrients to sprout its first growth.

And, of course, the fungi. An underground thread sidled across one of her roots, pulsing alarm. The fungi always knew first. This one blared: "not of this earth." Nettie understood the role of fungi as converters, decomposing what once was into a platform for what will be. She never understood, until now, their role as regulators. Fungi thrived when the forest thrived. They made sure the forest knew how to identify threats and regulate resources. They were everywhere, but their projects took shape over years, not seconds.

Another tendril, then a third and fourth grew towards her. The Keeper gave these two-legs access to their network, but the fungi needed more information.

Four tendrils became forty. Nettie wished she knew how to communicate with the forest, the fungi. They constricted around her. A threat, but one they could do something about. She felt fear, though the feeling was foreign in this new level of awareness. Mostly, she felt helpless.

Then, other sequences of feelings washed over her, pulsing outward from nearby. The sensation of a soft summer rain. The gentle zephyr accompanied by the playful song of finches. The warmth of dawn after the first frost of autumn. Feelings of safety and tranquility. Each signal pulsed with confidence and belonging, a young but promising two-leg who recently returned to the Grove after many seasons away.

Leesta! Nettie would have shouted gratitude if she knew how. Instead, she did her best to send the feeling she got when reading a book inside on a rainy day. Contentment.

The strings of fungi loosened.

Leesta responded with playful flashes of early summer sunlight, the promise of warmth to come. The strings of fungi loosened further.

All sensation was washed out by a giant pulse of hurricane force wind. Fire! Danger! Evil! Each burst of wind strained her branches to an extreme until she was sure one would break. As quickly as the storm started, it ended. Another pulse washed over her. The pride of a mama bear, the duty of a protector, a sacred vow to the earth and forest. Willow had joined their communion.

A moment later, Nettie blinked and almost cried in relief. She could see. She stood atop a delicate waterfall in a beautiful glen. Her hand was engulfed by Leesta's larger one. She smiled at Leesta. "Thank you."

In the relief of being able to see, Nettie had nearly forgotten their desperate situation. She quickly looked around, but could see no sign of battle. "Where are we? We have to get back!"

Leesta squeezed her hand tighter as she too looked around. "I think we're in Mother Silva's inner grove. At least our minds are. If the legends are true, Keepers can transport their minds to this place, while their bodies remain grounded. Kind of like the Pool."

Leesta pointed her chin, dragging Nettie's attention to two women picking their way through the glen towards them. Willow walked hand in hand with an older woman with gray green hair and ancient eyes.

Nettie knew who she was before Willow introduced her. "It's nice to meet you, Mother Silva," Nettie said with a curtsy that stole a giggle from Leesta.

Mother Silva nodded but it was Willow who spoke. All but the simplest words were foreign to the ancient tree. "Child of steel, we appreciate your offer of assistance. We could sense the God of Steel's boon on you the moment you set foot in the glade." Mother Silva shook her head gravely. "A mixing of your industry with Lo's bounty is a combination that results in destruction. I know of only one who has successfully melded both."

Nettie nodded. "Sucellia, the Greenginer."

Willow closed her eyes as she translated the meaning of Nettie's words into feelings.

"That's correct, child of steel," answered Willow, eyes still closed. "Sucellia taught that steel can work together with Lo to create. To protect."

"I'll do whatever I can to protect the glade, to protect your trees *and* my companions. They mean everything to me." Nettie stood straighter. "But, we have to act now! The Ach'Su will destroy us if we don't."

Mother Silva moved in front of Nettie and tendrils sprouted from her limbs to encircle the small Bricker. They didn't constrict or even touch her skin, hovering millimeters away, weighing and measuring. Finally, Willow spoke. "Always in a rush. In this place, we have the time we need. And our need is dire. If it weren't, the forest would never take such a drastic step." The tendrils danced around Nettie then sagged in disappointment. "This will not work. Sucellia had the power to commune with Lo. You do not."

"That's why I'm here," said Leesta. "Let me communicate for her."

Mother Silva smiled at Leesta. "Your voice has grown strong, child. The forest rejoiced when you walked back into this glade! What you ask is not simple. It can only work if the two of you become one."

"If you and Willow can do it, so can we," said Nettie. "Show us how."

Shoots grew from Mother Silva's hair. "I adore the enthusiasm of youth," said Willow. "So I won't tell you how long it took for Willow and I to become one." Leaves fell from Mother Silva's shoulder in what passed for a shrug. "You each accepted mortality and sacrifice to transform into something new. So, there is hope. Perhaps you're ready to evolve once more."

"Please, tell us how," said Leesta. The tremble in her voice sounded like reverence.

Willow sighed. "Very well. You have to forgive each other. Fully."

"But we've already done that," said Nettie. She looked at their entwined hands. "We've made our peace."

"That's not the hard part," said Willow. "You haven't fully forgiven each other because you can't. Not until you first forgive yourselves."

The green shoots atop Mother Silva's head wilted. "I've never understood this about two-legs. You are so hateful towards yourselves. A wolf doesn't hate itself for killing the hare. For that matter, neither does the hare hate the wolf. It's simply how things work. Be like the wolf."

"A wolf doesn't dwell in the past," murmured Nettie. "A wolf isn't cursed with remembering all the terrible things it did."

More leaves fell from Mother Silver's shoulders. "Exactly. Be the wolf."

Nettie felt Leesta's hand squeeze hers. If Leesta could look into her own pain, make peace with what caused her to leave home, then so could Nettie. She knew what she had to do, but it terrified her. All the mistrials, the wounds she inflicted that caused her to cringe, the insults she readily dished out. All of them paled in comparison to the one thing that truly warranted self hatred.

Pick, her little brother. The reason she hadn't returned to Brickolage to tell her parents. The reason she would never return to Brickolage. He died because of her. She dragged him along to chase her dream of solving the Triad Quest. How could she *ever* forgive herself for that?

Leesta squeezed her hand again and this time it felt desperate. Needy. Nettie squeezed back. If Leesta faced her own demons, Nettie had to try.

Nettie thought back to all the sleepless nights since Pick died on that bridge. All the dreams she had where she was able to save him only to wake up to crushing disappointment. Only to slink back into bed, hating herself all over again. For the first time, she faced that monster under the bed. For the first time, she turned a critical eye to it, like she would any other problem.

Pick wanted to be there. With her. Nettie told him in no uncertain terms that he was too young to follow her on the Triad. She even caught him the first time and dragged him back to Brickolage. She told her parents to keep an eye on him. Pick followed her again and didn't make his presence known until it was too late. He made his own choices. He was there because he wanted to be there.

Maybe it wasn't her fault. No. That was the easy way out. She could have done more to send him back. She should have done more. It was definitely her fault. She had to accept that before she could reach any level of forgiveness. It *was* her fault. She was the older sister. She held the responsibility once she agreed to let him tag along, whether he wanted to be there or not. Being honest, she wanted him there. He reminded her of home, of family, of belonging to something. She loved how enthusiastic he was about everything. He was annoying, but he was also smart. It was Pick, not her, that figured out the last piece of the Triad, the part about Malcolm Royce. Not only did he want to be there, he deserved to be there. Roanik was the reason why Pick was dead, but Nettie was the reason why Pick was there.

It was her fault, but it made her what she was today. Someone who protected others. Someone who dedicated her life to helping and making the world a better place. She was shocked at the realization. She realized, for the first time, that she respected herself. She liked who she was now.

Would she have taken it all back if it meant getting her brother back? In a second. But it didn't work that way. Pick's death made her what she was today, but so did his life. She wasn't about to spew any nonsense like Pick would have wanted her to live her life. He was too young for such sentiment. Yet, he was wise beyond his years. He would have made fun of her for carrying around a burden that wasn't helping her with her goals. Wasn't helping her save her friends.

Pick would have been the first to share that burden with her. To *take* that burden from her. That's who he was. He was better than her, but she became better than who she was because of him. It was long past time to accept her mistakes and allow herself some grace. To release the burden and become more.

She felt an icy hand of terror grab her by the face. If she let go, wouldn't that mean she would lose everything she had left of him? The guilt. The pain. They had replaced Pick. She knew it was stupid even as she thought it. Pick was never hateful like those things. Pick was excitement. Wide-eyed innocence. She could replace the horrible feelings with the good memories of him. So many flashed into her mind. The two of them carving their whistles, catching fireflies late in summer, fishing on the banks of the Rhune. Too many to count. That's how she wanted to remember Pick. To do that, she had to finally forgive herself.

She had to let him go

Sobs wracked her as she said farewell. It felt too quick, even a little cheap. She could memorialize him later, but this was the only way to help her friends. She had hung on for too long. Even as she wept, she felt stronger and better than she had in years. Even knowing the weight of what they faced, she felt lighter.

She squeezed Leesta's hand and whispered. "You can do this."

Leesta must have believed her. Her grip on her own hand tightened then strengthened. "*We* can do this."

Nettie and Leesta sighed and said, in perfect unison. "Yes, we can."

The two became one with the Northern Grove.

44

Grim

They pushed hard into the evening of the next day. Marina didn't ask another question the entire time. Her eyes were glassy with fatigue as she hit her sixtieth kilometer.

Grim ran behind her for the last thirty. Every kilometer he offered a way out. "All you need to do is head back to Krom," he bellowed at her back. He knew he wasn't being fair. There was no life for her back in Krom. He also didn't care. Another screw up like the one she made yesterday and all of them would die. They got lucky. Grim couldn't count on getting lucky again.

When they bedded down that night, Grim didn't assign Marina a watch. The woman looked at the rest of the group, head hanging in exhaustion and shame and made her way to her bedroll.

When the stew over the fire started bubbling, Grim looked to Krenzer. "Make sure she eats."

Krenzer cocked an eyebrow. "She could have gotten us all killed yesterday. Are you sure?"

"She did her time," said Grim. "We need her strong for

tomorrow."

Krenzer carried the stew to Marina and prodded her with his boot.

She took the offered stew and slurped it down like a starving raccoon finding untouched garbage. She put the bowl to the side and returned to her bedroll. Within moments she was asleep.

Grim was glad she didn't quit. If she could rein in her tongue, she would have real potential. He shook his head and realized he had become just like the drillmasters he despised when he was at the Bastion.

How did that happen?

* * *

Rose visited again that night. Grim shared how close they were to Loam but the Sage seemed distracted. He was about to ask why when he was shaken awake by Krenzer.

"What is it?" asked Grim. He blinked to adjust his eyes to the darkness. The embers of their fire offered the only light in the small glade.

Krenzer held a finger to his lips and pointed up.

Grim knew before he looked. Even from here he could smell it. Burnt butter. "Get the others ready. Quietly."

They were on the road before dawn. Marina looked his way and Grim nodded to one of the horses. He turned to face the six Krommians who followed him. "I don't know what today will bring, but there is a good chance we ride into battle. If that is the case, follow my lead. Do not act until I give the order. We ride doubled up. If we fight, I need you fresh."

They were ten kilometers closer to Loam when the sun peeked over the horizon. The light of early dawn shone a malevolent red.

"Do you smell that?" asked Krenzer.

Grim took a deep breath. The smell was undeniable. Smoke.

"Grim, we need you! Now!" shrieked Rose in his head. His whole body tensed as he was struck with an avalanche of emotion. He fell from his horse.

What is it? Bloody Grim shouted. *You need to let me know when we're under attack!*

We're not under attack, but we will be. Be ready.

Always.

Grim stood and brushed himself off. The rest of his squad stared at him like he'd grown a horn out of the middle of his forehead. "It's Rose. She needs us. Arm yourselves, we ride to battle."

They kicked the horses into a trot then a canter. The horses wouldn't last at this pace for long, but they didn't need to. Loam was only ten clicks out. The smoke thickened and they rode into it.

They heard the screams before they saw the crackling of the flames. They weren't screams of pain, but the screeches of attacking Ach'Su.

"Stay focused!" Grim shouted at his squad as their eyes turned skyward.

"Bloody hell," said Krenzer. "I only saw two of them last night. Now there's five. We can't defeat five."

"We're not going to be alone," said Grim. "The Liberators are attacking from the south. They're the anvil, we're the hammer."

"I don't care if the entire Krommian Army is waiting for us," said Krenzer. "We don't have a chance against five Ach'Su."

"You saw him fight, Krenzer," said Marina, speaking for the first time in two days. "Two weeks ago, I would have said an unarmed man wouldn't have a chance against a banglor. Then he fought three Vendri. Now I know nothing's impossible. If Grim says we can do it, we can do it."

The others straightened in their saddles.

Grim stole a glance at the Krommian woman. After two solid days of endurance torture, she stood up for him. He expected resentment, but loyalty?

She's a believer, Bloody Grim said. *I can feel your doubt. Let it go. Ach'Su are a worthy foe!*

Six months ago, he would have said a single Ach'Su was unbeatable. But now? Then the thought hit him.

What did Krom say about belief? Grim asked his battle twin. *Repeat his words.*

Bloody Grim's tempo sped up as he recited. *'Belief in yourself, belief in those fighting beside you. Before you go into battle, you have to know you are going to prevail.'*

To know we are going to win, we need a plan, said Grim. *Do you remember what everyone was talking about in Krom when we were leaving the city?*

The broadcast about Kavi? asked Bloody Grim.

Kavi and Harp. Do you remember how she manipulated the crowd, how she acted the puppeteer with those people's lives?

Evil but effective, said Bloody Grim.

It was evil because she didn't give them a choice. She turned inklings of belief into slavery. She offered a lie. A pretty lie of peace through servitude, but a lie nonetheless. We must offer a choice.

Then we will be gods!! yelled Bloody Grim into his mind.

Not gods, but we are Krom's champion. It will be enough.

"Grim!" yelled Marina.

"You don't have to yell, Marina," said Grim.

"Yes, I do," she said. "I called you twice and you just sat there, giggling."

Grim dismounted from Blue and he still stood as tall as those sitting in their saddles. "Everyone here knows I'm crazy." He said it with a grin, but the joke didn't land. "But I'm the kind of crazy we need right now."

Grim pointed into the smoky hell of the Northern Glade. "Before we go in there and face these Ach'Su, I need to share something with you. After I fought the Vendri, I had a..." What would you call what happened with Krom? A visitation, an audience? "a conversation with Krom."

"Bullshit," said Krenzer.

Grim held his eye. "Normally, I'd care less if you didn't believe me, Krenzer. But today is different. Belief is everything. You heard the rumors about this Heretic Squad and their run in with Harp. All of Grendar did. The gods are back. Krom appreciated my battles against the banglor and again against the vendri. He gave me a boon. Two, actually, though I see one as a curse."

"I knew it," whispered Marina.

But Krenzer laughed. "You! You are Krom's champion?"

Grim stifled the manic laugh of Bloody Grim. "Believe me, I thought it was crazy too."

"Prove it. What are the boons?" asked Krenzer, hopping out of his saddle.

526

"You've seen him fight, Krenzer. What else do you need?" asked Marina. She slung a leg over her horse to find the ground too.

The other Krommians dismounted and stared at him. Grim could tell they wanted to believe, but they weren't there yet.

"Come at me, Krenzer," said Grim. "Use a weapon, or try to tackle me."

"No, I'm not g—"

"Attack me!" shouted Grim.

The man lowered his shoulder and darted for Grim's legs. Krenzer looked like he dove through a pool of honey he moved so slow. Grim stepped two steps to the left then behind Krenzer.

To those watching, it looked like Grim blinked out of existence and appeared behind Krenzer. Marina sunk to a knee and bowed her head. The other Krommians followed suit.

Grim stood in the semi-circle they created around him and Krenzer. He offered Krenzer a hand. The man took it but only allowed Grim to pull him up to one knee.

"I'm sorry, milord," said Krenzer. "I didn't know."

Grim released the man's hand. "None of that milord crap, you hear me?"

Krenzer nodded.

Grim looked to the rest of his small squad. "Heads up, look at me. I have a crazy idea, but I need you to understand and come to your own decision about it. That's the only way I'm willing to do any of this."

"Tell us," said Marina. Her eyes shone with the light of a zealot.

They get to choose, Grim repeated.

You already said that. Get on with it, said Bloody Grim. *Our friends are running out of time.*

Grim wanted to ask, *Our* friends?, but Bloody Grim was right. They were out of time. He had to give them the choice and he wouldn't lie about it. But how?

"Quick story, then a choice," said Grim. "In my second to last mission as an Elite, my team was sent to scout an Astran fundamentalist group. Their leader was said to harbor godlike powers of persuasion. None of us believed it then, but we saw the result of his charisma." Grim looked to Krenzer. "I was high up on a ridge, but your brother saw it up close, didn't he?"

Krenzer nodded. "The Fourteenth Shield caught the short end of that stick. Kids grinding themselves against their shield wall. And the singing...he talked most about those horribly beautiful hymns. My brother hasn't had a full night's sleep since."

Grim wiped a hand across his forehead as if he could wipe away the memory. "A history lesson taught at the Bastion about the highlanders stuck with me. Those crazy bastards ran in to battle with the words, 'Rach'a den Bourg'. Know what it means?"

The smoke around them thickened. His time was up. "It means body and mind. The group of warriors was known as the Rachvellan, the meanest sons of bitches around. Their oath was not to a king, or a patch of land. It was to the men and women who fought with them. The Rachvellan supposedly had mystical powers. The entire unit fought with one mind. I believe we can do the same thing. I believe I can share my powers with all of you, as long as you believe I can."

All eyes were on Grim. "How?" asked Marina.

"Before the how, know that if you choose to do this, I will be in complete control. I will control your mind until I sever our connection. It starts with belief. Open yourself to me and give up your autonomy for the duration of the fight. You'll have to trust in me, in each other, completely. It may be our only chance."

"I'm in," said Marina immediately, her diagonal scars shone fiercely in the light of the building flames.

It didn't take long for the rest of the team to agree. All but Krenzer.

"No shame in saying no, Krenzer," said Grim.

"Of course there is," said Krenzer. "The only Krommian to turn down the chance to be a Rock Villain?"

"Rachvellan," said Grim. "Never mind. We're out of time. If you're in, you're all the way in. Now, for how it works."

Grim unsheathed his belt knife and drew a shallow cut along his palm. "Faith and commitment. Faith in me. Faith in yourselves. Commit with an oath. You can use Rach'a den Bourg, or you can say 'body and mind' to commit your willingness to hand over the reins. Understood?"

Marina unsheathed her belt knife and cut her own palm. "Understood," she said. She slapped her hand on his, took a deep breath and said, "body and mind."

You know what you're doing? Grim asked.

It's working! said Bloody Grim.

Marina and Grim convulsed. They said, in unison, out of two mouths. "Who's next?"

Seven became one and they sprinted into the glade.

529

45

Battle for the Northern Grove

The Loamian wolf soldier leapt towards the Ach'Su, twin blades flashing. The blades found nothing but air as the beast blinked and reappeared behind the wolf. The Ach'Su's black armored arm punched through the Loamian's chest in an explosion of blood and bone. The monster retracted the arm and the man sagged to the ground.

"Anything from Nettie and Leesta?" asked Rice in desperation. He looked back, but the two lay motionless on the ground with Willow. Rose shook her head once.

Grundle lumbered his way to the front to stand next to Piety.

Reaver fired his weapon twice, twin thunderclaps marked hot metal racing towards his target. In the chaos of the melee with the Loamian forces, the Ach'Su missed the threat of the lone marksman. Reaver's target staggered as his round passed through its armor and into its shoulder. The five Ach'Su scream in unison.

"They *can* be injured!" yelled Reaver to the Rangers in the branches above. "Time your strikes so they can't be dodged."

His declaration breathed life in the demoralized Ranger corp. Moments later, arrows rained down upon the five Ach'Su in synchronized waves. Most of the missiles were dodged, but not all. Two of the Ach'Su blinked away from one arrow only to be struck by another. Five mouths screamed again.

The Rangers cheered.

Their joy was short lived. The three Ach'Su holding the middle of the line opened their mouths, and concentrated waves of black energy crashed into the branches above. When the pulse of energy cleared, the three corps of Rangers and the branches they fired from had vanished, leaving no remains.

The Ach'Su advanced, the minor injuries inflicted by the ranged troops not slowing them in the least.

"Get Rose out of here!" Rice yelled to Gavin.

Rose shook her head, still standing over the prone forms of Leesta, Willow and Nettie. "No! This is where we make our stand. We fight here or Loam falls. I've seen it!"

Rice took a breath then pointed to Pyre.

Pyre's skin turned a deep magenta, camouflaging him in the fiery hellscape of the Northern Grove. A phoenix rose from the ground at the feet of the five Ach'Su. It made a pass across their line. Pyre staggered under the force of his conjuration.

Another cheer rose, this time from the Liberators, as the fire consumed the Ach'Su. The cheer ceased when the five creatures walked through the fire, untouched. Fire would not be fought with fire on this day.

The Ach'Su closed quickly. There were only three wolf

packs between the Liberators and the unstoppable warriors.

The five beasts blinked forward and engaged the closest wolf pack. Their armored arms were everywhere as they eviscerated the two closest Loamian warriors. The Loamians didn't offer a single strike before collapsing to the ground.

The band of Ach'Su closed on the wolf pack's back line, but before they reached the group they faltered. Green shoots sprung violently from the floor of the grove. The shoots wrapped around the legs of the Ach'Su. The five Ach'Su looked down and disdainfully broke from the leafy grips.

The distraction served its purpose.

* * *

Leesta sensed the Liberators sag with relief as the Grove finally fought back. While the Ach'Su were distracted with the tendrils, she quietly positioned five branches from the trees directly in front of the beasts. She bent those branches back behind their trunks. The tension of the wood stressed the branches close to breaking.

It would be worth it.

She needed to give Nettie as much time as she could. The branches she chose were not new growth, so they creaked as they were restrained, but Leesta knew the spread of their branches guaranteed the success of the trap she laid.

The Ach'Su walked right into it. As the five monstrous man-shaped creatures closed on the Liberators, Leesta let the branches slip. They flew towards the monsters before the creatures looked up from the weaker vines still pulling at their legs. The whooshing sound the freed branches made as they swept towards the Ach'Su caused the creatures to raise their eyes. The Ach'Su blinked to move out of the way of the trap, but the spread of woody branches was too wide.

The five Ach'Su were launched high into the air at tremendous speed. A late arriving group of Loamian Rangers sent arrows after them but even those missiles didn't have the speed to catch the catapulted Ach'Su.

Come on Nettie, thought Leesta. *I gave you some breathing room. Time for you to shine.*

* * *

Nettie flashed through the enormous catalog of engineering templates in her mental library. She looked for patterns that could mold wood without damaging it. Sadly, Sucellia's works were never documented. Even the Tinkerer didn't know how the Greenginer created her marvels.

It was time to improvise. Nettie had observed everything Leesta had done, learned everything she could from her brief commune with Mother Silva. Ever since she unlocked her talent as an architect, all her focus had been on design and construction. Materials were important, but only in so much as they impacted how high she could build, how strong the structure would be. She learned about statics in University and had an innate understanding of tensile strengths and material density. She'd always believed that material choice was important, but secondary to the design itself.

That dynamic had been turned upside down. As she linked

with Leesta, she knew materials were the *most* important thing. Not only did she have to choose wisely, but she would have to convince the materials to mold in the ways she needed. They never taught *that* at the University.

She started simple. If they were to protect the glade behind them from the fire in front, they needed a fire break. She sent the idea through Leesta, who was able to translate it to the trees. Leesta sent images to the trees to treat a line, ten meters wide, as if it had blight. Nettie, through Leesta, convinced the trees to migrate away from that patch of land. Leesta sent another image to the fungi below that same path, to increase the speed of decomposition so any leaves or broken branches were swiftly covered with mushrooms that ate through the fibrous material transforming it into non-flammable mulch.

To those watching it looked like a ten meter wide road magically sprung from the forest. Even the Loamians gasped at the odd sight.

You haven't seen anything yet, thought Nettie. She took on the challenge of building a defensible position next. Trees on their side of the firebreak leaned over and fit together like puzzle pieces to create a formidable ten meter wall, supported by broad trunks. Twin towers rose five meters above that. The Ranger corps running in from the southern grove scaled the towers and knocked arrows to bows.

Now for offense. Nettie's mind raced to the giant golems Rin summoned in the battle of Derkin's Ferry. She didn't have the materials for those, but she could build something similar.

She would need Mother Silva's help. Nettie shared her plan with Leesta and could feel her friend's inward sigh. After a series of disturbing images flashed back and forth, Nettie received confirmation from Willow in the form of two words. *We can.*

Nettie heard the shouts from the Rangers in the towers first. The sounds from outside the forest network were muted as if they came from a different room in a large castle. They were loud enough that Nettie understood their meaning. The Ach'Su were on their way back. They had taken to wing and flew right at them.

She wondered, for only a moment, why the monsters didn't attack another part of Loam. It could mean only one thing. Rose was their primary target. Nettie spared a moment to find the Sage. There, standing over her and Leesta's inert bodies. Through Nettie's sylvan sight, Rose thrummed with power.

Nettie wasn't about to let the Ach'Su reach the Sage. She gave the order and her three sylvan golems shifted, then patiently waited. Timing would be everything.

Arrows flew from the two towers with the buzz of a hive of angry bees. The two Ach'Su on the flanks lowered their heads and waded into the swarm. They hadn't used their darkness attack yet and Nettie could hear the muffled orders to evacuate the towers. The expected attack came in synchronized cones of gaseous night. Archers jumped the distance to the walls.

Nettie felt intense pain behind her eyes when the cone of darkness struck her towers. The trees who so willingly sacrificed the strength of their branches to protect their two-legged companions screamed as if they were aflame. The towers vanished into nothingness, leaving two giant holes in the wall Nettie had built.

The Ach'Su screeched in victory, the desolate sound magnified as it came out of five mouths at once. Nettie gave the order again to hold. Not until the Ach'Su passed the firebreak would she rally counter-defenses.

She didn't have to wait long. The Ach'Su saw the firebreak and dove towards the defenders on the wall.

Now! She sent the command to her sylvan golems. The three largest trees of the grove, besides Mother Silva herself, pulled their roots from the ground and moved. The forest golems rolled and tumbled like an avalanche. They extended all their branches in one direction, with one goal. Pull the three Ach'Su in the middle of the formation to the ground.

Their branches shot outwards as if the Ach'Su were selfish suns demanding growth. Three branches reached the middle beast before it could complete its dive. They wrapped around its wings, then its four legs, dragging it to the ground in the middle of the firebreak.

There were no living things above the ground in the firebreak, but there was an entire network of growth below it. The Ach'Su squawked in fear, for the first time making a noise the other four did not mimic. When it struck the ground, the roots under the break grew around the Ach'Su, then through it. Mushrooms popped up all over the beast, filling its mouth and ears before it could make a sound. Seconds later, the decaying giant beast was dragged beneath the earth.

The other four creatures looked back, with what could only be fear on their grim countenances. Nettie relished their terror. As they looked back, branches flew at the two in the middle. The Ach'Su navigated through them with the aerial agility of hawks avoiding the attack of a host of sparrows.

Just then, Willow called on the birds of the forest to join the fight.

Thousands of birds dive bombed the Ach'Su from above, managing to drive another into the firebreak. Half of its head was already decomposed by mushrooms as roots dragged it beneath the earth.

Three left. Nettie lined up her next defense. She was sure the trees could swing a branch with enough speed that the tip of the branch would fly off in a missile that could down at least one of the remaining Ach'Su. She issued the order too late and the three remaining Ach'Su transformed mid-air to land atop the wall she built. If she issued the order now, she would injure her friends. She watched in horror as the three man-sized Ach'Su tore through Loamians and Liberators.

* * *

On the wall, Rice wished for the tenth time in as many minutes that they had some suli to give them a chance in this fight. The three Ach'Su peered down the other side of the wall, looking for something. It had to be Rose. Even if the Ghosts couldn't stop the Ach'Su, the Liberators would do what was needed to give Rose the chance to escape.

The Sage would not fall here today.

"Right side trap," Rice yelled in his best tactician voice.

Piety slammed the handle of her mace on the wall and called her vicar skill. A golden shield made of light formed around their squad. It burned the Ach'Su and at the same time healed the wounds of everyone on their side of the wall.

The shield isolated the two Ach'Su to their left which allowed the team to focus all their efforts on the Ach'Su on the right. They didn't need to kill it. They only needed to throw it from the wall to land in the firebreak.

Pyre fired three flaming darts at the Ach'Su but the creature blinked, dodging. Pyre's skin and eyes were a light pink, his ether completely tapped. He looked exhausted, but he pulled the war staff from his back and planted his feet.

Grundle and Piety stood shoulder to shoulder, forming a barrier between the Ach'Su and the rest of the wall. Grizzly Grundle swiped a paw at the closest Ach'Su. The creature caught the strike in an armored hand then casually ripped the paw off at the elbow. Grundle bellowed in pain and the Keeper on the ground below screamed with him.

The branches which made up the wall below the Ach'Su shifted and reached for the Ach'Su, but the creature was too fast. It danced out of the way.

Piety closed, swinging her mace wildly in the hopes that chaotic strikes might more easily find one of the wickedly quick creatures.

The blades on the Ach'Su's left arm swept through the Astran woman's neck, cleanly decapitating her. The monster's expression never changed. Piety's head rolled off the wall to fall at Rose's feet, bumping against Leesta's motionless leg.

"No!" screamed Rice. Both fists glowed and he charged.

The Ach'Su showed no concern until two thunderclaps issued from Reaver's rifle on the far side of the wall. His rounds struck the Ach'Su in the same injured shoulder. It fell back for a moment, stunned.

That's all Rice needed. His fist swung into and through the stunned Ach'Su's head. Brain matter splattered Rice's face and he kicked the creature's body off the wall into the firebreak. He turned around to face the other two Ach'Su. He was numb. So much death. He refused to believe Piety was gone. He wouldn't believe it until he had time.

He wouldn't have time until the Ach'Su were dead.

Piety's vicar shield dropped when she died which was how Reaver's shots got through. The Ach'Su closest to the marksman blinked towards Reaver and the man drew his short sword. There was resignation in his eyes. The Ach'Su blinked behind him and snapped his neck.

Reaver fell, glassy eyes staring out at the forest glade.

Rice put his back against Pyre's and the two men faced the remaining two Ach'Su.

A wild roar came from the other side of the firebreak. It was so loud all eyes turned in its direction.

Then the Ach'Su turned in that direction, as seven Krommian warriors sprinted towards them at an inhuman pace, yelling with one voice.

* * *

"Rach'a den Bourg!" shouted Bloody Grim out of seven mouths. The enemy was dead ahead atop the bizarre looking wall. He leapt. All seven flew over the large gap in the forest to land on the great wall.

Grim screamed in pain as he watched Pyre fall, an Ach'Su's armored arm burst through his chest.

"Pyre!" screamed the Astran monk with glowing fists. The monk stood over him, desperately trying to heal him.

539

Pyre's eyes were wide. His hand found Rice's. "It's... okay," he choked out. "I never expected to make it this long. Finally...some rest."

Pyre shuddered then stilled.

Grim landed behind the Ach'Su as it swung for the back of Rice's head. The monk's movements were incredibly slow.

Not so the Ach'Su's. Grim barely had time to hook an elbow under the creature's arm and shift his weight to pull the beast down. The creature's sharpened vambrace cut into his forearm.

Grim strained with all his strength and barely managed to shift the beast. It must have to do with its mass. Its flying form was enormous, but all that mass had to settle into this man-shaped body somehow. Grim reasoned armor played a role. With his arm locked into the joint of the Ach'Su's armor, he brushed the thing's skin. It was like rubbing coarse granite.

Grim strained for a moment more, then broke his grip. He could feel the wound in his forearm healing as he drew the hand-axes from his belt. The creature dove low, scoring a strike against Grim's right shin. Krom, these things were fast! Even with his boon, they were faster than anything he'd ever fought save for maybe Kavi.

A boot kicked the creature in the face with impossible force, sending monstrous teeth flying from its mouth.

Grim grinned and his battle twin crowed. *They may be fast, but we outnumber them seven to two!* Krenzer's boot found the Ach'Su's face again and black blood poured from the creature's mouth.

Krenzer moved as fast as Grim himself. They all did.

Bloody Grim screamed and Grim screamed with him. His

hands went to his neck to stem the blood of a stab in the throat, but his skin was dry. He looked back to see the quietest member of his team of six, a man by the name of Libon. His lips puckered like a goldfish who had jumped from its bowl. He couldn't draw air from his sliced windpipe.

Grim screamed again. The pain was unimaginable. The only thing that could compare was the collar the League and Proust used to keep him in line. The only reason he kept his feet was the tolerance he'd built when tortured by the collar.

Grim felt Bloody Grim pull the others back to their feet, but not until another of his squad fell. This time it was Elias, the ugly man with an amazing singing voice. Bloody Grim wrangled the remaining squad quicker after Elias' fatal wound.

Krenzer struck again with his boot. Grim grabbed the Ach'Su by the hands and spun. Finally, the Ach'Su lifted from the ground. With a mighty heave he tossed the beast on to the ground of the firebreak.

Even Grim was shocked by the speed at which the roots and mushrooms consumed the fallen monster. He spared it only a side-eyed glance as he ran along the wall to assist a hard-pressed Marina. In the fraction of a second it took Grim to arrive, the fallen Ach'Su had disappeared beneath the earth.

The final standing Ach'Su twitched, shuddered, then paused.

They must feel the same pain we do when linked! Attack now! Grim shouted inwardly to his battle twin. Marina, Aubrey and Jurgen stabbed their gladiuses into the creature at the same time.

The Ach'Su used its remaining strength to push its blade

covered arm into Jurgen's belly. Marina and Aubrey stabbed again and again, using all the strength of Grim's transferred berserker skill.

Finally, it lay still.

No one on the wall celebrated. The butcher's bill was too high. Rice sat next to the bodies of Pyre and Piety with fat tears running down his face. His hand brushed over Grundle's severed paw, using all his healing power to slow the bleeding.

The battle of the Northern Grove was over.

They won, but Grim felt no joy.

46

Loops and threads

Kavi regained consciousness the moment he hit the snow. He opened his eyes and quickly shielded them from the glare of the sun. His dirty, bloody hands crunched against the surface as he sat up. The cold felt good. Pip's void gate winked out a moment later. Kavi instantly recognized the snow-covered road down to the bridge leading out of the Nest. After hundreds of hours shoveling it, every contour had been burned into his brain. His head whipped to the outbuilding where giant plumes of dust billowed through broken windows.

He looked desperately to see who made it out. Crystal knelt next to Stonez healing a broken arm as Stix looked on. Amity and Sliver worked together to stabilize Boost who's head lay on Jansen's lap. Felicity walked around the group with Pip and Jory. She gave what healing she could to get everyone back on their feet.

There she was.

The choice had been obvious. While they were in Vonderia, he and Clara did what they could to rekindle the fragile ember of passion which kept getting stepped on by life in the League, or buried by the mounds of emotional baggage that came with it. Being honest with himself, he had fallen for her. Hard. But they never had a free moment together. Thanks to the slag titan and her fiery minions, it took over a week for both of them to heal. Then, Pip went and got himself thrown in magic jail. All Kavi wanted was one day off to spend with her.

He rushed to her side and gasped when he noticed the sharpened end of a rocky tentacle poking through her chest. She trembled and her eyes searched around wildly. She gave him a bloody smile when she found his face.

"No, no, no. Felicity!" he shrieked. "I need you! Now!"

Clara's hand grasped her wrist. "I'm sorry...," she choked out. "I'm sorry we never got to be together." A bubble of blood pulsed from her mouth.

Kavi screamed.

Felicity looked at the wound and shook her head.

Clara's grip on his wrist was strong. "If you do...roll... back." She gave a wet wheeze. "...and I can't be saved...you save Tess, you hear me?"

She tried to pull another breath, but the air didn't come. She squeezed his wrist even harder. Her eyes widened in fear and she began to thrash. He watched helplessly as she suffocated and finally lay still.

No.

Not today.

He flexed that muscle in his brain until he thought his head was going to explode. Then he pushed some more. Time slowed then reluctantly began to reverse. Kavi strained as he paddled up the temporal stream, fighting the vicious current. Pip's gate opened and he flew backwards into the training cavern. He watched as the tremendous explosion of the vuori kraken sucked into itself. The creature reformed in a wriggling mass.

There! He watched the tentacle pull out of Clara's back and she was made whole. He saw other details too. Yantzy's team made it out of the cavern, so maybe some of them made it out alive. Varseid's team was a different story. They had dug in and he doubted a single member survived the explosion.

Kavi continued to back time up. He observed as he gave Ghost Squad the order to retreat. If he could only get back to when he was in the Aerie, he could call a general evacuation. The more he pushed, the more the current of time resisted.

Pip responded to Boost's question, "Yantzy asked the same question. What are we waiting for?"

Kavi strained. If he could push time back to when he positioned the squads, he could save so many lives. Then he hit the snag. The barrier was like a waterfall in the linear stream of time that couldn't be paddled past. No matter how hard he pushed, it wouldn't go any further.

He watched Tess stick her hands under the lip of the pit and focus. She shook her head. Kavi mouthed the words, even though Tess spoke them backwards. "Too much turmoil, it's not like the plant we encountered. It hasn't just been tainted, it feels like it's being controlled. Doesn't matter how many tranquility runes we use. This thing will not be pacified."

He pushed and flexed, but time refused to reverse any more. The current pushed back with impossible force. Time stopped and Kavi knew it was only moments before it resumed in its regular direction.

He looked at how Tess and Clara were positioned. They were furthest from him, positioned around the rim of the vuori's pit, about to set defensive runes. The other members of Ghost Squad took their traditional positions. Could he order one of the other Strikers to grab Tess while he grabbed Clara? He didn't think so. They were too far away. If he gave the order, he would lose *another* team member. He could order Clara and Tess closer. Kavi nodded, that's what he'd do.

He let out a breath, ready to let time resume when he saw movement in his peripheral vision from just behind Tess. What was that? He spun to face it but there was nothing there. Harp?

He couldn't hold it any longer.

Time resumed.

"It's a trap!" yelled Kavi. He looked to Pip. "Open a portal and order the retreat."

Pip looked at him, questions all over his face.

"Trust me and do it!" said Kavi. "Full retreat, all channels. Flee the Nest!"

Pip nodded and the portal appeared. He held two fingers to his ear and transmitted the orders. The rest of Heretic Squad started a slow but measured retreat to the portal.

Kavi calculated the distances. They would make it. He yelled to Tess and Clara, but either the noise from the vuori and its polyps was too loud, or they were too focused on their task. They never turned at his order.

He moved. Dancing and weaving between tentacles and attacks from the drones, he reached Clara and deflected the tentacle right before it pushed into her back. Yes! He threw her towards the portal

Even with all his speed, he could only save Clara.

The cold felt good as he pushed himself up in the snow. He looked over to Clara. The hilt of a jagged stone knife poked from her neck. Her eyes were wild and scared. "...save Tess," she whispered. Then, she was gone. Again.

"Harp, you will fucking pay for this!" he screamed at the top of his lungs. He flexed and pushed. And pushed. And the cycle started all over again.

He searched everywhere for the goddess as time backed up. He paused the time reversal hundreds of times making the herky-jerky movements even more unnatural and violent. No sign of Harp. Right before time resumed, he caught that movement out of his periphery, but it was too late.

Time resumed.

Clara died in his arms four more times. A stray arrow from Varseid's team took her in the neck. A falling stalactite clipped her temple. A drone enveloped in flame caught Clara in a deathly embrace. The original tentacle slipped through Kavi's defenses as he warded off these other threats.

She died every time. It didn't matter what he did, it was like she was marked for death. Every time she asked him to spare Tess.

He sobbed as he moved time back yet again. This time, he went for the ranger. His close friend. His betrayer. He loathed every step as he reached for Tess. He bodily picked her up and hurled her towards the portal, hating everything about her as she flew through the air.

Maybe he should just stay and die here with Clara. He caught that flicker of movement out of the corner of his eye again. This time it came from a different direction. Near the doomed Clara.

Harp. It had to be. He stopped time. He would catch that bitch this time. Make her pay. Even if he died in the process. He didn't turn his head, he just moved his eyes.

There, finally. The figure that had been haunting him. But it wasn't Harp. It was...him. He caught the stricken expression on his own face as he rushed to help Clara. What in the hell?

Was it some form of remnant from a previous attempt? Was that even possible? Was he somehow in both places at the same time? He focused.

Suddenly, he was looking out of two sets of eyes. Through one set, he observed Tess flying towards the portal. Through the other, he reached for Clara's arms to throw her. Simul-taneously. It felt like when he had the vision of the demon Marked when he was in the Pool. In two places at once. Could he control this? The explosion began.

He flew through the air and out the portal. He opened his eyes to Tess' slitted ones mere inches form his face. She looked furious. Clara lay next to her, tentacle sticking out of her chest. She was already gone.

Both of them out. That was new. So was the remnant. He felt a trickle of hope. Maybe he *could* he use the remnant? How?

"Why?" Tess asked.

He ignored her and flexed. Once again the river of time jerked violently backwards. He felt a slight headache the last time he struggled against the river of time. This time it felt like twin daggers pushed deep into his temples. He didn't think he had too many chances left.

Kavi raced to Clara again, knowing exactly where to stop to see his remnant. He stopped time and felt it when his remnant did the same. He moved just his eyes to look at his previous self, paused in his rush to save Tess. He focused, willing himself to be in both places at once, but the remnant pushed back. He focused harder. The remnant resisted. He made a final push and right before he slipped into both locations at once, he heard, in his own voice, "Find the cave in you." Then, he was seeing out of both sets of eyes again, right before the explosion shot him and Clara out of the portal.

He looked to Clara filled with hope, but the first thing he saw was the impaling, sharpened tentacle. He didn't wait for her to ask him to save Tess.

He held his head in pain as he forced time backwards again. "Find the cave in you." They were about to re-enter a giant cave. What the hell was he talking about? Why so cryptic? He hated games so his remnant must as well. That meant his remnant had only enough time to say one thing. The cave in me?

He raced towards Clara when it hit him. The cave in me.

He stopped time precisely at the moment his remnant would be near Tess. The cave in me? Was I talking about that odd liminal space where I have those bizarre chats with Holden?

Just like that, he was sitting in a chair. He looked up to

see the strange shrine of skulls not too far away. Across the table from him was another version of himself.

"Oh thank Krom," that version said. "Not all past versions of us figure it out. Surprisingly, we have plenty of time in this odd little place, so I'd be happy to answer any questions you might have, but it might help if I gave you a quick summary."

So weird. He was sitting here with a future version of himself. "Please," said Kavi.

Future Kavi gave a curt nod. "I'm in a timeline where this is my last chance to save Clara. Look at me."

Kavi squinted and examined his future self. Future Kavi had visible, blackened veins running through his face, neck and arms. The insides of his ears were crusted with dry blood. "You look like shit."

"We always say that."

"How many times have you done this?" asked Kavi.

"The obvious question and the start of the summary. This is my fourteenth time. I'm not going to survive it. The black veins showed up on my twelfth attempt, and the pain is no longer bearable. I want you to look at me, but squint and slightly cross your eyes until you can see two versions of me."

Kavi screwed up his eyes until he saw double. Shifting his eyes like that hurt, and the pain of his headache increased.

"Keep those versions of me in your mind's eye and close your physical eyes," said future Kavi. "This will help you see what we need you to see."

Kavi locked the image of the two versions of his future self. He closed his eyes. "You sound like Holden," Kavi said.

"Don't talk or you'll lose it," said future Kavi. "I want you to focus on the space between us. Do you see a wavy looking line?"

Kavi shook his head and opened his eyes. "I thought you were going to give me a summary."

"I will, but you have to see this first."

Kavi crossed his eyes again and stared. Then he closed his eyes and focused on the image of himself in his mind's eye and...nothing. Wait, there *was* something there, like a narrow line of smoke wisping off a dying fire. "I see it! How in the hell did you figure this out?"

"Excellent!" exclaimed future Kavi. "The first time I saw it, I had just gotten hit in the head from a rock thrown by one of the drones. That line is what Elana and the neuro-mages call a neural thread. I think of it like the core of your being, who you are."

Kavi's mind raced. "And you think with that thread, we can fuse," said Kavi.

"Exactly," said future Kavi. "Before you ask, yes, we can fuse with Clara and with Tess. But you're going to hate it and so will they."

"Why?" asked Kavi. "I've fused with both of them, I don't have anything left to hide."

"Of course you do," snapped future Kavi. "But that's not the point. You're going to hate it because the only way you can fuse with Clara is if you force it. You have to completely take her over." He held up a hand. "Yes, just like Harp did in the square. And the process is horribly violating. You have to remove every part of what makes Clara, Clara. Then, replace it with a picture you have of her. That's the hardest and creepiest part, because in your picture she can be our ideal woman. She can have all the great qualities and none of the ones that get on our nerves. She can be a sex slave.

She can be whatever we want her to be."

Kavi shuddered.

Future Kavi nodded. "Yeah, it's disgusting, but it gets worse. Because then, you fix whatever that image is in your mind and dominate what's left of her mind. Completely. You aren't sharing two versions, two narratives, like you do in a fuse. It's only you controlling her. To do it right, you have to basically rape her soul."

"That sounds horrible," said Kavi. He let out a deep breath.

"It was. The worst part was Clara watched the whole thing. Trapped and helpless." Future Kavi shuddered at the memory. "The first time I did it, she refused to look at me as I apologized over and over."

"But you got her out alive," said Kavi.

It was future Kavi who shuddered this time. "I broke something in her. She killed herself the second I turned away."

"You couldn't convince her to accept the fuse?" Asked Kavi.

"The moment we move back in the battle cavern, time resumes and we have three seconds. Do you think you could convince and teach either of them how to do a fuse in that amount of time?"

Kavi shook his head. Even if he slowed time, he wouldn't be able to explain it to her as she would be moving in regular time. "What else did you try?"

"I personally took Tess over and used her as a fused partner to help me get Clara out of there. That failed twice. They both died each time. According to a future version of myself, we've tried damn near everything else. As far as I know, there's only one thing left."

"What's that?" asked Kavi.

"You and I fuse, take them both over and run all three of us to the portal."

"That doesn't even make sense. How can we fuse? We're exactly the same."

Future Kavi shook his head. "No. When we reversed time the very first time, the timeline diverged. We are now separated by those differences, even if it's only a couple of minutes. We've each reversed time multiple times since, which created even more timelines."

"And if we fuse?" said Kavi. "We'll turn into a combination of what? Speed and speed?"

Future Kavi shrugged. "No idea, maybe we get even more power over time. Maybe we end up with the time to rebuild Clara and Tess in some other way. Maybe it kills both versions of us. Who knows?"

"We have to try," said Kavi.

Future Kavi nodded. "I want you to practice seeing the neural thread. I need you to do it enough times that you can see my thread without having to think about it. For us to fuse, you're going to have to reach for that thread by feel. Remember, the moment we get back in that cavern, you can't move. Any outside observation of divergent timelines will cause one of them to collapse. Not only do you need to grab for my thread, you have to do it the same time I grab for yours."

Kavi did the exercise until it became instinctive. The last time he opened his eyes, he could still see the thread floating just behind future Kavi.

"When we get back in there," said future Kavi. "I want you to say—"

"Move like wind," interrupted Kavi.

Future Kavi nodded. "Move like wind. Say it with the exact same timing we always do when we start our mantra. Then, reach for my thread and fuse."

"Should we try it here first?" asked Kavi.

"No. This is my last time. Even if it does work here, we have no idea what it will do to the river of time. I can't take the risk that a practice attempt here destroys our chance to save Clara and Tess." Future Kavi stared into his eyes. "Ready?"

Kavi nodded.

47

Revelations

He was back in the battle cavern. Time was stilled and so was he. *Move like wind*, he recited under his breath. He grasped for his future self's neural thread.

He felt the disorientation of the fuse. *It's working!*

Focus, said future Kavi. *I don't know how much time we have.*

Kavi looked out of two sets of eyes. Nothing moved. Yet.

A flash of light.

Kavi was a young boy of eight summers. He gallivanted around the inner bailey of Stonecrest keep with Grim and his brother Brink. Brink was only six. He followed Kavi and Grim everywhere they went.

It was so annoying.

This particular morning, he and Grim had come up with a plan. They would spar in one of the circles the guards had set aside for the kids. Once the bout was over, Kavi would pretend to be hurt and ask Brink to go get help. Once Brink left, they would flee down into the town, hopefully getting rid of him for the rest of the day.

It was the new huntsman, Carlin, that found them in town. He and Grim were having a great time playing knuckles with some of the bigger boys right outside of the blacksmith's shop.

"You lads best be coming with me," said Carlin. "Your ma is right furious with the both of you."

I was always such a selfish little prat. What I wouldn't give to see Brink again.

A flash of light.

Kavi was eighteen and back in the Bastion. It was the midterm sparring competition. First place was a given— Grim. Everyone else fought for second.

Kavi got lucky, he was on the opposite side of the draw from Grim. If he was good enough, he wouldn't face him until the final. His last opponent sustained an injury in her last bout and had to bow out. That gave Kavi a bye into the semi-finals, where he would face Thaddius Crumb.

Thaddius was not a graceful fighter. He made up for it with pure aggression and an unnatural ability to resist being thrown. He bull-rushed in most every fight, narrowing the circle to a small area his opponent had to fight within or risk stepping out and losing a point. It worked on most everyone but Grim who was even larger than the intimidating Thaddius.

Kavi had no idea how he was going to win the fight.

Ugh, we were so pathetic, giving up before the fight even begins.

Grim walked over to Kavi's corner before the fight began. He laid a heavy hand on Kavi's shoulder. "You're going to have to dance, do everything you can not to get caught in corner."

"It's a circle," said Kavi, with a grin.

"You know what I mean. Dive, jump, whatever it takes. Do *not* let him push you out."

Kavi nodded and walked to the center of the ring. The sergeant in the center raised his hand, looked at Kavi then to Thaddius. He lowered it. Kavi set himself but Thaddius charged with such ferocity that he found himself backpedaling. Within seconds he stepped out of the ring.

Pathetic. We didn't even have the guts to stay in for one point.

Who's saying all this hateful shit? Kavi asked of future Kavi. *If you remember, we won this fight and gave a Grim a run in the final.*

Both of us, replied future Kavi. *We've always been harshest on ourselves.*

Us, or the Lioness? asked Kavi.

Good question, said future Kavi.

Kavi won the next two points easily. All it took was a dive and a roll. On both occasions he punched Thaddius hard in the kidney. The brute had very little grace and fell easily. Kavi moved on to the final.

Look how sloppy our form is, said future Kavi.

We're not going to be able to complete the fuse if we keep hating on ourselves, said Kavi. *Remember our earlier fuses? The merge didn't happen until after we accepted the other person.*

Is it possible to fully accept yourself? asked future Kavi.

A flash of light

Kavi stood over a paralyzed Clara. The memory of a previous failed fuse attempt weighed heavily on him and he vowed to be ruthless this time. He invaded Clara's mind and began ripping out her personality piece by piece. All of her experiences with Trixie. Gone. All of her insecurities about her mother. Gone. All of her feelings for Ghost Squad. Gone. All of her feelings for Kavi. Gone.

In his mind's eye, Kavi could see Clara sitting in the corner of a dark, dank cell. She shook as she begged, "Stop it. Please! I can't lose any more. There's nothing left."

I can't believe you did that, said Kavi. *Only a monster could do that to her.*

Don't you think I know that! snapped future Kavi. *That's why I die after this fuse. But I can't think of another way to save her life. It's the only story I can tell to keep my sanity. Once we release her, her mind will go back to normal. Won't it?*

You're asking me?

It has to, said future Kavi.

Kavi looked closely at each and every part he ripped out of Clara. He realized that every one of her experiences, every interaction created the woman he had fallen for. He had already accepted all of her when they fused the first time, but things had changed as his feelings for her grew. They argued more as they grew closer. With those stronger feelings, he realized he injected more of himself into their relationship. Into how he saw her. His expectations had shifted. He began to expect the same from her as he expected from himself. But his standards were impossibly high. He hated himself when he didn't meet them. Was he doing the same with her?

He had no right to do that. She was her own person, not some extension of him.

We don't have the right to judge her like we judge ourselves, said future Kavi, *just because we care more for her.*

Maybe we don't have the right to judge ourselves so harshly either, said Kavi. *Do you remember what Dad said to us after Brink died? We sat in his study hoping the old man wouldn't* break into tears again.

I remember, said future Kavi. "Get out of your own way. You need to learn to like yourself before you'll ever realize your true potential."

Can you do that? asked Kavi.

Can you?

Kavi continued to dismantle Clara's soul, doing his very best to remember every piece so he could put it back together perfectly. He wept as he did it.

I don't know, said Kavi.

A flash of light.

A flood of images. Kavi helped his younger brother hold a sword for the first time as Brink looked on with hero worship. Kavi jumped in front of Ghost Squad to take on an entire line of kobolds bearing down on them. Kavi hugged his father as he wept over Brink. Kavi defended Clara and Trixie the first time in the Nest. A hundred images showed Kavi going out of his way to help someone.

Why do we spend so much time and energy remembering the moments of cruelty, the embarrassments? asked Kavi. We've done plenty of good.

Hating our failures make us stronger, said future Kavi. You heard it as many times as I did.

The Lioness is wrong, said Kavi. Hating our failures only teaches us how to hate. Perfection is the myth which prevents us from embracing that we're all imperfect. Imperfection is the cost of being alive. The cost of being able to think.

If Clara's taught us anything, said future Kavi, it's the beauty in being alive. That's what Mother never understood. Beauty comes from imperfection, it's the root of art and music.

You're right, said Kavi. Regardless of what the Lioness thinks, *it's okay not to be perfect. No, it's better than okay, it's what makes us human. It's what makes us interesting.*

I can accept that, said future Kavi.

Me too.

Their consciousnesses merged and they were back in the cavern. Kavi looked out of two sets of eyes. Time was still paused. He wiggled a finger and time remained paused.

Interesting.

He stopped and looked around. The vuori kraken glowed a pinkish red, close to exploding. He noticed an icy blue stream which looked like a children's drawing of water floating motionless in the air. It had a whimsical transparency as if the idea of materiality was a joke. Kavi reached to touch the wispy stuff and his hand went right through it.

It was eye level so he walked through it until he looked directly into the vaporish stream. When he looked to the left, he saw a transparent wall that pulsed with menacing energy. The stream continued past the wall, but Kavi knew he wouldn't be able to pass through the barrier. When he looked to his right, he saw future Kavi standing above Tess.

He raised his right arm slightly and future Kavi did the same in perfect synch. They were definitely fused. When they fused, this new power seemed to be showing him a physical manifestation of how he saw the currents of time.

Great, what to do with it? Kavi stared at the stream and noticed tiny specks of utter blackness. There were only three or four of them and he had to squint to focus on them. The motes looked almost like the void stuff Pip used to trap Harp. Kavi pulled out his dagger and gently poked a black speck. The tip of his dagger vanished. He pulled it back quickly, but the tip was still gone. *Okay. Don't touch the black specks.*

He relaxed his eyes and noticed an identical number of sparkling motes, just below each void speck. Partners in the stream. He gingerly poked the same dagger at one of these. The dagger stuck as if anchored there. He had to pull hard to remove it.

I've got a crazy theory, Kavi said.

I'm listening, said future Kavi.

I think the sparkly specks are timeline anchors. If we touch the anchor at the same time, you can stay in that body and fuse with Tess while I fuse with Clara.

And the black specks? future Kavi asked.

Timeline destroyers, said Kavi.

I was afraid you were going to say that, said future Kavi. He let out a sigh. *I wasn't going to make it anyway. And you know what? I've made peace with it. I'll destroy my timeline the moment you, Tess and Clara are out of here.*

Thank you, said Kavi. *I knew we'd do the right thing.*

It's what we do, said future Kavi. *The minute we interact with Tess and Clara, the timeline will resume. If we slow time, we can turn three seconds into about ten at our speed, but their minds can't handle anything more than triple speed. We have to be ruthless and work incredibly fast. That's the only way the three of you are going to reach the portal. Ready?*

Go! shouted Kavi. He reached out a hand to touch Clara and began to deconstruct her. He was as gentle as possible, but it was fucking awful. He had to rip out everything important to her. Until those anchors of self were gone, he would never be able to dominate the animal essence of her mind.

He gutted her personality while she watched on in horror. It wouldn't have been possible without their earlier fuse and untangling of threads, but because of them, he knew exactly

561

how to vivisect her soul. He removed the final piece and dominated what was left.

All of a sudden, he saw out of four sets of eyes. It took a millisecond to adjust. Then, he started to run. His Tess body spun to dodge a drone. His Clara body ducked and the sharpened tentacle passed over her head. His Clara body leapt forward and rolled, narrowly avoiding the bone dagger thrown at her neck. She dove to the right and avoided the falling stalactite as an errant arrow whistled harmlessly over her head.

His Tess body jumped and landed on the sharpened tentacle then ran along it then flipped towards the portal. Kavi's primary body followed behind both his female bodies. He would be last through the portal.

Tess floated through as Kavi felt the heat of the explosion behind him. He risked a look back when his Clara body reached the portal.

Future Kavi stood, looking into the building explosion. Kavi left as his future self reached for the black mote. As Tess then Clara passed through the portal, he felt his connection to their neural threads sever. He no longer had control of either of them. The force of the explosion pushed him through the portal and the world went black.

Kavi regained consciousness the moment he hit the snow. He opened his eyes and quickly shielded them from the glare of the sun. His dirty, bloody hands crunched against the surface as he sat up. The cold felt good. Pip's void gate winked out a moment later.

Kavi's head swiveled towards Clara and Tess. They were both there, as was all of Ghost Squad.

Clara and Tess stared at him with loathing.

Kavi stood, head bowed. "I'm sorry. What I did was unforgivable, but it was the only way I could save your lives."

Tess spit into the snow at his feet and walked away.

"You're an abomination," Clara said, then turned her back on him.

"I'm sorry," Kavi said again to her retreating back.

Then the seizure hit. He convulsed and darkness took him.

* * *

He awoke in the cave. The semi-circle of lit skulls surrounded him. The setting was so familiar now. He felt none of the panic he had when he woke here in the past. He looked for Holden. The man sat at the small table he and future Kavi had just shared. Holden's eyes sat on the table facing towards Kavi. He gestured to the empty chair.

Holden nodded to the empty chair. "Join me, young Lion."

Kavi pushed himself up from the shrine and stood. He had to hunch from his position on the high shelf. His eyes never left Holden as he dropped to the floor of the cave. "Who are you really?"

Holden smiled his sharkish grin, far too many teeth for his face.

"No more parlor tricks," said Kavi. "I've seen enough real monsters by now. It's time for answers."

Kavi flexed that muscle in his brain, wondering if it would work in the dream. Pain built behind his eyebrows. His eyes crossed when the piercing pain became unbearable.

Holden laughed. "I don't think so, young Lion. You've grown teeth of your own, but you'll never be strong enough to challenge me."

Kavi let the muscle relax and the pain began to fade. "Okay, who are you? A god? A Sage?"

Holden grabbed his eyes and popped them back into their sockets. They moved about crazily for a moment until they finally stopped to focus on him. The man's teeth faded back into his mouth and, for the first time, he looked almost like the farmer Kavi once knew.

Holden crossed one leg over the other as he considered his words. "Something like that. I was created to enforce a balance in this world. Certain...power brokers didn't appreciate the origin rules of this world. They decided to break them. I was tasked to inject a steadying force into the world to compensate."

"Created by who?" asked Kavi.

"By whom," corrected Holden.

Kavi glared.

"Fine. *Who* do you think would care about such rules?"

Kavi thought for a second. "Clearly not the gods. After having met one of them, they're no better than any other person with power. I assume they're the power brokers you're talking about. That leaves the Ancients." Kavi shook his head. "And what? I'm supposed to bring these gods under control to play by the Ancient's rules?"

Holden shrugged. "You were able to bring Harp to her knees in her own city."

"No," said Kavi. "I didn't sign up for any of this. I quit. I'm done being a pawn in the games of power."

Holden laughed, smacking the table several times. "I quit.

That's hilarious. You can quit as easily as I can. Besides, you're no longer a pawn, you've become a power player of your own. You're more bishop or rook now."

Kavi thought back to the most ancient of games that his father taught him so long ago. He was never a *good* chess player. He knew Holden referenced two of the back line pieces whose power stemmed from movement, but that wasn't enough to conquer the power of the gods. "I'm no god. Wasn't that the lesson your masters just tried to teach me? Choosing who lives and who dies is much worse than not choosing."

Holden nodded slowly. "But you didn't choose. You cheated, just like the other gods."

"I didn't cheat," said Kavi, pushing his chair back. "I made the only choice possible which allowed me to save my friends!"

"And were they happy about it? About the violation of their autonomy?" asked Holden.

Kavi shook his head. "No, it was the most horrible thing I've ever done, but it was the only way to save them."

Holden smiled and the shark teeth returned. "Abuse of power normally begins with the intention to do good. 'I only committed a small atrocity, because it was the only way to save my people!'—the rationalization of every dictator in history. It's a slippery slope, young lion. What if you took over another body, to save someone else's life, but it meant sacrificing the one you took? Sacrifice the autonomy of one, for the lives of the many. Just like Harp. That power is addictive."

Kavi nodded. He couldn't dispute the point. "What's the alternative? Let my friends die when I can do something?

565

I'll always make the choice to save my friends."

Holden grinned then stuck a finger in his ear, pulling out something that wriggled. He flicked it across the room and looked to Kavi for a reaction. Kavi refused to indulge him. "Fine," said Holden. "Let's talk hypotheticals. Would you save your friends if it meant, from that point forward, they had no personalities of their own? Let's say they became mindless automatons only capable of following your orders."

"You mean turning them into slaves?"

Holden nodded. "Would you save them then?"

Kavi shook his head. "That's not saving them at all. They might as well be dead."

"Exactly," said Holden. "What if, when you saved them, they fell madly in love with you? Anything you said, they would think was a wonderful idea and would blindly follow your lead?"

"Seems the same as slavery, no?"

"Agreed. Let's loosen the constraints." Holden pushed at the spot between his nose and his right eye until the eye began to pop in and out in a very disturbing fashion.

"Why?" asked Kavi. "This is an interesting conversation. Why distract me?"

Holden put his hands back on the table. "Apologies, it helps me put my thoughts in order and gives me insight into your emotional landscape which I can use to strengthen my argument. I'll try to stop. New hypothetical. What if, when you saved them through mind domination, it shifted their point of view. They would become biased to see things as you see them, fundamentally changing their thought process?"

Kavi absorbed that for a moment before responding.

"Would that be so bad? Isn't that what happens in every conversation? Don't we try to shift perspective so they see the world through the same lens we do?"

Holden shrugged. "Almost, except for two big differences. Do you know what they are?"

Kavi took another moment, longer this time. "Choice is one. In a conversation, one party always has the opportunity to walk away and not hear the other's perspective. I took that choice from them."

Holden shook his head. "Yes, you did. That's one, but the other difference is even more important."

What could be more important than choice? "I don't know. What?"

"In conversation, you articulate an idea, like I'm about to do," said Holden. His fidgeting ceased and he looked into Kavi's eyes. "The other person takes that idea and rolls it around in their mouth for a moment, as if tasting something new. They bring their own experience and personality to the idea and translate it through their own lens. They decide whether they can learn from it. Whether it shifts their own perspective. Whether it changes how they think about you. That is the beauty of independent thought. Take that from someone and..." Holden spread his hands wide.

Kavi felt his stomach drop. "Did I do that?"

Holden shrugged. "Maybe. When you took over their minds, you stole the choice from them. Worse, you planted something in their minds. That's something gods have been doing to their followers forever. It's called brainwashing. You planted an idea that their lives are more important than their autonomy. If they know that planted idea is there, it's not a lost cause, you can-"

Kavi! Rose's voice struck with all the authority of the fifth Sage. *Kavi, I need you right now!*

Wait! yelled Kavi. *I need to understand how to fix this!*

It was too late, the cave wavered in his mind's eye and disappeared.

48

The final Quest

Kavi appeared in the dream world, furious. He didn't even look at his surroundings as he confronted the fifth Sage. "Damnit Rose! I was finally getting some answers and you pull me here without my permission!"

"Silence, child!" Rose said with all the authority of her Sage power.

"No!" said Kavi. "I'm done being silenced."

Rose's eyes widened. "You've evolved your own authority," she said with wonder. Rose shook her head. "Then it's already begun."

"What's already begun?" Kavi asked, still angry.

"The final Quest, the battle for the world of Grendar," said Rose.

Kavi stopped and looked around. He was standing in a plush outdoor garden in full bloom. In the middle of the garden sat three comfortable couches. Grim and Nettie sat on one. Pip and Promo shared another. Gavin and a small man Kavi didn't recognize sat on the third.

Grim nodded to him. "Nice to see you, Kav."

Kavi smiled, walked over and hugged Grim and Nettie. "Good to see you, both of you! How we doing?"

Grim shrugged. "Same old same old. Fighting Ach'Su and receiving boons from gods."

Kavi pointed at him. "We're not leaving until I hear that whole story, but not yet."

He turned back to Rose. "Tell us more about this final Quest."

Rose looked around the group. "That's all of us, let's begin. Fifteen minutes ago...," she looked to Gavin who nodded. "Fifteen minutes ago, I received the most powerful calling I've ever received. I thought my mind was going to explode. When I woke, I knew all five Sages received the calling at the same time. When I tried to contact the other Sages, I discovered the calling was so powerful, it killed two of them. It was a mercy really, Arlo and Gerand were incredibly old and had gone completely mad."

She took a deep, shuddering breath, then continued. "We each received a piece of the final Quest from the Ancients, which means we may only ever have three of the five pieces. There is still hope, because I recognize the start of this Quest. It's made of snippets from previous Quests. What we thought was nonsense in those Quests, before the rhyming parts, were actually clues to the final Quest. See if this sounds familiar."

Rose's eyes went white and she intoned.

Three hungry snakes crawl the roads of Grendar
  The first what was, a glutton of innocence
  The second what comes, consumer of pain
  The third what ends. He writes the world in blood

"No way," said Kavi.

"That's the beginning of the Triad Quest," said Nettie.

Rose's eyes reverted to their natural color and she nodded. "I have other pieces too, but I don't know the order in which they are arranged." She looked to Nettie. "That's where I need your help."

"Any chance we can keep this amongst ourselves?" asked Kavi. "Let us figure things out before every yahoo in Grendar attempts to solve it?"

Rose shook her head. "No. Everything we have will be broadcast to everyone in Grendar. That was the edict of the Ancients. You'll be competing against the rest of the world to solve this one."

"It's worse than that. Much worse," said the small man sitting next to Gavin.

"Who are you?" asked Kavi.

The man ignored Kavi and focused on Nettie. "Not only will you have to compete against the rest of Grendar, you're going to have to compete against the gods too. And we cheat."

"Wait, *who* is he?" Kavi said, still waiting for an answer.

"He's the Tinkerer," said Nettie breathlessly.

"Then what the hell is he doing here? If we have to compete against the gods, it seems like a bad idea to invite the competition into the strategy meeting."

"He's loud and annoying," said Promo, with a look to Rose. "But he's not wrong."

The Tinkerer turned to face Kavi. "I'm here, Stonecrest, because I'm tired. I'm tired of my brethren, and I'm tired of the Ancients. Do you have any idea how old I am?"

The weight in the man's eyes was infinite. Kavi shook his

head.

"I'm seventeen thousand, three hundred and forty two years old and I'm exhausted. With all of it. I've accomplished everything I set out to accomplish, save for one thing." He held his hand up to stall Kavi's question. "No, that's not something I'm going to share with you. With any of you. However, I will help you, because the cycle has to end."

"What cycle?" asked Nettie.

"The Evolution Trials," said the Tinkerer.

"Oh...kaay," said Grim. "Want to share a little more on that?"

"Solve the final Quest and you might convince the Ancients that this world should continue to exist."

"What happens if we fail? Or if the Gods solve it before us?" asked Kavi.

The Tinkerer looked from face to face before his eyes landed on Kavi's. "The same thing that happened to my world. The Ancients scrap the entire experiment."

Thank you

Dear Reader,

I hope you enjoyed reading Heretic Squad, the second book of the Evolution Trials. If you enjoyed the story and look forward to more stories, please do me a huge favor and leave a review on Amazon.

If you're a regular reader, I'm sure you've read this before, but that doesn't make it any less true. Reviews are the lifeblood for self-published authors and I'm no different. I look forward to bringing you the next installment of the story soon!

Thank you so much!

If you would like me to notify you when the next book is released, please sign up for my newsletter or Facebook author page.

About the Author

Sean Kennedy graduated with a bachelor's degree in physics and did absolutely nothing with it. He became a coder, an entrepreneur and now a writer. He lives in Colorado with his beautiful wife, two daughters, a rescue mutt on trial for war crimes against squeaky toys, and a German shepherd who ratted her out for a tennis ball.

When Sean's not writing, you can most likely find him outside in the mountains.

You can connect with me on:

🌐 https://seanhkennedy.com

📘 https://www.facebook.com/profile.php?id=61552008412362

Subscribe to my newsletter:

✉ https://subscribepage.io/XlgsQy

Also by Sean Kennedy

Author of the popular Evolution Trials series

Evolution Trials:
   Ghost Squad
   Heretic Squad

Ghost Squad

The first book in the Evolution Trials series where we find out:

Who are the puppet masters behind the Ghost Squad trials?

Can Kavi make it through hell to find a way out?

In the shadow of his parents - what will Kavi be most remembered for? His swordsmanship, his brilliance, or something nobody expected?

Made in United States
Troutdale, OR
01/25/2024

17151903R00354